In the red velvet room
at Madam Labouille's

"No!" Elizabeth cried as he lifted her in his arms and moved toward the velvet drapes that enclosed the vast bed. "No! I didn't mean. . ."

It had all been a trick, planned so ingeniously, to lure him to his familiar place of assignation—to have him find, so unexpectedly, the young Elizabeth in the silken garments of a courtesan. To tease and torment Lord John—to drive him to the limit of frustration and frenzy—and then to withdraw. But something had gone awry . . .

Now they were inside the drapes. He was climbing the steps to the bed.

"No!" she gasped, writhing in his powerful arms. Fires were raging within her. She had to struggle as much against them as against the man himself.

"I will have you, Elizabeth." He flung her on the bed, holding her down. She struggled in his grip, knowing that each heaving breath thrust her breasts farther out of the filmy peignoir. She arched her body upward to break his grasp and then the buttons that held the peignoir gave way and she was utterly exposed to his gaze.

"Oh, God!" she heard him breathe. . .

PASSION'S PAWN

by
Annabella

&

A DELL/JAMES A. BRYANS BOOK

Published by
Dell Publishing Co., Inc.
1 Dag Hammarskjold Plaza
New York, New York 10017

Dell ® TM 681510, Dell Publishing Co. Inc.

ISBN: 0-440-06937-8

Printed in the United States of America

First printing—August 1978

BOOK I

Elizabeth at Eighteen

&

1

Elizabeth Stewart wrapped her cloak tightly about her as if to hug her excitement to herself. An irrepressible smile lit her pale oval face. Later, she would keep her expression demure, but it was all right if she allowed herself to look now the way she felt for she was alone in the huge, cathedral-ceilinged reception hall of Miss Holybrook's School for Young Ladies. It was the first time she had ever been alone there. She was aware of her smallness in the vast spaces that rose above her and stretched around her.

She was dressed and ready to leave the school where she had lived for the last ten years. Her trunk and valises and hatboxes were, even then, being loaded on the coach that had been sent from Polreath Manor to fetch her. Mr. Hurford, the business manager for the Lord of Polreath's affairs, was making the final arrangements with Miss Holybrook for her departure from the school.

Elizabeth moved across the floor to stand before the portrait of the Lord and Lady of Polreath. He looked lean, dark and, somehow, mysterious. Next to him was Lady Sarah, small and lovely, with dark hair and a look of intensity in her smoky eyes.

From the time that Elizabeth had learned that every year each patroness chose one of the girls from the graduating class to sponsor during the coming Social Seasons, she had prayed that when she graduated she would be chosen—by Lady Sarah. That was the secret wish of every girl in every graduating class.

Even the austerity of Mr. Hurford, who had come to the school in February for the final interview with the girls under consideration, could not dampen the enthusiasm of the girls to be sponsored by Lady Sarah.

Mr. Hurford was slightly ominous—tall and dark-featured and thin, and yet he seemed looming and spectral. Aesthetic was the kindest description that could be given him, and that not really applicable, for the hard expression in his narrow eyes and on his tight mouth had nothing of the look of the aesthete.

He was spare of words, and his silence was intimidating rather than monastic. Still he had come as envoy from Polreath Wood in Cornwall, and Polreath Wood was known, at least by reputation, even as far away as the school. The holding of Polreath was an ancient and greatly honored one. And Lady Sarah of Polreath was known to be held in highest regard in Court circles, and by King William himself. Her father, until his death, had been an intimate of the King.

Elizabeth, in spite of the fact that she was an orphan and her real parentage unknown—or perhaps because of it, since it was somehow accepted that she was high-born—had been looked upon with favor by the other two patronesses as wall as by Lady Sarah. The other two were Lady Grey of Beacon's Green and Lady Weatherford.

The dowager Lady Grey was the most formidable woman Elizabeth had ever seen. She was sure that each of the other girls under consideration, the same as she, had quaked in every fiber during their sessions with her, dreading that the steel-corseted lady might find her acceptable.

In striking contrast was the timid Lady Weatherford. Elizabeth did not fear her, but she feared whatever it was that had made of her the timid, wary creature that she was. It was assumed that it was her life with her husband that had brought about her present state, although nothing untoward was known of—or spoken about—Lord Weatherford.

Elizabeth stood before the portrait of the Lord and Lady of Polreath on the wall of the reception hall as if she stood before a mirror. She was trying to see herself through their eyes—or rather, in truth, through the Lord of Polreath's eyes, since she could assume that the Lady of Polreath did not find her displeasing. She remembered a remark attributed to Henry VIII regarding Anne of Cleves that she had read once in a book that was being surreptitiously passed around at Miss Holybrook's—it was certainly not a school text. She couldn't remember the remark exactly, but it was something like, "Judging from her tits and her belly, you wouldn't know she was a woman." It made Elizabeth blush to think the words, but they gave her a yardstick by which to measure what men evidently wanted in a woman. Well, she had a bosom. Even Henry VIII couldn't have faulted her there. He might have been disappointed by the flatness of her stomach. No matter how much she ate, she couldn't seem to round it out. And her hips and flanks were too slender and boyish, she thought. She supposed her body was properly proportioned, her legs as long as they should be for the length of her torso. They were shapely but slim. She would never have dimpled knees, but if it were a choice between dimpled knees and her trim and well-turned ankles, she would choose her ankles. An inadvertently lifted or windblown skirt didn't show a knee.

She didn't know what color to call her hair. It wasn't brown, and it wasn't blond. Ash, she supposed. That wasn't any color at all, but any faintest light would bring out the radiance in it and make it shine a pale gold, and there was an abundance of it that rippled in soft waves when it was out of its pins.

Her eyes were green—a green that changed color with her mood. Her eyebrows and eyelashes were so dark that when her hair was covered she looked more like a brunette than a blonde. Her nose was fine-boned and straight with a slight tilt that showed the hauteur of her nature rather than sauciness. Her mouth was the most expressive feature of her face. It was full, especially her lower lip. And it was as quick to show her mood as her eyes—a bit too quick to pout sometimes, perhaps.

Elizabeth realized that she was looking straight into the intense, brooding eyes of the Lord of Polreath in the portrait. She blushed, much as if she had caught herself staring at the man himself, and turned aside.

She heard voices outside the door of the reception hall and quickly moved away from the portrait. The voices were those of Miss Holybrook and Mr. Hurford. Their business was finished. It was time for Elizabeth to leave. Her pulse quickened. It was the moment she had waited years for—the moment when she would be forever rid of Miss Holybrook's School for Young Ladies!

"The coach is ready, Miss Stewart."

The bony frame of Mr. Hurford towered suddenly in the doorway, his small eyes glinting, thought Elizabeth, as though they held some disagreeable secret.

2

The heavy coach swayed and jolted over the narrow, twisting lanes that served as a high road. The night was dark and bleak beyond endurance. The winds howled incessantly, moaning at times and sometimes rising in a thin, piercing whistle that drove slivers of pain through Elizabeth's ears. She felt that she was again a-sail on a restless, heaving black sea.

The coach leaned precariously to the right or the left as the horses rounded the zigzag curves of the road without at all diminishing their breakneck speed. What was the need for such speed? It was that, as much as the threat inherent in the legends of Bodmin Moor at night, that frightened Elizabeth. And she was alone with three men who were strangers to her.

In the dark she could see little except, now and then, the eerie gray ribbon of road when an extended curve stretched ahead. There were no trees, and the barren high country, roughened by scrubby growth and sharp outcroppings of rock, stretched far beyond any distance her eye could see.

There was no moonlight, but intermittently something in the atmosphere produced an uneasy distinc-

11

tion in the dark, and she could make out the long, thin face and stern, upright form of Mr. Hurford sitting facing her, stiffly silent, offering no warmth of companionship. The man frightened her. The very fact that he kept his distance alarmed her. She'd seen a man keep his distance once before, and then . . .

Once, beyond the coach and the road, Elizabeth made out the eerie blackness of a burned out field of gorse. The spiny, charred remains of thousands of elongated, needle-sharp spikes thrust out in petrified black menace. Elizabeth shivered. She could sense the spiky fingers clutching at her skirts if she were forced to take flight across such a field.

She listened to the clap-clapping rhythm of the horses' hoofs. What if one of the horses threw another shoe? There would be still another delay. They would have to stop where they were until the shoe could be replaced. There had been two delays already.

At the very beginning of their journey, it had been discovered that the brake was not working properly. Elizabeth had had to stand about while it was being repaired. They had not been too long started again when a horse had thrown a shoe. Again she had had to stand about, this time on the roadside well beyond the limits of the village. Darkness had come upon them while she waited, shivering in the cold of the ceaselessly blowing winds. The torch, ready in its clamp by the driver's seat, had been lit, but it did little to lighten the dark. Elizabeth had started at every sound and movement in the empty wastes around her, expecting momentarily that the torch would be extinguished by the force of the winds.

If not for the delays, they would have been beyond the moor by nightfall, she was told, but both repairs had taken undue lengths of time. No one on honest business would choose to cross the perilous moorlands

after dark. It was dangerous enough to travel those
God-forsaken stretches by day.

They had met no one on the road since the first
coming of night. They had passed no villages that
Elizabeth could see, and no isolated farmsteads. It was
as if she and the silent Mr. Hurford inside the coach,
and the two outside on the driver's seat (Dax and
Oxford, she had heard Mr. Hurford address them)
were alone in the world surrounded by the dead and
burned-out fields, hounded by the shrieking, howling
might of the winds.

The drivers were armed, and Elizabeth strongly
suspected that the seemingly imperturbable Mr. Hurford had a pistol concealed beneath his coat. Her
knowledge of firearms was nonexistent, but even her
inexperienced eye had seen that the heavy shotgun
bracketed on Dax's side of the driver's seat had had
much use.

Elizabeth tried to turn her thoughts from speculations of possible dangers and to fill her mind with
soothing things. She was free of the school, at last, and
free of that monstrous creature, Miss Goodrod, who
passed herself as a woman, but was not! Elizabeth was
as glad—more so!—to leave the school behind her as
she had been to leave India behind her—and for the
same reason. What was it about her body that attracted
those she least wanted to attract? Was there something
in the way she moved, or walked, or breathed? Was
there something in her that she was not aware of, but
that was so evident to others? Elizabeth had had almost a lifetime of torment from such thoughts. She
would not let herself dwell on them now!

The journey she was on would take her to a corner
of Cornwall far removed from Miss Holybrook's School
for Young Ladies. It would take her to London for the
season and to Brighton when court was in residence

there. This year—1830—would be *her* year! She would
mingle with royalty and those of noble blood and
ancient lineage. She was about to enter a whole new
world. In that new world she would have a place that
was her own. It would be a place of pride and self-
respect—she was determined that it would. Never
again would she be physically used! Never again
abused! She would kill the first who tried.

Suddenly Mr. Hurford got to his feet in the lurching
vehicle and, leaning over, jerked down the window of
the door on Elizabeth's right. The wind burst in with
a howling roar, but above the roar she heard the shouts
of rough male voices and the pounding of the horses'
hooves.

Three men on horseback, one carrying a staff with
a white cloth tied to it, were riding full gallop toward
their own flying horses. A horde of men on foot, some
waving torches aloft, crested the ridge of a nearby rise
and stormed down toward the coach in the wake of
the riders, yelling as they came.

"It's the tinners!" Oxford shouted, and Dax took up
the cry. "It's the tinners! They've come!"

"Be calm!" Mr. Hurford shouted from inside the
coach. "Pull in—pull the horses in! They'll shoot the
lead horse and that will be the end of us. Pull the
horses in, I say! We'll show a willingness to talk."

Panic flooded Elizabeth. Three men against that
horde—they hadn't a chance!

The approaching riders were within feet of the
coach, and the running men streaming behind them
were closing in the space between. A blast from the
shotgun crashed through the air, but the horde came
on! The coach lurched sickeningly and crashed into
the low, overgrown stone wall to the left of the road.
Elizabeth was thrown to the floor, striking her head
on the frame of the window. She crouched where she

was, stunned with terror as much as with pain. The horses screamed and neighed in fright. They lunged and snorted, trying to pull themselves and the vehicle from the scrub and growth that overran the crumbling stone wall. More shots blasted through the air, the earsplitting sounds crashing over and above the other sounds of tumult.

Mr. Hurford swiveled in his seat and flung open the small communications panel above the seat. "Hold your fire, Dax! We'll talk, I said! Can't you see they're flying white? Hold your fire!" He pulled himself upright by the handhold of the door. "Come, get yourself up!" he ordered Elizabeth.

As he was opening the door to emerge from the coach, the foremost of the riders plunged toward it, rearing his horse with a stout hard pull of the reins. "We came for talk, your lordship! We came wanting talk!" His voice was harsh and ugly. "It's a poor day when you refuse us talk! You fired on the men, and me riding before them flying white! I'd heard different of your lordship, and expected different!"

Mr. Hurford got the door open and stepped out on the footrail, which had sprung out with the opening of the door, the height of it making him equal in height with the mounted rider.

"His lordship is nowhere here," Mr. Hurford said. He gestured toward the inside of the coach as if inviting inspection.

Shouts, yells, and curses burst in a swelling crescendo from the crowd. "Charlie's hit! They've shot Charlie! They've killed Charlie!"

The coach was being boarded. It dipped and bobbled crazily with the weight of the cursing men as they clambered up onto the driver's seat and overpowered Oxford and Dax and hauled them down. The coach righted itself and was still, its stillness accentuated by the earth-moving struggling and scuffling that was going on around it.

A horrible screaming rose on the air. Elizabeth cringed, terror rendering her almost senseless.

The screaming stopped suddenly, and then a single scream rose—a high-pitched, rising sound that thinned to a single ghastly note and pealed off into the black heavens.

The sounds of struggling ceased. The horses stopped lunging and were restlessly quiet, as if they were being held. There were no loud curses, no disturbing of the quiet. Only the wind continued its noisy howling and moaning unabated. The quiet was worse, and more ominously portentous, than the scuffling, struggling, and screaming that had gone on before. Whatever it was that the mob had been bent on doing to Dax or Oxford—or both—it had been done.

The three men on horseback had dismounted, and Mr. Hurford was now on the road beside them. The man who was holding the staff to which the white cloth was tied tossed it away with a snort of disgust and grabbed a torch from one of the men in the crowd. "I'll see it for myself whether his lordship is nowhere here. I have it on good information that he is. It's a new Lord of Polreath that I'm learning about tonight— as you'd have it!—that he'd hide behind the skirts of the likes of you!" He pushed Mr. Hurford roughly aside and jerked open the door of the coach and thrust the flaming torch inside.

The flame of the torch was hot on Elizabeth's face. She tried to move away, but she was jammed against the door. With a bellow of rage, the man flung the torch upward in a wild, swinging motion as if he would club her with the flaming end of it.

"By the gods!" the man screamed. He was savage in his anger. He grabbed Elizabeth's arm and jerked

her up to a sitting position. With one strong motion, he
was on the footrail of the coach and had pulled her to
her feet in the high-ceilinged vehicle. He thrust the
torch upward toward her face. "Look ye!" He swung
the flame toward his companions and then back to
Elizabeth. "It was his lordship was to be traveling this
coach this night—so I had it on good information." He
jerked Elizabeth forward so that she was framed in the
door. "Is this his lordship? This sniveling . . . "

The two who had ridden with him exploded in fury.
Both turned on Mr. Hurford, one grabbing him by the
collar of his coat. "Where is he? You'll tell us where he
is! We'll not be made dupes of! Where is he?"

The three dismounted riders showed no interest in
Elizabeth except as the cause of their fury, but several
men from the mob sidled close in a semicircle about
the door where she was still held in the grasp of the
man who had discovered her. Her face and upper body
were clearly illuminated in the glow of the torch.

The lewd chuckles and sly, leering comments whispered among the men near Elizabeth drew others from
the crowd. One, bolder than the rest, laughed out in
raucous glee. "Damn me bones!" he swore, pounding
one of his fellows on the back and looking about at
those who crowded around him. "It's a trade I'll make
with a will! What say ye, lads?"

He turned back to Elizabeth, his leering, grinning
face moving up and down as his eyes traveled over her
from head to foot and back again to her face. His
eyes stayed on her face a long moment and then traveled slowly and deliberately down to her bosom. The
contours of her breasts were totally obscured by the
fullness of her cloak, but she felt that they were exposed in nakedness to his lustful, evil eyes. She felt
the skin of her breasts tighten involuntarily, and felt
the nipples harden. Hot, furious blood surged through-

out her. Her face—all of her body—was suffused with it. Angry flushes prickled the skin of her face and throat. She felt a stronger hatred for the man than she had ever felt for anyone in her life. Her body was reacting to his bestiality as if it were passion that he roused in her!

The man laughed aloud at the sight of Elizabeth's reddened face, and her fury deserted her as fear and panic seized her. He made a move toward her and she shrank back, trying to pull her arm from the grip of the one holding her. Others from the mob moved closer. Sly, drooling faces peered up at her. Bold eyes raked over her. Some of the men licked dry lips, breathing hard through open mouths. Elizabeth's body trembled violently, her heart pounding beneath her ribs.

Dirty hands reached toward her. The leering mouth of the man below her opened wetly as his hand went under her skirts and gripped her ankle so tightly that she could feel each finger through the thin leather of her boot. The fingers relaxed and the hand slid upward and was above the boot, on the thin material of her stocking. Elizabeth screamed. She writhed and struggled in the grip of the two men holding her. The hand on her leg had her in a viselike grip, and the man's other hand was under her skirts, sliding upward above her knee. Other hands were grabbing at her, jerking at the folds of her cloak so that she was pulled off balance and then jerked upright again, but always the pull was downward and, except for the man whose dirty hands were on her legs, she would have toppled forward.

Suddenly the man with the torch made a wide swing with it, scattering the men at Elizabeth. They yelled in pain, some beating at their clothing that had flamed up at the touch of the torch. One was tearing wildly at his flaming hair. His shrieks tore through the night as he turned suddenly and ran, senseless and screaming, into the darkness of the moor.

"Hold off! Hold off!" The torch was held aloft, in readiness to swing again. "I didn't bring you here to-night to satisfy yourselves on a woman—it's business that we're on!" He gave Elizabeth a violent push back inside the coach and jumped down from the footrail and slammed the door.

Elizabeth was crouched against the door again in convulsions of sobbing. Mr. Hurford had made no move to help her. He'd stood the while beside the dead Charlie, watching what the men were doing to her with cold, stony eyes.

"Our business has taken a turn!" the man with the torch cried out. "We have been betrayed!"

The man who had worst tormented Elizabeth made a lunge toward the coach. He pounded heavy, furious fists against the side of the coach, giving it a savage push. He and others near him grabbed handholds where they could and shook the coach violently, rocking it from side to side in increasingly wider arcs. The coach jolted wildly as the horses reared and plunged, straining against their traces in fright.

A wild panic from a new source overcame Elizabeth. She was alone in the coach, and the horses were maddened with fright! If they got the vehicle free and bolted, she would die, flung into the sharp needles of the charred and blackened gorse, or smashed, along with the coach, crushed and broken against the stone wall!

They'll kill me, Elizabeth thought wildly. They're trying to kill me!

The leader was again at the crazed men, swinging the torch in wide swathes. He yelled a harsh order, and some men from the crowd rushed forward and tussled with the men trying to wreck the coach, finally breaking their holds and pulling them away.

"If I have to pull my gun to keep order, I will!" The man threw the torch aside and put his hand beneath his coat. "What's one life or two to me when it's hundreds I'm after saving?" He turned on Mr. Hurford. "Who put you onto our plan? Speak! Point out the one among us who betrayed us!"

"I know nothing of 'plans,' nothing of 'betrayal.'" Mr. Hurford's contemptuous tone put such doings beneath him.

Elizabeth's tormentor swung on the leader. "You told us *he* was coming—home from London by way of Launceton road, you said! We've waited all day and half the night, freezing our cocks on those cold rocks yonder, with nothing for our comfort but your promise of setting things to rights so we could fill our empty bellies. And what has your promise come to? Nothing! Nothing, except that we've been made fools of! The men'll not stand still for it—not the men in my section. We'll find his lordship ourselves—and not for the *talk* you set such store on!"

"Hold your temper, Gidney! Yours and your men's as well! I've no liking for what I've seen from you tonight, nor for what I've heard. That kind of talk puts a rope around a man's neck, not food in his belly!" The man's voice rose loud and commanding as he turned to address the crowd. "We've not come this far and done this much to ruin it all by making disagreement amongst ourselves. I'll handle any disagreements later. Right now I want the one who informed on us!" His hard eyes moved from face to face among the crowd.

The men returned his searching gaze, bold-faced, defiant, each determined to prove, by refusing to be intimidated, that he was not the guilty one. Some began to look around, examining the faces of the others.

"It was Charlie was shot." The flat statement came from the midst of the group.

"What do you mean by that?" The question was angrily put by someone close to the speaker.

"I mean it was Charlie was the one shot, and maybe there was a reason."

"By God's eyes, I'll see your blood for that! I was friend to Charlie, and knew him! He was a decent man and a good . . ."

"He was go-between between us and them. And the man who was his contact was the same one that shot him. I figure a man who'll betray one side won't stop from betraying the other. I say both was playing both sides and had to kill the other or himself be killed! It come down to a case of which could be the quickest. You all seen Charlie running out ahead when we hadn't got the signal yet to come running. And I say Dax was aiming straight to kill Charlie! Or why hadn't he shot sooner? It don't make sense to let three come at you riding, and get nearly on you while you sit holding a gun idle in your hands, and then let off and shoot somebody a good hundred yards behind them that's on you! If you got an explanation for that, I'm waiting to hear it!"

The crowd was silenced.

Out of the silence a rustle of movement was heard. Oxford came through the crowd, weaving a twisting way among the men, who made no move to hinder him. Elizabeth gasped and clutched her hands to her breast. She had thought him dead! Mr. Hurford was even more shocked than she. His face had gone a startling white.

Oxford stopped before Mr. Hurford. He said, "It's truth what the man says. It's something I should have suspected myself, and from long before the time we left the manor to go to Launceton to fetch the lass. It's a queer way that Dax's been acting for these two months past, since the mine was closed. He's been off from home times he shouldn't've, and he's been snooping 'round in places where he had no cause to be. Even not thinking on that—just taking in consideration what happened today. I'm a coachman and a driving man, Mr. Hurford. I don't put a vehicle on the road with brakes that don't hold. Now, a horse of mine will throw a shoe—any horse will, given rough enough a way. And it was the Lord's own time Dax took tonight, setting things to rights. Seems now he was holding up a-purpose . . . "

Oxford was interrupted. The man who obviously was in command turned to Mr. Hurford. "My name's Calvin," he said. "No doubt you've heard it."

"I've heard it."

"I'm sending a message to his lordship. Tell him my business with him isn't finished—I'm sending him proof and token." He turned his head and called out, "Bring that one here! Him that shot Charlie!"

There was a stunned silence, and then a rustling. Several men came through the path that opened before them. They carried the lifeless, bloody body that had been Dax.

Elizabeth cringed, wanting to hide her eyes from the gory, awful sight, but at the same time she was compelled to stare.

"Tie him on up front there!"

Again the coach dipped and bobbled in swinging jerks with the weight of men clambering about. Elizabeth felt violently ill with the realization of what they were doing. A dead man would travel the rest of the way with them—a bloody mass of deadweight tied onto the driver's seat beside Oxford! She shivered, seeing in her mind the mutilated corpse, its dead eyes opened wide and staring as its head rolled, its weight shifted about by the swayings of the coach in spite of the binding ropes, lurching sometimes forward, sometimes back to thud against the coach, sometimes touching Oxford!

The man Calvin was speaking again to Mr. Hurford. "It was not my purpose tonight to see murder done . . ."

Mr. Hurford interrupted stonily, "But it's murder that's been done, and it's not the first time murder has been done at your instigation and in the name of Cause."

The tinners had been silent. Now one spoke out. "It's murder his lordship is causing to be done, for it's murder to let women and children starve to death! It was a death sentence put on our wives and children the day the mine was closed. How are we to feed them?"

"It was for your own safety's sake that the mine was closed." Mr. Hurford's voice was cold.

"The mine *is safe!*"

Others joined in.

"Safe enough for tinners!"

"And there's tin there still!"

"Aye! More tin than has ever been mined out of it yet!"

"His lordship was almost killed in the mine." Mr. Hurford's voice had a final sound.

"It wasn't the fault of the mine!"

"Let his lordship stay aboveground where he knows how to keep his footing!"

"Aye! Leave the mine to the tinners!"

"We're willing to risk it!"

"That's right! If we're willing to risk it, who's to say us no?"

"You know who!" The voice was high-pitched and whining, but venomous overall. "Her ladyship!"

"Aye, and that's right. It's her doing that it's closed!"

"Behind his back, she closed it!"

Mr. Hurford said, "The Committee of Engineers condemned the mine."

"Committee of Engineers be damned! They weren't Cornishmen! English toadies of her ladyship! What do they know of Cornish mines?"

"Stepped their fine English boots in a few inches of water and turned tail—that's the story of it."

"They never went beyond the passage!"

"There's always a bit of water."

"Midland coal mines they might know—let them keep their inspecting for the Midlands! It takes a coast man to understand mining under sea. It's not right to bring in strangers to pass judgment on something they don't know anything about."

"We've our own engineers among us. They know the sea, and they know how we work with it. Let them pass judgment!"

"Aye, that's the way it should be! That's fair!"

"That would have been the way of it," the waspish voice put in. "If his lordship hadn't been hurt and taken from home up to London. Him unconscious, and her having the say in that, too!"

"That's right! But he's coming home now, and we're not taking the say-so of any English Committee of Engineers! We'll hear it from his lordship that the mine is closed, or . . ."

"That's enough!" Calvin's words were an order. "You've spoken your piece. Hold your arguments for his lordship's hearing—you'll get it. You have my assurance on that." To Mr. Hurford, he said, "You brought tonight's bloodshed on yourself by not keeping your man under control, and if you bring more, we'll not stop short of it either! We were fired on while flying white. You know it, and we know it! And the lass there knows it." There was a surprising softness in his voice when he made reference to Elizabeth, considering the rage he had shown when he had discovered that it was she in the coach instead of the Lord of Polreath. The softness was replaced by contempt when he continued, his hard eyes on Mr. Hurford. "You're free to go your way. Take the scared little lass and go. But don't mistake me—I'm serious in my purpose! I've had success in my dealings up to now, and I'll have success in this. Right is on my side!"

Mr. Hurford disdained to answer. Oxford opened the door of the coach for him, and he climbed in and took his seat. Elizabeth scrambled from her crouched position at the window and pulled herself onto the seat facing him, pulling her ripped and torn skirts over her legs to cover them. Oxford closed the door tightly and secured the footrail before going forward to climb up to join the dead Dax on the driver's seat.

"Haul them out, men!" Mr. Calvin shouted. "Haul away!"

The coach was pushed and pulled and somehow jerkily maneuvered out of the wedge of the brush and growth of the stone wall and onto the road. There was a loud snapping crack from several whips, and the horses bolted. The coach almost catapulted end over end when the slack in the traces was taken up by their forward plunge. Elizabeth was almost thrown to the floor again but managed to stay on the seat.

Looking back to reassure herself that the mob was not following, Elizabeth saw the inert dead form of Charlie lying beside the road. She shuddered remembering another form of a man lying inert by a roadside in a ditch . . . that one muddy and rain-soaked, blood-soaked . . . the road far away across a wide ocean . . .

Even after the vengeful mob had been left far back

on the road, Oxford did not decrease the speed of the coach. It was as if he were trying to escape from the horror that was lashed, swaying and bumping and all unknowing, onto the seat beside him.

3

Huddled and miserable, Elizabeth was scarcely aware of the turnings of the coach. After an interminable time, they were out of the moor. The road became wider. They drove through sleeping villages and quiet countryside, and finally along the coast, high above the crashing waves of the sea before turning again inland. They passed close by a Norman church—she could see its spire rising solidly. They must be passing through the village of Polreath Wood. The sound of the crashing sea receded as they left the village behind.

Throughout, Mr. Hurford had sat more stiffly silent than ever. There was anger in him now. Elizabeth could see it in the coldness of his eyes. He hadn't spoken to her, except at the beginning, to tell her to cover herself, his eyes on her knees. She'd looked down quickly. She had been very careful to arrange her cloak so that not even the stuff of her dress showed in the rips that the grabbing hands of the miners had torn in it. It was still so arranged. Nothing of her was revealed except her face. Even her hands were covered with gloves. Still, he kept his eyes on her legs until she rearranged the folds of her cloak over them, which she did with suddenly trembling hands. Was the man mad?

From that time, he sat with his face stiffly straight toward her. Elizabeth kept her head averted. She could feel it the times when his eyes were on her face. She sat tight and uncomfortable, all too conscious of herself, under his cold, appraising scrutiny. From time to time, all during the ride, his eyes returned to her face.

Would they never reach the manor and safety? How long could she stand the torment? His eyes seemed to blame her. How could she be held to blame? For what?

They turned off the main road. Mr. Hurford spoke to Oxford through the slot. "Take the back lane, Oxford."

They turned off onto a small lane just barely wide enough for the coach to make its way. It was dark, and the shrubbery and brush crowded against the coach, scraping raspingly along the sides of it. Overspreading limbs of trees, tangled with heavy, looping vines, made a tunnel of the lane.

"Stop! Halt!" a voice shouted out of the darkness, and three men appeared from the concealing brush and stood in the way of the coach, which they couldn't identify at first. The torch had been torn from its clamp by the miners and thrown in the dust of the road. No one had given thought to it when they had taken up their way again.

"It's all right, Mr. Hurford . . . Miss . . ." Oxford said quickly. "It's the watchmen."

"I know who it is!" Mr. Hurford's voice was clipped. "Have them take Dax! Answer no questions!"

"Ho there, Oxford. It's you come home, is it?" And then the speaker must have come close enough to see Dax. "What's that? What's happened to Dax? God above, look at the sight of him!"

"Answer no questions!" Mr. Hurford repeated his order. "Help them with Dax. Keep quiet! You understand? Quiet about everything! I'll make any explanations that need to be made after I've seen his lordship."

Dax was taken down much more gently than he had been put up there. Elizabeth could feel the movement of the coach as the men moved about on it, but the movements were not jerky and sharp. There were low exclamations and low, shocked questions from the men, but Oxford answered them nothing.

The men moved away with their burden, and Oxford made to climb back onto the driver's seat. Mr. Hurford suddenly stood up and swung himself down from the coach.

"Go with the men. I'll drive the coach to the house."

Elizabeth could sense the amazement and consternation on Oxford's face. He stood for a moment, as if unsure of what he'd heard, and then stepped back a pace or two. "Yes sir, Mr. Hurford," he said. He cast a glance toward Elizabeth before stumbling off through the dark after the watchmen and Dax.

Mr. Hurford maneuvered the coach backward, using the whip to direct the horses. They shuddered in their traces, trying to do the impossible thing demanded of them, frightened into obedience by the snapping, stinging flicks of the whip on their rumps and withers.

The narrow, dark passage was negotiated, and they were back on the road. They soon turned off the road and stopped before a pair of tall iron gates set in a high stone wall. The stone wall extended to a corner to the right beyond the gates and served also as the outer wall of a large gatehouse, the second story of which rose above it.

The double gates swung open from the middle and they drove through. "Evening to you, Mr. Hurford," Elizabeth heard a muffled voice declare hurriedly.

There was surprise in the voice that the speaker tried to suppress. She looked back to see the gates swinging shut again. A figure that was no more than a shadow closed them securely and drew the heavy iron bolt and padlocked it. A sense of fear seized Elizabeth, now that the gates were locked behind her.

The avenue along which they drove was also closely grown with trees with overhanging limbs tangled with vines. The avenue was not straight, nor was it on level ground. They made several curving turns and were pulled up small steep hills by the straining horses, urged on by the stinging flicks of the whip, and held back by them on the sharp descents. Elizabeth lost all sense of direction. Once she thought she heard the crashing of the sea.

They came up on another stone wall. It was lower, and where there might have been a gate, there was a wide, high archway. The coach ground jarringly over an iron bridgework laid flat on the earth beneath the arch, and they were on the gravel of a court.

Elizabeth could sense the manor house, more than see it. The huge, shadowy shape of it towered in uneven heights far above. She could not make out the extent of its height nor of its width. It looked like a huge stone fortress-castle with towers rising above its every corner.

Mr. Hurford pulled the horses to a stop at a door set into the wall in a recess, to the side of which rose one of the towers. He climbed down and came around and opened the door of the coach.

"Keep quiet!" he said, his words an order. "The household is asleep. I do not want the lord and lady disturbed!"

Every instinct in Elizabeth cried out in warning. She huddled in her corner, not moving, staring at Mr. Hurford, apprehension growing to alarm at the sight of his eyes. They were cold and stony still, but there was something else in them now—a brightness, as of fever.

"Come down, Miss Stewart!"

Quaking in every fiber, Elizabeth climbed down from the high coach. He did not touch her to help her. He turned from her and unlocked the heavy wooden door. It was of thick, deep slabs of wood, held solidly together by wide, heavy crossed iron strips studded with heavy nails. He opened the door and pushed her roughly inside.

Elizabeth could see nothing in the pitch-black. She heard the door thud to a close and heard the iron key turn in the lock. She stood frozen in fear.

Mr. Hurford's cold hand grasped her arm tightly, fingers pinching her arm, hurting it. He pulled her, stumbling and halting, along the passage. They descended narrow, twisting stone steps set between damp stone walls. They were too narrow for two to descend together, and he pushed her along before him. Her feet slipped on the slimy wet stones, and she would have fallen several times except for his grip on her arm.

Once down the steps, he pushed her ahead along a narrow passage cut through stone. They made several turnings along the long way. Finally Mr. Hurford shoved her roughly against the wet stone wall and reached around her to unlock another door. He opened it and shoved her inside. She stumbled forward, lost her footing, and fell. She heard the key turn in the lock.

Elizabeth's mind was in a daze from disbelief and shock. She couldn't take in what was happening. Was she crazy? Had she suddenly gone mad? This could not be happening! She was in a dream, a nightmare!

She heard the sound of gliding footsteps fading away, muffled by the close walls of the passage.

Elizabeth sprang to her feet, stricken by terror. Mr.

Hurford was leaving her locked alone in the room! She sprang in the direction of the door and found it by scrabbling with her fingers along the wall. She pounded on it, screaming for Mr. Hurford to come back. She stopped pounding and listened for the sound of footsteps coming back. There was no sound except the slithering oozing and dripping of water somewhere inside the room where she was.

Elizabeth was afraid that her mind would snap. She could see nothing—not even the dim outline of anything. She could smell the dankness of the stone walls, and she could hear the sliding of water down slime-covered stone. She turned from the door, whimpering, almost senseless with terror. She pressed her back against the wood of the door, not daring to risk losing the sense of where it was in the dark. Oh God, where was she? What was happening to her? She strained her ears for any sound of footsteps. He couldn't mean to leave her here! He must come back!

But he did not. Elizabeth didn't know how many dragging moments and hours she kept upright, cringed against the door. When her mind and her body could take no more of terror, she slid in a swoon to the floor.

Elizabeth was brought back to consciousness as the door was pushed open. Her deadweight was against it, and she was being shoved, inch by heavy inch, to give space for entering to whoever was outside the door. Her face was pressed on the stone floor. She felt first the pain in her cheek as it was scraped over the rough stone, and then her face was in cold water. Full consciousness came to her when she almost drowned in the water. She pushed herself up by her hands and looked about, trying to place where she was. And then she remembered! She crawled quickly away from the door, staying close down on the floor, peering in the direction of the door.

She could see nothing. She heard footsteps moving across the room. She heard the strike of flint. Then the glare of light flared out, momentarily blinding her. She blinked her eyes against the pain of the light. When she could open them, Mr. Hurford was standing in a corner of the room, looking across and down at her. His face was as cold and stony as ever. The bright, feverish look began to grow in his eyes, but the expression on his face did not change. He was standing next to a low table. A platter of food was on the table.

"Get up!" he ordered. "I've brought you food! Eat!"

When Elizabeth did not move, he strode over to her and jerked her forward. He pulled her, on her knees, across the stone floor.

The food was hot, and when the steaming scent of it reached her, Elizabeth felt saliva pour into her mouth. Her stomach knotted in pain. She was starved, ravenous, and she had not known that she was. She had given no thought to food. She had had nothing to eat since noon of the day before. She fell on the platter like a starved animal, eating with her hands, shoving handfuls of meat and boiled potatoes and greens into her mouth, swallowing half-chewed gobs that almost choked her.

She felt herself jerked away from the steaming platter by her hair. Her gorge rose, and the food with it. She was choking and gasping, or trying to gasp, to get air. Her head was pulled sharply back, her throat arched upward. If he continued to hold her so, she would choke on the food in her throat!

He threw her head forward with a sweep of his hand. Elizabeth knelt there on the floor, head almost down to her knees, trying to gain her breath, trying not to lose the food, trying to keep her sanity. She felt a faintness coming over her. She could not give in to faintness! She would die if she did! She would choke to death on the food in her throat.

Elizabeth stayed where she was, swallowing as often as she could summon enough saliva to allow her to swallow, slowly forcing the food down. She needed strength. She needed reason. She was being treated like an animal, and she was acting like one. She knew it, but she also knew that an animal's instinct for survival was more knowledgeable than a human's. She would make use of it.

Hurford looked down upon the sorry creature at his feet, contempt on his face. A slow, sneering smile thinned his lips. His thoughts pleased him. This time he would have his way—Lady Sarah be damned! The thing before him—at his feet—was no prize, but she could be made to do.

As for Lady Sarah, he could handle that madwoman. Hadn't she thrown herself at him? She knew what he wanted from a woman, and she wanted him to want it from her. The sneering smile tightened. All he wanted from Lady Sarah was the money that she swore would be his. He would have it if she would keep her craziness under control and let him manage things. It was her interference—always her interference—that made their schemes go wrong! This time he wasn't listening to her—this time he would call the tune. He'd been quick enough to promise her that he would get rid of Miss Stewart. What was a promise? He would get rid of Miss Stewart—when he was finished with her! Let her ladyship snap her darting brown eyes at him, let her toss her faded brown hair at him. Let her threaten even as she beckoned. Her threats were less nuisance to him than her beckonings. He had proof against her ladyship of most of her sorry dealings. All she had as proof against him was her word, and she was a woman known to be mad!

Looking up at him, Elizabeth had the sensation of looking at a caricature of a man.

"There's more food, Miss Stewart," he said. "You've not finished your food."

Elizabeth's senses were stunned again. The man was mad! He'd stopped her from eating, and now he was telling her she hadn't finished eating!

Elizabeth stayed exactly where she was, on her knees, facing away from Mr. Hurford now. Some instinct told her to follow in whatever direction he led. "I'm not hungry anymore," she said, head bowed, as if in meekness and submission.

"Then rise!"

Elizabeth tried not to show the astonishment that she felt at so lordly, so regal a command. She pulled herself to her feet, holding onto the edge of the table in order to do so.

It was another Mr. Hurford that she saw when she was on her feet again and facing him.

Mr. Hurford stood outlined against the door. He held a whip in his hand. Elizabeth remembered how he had used the whip on the horses, forcing them to do something totally unnatural to them—forcing them, with the whip, to guide the coach backward on a narrow dark lane.

Elizabeth knew that she was in the presence of something unnatural, something evil. But Elizabeth was Elizabeth. She had been through unnatural things before, and she had survived.

"Mr. Hurford," she said, lifting her head and trying to stand straight. "I was brought here to be guest of the lady of this house, at the invitation of the lady of this house. I demand an explanation!"

The whip flashed. It flicked toward Elizabeth. It did

not strike her, and she knew that it was not an accident that it did not. He had not meant it to. It flicked again and touched, just barely, the material of her cloak, leaving a short, neat slash, as if the material had been cut by scissors.

Mr. Hurford stroked the whip in his hand. "This is your explanation, Miss Stewart." He turned and left the room, locking the door behind him.

Elizabeth, appalled, unbelieving, heard his footsteps gliding mushily along the damp stone of the passage. He turned a corner somewhere along the length of the passage and his footsteps became muffled, dying echoes.

As if in a state of fascination, Elizabeth stared down at the slash in her cloak. ❧

4

The place where Elizabeth was could not be called a room. It was nothing more than a hollow the size of a small room, chiseled out of stone. What had been its original purpose, she couldn't guess, unless it had been a dungeon. In it there was only the low table, a stool, and in one corner that was on a higher level of the rough floor, a matted bunch of dried and rotted straw. The floor and the high ceiling were uneven, as were the walls. In places, water stood in slimy, stagnant pools. Water oozed from the stone of the walls and rolled and slid down the uneven cracks and crevices to the floor, and some seeped on through the floor to some level below.

On the low table, beside the platter of food, were a pewter pitcher of water and a stack of thick candles. Whether Mr. Hurford had brought the candles when he brought the food and water, she didn't know.

Only the fact that she had light in the room kept Elizabeth from going mad. That, and the fact that she had a timepiece and could watch the hours and know when day had come, and then night again. For it was that long that she was alone there before Mr. Hurford

returned. By the time he did, she was numb with cold
and despair, convinced that she had been left to die.
But why? What had she done? What was the reason
for this plot against her?

She heard the echoes of distant footsteps and then
heard the gliding footsteps. The door was unlocked
and opened, and Mr. Hurford, carefully and deliberately locking the door behind him, advanced into the
room and to the table. He carried another tray. He
exchanged it for the one that was there, retraced his
steps to the door, unlocked it, went out, and locked it
behind him. He had not glanced in Elizabeth's direction and had not uttered a word.

Only when she heard the heavy key turn in the
rusty iron lock did Elizabeth fling herself from the
rotted straw and rush to the door. It was as if she had
been held in a vise of terror until the greater terror of
being left alone again had released her. She pounded
with her fists on the rough wood of the door, screaming
and shrieking. She continued shrieking even after no
sound was coming from her raw and aching throat. She
slid down the door, feeling the sharp prick of splinters
on her cheek and forehead and on her bleeding palms.
She cried aloud with bone-wracking sobs. The sound
of her crying filled the space around her, echoing and
resounding on the stone walls, her own utterances
closing in on her and smothering her.

It was another full twenty-four hours before Mr.
Hurford came again. This time Elizabeth was at the
wall beside the door when he reached it. She'd been
there from the first sound of echo that she had heard.
Her heart pounded. She had planned that she would
slip through the door when Mr. Hurford opened it.
She prayed that he would open the door as confidently
as he had before—with no thought that she might be
there, poised to slip through, behind his back as he

entered. Where she would be when she was outside, she didn't know, but anywhere would be better than a moment longer in the place where she was.

The key scraped in the lock. . . . The door remained closed. Elizabeth waited, breath bated, heart pounding so fiercely that she was afraid it could be heard beyond the door.

When she thought she could stand the suspense no longer, Mr. Hurford's voice came, muffled but audible, through the wood of the door. "Stand away, Miss Stewart!"

Elizabeth's tensed body sagged. How had he known? How *could* he have known! Her utter helplessness overwhelmed her. Tears spilled down her cheeks. She backed away from the door.

Mr. Hurford then entered. He closed and locked the door. He did not carry a tray. He held the whip before him, stroking the leather-wrapped butt of it.

"That was not clever, Miss Stewart." He toyed with the whip, flexing it between his two hands. "Quite naïve and obvious. You wouldn't want to anger me, you know, presuming that I could so easily be tricked."

"I demand to see her ladyship!" Elizabeth screamed. "I am here at her invitation! I demand to see her! She was expecting me! She will wonder where I am! You can't get away with this! I demand . . ."

"How do you know that, Miss Stewart . . . that her ladyship expects you?"

"You yourself delivered her invitation to me!" With those words in her ears, Elizabeth realized that he was the only person in the world who knew that the invitation had been delivered to her and that she had accepted it. She had not apprised Miss Goodrod of her destination when she had left Miss Holybrook's.

The driver—Oxford! He knew that she had been brought here!

"Perhaps her ladyship does not expect you, Miss Stewart."

"What are you trying to tell me? That it was all a hoax? I don't believe it! The driver—Oxford! He didn't look like the kind of man . . ."

"What do you know of Oxford, Miss Stewart? I wasn't aware that you knew him."

Hope left Elizabeth. She didn't know Oxford. He'd seemed a kind man, but it was all too obvious that he was in on the scheme, whatever it was—or why hadn't he done something?

"What do you want from me?" Hysteria sent her voice ringing against the stones. "What do you want from me!"

Mr. Hurford said in a voice of deadly calm, "You overexcite yourself, Miss Stewart."

"Overexcite myself! You must be mad! You bring me here—an invited guest—and then you throw me in this dungeon! You leave me alone here to rot! And when I question it, you tell me that I *overexcite* myself! You're a lunatic. You're mad!"

"Calm, Miss Stewart." Mr. Hurford looked at her, eyes passing from her face, slowly down the length of her to the hem of her cloak. "You wear your cloak still, Miss Stewart. Aren't you overwarm?"

"No! I'm not! It's cold in this. . . !"

"I feel you must be overwarm. Remove your cloak, Miss Stewart."

"No!"

"The cloak, Miss Stewart."

Mr. Hurford stood in the center of the room. He did not look at Elizabeth. He flicked the whip in different directions, not at anything in particular. He might have been merely amusing himself. But he could reach every farthest distance of the room from where he stood. The clicking of the tip of the whip against the stone of the walls in various directions proved it.

"The cloak, Miss Stewart," he repeated.

"I won't take it off! No!"

The whip flashed, and a long slash appeared in the wide sleeve of the cloak. Elizabeth had not even felt the sting of the lash. She had not seen the whip coming toward her.

"As you can see, Miss Stewart, it would be easy enough for me to remove your cloak."

The whip sang out and slashed through the folds of the skirt. Elizabeth froze, too terrified to make a sound or a movement. The whip hissed, and the collar, close at the neck, fell away to hang down her back, cut neatly away from where it had been sewn.

"The cloak, Miss Stewart. . . ?"

Feeling paralyzed, Elizabeth fumbled at the fastenings of the cloak with fingers numb, and yet shaking so hard that she could not manage the clasps.

Mr. Hurford watched silently, the sneering smile thinning his mouth.

"They don't know I'm here, do they?" Elizabeth sobbed. "No one knows I'm here, except you and the driver who brought me."

"Oxford left us on the lane, if you remember."

Dry sobs jerked Elizabeth's shoulders. Not even the driver then . . .

"Only *we* know, perhaps, Miss Stewart."

The clasp below the one that Elizabeth was fumbling with fell away and made a soft clatter on the floor, neatly severed by the whip. Elizabeth jumped away. Suddenly the deadly, hissing whip was around her everywhere, not touching her, but close enough that she could feel small rushes of wind on her cheeks, her hair, her hands.

"I want to see his lordship!" she screamed. "I want to see Lady Sarah! You'd better take me to them, and take me *now!* They'll find out what you're doing, and when they know . . ."

"Do they not know, Miss Stewart?"

"They couldn't! Why would they do such a thing? They *wouldn't* . . ."

"You could say, Miss Stewart, that you have her ladyship to thank that you're alive at all."

Mr. Hurford's sneering smile thinned to an ugly grimace as he thought of this second scheme gone wrong because of Lady Sarah. The scheme to get rid of his lordship had come to nothing more than his being hurt—had come to nothing more because of her! The failure of that plan, as well as this, was due to her and to none other!

He'd performed his part perfectly. He'd had it all so carefully planned and arranged. He'd exactly calculated the distance at which the man-engine must break from the timbered scaffolding. He'd exactly calculated the weight and stress necessary to make the man-engine snap the ropes that he had cut partway through, and fall to the bottom of the shaft. He'd exactly calculated the timing. He'd made his careful arrangements with Charlie. Charlie was to come for him with an urgent message just as he and his lordship stepped onto the man-engine, a message calling him urgently away, leaving his lordship alone to take the fall.

And then that damned Daly had shown up! *She* had sent him on some stupid pretext, knowing he would dog his lordship's every step, watchful of his safety. Knowing that his lordship would listen to Daly when he would listen to no other. It was Daly who had insisted that his lordship go down by ladder to the first level and take the man-engine from there. As a result,

the fall was only twenty feet, and Daly had taken the
brunt of it.

Damn the man! He'd come out of it without so much
as the breath knocked out of him! It was only a freak
of chance that some of the timbering had caved in on
his lordship, crushing his chest and leaving him with
several broken ribs and internal injuries.

Lady Sarah hadn't wanted his lordship dead all the
while she'd been plotting his death! Or the fool had
changed her mind! She could have brought suspicion
on his head with that one, what with being so anxious
to see that Daly came to the mine where his affairs as
bailiff never brought him. The woman's madness
would ruin them both yet!

Now here was the second scheme gone wrong—and
her ladyship to thank for that, too! Miss Stewart was
in her debt for being alive, no less than truth in that!
But it wasn't for the sake of keeping her alive that
Lady Sarah had interfered. There was no question but
that she wanted Elizabeth Stewart dead. It was for his
own sake that she had put her fine hand in. She had
insisted that Dax act as go-between. It wouldn't do
for Mr. Hurford to be seen about with Charlie, she'd
said. It was too soon after the accident in the mine,
and some might remember how thick they had been
then. He had seen the merit in her argument, and he
saw it now.

Still, he wished he hadn't listened. If he'd handled
Charlie, Charlie would have done what he was supposed to do. He wouldn't have had the guts to try to
outfox him as he had tried to outfox Dax. The two
stupid bastards! Neither one had a wit in his head, and
there were both of them, trying to play it grand at
being spies and double-spies! Served them both right
that they were dead. And it served her Ladyship right

that Miss Stewart *wasn't!* Let her stew in her own juice, knowing that she was still alive, and that he had her where he had her. Let her know that he was taking his pleasure of her—and let her worry about Oxford's finding out!

Oxford! That was another instance of her madness! Did she think he didn't remember the grudge she had against Oxford? For propriety's sake, Oxford must go to Launceton, she had said. Damn her to hell! Where was her own propriety? She'd wanted Oxford killed, along with Dax and Miss Stewart. She hadn't fooled him on that from the start! Did she think he didn't remember how Oxford had fouled her little scheme to get rid of his lordship's bastard Colin? Damn the brat, too! Damn them all! When he got his hands on the money Lady Sarah stood to inherit—and he would!— he'd show them that a man didn't have to be born to place to be a man!

All the hate in Mr. Hurford concentrated on Elizabeth. Groveling, puling wretch! Little fun she promised—she'd give in before the whip was limbered!

"Are you saying that this is his lordship's doing?" Elizabeth stared in disbelief. "Are you saying that he wanted me dead, and her ladyship prevented him? What has his lordship got against me? What *can* he have against me? I've never seen him in my life!"

"Why give the Lord of Polreath so many of your thoughts, Miss Stewart? I doubt that you are in his."

The whip flashed, this time slashing through all the layers of her skirts and stinging her ankle.

Elizabeth screamed and hopped to one side.

"That's better, Miss Stewart. Dance for me!"

Elizabeth bent forward, screaming like a hysterical banshee. She was beyond control. "I want to see his lordship! I *demand* to see him! I have the right to know why he is doing this to me! I have the right..."

"If you wish to send a message to his lordship, Miss Stewart, dance for me!" Again the stinging whip flashed and cut through to her leg. Even as Elizabeth whirled and tried to run, the whip sang out twice in rapid succession, and two more clasps of her cloak plinked on the stone floor. "Dance for me, and perhaps I'll see that his lordship gets your message."

The whip continued to lash out, and no matter the direction Elizabeth whirled and ran, it found the clasps until the last one fell to the floor and the cloak hung open from neck to hem. The tip of the whip had touched Elizabeth's skin only once, and that was when it had plucked the clasp from the neckline. Elizabeth choked and almost strangled, grabbing at the burning skin of her throat.

"Drop the cloak, Miss Stewart."

In her mind, Elizabeth felt the burning, cutting sting of the whip circling her neck. She knew that she would feel it in reality if she didn't do what he said to do. She loosed her hands from her throat and let the cloak slide to the floor at her feet. She felt that she was already naked before him. She knew that her dress—all of her clothing—would be slashed and ripped from her before he was through.

"Leave me alone!" she screamed. "Leave me alone! Leave me alone!" She screamed one piercing shriek after another, swinging one way and then the other, running from one wall to the next, the lashing, hissing whip everywhere around her.

Elizabeth could feel the stabbing, stinging lick of the whip on her skin each time it sang out now. Slashes and rips appeared in her dress each time it struck. The sleeves were in strips of material, still bound at shoulder and wrist. There were rips the length of her skirt. She felt the sting of the whip on her back and shoulders and felt the cold air of the dank room on the skin of her back as the material parted.

And then she felt the first sharp sting on her breast. She screamed and looked down, bending forward and clutching her bosom. She expected to see blood streaming, but there was only a slight reddening of the skin where the whip had made contact. She bent farther over to protect herself. "Please don't!" she cried. "Please! Please don't!" She sank to the floor, sobbing hysterically and pleading.

Mr. Hurford's eyes glittered. He sucked in his breath rapidly. A look of sardonic satisfaction was on his face. It had been better sport than he had expected. Let there be more then!

Slowly he controlled his breathing as he looked down at the crumbled figure at his feet. Slowly his eyes lost their feverish glitter. Nothing then was different from his normal appearance. He had stood, throughout, as stiff and straight and solemn as if he had been in attendance at a bier.

"Yes, Miss Stewart," he said, "I think I *shall* leave you alone . . . for now. If I see all of your dancing today, what shall I have for my amusement tomorrow?"

With the sharp toe of his boot, Mr. Hurford turned Elizabeth so that her upper body faced him. He inserted the toe of his boot in a rip in her bodice and pulled upward and away, ripping the material until Elizabeth's full breast was exposed. The rough sole of the boot grazed Elizabeth's nipple as his foot crossed over to expose her other breast. Elizabeth tried to wrench herself away, but he pinioned her shoulder to the floor with the long butt of the whip.

"If you don't dance to suit me tomorrow, Miss Stewart," Mr. Hurford said, "those breasts that wink so prettily at me now may lose their rosebuds." He brushed the sole of his boot across one nipple and then across the other. "That's something for you to think about until I come again."

He removed the butt of the whip from Elizabeth's shoulder. She moaned and turned away from him, hiding her naked breasts and face against the stone floor.

Elizabeth wished that she would die. She prayed for death. Please God, let me die before he comes back.

She heard his footsteps as he walked across the room and then turned and walked to the door.

"I'm taking the lighted candle and the flint, Miss Stewart," Mr. Hurford said. "For your sake. Contemplation is better done in the dark."

Elizabeth heard the key turn twice in the rusty lock —once unlocking, once locking—heard the slithering footsteps receding, heard the echoes and heard them fade.

Please God, she prayed, let me die before he comes tomorrow! ☙

5

Oxford usually finished his morning inspection of his coach horses and got himself out of the stable area and to the coach house in short order. Heller, the head of his lordship's stables, had a high-minded way about him that Oxord didn't like. And didn't have to put up with. Wasn't he head coachman, and equal in importance to any groom?

This morning he hung around so long that Heller finally remarked, "Be ye still about, old man? Things taking care of themselves, are they, over at the coach house?"

Oxford was hanging around for a reason. The little girls—Lady Sarah's wards—would be coming to see their ponies exercised. They came every morning. He had expected, for two mornings now—the two mornings that had passed since they'd fetched Miss Stewart to the manor—that Miss Stewart would come with them. Each year, the little girls were allowed to contribute to the entertainment of Lady Sarah's guest from Miss Holybrook's school. One of the things they always did was bring the young lady to the paddock to show off their ponies. Oxford hadn't seen hide nor hair of

Miss Stewart—neither at the paddock nor anywhere else—for the two days she'd been at the manor. He had a strange feeling in himself that things weren't right where she was concerned. He busied himself putting a lead rope on Nero, the horse that had thrown a shoe on the way back from Launceton. Oxford started with him toward the paddock.

"What are ye about?" Heller asked indignantly and loftily. "That horse don't exercise in this paddock. He's too heavy a tread to be mixing with my saddle horses and ruining their turf! You want to walk him, you take him to his own paddock where he belongs to be!"

"I intend to walk him just the bit of time it takes to see if he's any way lamed. I aim to put him to the long coach to carry poor Dax and his twin to the chapel . . . poor fellows." He kept on walking toward the paddock. "Will you be coming for the funeral, Heller?"

"Aye. I'll be coming. All us'll be coming."

Heller said no more about Nero's ruining his turf. Which was what Oxford had hoped for when he'd purposefully mentioned the funeral. Heller had had a fondness for the rascals, Dax and Jax. Jax, poor demented fellow, had taken his lordship's horse, Juniper, and tried to ride off on him. He was the fastest horse in the stables, and Jax was after catching the labor leader, Mr. Calvin, and killing him. He blamed him for Dax's death, and, in a way, perhaps he was to blame. Jax had gotten himself killed for his trouble. The horse had thrown him. Juniper was a devil horse. Only two who could put a finger to him were his lordship and Heller, and Jax should have known better than to try to sit him. Poor fellow. He was out of his mind with grieving for his twin and not thinking of consequences.

The little girls were coming up now. Oxford timed

his steps so that he passed the rail fence just as they reached it. He touched his forelock twice. "Morning to you, Miss Patience. Morning to you, Miss Hope." He was bold to speak before being spoken to, but he was compelled. He had to be even bolder. "Be ye not likin' the young lady from the school visiting this year? Ye've not brought her to see your fine ponies."

The older of the girls looked at him scornfully. "You're as foolish in your head as ma'am says you are!"

"Ma'am's not having anyone this year from Miss Holybrook's," her sister added, aping the older one's scornful tone.

Oxford stopped. "Be ye sure now?"

The voice of one of the nurses, following at a distance behind, called out, "Miss Patience! Miss Hope! Come along quickly. You mustn't engage in talk with the people."

Both girls gave Oxford a spiteful, baleful look. "We won't be allowed to watch our ponies now," Patience snapped meanly. "All because of you!"

Oxford stood staring after the little girls as they walked away. He was right then. Something mighty strange was going on with the lass, Miss Stewart. He was standing at the rail, puzzling what to do when he saw the tall, thin figure that was the Lord of Polreath striding up. The man had a way of seeming to materialize.

Oxford bowed, tugging hard at his forelock.

The Lord of Polreath stopped. His greeting was curt.

"Good morning, Sir, my lord." It was never possible to guess what his lordship's mood was. He seemed always angry. It was the look he had, stern and forbidding. Lord John was a young man, for all his shock of white hair that had its original dark color only at the edges on his neck and in the sideburns.

Oxford had known Lord John all his life. He had been born at the manor himself, and was a lad of thirteen when the heir to Polreath was born. The heir had been a wild one in his youth, but there was nothing of his old mischievous wildness in him now . . . hadn't been since he'd come back from India ten years ago. All the bright sparkle of love of life that he had used to have was gone from him. Must be due to the wars he'd fought that it was gone. He'd come back from India no longer a boy, but a hard and angry man. He hadn't been old in years, but his hair was already beginning to turn white even then, and it wasn't many months before it was as it was today. His lean, hard body had the same angry look as his features.

"I don't want time lost this morning, Oxford. The funeral service will be at ten sharp."

"The coach will be ready, my lord." His lordship had wanted the funeral to be held the day before, but because of the condition of Jax's wife, who was near time of birth with a baby, it had had to be postponed.

"See that it is!"

"Yes, my lord." Oxford tugged at his forelock, bowing again. He shuffled about, not turning to go, as he knew he was expected to do. His feeling about Miss Stewart held him there. He'd brought her to Polreath, had driven her there all the way from Launceton, been with her through the scare the tinners had given them and the terrible thing they had done to Dax, and somehow all of that obligated him to her. If something was wrong and he didn't do anything about it, he'd blame himself all his life. It was the same feeling he'd had that day a few years back when the boy Colin had been lost on the cliffs. If he hadn't made himself bold to go to his lordship that day, the boy would have drowned.

"Excusing myself, my lord, but will Miss Stewart be

riding, or should I see to room for her in one of the carriages?"

"Miss Stewart . . . ?"

"Her ladyship's guest, my lord. Such as she has one every year this time from the school what she patrons."

The tall man stared down at him, his black brows drawn together in a questioning, black frown. "She won't be attending," he said shortly. He looked about in a distracted manner and then turned and walked back toward the manor. Whatever it was that he had come to the stables to do, he didn't stay to do it.

Oxford was relieved of the burden of Miss Stewart's well-being. He knew the cause of the angry frown and the distracted manner. Lord John hadn't heard the name "Miss Stewart" until he'd heard it from him. Something *was* wrong, but Lord John would get to the bottom of it, and hard day it would be for whoever was the cause of the wrongdoing!

Oxford went about his business shaking his head and muttering to himself. Who would it be else than her ladyship would be the cause of the trouble? Nobody. It was always her was the cause of trouble when it came. Good as she might be, and goodhearted as she might be . . . and she was both, in some ways.

Take the trouble she put herself to over the school. The school couldn't have a better patron than her ladyship if the number of its patrons ran to dozens. Every year, come near graduating time, she traveled to the school herself or she sent Mr. Hurford to choose the most deserving among the graduating ones to be companion to her for the summer at Polreath Manor part of the time and at her own family seat at Dunmavern in Scotland part of the time. The girl would stay with her through the season in London and later at Brighton. It was a proud young lady who entered society by the side of Lady Polreath. It was a most signal

honor to the girl chosen, and no mistake, no matter
how high the rank of her own family. Few there were
that outranked Polreath, saving maybe the king's own
kin.

Oxford's puzzlement grew stronger in him. People
didn't just disappear like they'd never been.

Sarah Broughton, Lady Polreath. (Her husband was
an earl. It was one of his idiosyncrasies that they must
be addressed by their given names.) Sarah Howard
Broughton—Lady Sarah—stood at a tower window
staring down at a garden that was not visible from
her own apartments. It was her husband's private
garden. He walked there sometimes, meditated there,
brooded there. Usually it was deep twilight when he
could be seen moving along the paths, head lowered,
his hands grasped behind his back. The times that he
used the garden were rare. Even so, he allowed access to the garden to no one, except the gardener he
had chosen to tend it. He little knew the hours that
his wife spent where she was now, leaning into the
small window—deep and barred—gazing down upon
the garden.

There had been another garden that Sarah had stood
in a window and gazed down upon. She had been a
child then. She had been Sarah Howard. She was an
Honourable in her own right, for she was decended
from the line of the third Duke of Norfolk. Her family's
claims to descent had been disputed, and more than
once, though not in her lifetime; but they had fought
for and won the right to keep the position that they
held among their aristocratic peers. The privileges of
rank had been instilled in Sarah from the time she was
born. Her actions were based on the assumption of
privilege, and were in no way governed by the dictates
of law. If it seemed madness to others, to her it seemed

right and natural. It had been so since she was six, though she was seven when she became aware of it.

From the window of the day nursery, Sarah looked down on the topiary garden. She was fascinated by the garden, and it was forbidden her. It belonged to her older brother Robert, who was eight. He was lordly about what was his, and jealous of his possessions. The garden had been a present to him at birth from the lawnskeeper. It had really been only the promise of a present, for there hadn't been a single topiary in it at the time—Sarah had heard the story often. It had been only a part of the wide lawns. Now it was a wonderland of things almost unbelievable to the eye. There was a church, complete with spire. There was a Hansel and Gretel house. There were chairs and sofas. There was a clown with balloony trousers and a sailor with twin-peaked cap. But most wondrous of all, to Sarah, were the animals and fowls. There was a mother goose with goslings following. There was a falcon lifting, great wings spread. There was an elephant trumpeting and a tiger crouched to spring. There was a great risen bear and a wild boar on the attack. There were gentler ones—a lamb, a curled and sleeping puff of a cat. . . . And all of them clipped from growing green hedge.

A sparkle of sunlight on metal caught Sarah's eye. She leaned farther over the casement trying to see again what it was that had caught a glint from the sun. And she saw what it was. There! There by the haunch of the tiger gathered for the spring lay a pair of the gardener's shears!

Wild excitement filled Sarah. Her hands itched to hold the shears—to clip—oh, just the tiniest bit of a clip—one of the topiaries. She had watched the gardener—the special one who tended the topiaries, who was such a genius at shaping them—teach Robert how to use the shears. She had watched the two of them as they stood close to the topiary that was to be clipped, the gardener's head bent down to Robert's as he explained it all to him. She had seen them back off a distance and look at the topiary, and then walk up to it again . . . had seen the gardener pass the shears to Robert . . . had seen Robert clip—such a little bit that she hadn't seen any change in the shape of the topiary —seen him clip again, and sometimes once again before he and the gardener backed off a distance again to observe what he had done. She had seen the gardener nod approval—say a few words to Robert that were words of praise—for Robert would nod. Then they would move up to the topiary again. She had seen Robert handle all the implements in the gardener's basket, from the smallest clippers to the largest shears —the ones that looked as if they would be half his height if they were upended on the ground beside him. Sarah had burned with envy.

Of a sudden, Sarah's mind was made up. She was going to go into the topiary garden. She was going to clip a topiary. Just the least bit. Just the littlest bit. She wouldn't make any change in the shape of the topiary. No one would ever know that she had touched it. When she finished, she would return the shears to where the gardener had forgotten them.

Sarah went to the door of the nursery and listened carefully, holding her breath. She heard no sounds. It was the quiet time of the afternoon. Everyone was sleeping after heavy dinner. She was supposed to be asleep herself. Robert, of course, was not sleeping. He was privileged in everything. He and his tutor were probably at darts in the billiard room, or at billiards.

Sarah was a small child, darting and birdlike in her movements. She skipped rather than walked, flitted rather than ran. Her mother teasingly laughed that her mind skipped and flitted the same as her feet, with no more attachment to solid reason than her feet had to the ground. Her father would tweak her chin and say that he wouldn't have her any other way; he wouldn't have her weighted down by brains to earthly cares. She was his little hummingbird and his delight, and that was all that was required of her.

Sarah was soon poised on the edge of one of the gravel walks that bordered the topiary garden. She dipped one small slippered toe onto the closely clipped grass of the lawn of the garden, but then she quickly pulled it back, afraid for a moment of the trespass she was determined on. She braced her shoulders with a twist and tossed her dark curls and cast her narrow bright brown eyes toward all the corners of the garden and the paths around it. There was no one to be seen. She lifted her chin and hummed softly to herself—it helped to pretend to herself that she wasn't scared—and stepped onto the grass. Then she ran on winged feet straight for the shears. She stood beside them, she in the shadow of the topiary, the shears just beyond the shadow. It was not a bright day, but now and then a shifting in the clouds would release a ray of sun that would catch the metal of the shears.

Sarah held her breath and leaned forward and down and grasped the shears by the handles. The metal felt cold to her hands and brought back some of her fear at what she was doing. She tightened her grip on them to warm them and looked about at the topiaries, trying to decide which one she would like the most to clip. One of the big ones, she decided, so that if she slipped and made a mistake, it wouldn't be so quickly noticed. She would clip one of the eaves of the Hansel and Gretel house. She could reach that high. She started on tiptoeing feet toward the topiary, holding the shears pointed straight in front of her.

She was startled and stopped in her tracks by Robert's angry scream.

"Come out of there! Who told you you could go in my garden? Come out of there this instant! If you don't, I'll call Papa!" His rage grew beyond bounds—even for him—when he saw the shears in her hands. "What do you think you're doing!" he shrieked. He was running toward her. "Give me those, you brat! I'll have Papa whip you! You're a sneak! You're no better than a sneak! Give me those! I know why you sneaked in here behind my back—you wanted to ruin my garden! You're mean and jealous! Give me those before I go tell Papa and he has you whipped!"

Sarah tried to tell him that she was only going to clip the tiniest bit. She tried to tell him that she knew how to do it because she had watched him so many times. She tried to beg him to let her clip just one little time . . . just one little time. But he kept screaming over every word she tried to say.

"Papa will have you whipped for trying to ruin my garden! Don't think he won't!" He was almost up to her. "Give me those!"

"Take them!" Sarah screamed. "You're hateful! You're hoggish and stingy and hateful! Take them!" She threw them at him with all the force in her.

The shears flashed in an arc from the sideways swing of her arms. One of the points caught Robert in the throat. He grabbed at his throat, whirling from the impact. His body turned and he fell on his face on the grass. The shears had become dislodged and lay partly under him. Blood spread from his throat onto the grass.

Sarah ran. She didn't stop running until she was

back in the day nursery. She stood just inside the closed door for a while, trying to stop her trembling, trying to catch her breath. Her eyes were glued to the window that faced on the topiary garden. Finally she glided across the rug and leaned over the casement and looked down into the garden. Robert was still lying the way she had seen him last. There was more blood now than there had been. There was a big pool of it under his face and head and throat and even his upper body. The part of the shears that she could see was covered with blood.

Sarah felt herself swooning, but she was jerked back to her senses by a scream. It came from the gardener. "Master Robert! God above! Oh, no! God above!" He had run across the garden and was kneeling beside Robert.

Suddenly the whole house was shaken with the running of feet and swollen with the bursting forth of excited voices and screams and crying. Sarah fainted.

Sarah was ill of brain fever for a long time—eight months. Her birthday came and went while she was ill. When she was herself again, she was seven.

Many changes had come about while she was ill. The topiary garden was no longer there. In its place there was a rock garden. The gardener whose special skill had been in shaping topiaries was no longer there. He had blamed himself for Robert's death—and perhaps others had, too. He'd forgotten a pair of shears —had left them lying about—and Robert, without any supervision, had decided to work on his beloved topiaries and had fallen on the sharp, pointed tips of the shears. One had pierced his jugular vein. The gardener had been pensioned off. He was not held accountable, but the fault lay with him, and his own grief had sharpened the grief of the stricken father and mother at the

death of their only son. He had wanted away from the
place of his misery, and they had wanted to be rid of
the reminder.

Even after Sarah was well, she continued to have
nightmares. Her mother and father attributed the
nightmares to the fact that she had seen Robert lying
dead in his blood on top of the shears that had killed
him. She had been napping and had been awakened
by the gardener's screams and had run to the window
and had looked down and had seen Robert. It was obvious that that was what had happened because she
had been found lying unconscious on the floor beneath
the window. The shock had given her brain fever and
the prolonged nightmares that she still suffered. Her
mother or her father—sometimes both of them—would
sit beside her bed. They would hold her hand and
smooth her brow and whisper reassurances to her.
Sometimes her father would pick her up from her bed
and walk back and forth the length of her room, holding her close to him as if he would protect her with his
arms from any threatening evil. She must get well, he
would whisper; she was his treasure now, his last hope.
All that he had expected of Robert he expected of her
now. All that would have been Robert's would be hers
now. She must get well. She must fit herself for her
inheritance. It was her duty. She was a Howard. She
must never forget that.

With every day that passed, Sarah was brought to
more fully understand the very great extent to which
she had benefited from Robert's death. She was all supreme now. She didn't have to take second place to
anybody. She wasn't going to be the poor relation,
the inheritance would be hers. Robert had taunted her
that she would be nothing more than a servant in his
household when everything was his. But now that day
would never come. He was dead. If she had it to do

over again, she would kill him on purpose. That was the way to get what you wanted—get rid of the people who were keeping you from getting it.

Her father thought that he had secured the inheritance for his only offspring, but that offspring was female. When his younger brother laid claim to the title and the holdings, both were awarded him. But it was only a waystop, and the fortune would still be hers; her uncle had no heirs and she was the last of the line. &

6

At some point during the dragging hours in which she was alone in the dark, Elizabeth had found a reserve of strength. She had forced herself to eat every scrap of food that remained on the platter and had forced herself to drink the water, already rancid in the stale atmosphere of the room.

When she heard the first whispering of distant echoes, Elizabeth stationed herself in the place she had decided on. It was opposite the bed of rotted straw and would be out of the light of the candle that Mr. Hurford would surely bring.

Crouched and ready to spring, Elizabeth listened to the approaching echoes of Mr. Hurford's footsteps. At the turning in the narrow passage, where, before, his footsteps had become gliding whispers of sound, they did not. The man was sure of himself now, for the footsteps sounded sharp and ringing—the steps, not of someone gliding stealthily forward, but of someone walking determinedly and forcefully, doing nothing to hide the fact of his approach.

He thinks he's broken me, Elizabeth thought. That's

good. It will give me advantage. Let him be as sure of himself and overconfident as he will!

Elizabeth didn't think of rescue. She was too far into despair to expect it.

Her heart tightened as the ringing footsteps neared. Her breath shortened as her body tensed. The sound of footsteps stopped abruptly at the door. A key grated in the lock.

The door opened and the tall form of a man appeared.

Elizabeth was on the man entering the room before he was well into it. A snarl that might have come from a tigress at bay came from her throat as she sprang. She was onto the man, legs around his waist, holding her locked to him. Her broken, jagged nails were clawing at his face. Her teeth were trying to close on his throat, searching for the jugular vein.

With one vicious twisting of his body and one savage slash of his arm, the man threw Elizabeth from him and sent her sprawling to the floor.

Elizabeth was up and in a squatting position on the balls of her feet, toes pushing against the stone, ready to spring again. Her matted hair covered half her face. Her eyes blazed with all the glittering hatred of a cornered cat. She was waiting for that instant when Mr. Hurford would fling himself toward her. When he did, whip flying or no, she would be ready.

The man turned and Elizabeth sprang. She sprang with all the strength of a madwoman, straight for his chest, knees catching him in the abdomen. He staggered backward and Elizabeth made ready to spring again. She would attack until she knocked the breath from him! And then she would strangle him with her two hands! She knew how and where!—she had tried it on her own throat, wishing she had the courage to kill herself.

Instead of swinging forward to overpower her, the man swung out behind him and threw the door wide so that light from a candle in the doorway came into the room.

It was not Mr. Hurford! A tall man with a shock of white hair, black-edged, with angry, lowering black eyebrows and stabbing, piercing gray eyes towered over her. The gray eyes flared momentarily and then narrowed as he peered down at her. He stepped backward away from her. He shook his head in confused fashion, brushing one hand across his eyes.

Elizabeth could not have seen anyone at that moment as anything except enemy. She took the opportunity to spring again, but because he had moved away, her spring was short and she was not able to hit his chest with her knees as she had planned. She slid down his body, arms clutching around his legs. She jerked hard at the backs of his knees, hoping to make him topple forward. She would spring on his back and beat his face against the floor!

But his knees didn't bend, and she was on the floor. His hands, like vises, closed on her arms and jerked her to her feet. She twisted away and he caught her around the waist and chest. Her back was crushed against him. His arms were like rods of iron, the one across her breasts hurting them cruelly. She screamed, arms flailing wildly, hands over her head and backward, trying to claw out his eyes. His arm tightened across her breasts, and she could not endure the pain. She wanted to claw at his arm, to pry it away from her, but the pain was so intense that she could not. She felt herself drowning in a sea of unendurable agony. All of her determination—all of her desperation and strength and will—could not keep her from sagging against him.

When Elizabeth opened her eyes, she was lying on

the floor and the man was striding back and forth across the room. She had come from unconsciousness slowly. She had come back to the rhythm of his pacing footsteps, back and forth, back and forth.

When first she opened her eyes, slowly, carefully, only slits, his back was to her. His every muscle—and they were all revealed by the riding clothes that he wore—showed a sinewy, hard strength. His hands were clenched in fists at his sides. He turned suddenly, as if aware that she was watching him.

The man stood above her, but he did not move toward her. He looked down at her from the distance where he was.

"If you are ready to make some sense," the towering man said, "I am ready to listen."

At the cold, uncaring tone of his voice, Elizabeth's will asserted itself. She sat up, flinging back her hair, eyes spitting fire.

The gray eyes narrowed again, and the man shook his head and brushed one hand across his eyes as he had done before. But the change in him was fleeting. His eyes were immediately hard and impersonal again, and cold.

"I want to know how you came to be here," he said. He might have been a magistrate in a court, and she the accused.

Elizabeth sprang to her feet. "My Lord of Polreath!" she said, the sarcasm in her voice as strong as she could make it. She curtsied as low as she could without losing her balance. "It *is* my Lord of Polreath?"

The gray eyes did not show any expression now as he looked at her. They were colder than any eyes she had ever seen. They were gray, but they had only the noncolor of ice.

He repeated, "I want to know how you came to be here."

Elizabeth flamed at the accusation in his tone.

"I'll tell you how I came to be here! I came to be here because you *planned* that I would be here! You used me to save your own neck! No, that's not right. You didn't plan for me to be here at all. You thought they'd kill me! And when they didn't, you had no choice but to bring me here and throw me in this prison! If you'd had your way, they'd have killed me out there on the moor, thinking I was you. You want to make it seem that I came here of my own free will. You're pretending something to keep the blame off yourself!"

Elizabeth couldn't keep the sense of what she was saying straight, and her sentences came out all helter-skelter.

"You make it sound as if I'm here by choice and against your will! Well, I'm not here by choice—not by mine! Do I look as if I'm on a pleasure jaunt?" She flung her arms wide, knowing that her breasts and legs were exposed by the tears and rips in her dress.

The man did not react in the way any other would have at the sight of her nakedness. He moved lithely and quickly to the corner where her cloak was crumpled on the floor, picked it up, and threw it at her. "Cover yourself!"

Elizabeth made no move to pick up the cloak lying at her feet. "I'm sure you're not much offended! I'm sure you're seeing exactly what you knew you would see when you came here! Or was the shock that I saw on your face because you had expected to find me dead? I have Lady Sarah to thank that I'm not. You'd ordered him to get rid of me altogether. Perhaps you don't know your man as well as you think you do!"

Elizabeth couldn't control a frenzy coming over her. "Or do you?" She twirled about, the strips of her skirts whirling about her legs as she turned and twirled before him. "Did he learn his appreciation for erotic dancing from you?" She turned faster and faster, arms above her head, tattered strips flying, her lower body exposed almost to her waist, her breasts bare between the long tears in the bodice of her dress.

Unmoved by what he was seeing, the stone-faced man grabbed her wrist and twisted her arm savagely behind her as he pulled her to a rough stop before him. She yelled like a banshee and twisted free, whirling back to attack with kicking feet and clawing hands. Before he subdued her this time, the sleeves of his own coat were in strips. Her fingers on them had been like sharp iron claws.

Long after there was any use in it, Elizabeth panted and struggled. The man stood as if he might have been rock, holding her pinioned against him while she fought to free herself so that she could attack again.

Elizabeth sobbed suddenly. She couldn't stop herself. Her breath came in heaving, sobbing gulps. She hated herself for crying!

"How could you let him do what he did to me?" she sobbed. "What kind of man are you?"

"I'm the kind who can tame a wildcat when I have to," he said coldly. His hands were on her bare flesh, but they were not caressing hands. Elizabeth suddenly became all too aware of his hands on her naked flesh. "Let me have my cloak." She was crying softly now. "Please. Let me have my cloak."

Without a word, he released her. She staggered as she moved away from him. He made no move to support her. She picked up the cloak and wrapped it around her.

Some of Elizabeth's will asserted itself after she was covered. "If you don't want me to dance for you," she asked, "then what is it you want?"

"I want to hear less of your ravings and more of the truth."

"Why won't you believe me?" she cried. "What's wrong with you that you can't see what's before your eyes? How do you think my clothes got like this?" She threw the cloak open to indicate the strips of her skirt.

For answer, the rocklike man looked down at the strips of his sleeves and then looked at her.

Fury filled Elizabeth. "I didn't do this to myself! Do you think I'm crazy?"

"That has been my impression so far."

"You must be the devil's own spawn! You're worse than *he* is!"

"Who is the 'he' to whom you refer?"

"Who *is* he? Who else *would* he be except the one you sent to do your dirty work!"

"That would be. . . ?"

"You know very well that I'm speaking of Mr. Hurford!"

Impatience sharpened the man's cold features. "I've had enough of your ravings." He turned to leave. "I'll send clothing to you. Dress yourself!" He turned back. "Are you hungry?" he asked, surprising Elizabeth. "I see no evidence of food. Have they been feeding you properly?"

"Oh, yes! Yes, you can be sure that Mr. Hurford has been feeding me! He doesn't want to lose his little plaything!" Elizabeth heard a cackling laugh come from her throat. "Performance is scheduled for midnight—perhaps you'd care to join us?"

The man's face showed disgust. He turned on his heel and left. He had been gone some time before Elizabeth realized that he hadn't locked the door. ❧

7

Elizabeth had been outside the door and then had gone back into the room a dozen times.

It was a trick—he'd left the door unlocked on purpose! He wanted her to get out, to go running from there like the lunatic he thought she was. He wanted her to be taken for a madwoman and locked in the madhouse at Truro.

And, because she couldn't stay in the awful place any longer, Elizabeth was going to run headlong into his trap.

She had made up her mind. She was outside in the passage when she heard the telltale echoes of footsteps. She whirled to run in the opposite direction, deeper into the dark passage.

A voice called out dimly. "It's me, Oxford, that's coming, Miss Stewart! Don't be none alarmed!"

Elizabeth stopped. She stood shivering with a mixture of apprehension and relief. Now she couldn't make up her mind whether to take her chances running or to trust her former instincts about Oxford and wait there for him.

"His lordship's sent clothes for you to wear, Miss."

Oxford's advancing voice was obvious in its embarrassment at the words he had to say. "If you'll just keep yourself inside, out of sight . . ."

It wasn't a scheming, evil-minded man who called those words to her. Elizabeth darted back into the room and stood behind the door.

". . . 'til her that's coming with me can bring them in to you. . . . Follow up close there!" he called out in a stronger voice, turning his head as he did so, apparently, for his voice suddenly became fainter. "Follow up!"

Elizabeth heard the echoing footsteps of what seemed to be an army. She froze.

"Don't alarm yourself none, Miss Stewart!" Oxford called out. "It's just them with me that his lordship's sending for your company."

The footsteps were in the near section of the passage. They stopped at the door.

"Be ye there, Miss Stewart. . . ?"

Elizabeth trembled. Her voice shook. Please God, she prayed, don't let this be another of his treacheries!

"I'm here, Oxford."

"It's Lizzie's her name, what'll be comin' in. Her's to keep you company and see to your needs 'til I comes back. It's Thomas'll stand outside in the passage here."

Elizabeth's mind was all confusion. She couldn't bring a response to her lips.

"Be ye all right, Miss Stewart?"

At the concern in his voice, Elizabeth began to cry. It was the first kindness she had been shown.

"Get yourself inside, girl!" Oxford's voice was sharp and scolding. "You wasn't sent here to stand about gawking!"

A young girl in maid's uniform came skipping into the room. She paused, looking around, and, not seeing Elizabeth behind the door, asked in lilting, breathless tones, "Where is it you've hid yourself, Miss Stewart, ma'am?"

"I'm here." Elizabeth moved a little away from her place of concealment, keeping out of sight of the men at the open door.

"Oh! There you are, to be sure!" Lizzie's eyes flew wide when she saw Elizabeth's state, but she made no remark. She flew back and forth between the door and the table, bringing in things that Oxford and Thomas handed her—a bundle of clothing, a washbowl and water, a brush and hand mirror. Elizabeth watched as if in a trance. "I'll just close the door now," Lizzie sang out to the men. "Miss Stewart and me, we need our privacy!"

"I'm going now, miss," Oxford said. "But I'll be comin' back with dinner for ye, soon's I'm done at the funeral. Don't you worry none, Miss Stewart. Thomas'll be just outside here all the time. He's a young one, but all brawn and muscle!"

Lizzie giggled, then hushed herself quickly with her hand over her mouth.

Elizabeth wanted to call to Oxford to stay, but she could only stand, gaping and dumbfounded, watching Lizzie.

When Lizzie had everything at the table to suit her, she turned around and looked Elizabeth over. "Oh, my, Miss Stewart! What a sight you are, to be sure!"

Elizabeth, still dumbfounded and not quite able to take in all the bustle going on about her suddenly after days of being alone in the dark and quiet, responded automatically to Lizzie's exclamation. Her hands went to her hair, her face. Her hair was a mass of tangles, and the skin of her face was raw in places where it had been scraped on the wood of the door and on the stone floor. Her hands, also, were cut and bruised.

"Now never you mind. I've everything as's needed

to set you to rights." Lizzie cooed. She moved on
dancing feet around Elizabeth, unbuttoning buttons
and undoing clasps. "First order is to get you out of
these rags!" She made a clucking noise. "Shameful!
Purely sinful! Good stuff, every inch of it—and all
gone in ruin!"

"Where did Oxford say he was going?" Elizabeth
asked. She shivered, remembering the word *funeral*,
and remembering Dax. She was afraid that Oxford
would be leaving the manor to go all the way to Polreath Wood where she had seen the spire of the Norman church.

"Oxford's the one drives the corpses to the chapel
when there's funerals here. They're burying Dax and
Jax today. Had to put off the burying 'til Jax's missus
could calm herself from hysterics, she took on so!"

"Jax. . . ?"

"Jax and Dax. Twins they was, and two worse rascals you never could hope to meet! Came to the end
was always said they'd come to. Dax got himself cut
up and killed in a fight with the gypsies . . . them as
always come around this time of year with their sneak-
ing and stealing, and it's only the biggest kind of fool
doesn't steer clear of them . . . and Jax got the same
for himself when he went over to the gypsy camp to
take revenge. They was close, the twins was."

So that was the story they were putting out—that
Dax had been killed by gypsies.

Lizzie had Elizabeth's dress off and was unbuttoning her chemise. "My, isn't it pretty! Wasn't it, should
say! Is the handwork all your own, Miss Stewart?"

"Did you say Dax was killed by gypsies?"

Lizzie giggled. "That's the way we're supposed to
tell it. But that's not the way of it. It was something
to do with his lordship's mines. His lordship owns half
the tin mines in Cornwall! Did you know that, miss?

He's rich, oh, my yes! Something peculiar going on at the mines, but we're never told about it here. Things to do with business." She minced and continued in a voice exaggeratedly prissy. "Shouldn't be talked about in a league of her ladyship! Might be heard by her and soil her dainty ears! Humph!"

The saucy girl had better learn to repress herself, Elizabeth thought, or she'd feel the strap taken to her back.

Lizzie finished unbuttoning the chemise, untied the ribbon, and started to slip it over Elizabeth's shoulders. "Oh! Oh, my! Just look at those bruises—why, there's scratches and cuts all over you everywhere! Rats *have* been at you—wasn't a lie about that! You come over to the table and let me wash you up!" She patted Elizabeth's shoulder. "Scarifying things, rats! Hateful too!" She shuddered. "But they won't come back, not while there's light!" She crossed over to the table on airy feet, kicking out at the abominable bed of rotted straw as she passed it. "It's a noxious place, this, to be sure! Just come over here now, to the light of the candle, so I can see to wash you."

Elizabeth stood while Lizzie washed her, she chattering all the while and making clucking noises about the cuts and bruises on Elizabeth's body. "Just grit your teeth hard, now. I'm going to swab you down with liniment. It'll sting, but not for long."

"Oh!" Elizabeth jerked away, gasping in pain when the liniment touched the open cuts.

"Bend yourself over and hold onto the stool. It'll give you something to grip your hands on so I can put the liniment on. You don't want to have rat fever, do you, when you get up to London?"

Elizabeth gripped the edge of the stool hard, cringing and trying not to cry out while Lizzie swabbed every inch of her body. When it was done and Elizabeth could unclench her teeth, she said, asking, "London. . . ? Did you say London?"

Lizzie giggled, all breathless excitement. "Yes, miss. It's to London we're going, Miss Stewart!" Her eyes widened as round as saucers. She whispered, "Oxford told me. Now don't let on to them that I gave it out to you." She couldn't contain herself and her voice went back to its sprightly breathlessness. "Imagine it, miss—London! I never thought I'd see the day when I'd see Londontown!"

The chapel was a small stone structure built on the pattern of the Norman church in Polreath Wood. It was covered with moss and lichen, the ancient stones mellowed.

There was a large crowd gathered when Oxford pulled the horses to a stop at the door. A number of the sturdier men came forward from the crowd and tugged the wooden coffins from the back of the coach and sweated under them, carrying them to place them end-to-end in front of the altar inside the chapel. In back of the altar, the Right Reverend Colfax, Bishop of Polreath, stood. The Lord and Lady of Polreath were seated in high-backed chairs to his rear.

A young woman, far gone in pregnancy, was supported down the aisle by an ancient crone. The young woman seemed not to be aware of anything around her, nor of what she was doing, or being led to do. The old crone seated her in the first pew, directly in front of one of the coffins, and sat down beside her. An old man joined them in the pew.

People from the crowd outside filed in and took seats in the pews until all the space was taken. Those who didn't have seats stood in the aisle and at the back. The overflow stood outside, close about the open

door. All of Polreath's people had been excused from
duty so they could attend the funeral.

The atmosphere in the chapel was soon stifling because of the crush of people.

The Right Reverend Colfax raised his hand for
silence. He began to intone the funeral sermon, his
voice droning on in monotone. He finished the sermon
and bowed his head. All of those in the congregation
bowed their heads. The prayer was intoned in the same
flat monotone, the voice droning on. ". . . returned to
earth and returned to dust . . ."

A wild shriek rose that pierced the very ceiling. The
pregnant woman flung herself from her place in the
pew and flung herself upon the coffin in front of her.
"Jax! Jax! Jax!" she shrieked. Every head in the congregation flew up, mouths agape, eyes staring. The woman
was trying to pull the body from the coffin! "Jax! Jax!
Jax! Oh, he's so cold! He's so cold!" She somehow got
her arms around the corpse.

The dead man's head and torso came up from the
bed of the coffin, and the congregation screamed out
in one voice.

The ancient crone and the old man came out of
their shock and were at the woman now, trying to pull
her away from the body. She would not let go of it,
and the stiff head and shoulders of the dead man
jerked grotesquely up and down as the tug of war
went on.

"Clear the chapel, Mr. Hurford!" The voice of the
Lord of Polreath roared out over the stunned and
shocked silence that gripped the staring, mesmerized
congregation.

"Heller!" Mr. Hurford's voice rang out. "Oxford!
Clear the chapel! Everyone—outside!"

Heller and Oxford were on their feet and in the
crowd of people, all standing now, pushing forward,

or trying to push forward. "You there, Davey!" Heller shouted to his head stableboy, "Get those people away from the door! Outside, everyone! Outside!"

Heller and Oxford pushed and shoved at the straining crowd. The people had turned their bodies toward the door at the front of the chapel at his lordship's first order that the place be cleared, but their heads were all turned backward as they stared in fascinated horror at the corpse rising and falling in the clutch of the woman who was being pulled away, only to heave back again.

"Clear this place!" The Lord of Polreath was standing in front of his chair now. His face was black with anger. Hearing him and seeing him, the people made a mad scramble toward the door, each wanting to be first out. Feet stumbled and people fell, others falling over them, still others climbing with booted feet over the fallen ones. Screams and cries were heard as hands and faces were trod upon. The jam at the door made it impossible to get through . . . until Mr. Hurford was out of the chapel by a side door and had lashed with his whip into the people crowding the door from outside. The people fell away and those inside the chapel streamed through the doorway, some crawling, some staggering up from the floor where they'd fallen or been pushed, blood pouring from cuts made by boot heels.

A crash sounded inside the chapel. Those still within turned to see a sight that chilled them to the bone with horror and gave them nightmares for many nights afterward.

The coffin had been pulled over by the hysterical, screaming woman. It had toppled over atop her, spilling out the grotesquely stiff body of the corpse. The stiff body, cold and pale, was on its side, propped by the woman's writhing, twisting form, which was partially hidden by the coffin. A wild shriek went up from her and her body gave a mighty heave, pushing away the corpse and dislodging the coffin. A great gush of blood poured from under her dress, soaking her and the floor around her and spreading to the corpse. Another wild shriek rose as she grabbed at her heaving abdomen, pulling up her skirts and beating at the mound of her stomach with her fists. The bloody head of a babe appeared between her legs. With a howling scream and a wild arching of her back, the woman spewed forth the babe, the umbilical cord stopping it in its roll from the mother's womb.

At the sight of the child, the old crone—midwife she was to the women of Polreath—came to her senses. She was on the floor between the crowd and the bloody scene, skirts spread around her as she went to work at her trade, biting and severing the umbilical cord, twisting and knotting the end of it, and pushing the length of it back inside the woman, clearing the mouth and nostrils of the child of blood and gore, sucking and spitting, pounding the child and yelling at it the while, "Take breath! Take breath!"

Those still inside, shaken and sickened, allowed themselves to be pushed outside by Heller and Oxford until finally the chapel was cleared.

The people stood in groups and clusters, shaking their heads, speaking now and then, but only in shocked whispers. Much as most of them wanted to get as far from the scene of sacrilege as they could, they knew they must stay. There were two bodies in the chapel that had to be taken to the burial ground and put in the ground. That was the way of it: the dead had to be buried.

Inside the chapel, the old man, who had been allowed to remain, knelt beside the fallen corpse of his son. He wiped him as clean of the blood that had brought forth his own son as he could. Heller and Oxford righted the coffin and returned Jax's body to it. The woman lay unconscious. The newborn yelled in mewly, gaspy cries in the arms of old Mrs. Vellin, the midwife.

"Bring the long coach to the side of the chapel, Oxford," the Lord of Polreath said. "The coffins will be taken out by that door. Heller, have Davey come in to help. And tell Mr. Hurford to come in." When Mr. Hurford appeared, he said, "See her ladyship to the manor, Mr. Hurford."

Lady Sarah had sat unmoving, and seemingly untouched, throughout all of it. She stood now, took Mr. Hurford's arm, and swept from the chapel. Her bright brown eyes were straight ahead of her as Mr. Hurford escorted her through the clusters of people. Her straight, thin, rather short figure was regal in its black. Her lifted head and pointed features also were regal in their removal from all things untoward.

"Always the lady," someone whispered after she had passed. "Her ladyship's always the grand lady." ℰ℘

8

Elizabeth left Polreath as she had arrived, in the dark of night. She was led out of the dungeon along the same way she had been taken there. It was Oxford who led her out, lighting the way with a lamp, Lizzie and Thomas following behind. It was not the coach she had ridden in before that stood waiting at the entrance, but a fine traveling carriage with matched bays in the traces.

Elizabeth was still in a state resembling shock. She could not make her senses balance. What was he doing, the Lord of Polreath? He'd had her incarcerated as if she were the lowest kind of common criminal, the most demented and dangerous of lunatics, had let Mr. Hurford take the worst kind of advantage of her, and then had reversed himself and—apparently—had forbidden Mr. Hurford to come near her, had sent Oxford to reassure her, had sent Lizzie to maid her and Thomas to guard her, and now was sending her off to London. He was as mad as Mr. Hurford!

A terrifying suspicion lodged itself in Elizabeth's mind. He was removing her from the protecting presence of Lady Sarah! Hadn't Mr. Hurford said that it was only because of Lady Sarah that she was still alive?

Elizabeth's thoughts were torn, her relief and sense of rescue mixed with apprehension.

There was no one in attendance on the horses at the carriage, yet the bays stood patiently still, much as if they had minds to think and had heard and remembered an order earlier given—Wait there quiet now!—from Oxford.

"Ye'll sit front with me, Thomas," Oxford said, "as I've told you. Hand Miss Stewart into the carriage! Mind your manners!"

Oxford waited until Elizabeth was settled in the seat, facing forward, as she had sat in the coach.

"Ye'll sit inside with Miss Stewart, girl! Facing!"

Lizzie had been hopping about eagerly. Now she climbed up nimbly and seated herself on the seat opposite Elizabeth.

"Up with you, Thomas!"

Thomas climbed up onto the driver's seat, high up in front of the carriage.

"Ye'll learn a thing about a driving man this night, nephew!" Oxford exclaimed, climbing up and seating himself.

Elizabeth heard the flick of a whip, slicing only at air, heard a cluck from Oxford. The bays made a smart turn, and the carriage was moving away from the manor house.

The avenue did not seem as long to Elizabeth as it had seemed when she had come over it with Mr. Hurford. They were at the gatehouse before she had expected that they would be.

The carriage stopped when they reached the gatehouse. Elizabeth thought that Oxford had stopped to await the gate's being opened to allow them exit. She had her eyes on the gate—anxious inside herself, as she had been all the way along the avenue, afraid they would be stopped. She was expecting to see the same shadowy figure open the gate that she had seen when Mr. Hurford had driven her through it. But no one was near the gate. She heard a small, piping voice. "Sir!"

Elizabeth looked around. The door of the gatehouse was open, light spilling through. A child—a boy—small of frame, dark of hair and eyes, stood framed in the doorway. "Sir! You won't be long away?"

"I'll not be long, Colin, no. I'll be home again within the month."

The child ran forward and flung his arms around the waist of a figure that Elizabeth hadn't seen; the man had been on the steps and in the shadows. The man reached down and lifted the boy, clasping him to himself in tight arms. "Take good care of Jason while I'm away," the man said. "Take good care." His face went down to bury itself in the boy's black hair. "And of yourself. Take care!" He put the boy down and away from him. "Inside! Go inside! . . . Daly!" the man called out. A sturdily strong man of medium height came into the light of the door. He spoke to the child. "Be grown a lad as you are, Master Colin," he said. "His lordship will be home again within the month. If his lordship says it, so he will. Let him go in peace of mind."

Without a word, the boy walked away from the man on the steps and disappeared inside the door. The door closed, closing off the light from within. The figure on the steps did not move. The man remained standing there, facing the closed door.

"It's all in readiness we are, your lordship, sir," Oxford said, his voice hesitant.

"I'll see to the gate," Daly said and strode off toward it.

The man on the steps turned abruptly and came down the shallow steps. He walked firmly to the carriage and climbed in and sat himself beside Elizabeth. Thomas, who had been standing in attendance beside the open door of the carriage, closed it, made sure the steps had returned properly to their place beneath the carriage, and sprang back up to the driver's seat beside Oxford.

The drive along the dark roads was made in silence except for Oxford's voice singing out to the horses and then lowering to explain to his nephew the intricacies involved in handling horses as fine as those he was driving.

The Lord of Polreath ignored Elizabeth completely. He did not give his reasons for doing what he had done before, and he did not give his reasons for what he was doing now. He did not try to absolve himself of blame for the heinous treatment that Elizabeth had suffered at the hands of the tinners nor at the hands of Mr. Hurford. His attitude seemed to be that she could think him guilty or not, as she chose, and that whatever she thought did not matter in the least to him.

Elizabeth sat in resentful silence beside the silent man. He was the coldest, most unfeeling man that she had ever met!

It was daylight before they reached Penzance. Even in the early dawn, the port city was bustling. Large and small vessels crowded the harbor, sailors and dockhands swarming over them and over the long piers. The wharfs were stacked with boxes and bales, wooden crates and barrels, some having been unladen from lately docked vessels and some waiting to be laded.

Even the awesome presence of the Lord of Polreath

could not restrain the irrepressible Lizzie. She squirmed and wriggled about on the seat, exclaiming at everything, peering through each window in turn, trying to see everything at once. Elizabeth was as eager to look about as Lizzie, but she sat in stiff dignity, nursing anger and resentment toward the hateful, silent man beside her.

"There she is, sir, your lordship!" Oxford called out. "Begging your pardon for speaking. See, Thomas? See that emblem on that tallest-masted ship there? That's his lordship's 'signia. That ship you're looking at is a Polreath ship—finest in the harbor, as ye can see! And not the only one of Polreath's of its like. Sails clear to India and the South Seas and on beyond, she does. Not a harbor 'round this world hasn't seen his Lordship's 'signia. Look around, see, do you see it on any of the littler boats? Might be others of ours here."

The Lord of Polreath leaned forward and spoke into the tube. "Stop the carriage."

Oxford pulled the horses to a stop, and his lordship opened the door and descended from the carriage.

"I don't want the horses in the crush," he said to Oxford. "Stable them and rest them. I want all ready to leave at first dark." He walked off toward the tall ship.

"Oh, my, Miss Stewart!" Lizzie breathed in awe. "Oh, my! Just imagine having boats that's your very own. Why, you could go anywhere in this world you wanted!"

Oxford had turned the carriage back the way they had come. He was speaking in a stern voice to Thomas. "Next time his lordship orders this carriage stopped, Thomas," he was saying, "you be down off this seat and opening the door for him before he puts down the tube! You hear? You don't sit gawking about when there's something needs doing for his lordship!"

Oxford had crossed the wide esplanade that sep-

arated the main street of the town from the harbor-
front. He turned onto the street and stopped before a
large, stately, but rambling building. *The Queen's
Hotel* was painted at the bottom of a wooden sign
that hung from an iron rod extending from a corner
of the building. Above the words a crouching lion was
painted, the paint faded and chipped, daily eroded
by the ever-blowing salt winds.

A dozen attendants from the hotel, it seemed, were
at the carriage, opening the door, assisting Elizabeth
down, assisting Lizzie, taking down the luggage. All
of this done without orders from anyone. When Elizabeth was on the wooden walk outside, she saw the
reason why. A small coat of arms of the House of
Polreath was imprinted on the door of the carriage.

A man in black morning coat and tight black pants
buckled at the knees over white stockings stood at the
door. "His lordship's suite is in readiness, madame," he
said. "If you will follow me, please."

Elizabeth was thankful that the hooded velvet cape
that his lordship had provided for her covered the
ill-fitting dress beneath it. The precisely formal man
who was being so obsequious now was the kind who
would be quick to sneer once his back was turned.
She lifted her head like the grand lady he thought she
was and indicated that she was ready to proceed.

Breakfast had been prepared and was ready on a
table before the fire in the sitting room of the suite,
servants in attendance.

"I hope everything will be as you would like it to be,
madame," the man said. His enunciation of the term
of address had altered. Elizabeth had pushed the hood
from her face, and she looked as young and uncertain
as she was.

The man looked around at the footmen bringing in
the luggage. There was little of it, and there was not

a lady's hatbox nor wardrobe trunk among the pieces.

"My mistress is Miss Stewart," Lizzie said—a little too sharply, Elizabeth thought, considering her position, "close friend to Lady Sarah of Polreath. Miss Stewart's trunks and boxes came loose due to the bumping on the road and fell off. It's bad roads you've got, coming into your town. We left everything where it fell, being it was all ruined in the mud. Miss Stewart will be needing the best shoplady you can offer, immediately she's had her breakfast. Tell the shoplady she's to bring lots of everything so Miss Stewart can make her choice! Tell her if she brings leftovers from last year, she'll be sent back with them! Miss Stewart will want the latest in fashion—we're on our way to London!" She finished her speech on a boastful, condescending note.

Elizabeth was hard put not to gape at Lizzie. How had the girl so suddenly become so worldly? she wondered. And then she realized that Lizzie had been parroting as best she could what she had been coached to say.

The man bowed and went to the door where he bowed again before he disappeared.

"If you're ready, Miss Stewart, I'll just freshen you for breakfast," Lizzie said. She opened the door into the bedroom for Elizabeth and closed it after them.

"Madame indeed!" Lizzie sniffed, as if herself offended. "I was quick to set him straight on that! You know, Miss Stewart, when they call you 'madame,' the way he said it, that means they think . . ."

"I know what it means they think!"

Something had been puzzling Elizabeth—the readiness of the hotel suite and the staff for their arrival. "How did they know we were coming, Lizzie?"

"Why, someone was sent from Polreath to ride ahead to make it known. 'Twouldn't do, Miss Stewart, for his

lordship to come unexpected some place and find
things not ready with his comforts!"

Elizabeth and Lizzie spent the day in a flurry of
shopkeepers and dressmakers, milliners, cobblers, and
linen seamstresses. They didn't see anything of Penzance that they hadn't seen when they rode into the
town, but when they left Penzance that evening, Elizabeth was properly dressed from the skin out. A trunk
and hatboxes held several changes of costume.

Elizabeth hadn't seen the Lord of Polreath all day,
and he wasn't in the carriage when Oxford and
Thomas came for her and Lizzie. Maybe he wasn't
going on to London with them, Elizabeth thought,
glad to be relieved of his presence. And then something that she hadn't even considered occurred to her.
Where in London was he sending her?

"His lordship's ridden on ahead," Oxford said. "Likes
riding, his lordship does. He's not much of one for
sitting confined too long in a carriage."

Their next stop was Plymouth. Elizabeth vaguely
recognized the harbor there. That was where she had
landed when she had come to England ten years before. Again there were ships in the harbor bearing the
Polreath insignia.

An angry frown creased Lord John's forehead. It
deepened every time he glanced toward the carriage.
Damn the girl, and twice damn her!

How old had Hurford said she was . . . eighteen?
That much information he had listened to from Hurford—that and the fact that she was, indeed, a spring
graduate from Miss Holybrook's school, that her parents were not living, and that she had attended the
school under the auspices of a guardian whose name
Hurford did not know. There had been no further
discussion.

Lord John did not discuss Lady Sarah—not with Hurford nor with anyone. Any explanation for what Sarah had done would have been as good as any other. There was no accounting for her aberrations. He was only thankful that he'd found the girl in time, before Sarah had killed her. Sarah would succeed someday in killing somebody, and, unless the king himself intervened in her behalf, there would be a trial. Lord John could not afford to let that happen. For his sake, he didn't care, but he owed Sarah the protection of her good name, if nothing else. For almost ten years, he had lived a lie, fulfilling that obligation. If all came down in ruin on her head, it would be her own doing. But it was because of him that she was the way she was. Others had told him that Sarah had been the way she was long before he had ever known her, but he could not see himself as without guilt where she was concerned.

Sarah could afford to be any way she wanted to be. She would expect the king to intercede for her if she needed his help. And likely he would! Good old Billy! Doddering old idiot! He'd probably do it. He was a sentimental old fool. Sarah's father had sailed with him and had later been one of his old naval cronies until his death. As a child growing up, Sarah had often visited the king at Bushy Park when he was duke and living there with Mrs. Jordan, the actress, and their children. The king—then duke—had adopted a very paternal attitude toward Sarah when her father died, and he still had a strong interest in her welfare. Sarah had every right to feel complacent where the king was concerned.

John put thoughts of Sarah from his mind. He tried to think about Margaret. Margaret couldn't make him forget, but she could entice and please him so that all else could be pushed aside from his mind—at least momentarily.

What was it about the girl? Why did she make him think of Santha? She was nothing like Santha, certainly. Santha had been small and dark. The girl was taller, with hair that was no color—light . . . ash, he supposed the color would be called. She had nothing of the look of Santha—except perhaps in the bearing that she had.

He'd never seen the girl before—he knew he hadn't! Why did it seem that he had? Why did his heart wrench painfully every time his eyes fell on her, all the remembered hurt come back? God, how he wished he'd never set eyes on her! Why couldn't he free his mind of the sight of her haunted green eyes, eyes that were haunted one instant and spitting fire and fury the next. He was a man who had known many women, slept with many women. He'd never known one before that he couldn't even sit next to without having every lustful urging in him rise. It wasn't the remembrance of her young breasts and thighs that made him want her. It was the whole of her, the pliant softness that he knew was beneath the defiance that she showed in the proud way she carried herself, slender body straight, head lifted. She'd looked like a snarling alley cat the first time he'd seen her, but she was a beauty with her abundant hair and slightly tilted nose, her petulant mouth and big green eyes. He chuckled suddenly. Margaret would be none too pleased when she saw what he was bringing her for houseguest.

The horse pranced beneath him, and he jerked sharply at the reins. He was immediately impatient with himself for his rough treatment of the animal. The horse was only reacting to his own agitated state, his discomfort in the saddle. With a flick of his crop, he set the horse to speed and they raced ahead and

out of sight of the carriage. Fool that he was. He
wasn't escaping her by flying off ahead of her! Why
in God's name had he decided to take her to Margaret?
He could have sent her back where she came from.
He'd take her at the first opportunity—rape her if he
had to! That would rid him of whatever it was that
plagued him. Even as he swore to himself that he
would rape her, he knew that he would not. Something
about her—the strong feeling or *déjà-vu* that he had
so often when he looked at her—would prevent him.
He almost stood in the stirrups, urging the horse forward. Damn the girl!

The party stopped also at Sidmouth. After that there
was the long, long ride over inland roads. The journey
was broken by overnight stops at inns along the way.
Elizabeth thought the miserable trip would never end.
She hated the Lord of Polreath more with every mile
they put behind them. He had not joined her in the
carriage once since they had left Penzance. He had not
spoken to her, except to nod a brief good morning or
good night. When he did condescend to glance in her
direction, it was with that same angry, doubtful appraisal and shaking of the head with which he'd looked
at her the first time he saw her. It had been especially
so when they had been at the harbor in Plymouth.
For his part, he seemed as anxious to be rid of her as
she was to be rid of him.

At long last, the spires of the cathedrals of London
and the rising heights of its towers could be seen in
the mist in the far distance.

"London!" Oxford called out. "Look ye in the distance there! We're nigh on London!"

"London . . ." Lizzie breathed, for once overcome.
Her voice was reverent. "There's London, Miss
Stewart . . ." &

BOOK II

Love and Abandonment

&

9

The streets were teeming with milling, foul-smelling crowds. Some of them were impassable until the way was cleared by Oxford, laying about the ragged beggars and idlers and the street urchins with his whip, calling out to them to make way for quality, stinging many of them with the whip and sending them stumbling and sliding in the mud of the streets and in the filthy, malodorous water that stood in the ditches on either side of them.

Clods of dirt and mud pelted the carriage, thrown by grimy, claw-fingered hands. Gaunt faces spat in the direction of the carriage.

"Close the curtains, girl!" Oxford yelled to Lizzie. "This end of London's no sight for Miss Stewart to be seeing!"

Elizabeth was shocked and appalled and disappointed. This was London? The grand, the glorious London?

Lizzie jerked the curtain across the window that she was staring through. She was disappointed, too, and angry. "Leave the sight of it for them as it belongs to!" she said.

After a while they were on smoother streets, with cobbles bouncing from under the wheels of the carriage. "We're here, Miss Stewart," Oxford's voice came sedately through the tube. He was slowing the carriage to a stop.

Lizzie peeped under one of the drawn curtains. "Humph!" She opened all the curtains. "Don't look near so grand as what you'd expect. Just little houses stacked in a row! You could put the lot of them in a tower wing of the manor!"

Elizabeth didn't share Lizzie's feeling of scorn. She loved what she saw. They were on a street faced on one side by a row of stately four-storied mansions, facades sparkling with cleanliness. On the other side of the street there was a park with lovely green-leafed trees and well-swept, neatly trimmed paths. There were benches along the paths, and flowers bloomed on the bushes and in the beds laid out in formal patterns.

Oxford stopped the carriage before one of the mansions. The Lord of Polreath's horse was being led off by a groom. The Lord of Polreath's back was disappearing inside the gleaming mahogany door.

After some time, while those in the carriage waited, the large mahogany door swung inward. A woman appeared in the door and stood there for a moment. Then she came forward.

Elizabeth thought that she had never seen anyone so beautiful. The woman was tall and slender with a cloud of black hair. Her eyes were a bright blue, rather deep-set in their jet-black lashes and brows, but brilliant and flashing. Her nose was straight and long. Her mouth also was long and more thin-lipped than not. Her features, taken separately, were not perfect, but they combined to form a face of exceptional beauty. Her expression was lofty. She was dressed in

a gown of bright rose color, the bonnet matching. The
toes of her satin slippers were of the same shade. She
carried herself with arrogance, and when she was
nearer, Elizabeth saw a hardness of the eyes and a
tightness in the mouth that hadn't been there on first
glance.

"I'm Lady Margaret," the woman said. "I've come
to make you welcome to my house."

"It ain't fit and proper to announce your own self
by title!" Lizzie hissed in a whisper, "But it's just like
her to do it!"

Elizabeth jabbed at Lizzie viciously with her elbow.
"Be quiet!" she hissed herself, between gritted teeth.
Her attention was on the woman. All of her first im-
pressions had reversed themselves. The woman was
not beautiful, she was mean and spiteful. Her eyes had
narrowed when she had seen Elizabeth fully. A sudden
malicious anger had flashed behind the lids hooding
the bright blue eyes.

But the anger was bridled. "You're Miss Stewart, I'm
told. Welcome to London. Do come in."

Elizabeth knew that she was not at all welcome to
London, nor wanted to come in. And even if she had
been, it would not have changed her feelings toward
the woman. She hated her! The woman's brilliant
beauty made her feel drab in comparison. But more
than that, she knew instinctively that here was an
antagonist, and a dangerous one. Why? Whatever for?
She hadn't asked to be brought here!

"*Do* come in!"

Elizabeth realized that she had been standing on the
walk, like the simpleton that the woman seemed to
think she was, simply staring at her. "Thank you," she
said, with all the dignity she could muster. "Thank
you very much."

Every appointment in the house was as grand as the

lady of the house. The rooms were large, the furnishings massive, the upholsteries of the richest of materials, the crystal of the chandeliers reflecting myriad lights from their myriad prisms. Fresh flowers stood in silver and crystal vases everywhere. The sweetness of the flowers was cloying to Elizabeth.

The Lord of Polreath was nowhere to be seen.

Who was the woman? His sister? A cousin?

He had no right to simply dump her on somebody without even telling her who the person was—and in a place where she wasn't wanted! Lady Margaret's words might have been cordial, but her face had made it quite plain that she felt the opposite.

Lady Margaret said, "Mrs. Wooley will show you to your rooms. I hope you will find them nothing lacking. We were hardly prepared . . ." She trailed off, the rest of the sentence unsaid, the meaning as clear as if she'd shouted it. "I'll send your footman up with your bath. I'm sure you will want it immediately after your long journey." Her speech made Elizabeth feel as if every mote of dust between Polreath Wood and London was on her person. "We will dine at four. We do hope you will join us!" She stressed the last, her voice somewhat raised, as if intended to reach the ears of someone out of sight but near.

After the black-clad Mrs. Wooley—evidently the housekeeper—had left them, Lizzie closed the door and turned to Elizabeth. The sauciness of a devil's imp was in her eyes. "My, Miss Stewart! How the tongues would be waggin' back at the manor if they knew I was standing this minute in Lady Margaret's house!" She twisted about, looking at the room around her, a smile of victory dimpling on and off her mouth as if being there were an accomplishment of her own.

"Whose house is it?" Irritation made Elizabeth's voice sharp. "Who *is* she?"

"Why his lordship's mistress, to be sure!" Lizzie chirped.

"What!" Elizabeth bristled with anger. How *dare* he bring her to the house of his *mistress!*

"Lady Margaret Litchfield, she is, and they say she's very rich, but she's not married now, and they say she never will be again until she marries his lordship himself. She's set her cap and is determined. Her that used to be Lady Sarah's best and dearest friend! Course the fault they're not friends anymore can be laid to Lady Sarah and not to Lady Margaret. Lady Sarah . . ."

"Don't run on so, Lizzie!"

Elizabeth moved impatiently about the room, tugging at the ribbons of her bonnet. She felt stifled. "Get me out of these things!" Lizzie tripped over to her and began undoing the clasps of the traveling pelisse that Elizabeth wore. "How do you know so much about her? You shouldn't repeat backstairs gossip!"

" 'Twasn't to say gossip, Miss Stewart. Lady Margaret lived . . ."

There was a rumbling and clattering in the hall outside. "That must be Thomas with the bath!" Lizzie said, interrupting what she had started to say. She ran to the dressing room to open the door that opened on the hall from it. Elizabeth followed. Thomas was awkwardly managing a large conglomeration of unwieldy-looking things. There was a full-sized metal tub on a low, wheeled platform. The tub was lined with porcelain painted to represent a shallow waterfall cascading into a grassy pool in a wooded glade. There was a small brass stove with a coal fire burning steadily behind its filigreed door, a low cart with covered kettles of steaming hot water, and something that looked like a tea cart on which were towels and bowls of soap and bottles of lotions and hand-painted jars of creams, the paintings on them companion pieces to the painting in the tub.

"Don't stand about so, Thomas!" Lizzie said sharply. "Would you be wanting Miss Stewart to have a cold bath?" She bustled busily about, helping him. "Thomas *will* stand about!" she said to Elizabeth, "but he *is* a good footman, for all that he's just started being one. You'll see, Miss Stewart, how fast he'll learn! I'm going to show him this once how to prepare a bath properly, and then . . ."

Thomas was still standing in the door, looking embarrassed, tugging at his forelock. Without Lizzie's saying it, it would have been obvious that he was not accustomed to something so intimate as preparing a lady's bath. Elizabeth turned and went back into the bedroom. It was her presence that embarrassed him.

Lizzie came to the door. "I'll just finish helping Thomas," she said breathlessly. "We'll have your bath ready in no time!" She closed the door. Soon there came from the dressing room the noise of the trundling of the heavy pieces and the splashing of water. Then there was silence. It lasted so long that Elizabeth became impatient. She was too irritated with the Lord of Polreath and that woman, and too at odds with herself to keep still. She'd been pacing back and forth and stopping to look out the window and then pacing back and forth again. Now she went to the door of the dressing room and opened it. And stopped short one step inside the room!

Lizzie and Thomas were in back of the tub. Elizabeth couldn't see all of their bodies, but she could see enough to recognize quite well what was going on behind that tub! Lizzie's legs, completely bared of skirts, moved in quick jerks up from the floor and down again, arching from her heels as she thrust her body up to meet Thomas's. Thomas's legs, trouser-clad, moved in jerks the reverse of Lizzie's movements as he strove over her, driving himself into her upward-thrusting pelvis. Their movements became faster, their comings together more forceful. Lizzie started to utter sharp gasps and small moans each time he drove deeply into her. Thomas's breathing became a series of short, hard animal grunts. Elizabeth's face flushed with hot embarrassment and anger. She drew quickly back and closed the door. As she did so Lizzie emitted a muffled scream and Thomas grunted out all of his breath in one explosive burst. Elizabeth flung cold hands over her hotly flushed cheeks and ran to the window and leaned out into the fresh air. The nerves deep in her groin had tightened and then released from tension, sending a sweet spreading sensation through her lower regions. She knew that she was a woman with strong sex motivations, but it shamed and humiliated her to feel vicarious thrills.

Elizabeth was still standing in the cooling air of the window when Lizzie came to announce, "Your bath's ready now, Miss Stewart." She spoke with the same quick breathlessness with which she usually spoke, but this time Elizabeth knew the reason for the breathlessness and scarcely subdued excitement. She wanted to whirl on Lizzie in hot anger, but she held herself in check. The anger that she wanted to take out on Lizzie wasn't toward Lizzie. She'd known for some time what was going on between Lizzie and Thomas. They tumbled every time they had the chance. She should have known what she would find when she opened the door on them.

There were three for the meal—the Lord of Polreath, Lady Margaret, and Elizabeth. There were five in attendance—a footman in back of each chair, the butler, and the serving maid. The meal was had mostly

in silence, what conversation there was being about
the food, and that mostly questions from Lady Margaret
to "John," as she seemed fond of repeating, inquiring
whether each dish was to his liking. His answers
were short and distracted, even rude. Lady
Margaret smiled brilliantly at him often, ignoring Elizabeth
for the most part. Course after course was
served. They were two hours at table. After the uncomfortable
meal was finally over, Elizabeth excused
herself and fled upstairs to her rooms. She felt insulted
and furious. Lord John had been scarcely civil, either
to herself or to Lady Margaret.

Elizabeth was too agitated to compose herself to
read or to rest. She was too agitated to direct Lizzie
in the disposition of her things, which Lizzie was
busily unpacking. She went from one window to another,
looking out at the gathering dusk. She decided
that she would take a walk. She wanted to be out of
that hateful house! "Come, Lizzie, bring my pelisse.
And put on your shawl. We're going for a walk!"

"By ourselves on London streets, Miss Stewart?"

"What's wrong with that?"

"I'd better pull the cord for Thomas."

"Just come with me, Lizzie!"

Lizzie dropped the nightshift she had just taken
from the trunk and ran to get Elizabeth's pelisse and
her shawl. She was learning that Miss Stewart had a
temper. There had been signs of it before, but this
was the first time she'd looked near to losing it altogether.

They went out the door and started down the hall.
The sound of voices raised in anger came from a door
they were approaching. Elizabeth slowed and stopped.
Only one voice was raised in anger, she realized as
she listened—Lady Margaret's. Lord John's voice was
controlled, but cold and insulting.

"You're behaving like any street slut!" he said. "At least show the courtesy expected of someone in your position."

"I want her out of my house!"

"She'll leave the house when I'm ready for her to leave it! And that will be when I know where she goes from here!"

"What am I supposed to do with her? Tag her along with me wherever I go? For God's sake, John . . ."

"That's not a bad idea. Introduce her to society." A mirthless chuckle came from him. "Why not? Your friends might be amused. She would be a diversion, I think. There's not been much of excitement lately at court. No new faces. Yes, Margaret, I think that's the right idea. Sponsor her at court."

"I'll do nothing of the sort!"

"You won't. . . ?" His voice held a deadly edge. ". . . You won't, Margaret? I say you will!"

"You couldn't ask that of me!"

"I'm not asking it, I'm demanding it!"

"You want me to sponsor your latest conquest at court! You want to make a laughingstock of me! You've brought her to my house, but that's not enough for you. You . . ."

"You should know as well as any, Margaret, that I am not addicted to simpering young girls."

"She's far from simpering! She's a little Miss Lady Snobnose if I ever saw one. She turns her nose up at me in my own house! I won't have it!"

"You're not pretty when you're vicious, my dear. Jealousy doesn't become you. Especially jealousy misplaced. In this case, it is. You should know that I like my women older, experienced . . . like you, my dear."

"You're insulting!"

"Am I? Come, show me your wiles. Prove that what I say is true."

"You speak to me as if I'm the lowest kind of whore —and you expect me to come crawling to you!"

"Are you refusing me?"

The woman started to weep.

"How can you be so cruel? You know how much I love you, John. Haven't I always? How can you treat me . . ."

"Come, Margaret! If you want me to leave, that's the best way to go about it."

The woman's next words were muffled, as if she had thrown herself against him and spoke against his chest.

"Don't go! Please don't go, John! I never see you anymore! You come so seldom now. Please, John!"

Elizabeth jerked herself way from the door and almost ran to the stairs.

"Come, Lizzie! Come!" she hissed. Her face was flaming. She was furious. Knowing what was going to happen in that room wasn't what made her mouth tremble with anger and her heart pound with hate, she told herself. It was what he'd said about her. *Simpering*, he'd described her! She would be a *diversion*, an *amusement* for Lady Margaret's friends at court. Oh, he was insufferable! She hated him. She hated him worse now than she had before.

She'd pay him back measure for measure! She'd find a way! ᴄᴏ

10

Elizabeth's heart pounded harder in her breast than her footsteps pounded on the marble staircase. The blood inside her veins pulsed and throbbed with fury. And yet an unbearable envy and jealousy (for something she didn't want, and wouldn't take if offered, she told herself, teeth clenched and mouth tight) caused a tightness in her groin and an ache in her lower regions that she had to steel herself against and that made her breath come in short, hard gasps. She had to stop at the bottom of the stairway and hold tightly to the carved and gilded newel post to try to gain composure.

"Ah-h-h . . . Lovely . . ."

Elizabeth jerked her head around toward the sound. A man was standing in the doorway of the small salon.

"Lovely . . ." he repeated. He smiled and bowed. His every movement seemed to Elizabeth exaggerated and false, his smile sardonic.

"Who are you?" she blurted, too embarrassed at the picture she must present to think of manners.

"I'm a friend of the Lady Margaret," the man said. "I assume you are the same." He stepped into the hall

and extended his arm back through the open doorway.
"Will you join me while I await her ladyship?"

Elizabeth swept past him and into the salon, leaving
Lizzie behind her on the stairs to do as she would.
"You may have a wait of some time," she said haugh-
tily, not glancing at the man as she passed by him.
"Her ladyship is entertaining."

The man laughed. His low, intimate laugh clearly
said that he read from Elizabeth's intonation of the
word the kind of entertaining Lady Margaret was
engaged in.

"I expected as much," he said. "I saw a lackey in
his lordship's colors when I left my horse to stable."

"I'm sure I don't know whose lordship you have in
mind," Elizabeth said loftily. She had a suspicion—
more than a suspicion—she was sure that the smirking
man knew the reason for her discomfort that had been
so plainly obvious when she had descended the stairway and had stood grasping the newel post while she
tried to gain composure.

"I'm equally sure that you do," he said. He walked
over to a low table before the fireplace. On it there
was a large assortment of heavy crystal decanters,
glasses, and goblets. "Will you join me in a . . ." He
lifted the top from one of the decanters and sniffed it.
He cast a sideways look at Elizabeth. ". . . in a toast,"
he said, "to the fortunate . . ." He stopped short of
saying *couple*. But he might as well have said it. The
word rang in Elizabeth's ears. He replaced the top on
the decanter, lifted another, and sniffed it. "Very
good," he said, "Both very good, but then one wouldn't
expect anything else. A lady of inestimable taste, the
Lady Margaret. . . . In all things." He smiled at Elizabeth, a mocking, knowing smile. "Brandy? Or would
you prefer sherry? There's also . . ."

Elizabeth cut him off. "Brandy is stronger, isn't it?" she asked.

His eyebrows lifted. "I believe it is."

"Brandy then!"

He smiled and poured two glasses of brandy. He handed one to Elizabeth, bowed, and touched his glass to hers.

"To the waiters, or the lovers?" he asked.

Elizabeth drank her brandy down in one gulp. It burned all the way to her stomach. She had to press her hand over her nose to keep from sneezing. The fumes had been overpowering. She sat down on the sofa and put the empty glass on the low table before it.

The man laughed and poured her another.

"You're mistaken if you think I was waiting," Elizabeth said. "As a matter of fact, I was on my way out."

"Yes, so I see," the man said. He eyed her pelisse and bonnet. "Out of here . . . but out to where? Anywhere? Or just out?"

Elizabeth had downed the second brandy. When tears came to her eyes, she told herself it was from the fumes. The man saw the tears. He put his hand on Elizabeth's shoulder. The tears rolled down her face.

"After a while, it gets easier," he said, "the waiting. Or perhaps the pain dulls and it seems easier." He patted her shoulder. He removed his hand, sighed deeply, walked to the mantelpiece, and rested one hand against it. "I could tell you a great deal about waiting," he said.

He didn't seem as offensive to Elizabeth now as he had seemed before. "Are you in love with her?" she asked.

"In love with Lady Margaret?" He made a vague

gesture. "Is enslavement love? No, I don't love her. I hate her. I've lost everything because of her. My family has disowned me. Not because of her—she's a Litchfield, after all. No, they've disowned me because I'm running after Polreath's leavings. She throws a few crumbs in my direction and I snatch them. She does it to try to jolt Polreath into making a declaration, and he can't even be bothered to notice. She's as helpless to leave him as I am to leave her. Love? No. Not love. Addiction. The worst kind. Worse than addiction to morphine. The only way to assuage it is to indulge it, and the more you indulge it, the more helpless you become to throw it off." He turned to face Elizabeth squarely. "Don't let it happen to you," he said. There was no smirk on his face, no mockery in his eyes. "Run," he said. "You were right to run. I never should have stopped you. Save your life. Get away from him."

"He means nothing to me," Elizabeth said. "I don't need to run from him."

He looked down at her. He shook his head slowly. He didn't believe her.

"If I should run," Elizabeth said, "it wouldn't be yet. I owe him a score."

"He can't be touched," the man said. "Forget it. You'll only become the more deeply entangled."

"Nothing could entangle me with him!"

"You already are entangled or you wouldn't want so badly to even the score. I tell you again, forget it. The man cares for nothing and no one . . . except his son. . . . You know his son?"

"No," she said. Then she remembered the child at the gatehouse. She remembered the desperation with which man and child had held each other, the obvious love that had surged between them, the pain that the parting had caused in each of them. "I've seen him once," Elizabeth said.

"The only way you could avenge yourself in a way that would touch him would be to harm that child. Even Margaret wouldn't stoop so low, though I expect at times she's been tempted. . . . You wouldn't stoop so low. I'll say further. . . . You wouldn't harm anything that was his. Because it was his."

"You are quick to take liberties," Elizabeth said. "You know nothing of me nor of my character."

"I'm a student of physiognomy."

"A practice I distrust entirely."

"Perhaps I can change your mind."

"I doubt it."

He stared openly and appraisingly down at her face. He was so long about it that Elizabeth became uncomfortable under his eyes.

"I'd say you've the daring to play a trick on his lordship," he said finally.

"To what end?"

"You've a score to settle, you said."

"I intend to settle it in full and not in measure by playing tricks."

"That's what I have in mind," he said. He stared at her a while again. ". . . I'd say you have a strong sense of adventure, a love of daring. You'd have to have a sense of daring for what I have in mind."

"What is it you have in mind?"

"Let's talk about a few other things first. . . . What is he to you, exactly? Not speaking of feelings now . . ." He held up his hand when Elizabeth started to protest that she had no feelings for him. ". . . family relationship. Is there such?"

"No!" Elizabeth's face flamed. "After you've just accused me of an entanglement with him, what you suggest is monstrous!"

"Monstrous perhaps, but not uncommon. I could name you five families on this square that harbor relationships within them that are not . . . familial . . ."

"I don't want to hear about them!"

"You are not related to Lord John?"

"No!"

"I was so sure you might be. I thought perhaps that might explain . . . I understand he's kept an unaccustomed distance where you're concerned, not so much as sharing a carriage seat with you on your journey here. . . . He's not one to lightly toss aside a delectable . . ."

Elizabeth's face flamed again, but this time for a different reason. How much humiliation was the despicable Lord of Polreath going to bring to her? Here was a total stranger telling her that it was common knowledge that his high-and-mighty lordship couldn't bear her company!

"I have many ways of knowing many things that might remotely touch on the Lady Margaret," the man said. "Your mode of travel isn't common knowledge, as I can see you think it. As far as I know, the knowledge is private to me and those in whose company you were traveling."

"It's a comfort to know that I retain some privacy," Elizabeth said stiffly.

"My apologies for making you think otherwise, even if only for a moment. . . . You've not answered my question as to your connection with the Lord of Polreath."

Elizabeth had no answer. She didn't have any connection with him. "My connection with the House of Polreath is through Lady Sarah," she said.

He looked at her, plainly puzzled.

"It is also personal and private," Elizabeth said.

He inclined his head. "My apologies for any intrusion. None was intended." He brightened. "So you have a connection with the House of Polreath through

the Lady Sarah . . ." His eyes twinkled. It was the
first gaiety that Elizabeth had seen in him. ". . . and
you have a vendetta against the Lord of Polreath.
How suiting! . . . Her ladyship will never know of it,
of course, but the little game I have in mind would
please her greatly, I think."

"Now it's a game, is it? Before it was a trick."

"You'll have to be game to help me perpetrate the
trick."

Elizabeth made a wry face.

"No appreciation for puns," he said. "Pity . . ." He
took a seat on a satin hassock at Elizabeth's feet
and leaned his face close to hers. "You're daring and
you're adventurous, and you'd risk a lot to get what
you want. It's there. It's all right there in your face.
. . . Have you ever been to the Haymarket?" he asked.
Elizabeth shook her head. His eyes bored into hers.
They were almost violet in their intensity. "There's a
certain house there," he said, "that I know intimately
—quite intimately, as does his lordship. We go there
together often. It's a house of . . . entertainment. You
see, his lordship is aware that I need a bit of . . .
frivolity, shall we say, after a disappointment such as
I'm experiencing now . . . and he—well, he always
needs more of everything. Not even Margaret . . .
Well, at any rate, often on nights such as this, we go
to the Haymarket to Madame Labouille's house there.
Quite the most elegant of its kind in the city, as you
may well imagine, knowing that it's a favored haunt of
his lordship . . ."

Elizabeth interrupted him. She had heard of the
Haymarket. Some of the girls at school had brothers
who had bragged to them of their visits there. "What
help could I possibly be in a trick that has to do with
a brothel?"

"Aha! Perhaps your daring is even greater than I

thought. No shrinking from the word, eh? Good!" His
eyes became even more intense, gleaming into hers.
". . . *You* would be the joke!"

Elizabeth drew back from him. "Are you suggesting . . . ? Surely you're not . . ."

"Oh, but yes I am!" He leaned farther toward her;
she remained pulled back from him. "I can arrange it—
I can arrange everything. If we leave now . . . It will
take some time . . . not much, but some. Everything
must be exactly so. The proper room . . . I know the
perfect one. The proper wines and most delicious supper at hand. The most enchanting . . ." He looked
at her pelisse. "What are you wearing under that?"

Elizabeth pulled her pelisse closer about her as if
she were naked underneath it. "Not anything that one
would be likely to wear in a brothel, I shouldn't
think!"

"I was sure not. But that's no hindrance. Madame
Labouille will let me select from the wardrobe." He
stood up and took her hand to pull her to her feet.

Elizabeth held back. "What am I supposed to do?"
she asked. "I can guess that you intend for him to find
me where he would expect to find one of the . . ."
She stopped. The only words she could think of to
call them were the two that she had heard Lord John
and Lady Margaret say earlier, and for some reason
remembering hearing them say them threw her into
confusion.

". . . ladies of the house," the man prompted.

". . . But is that all of the trick?"

The man made a slight gesture with one hand, as if
he would ask her the same question. He smiled at her.
"I'm going to supply the stage and arrange the setting,"
he said. "The production is up to you."

Elizabeth looked into his smiling eyes. They were
smiling only on the surface. What she saw in the

depths of them was no smile. She didn't know what it was, but whatever it was it sent a chill through her. "Why do you want to do this to him?" she heard herself say. Something had tightened inside her that made it hard for her to speak.

"But, my dear, I'm not doing it to *him*."

The hardness in his voice made the chill come over Elizabeth again. "You hate her that much?"

"That much, and more."

Elizabeth tried to pull her hand away from him, but he gripped it the more tightly. "Aren't you game? Or was all your talk pretense and bluster?" he asked.

His voice dared her. The intensity of his eyes made her hatred for the Lord of Polreath only a shade beside his for Lady Margaret. . . . Or so he seemed to think it.

Elizabeth stood up. She could hate as deeply as any. "I'm game," she said.

Elizabeth had never been in a place of such opulent and overdone splendor, nor had she ever been dressed —or undressed—in garments fashioned of such soft and luxurious fabrics and made to such exquisite—and purposeful—design. She was alone in the room that Ronald Asquith had cajoled Madame Labouille into preempting for their use. (The man was Ronald Asquith. His father was a baron, Lord Mowbray, who had large holdings on the east coast of England, to the north toward Berwick. That was the inheritance that Ronald had lost. It wasn't an irrevocable loss, Ronald had told Elizabeth. He had talked in a continuous stream of words all through the drive to the Haymarket. His father might relent—would relent under certain conditions. Ronald had admitted that his father, because of his mother's urgings, was ready to forgive him the moment he had proof that Ronald had given up his unsuccessful pursuit of Lady Margaret. That proof was in the form of marriage to a lady whose father's estates adjoined his own father's. Ronald was not prepared to accept his father's terms.)

The room in which Elizabeth was alone—and had been for a while—was large. From the center of the ceiling fell crimson velvet drapes that formed a square. The crimson velvet was overlaid with gold satin. Sprinkled about the satin were cut-out designs of fleurs-de-lis, so that, in a reverse of tradition, they were not themselves of gold. The squared drapes concealed a bed—an enormous bed. It was on a raised dais. Three steps led up to it on the two sides. The mattresses and pillows were of down, and the bedclothes were of softest silks and satins, white and gold. The ceiling was mirrored, but with tantalizing, distorting prisms. Incense emanated from some concealed place within the space enclosed by the drapes. It did not penetrate into the rest of the room. There was a rich headiness in the scent and a strong presence of musk.

There were four sections of the room around the squared drapes, making a room within a room. The sections were partitioned by screens depicting scenes from classical erotica, all in sensuous pastels and flesh tones. In one section there was a table set for supper for two. A cloth of whitest damask covered the table to the floor. The goblets were of beaten gold, as was the plate. The china was embossed with the fleur-de-lis. The lighting was softest candleshine. In one section there was an inlaid card table and all of the accoutrements for various games of cards and chance. (Did anyone ever use them, Elizabeth wondered.) One section was a "conversation corner." In it there was an inviting wide sofa and equally inviting chairs. There was a small smoking table and a sideboard with an

array of wines and brandies and sherries, and coolers
for champagne. That was the place for getting acquainted, Elizabeth supposed, if the assignation was
the first for the two involved. The fourth section gave
Elizabeth a feeling of queasiness, even of apprehension. It was bare of any furnishings. It struck a strange
note in the midst of the richness of furnishings in the
sections around it. Ronald had been casual about it,
and that had made her more apprehensive. "One never
knows what some people might require" was all that
he would say about it.

Ronald had chosen for Elizabeth from the wardrobe—which Madame Labouille apparently kept in
readiness for any emergency—a nightshift of such softness and creaminess to the touch that it seemed that
it must melt away in the fingers before it could clothe
the body. It was of the color of Elizabeth's skin. Over
the nightshift she wore a peignoir of the same creamy
color. It was of chiffon. It was fashioned with a dar-
ingly low décolletage. But, except for the swell of
Elizabeth's breasts above the low neckline, it was not
revealing. That is, as long as she stood perfectly still.
It was gathered in soft folds over the shoulders and encased Elizabeth's upper arms and bosom in soft folds.
The folds were caught in a tight band under the bosom
and then fell loose again to the floor. It was a garment
meant to inflame a man's senses, for it gave promise
of revealing what it hid. The nightshift under the
peignoir hid nothing. On Elizabeth's feet were soft
slippers of padded gold velvet. Overall was a flowing
cape of gold velvet, of such a lightness of texture that
it floated when she moved. It was fastened at the neck
with a clasp of filigree gold and pearls. A small ruffle,
heavily embroidered in gold, circled the neckband and
stood upward as if to frame the face in a setting. When
the cape was in place Elizabeth was completely cov-

ered, except for her face and head. There was just one
thing that concerned her: there were no slits for her
hands. In order to use them she had to open the cape.

Ronald had been gone for some time, and Elizabeth
was becoming more and more nervous. She was also
becoming more and more angry—angry at the arrogance that the Lord of Polreath had shown toward
her that had made her resort to what she was doing. It
was no more than he deserved, and she wasn't sorry
that she was doing it, but she wanted to have her moment of triumph and have it over with. She wasn't
feeling as comfortable about the whole thing as she
wished she were. For one thing, she didn't have the
faintest idea how a woman went about seducing a
man. And she wasn't at all sure that, no matter how
hard she tried, nor what kind of wiles she used, she
would succeed in seducing the Lord of Polreath. . . .
Not that she intended to go all the way through with
the lovemaking. She was going to get him to the point
of torment and then laugh in his face.

The plan was that Ronald would return to Lady
Margaret's house (which he had). There he would
greet the Lord of Polreath when he descended from
the upstairs regions, where Lady Margaret usually
remained. The two men would have their usual brandy
or two. They would have some talk about the latest
hunt or whatever interested them at the moment, and
then one or the other of them would suggest that the
Haymarket was as good a place as any to while away
the remaining hours of the night. Ronald had assured
Elizabeth that this sequence of events was practically
a ritual by now. When the two men arrived at Madame
Labouille's, Madame Labouille—who, with all the
exuberance of her Gallic sense of fun, loved a joke,
and who had no idea of the evil intent behind the one
being played in her establishment that night—would

regale the Lord of Polreath with tantalizing descrip-
tions of the charms of the delightful creature that she
had in reserve for him. A jewel . . . the rarest of jewels
was awaiting his pleasure! Madame Labouille would
usher him into the room and close the door behind
him, herself outside. Elizabeth would not be in his
sight when he came into the room. She would be
waiting for him in the "conversation corner." . . . Later,
after she had been triumphant, she would pull the
cord that would summon Ronald, who would be
waiting in Madame Labouille's apartments . . .

Elizabeth's lips curved downward in a grimace of
disdain and satisfaction. What a look must come on
the Lord of Polreath's face when Ronald Asquith
showed himself to slap him on the back in a great
show of camaraderie and force him to laugh at the joke
they had been clever enough pull on him!

It must be near the time when the Lord of Polreath
would be coming. Elizabeth went into the conversation corner. She poured herself a brandy—a big one—
and drank it down. It burned just as much as the first
one she had had at Lady Margaret's house. And the
fumes choked her just as much and made her want to
sneeze. She was glad for the momentary discomfort—
it meant that the brandy was affecting her.

Elizabeth heard the door open. She heard a few
murmured words. She heard the door close softly. She
stood rigid by the sideboard. She turned to face the
opening between the screens that partitioned that section of the room from the rest of it.

For a moment there was silence. Then: "If you've
taken to bed already, you overextend yourself," the
Lord of Polreath said. "I am not so eager. Show yourself! We'll toast the night."

Elizabeth gritted her teeth. The conceit of the man
—was there nothing in which he was not arrogant! She

didn't move. She was not going to him. That would put the whole thing off to the wrong start. *He* was to come to *her!*

She waited. She waited such a long time, while nothing happened and no sounds were made, that she thought he must have left and that she hadn't heard the soft catching sound of the lock of the door when he opened and closed it. And then she heard him ejaculate impatiently. "You have so much to offer that you think I must come seeking—is that it? You make a mistake, my girl. But keep to your bed, for I've lost my taste for anything other than the drink I'll have." Elizabeth heard him crossing the room toward where she was. "And then I'll bid you good night and leave you to contemplate the ways of men at your leisure," he said, and with that he was inside the screen and standing face to face with Elizabeth.

Elizabeth clutched the edge of the sideboard. The Lord of Polreath stiffened with a jerk and stood frozen where he was.

"I was going to have a brandy," Elizabeth said. She tilted her head and smiled at him. "Will you join me?"

He didn't brush his hand across his eyes as he usually did at first sight of her. He looked her up and down. His eyes traveled angrily over the length of her. He was not undressing her with his eyes. Only scorn was in them, not lust—not even the beginnings of excitement. Elizabeth felt her resolution quiver. She turned to the sideboard and poured a drink, turned back to him, and lifted it. She smiled again. "Are you sure you wouldn't care to join me?"

He strode over to her and took the glass from her and put it down on the sideboard. His movements were not gentle. The brandy sloshed over onto his hand and onto the top of the sideboard.

"Where are your own clothes?" he demanded. "Put

them on! Get out of those trappings and put your own clothes on!"

"Look what you've done," Elizabeth said, pouting and looking up at him from under lowered lashes, "You've spilled my brandy. Why you've got it on yourself, too." She brushed her hand over the back of his, lingering her fingers in a slow, soft movement across his hand and fingers. She moved close to him. She pressed herself against him, pretending that her only intent was to wipe the brandy from his hand. She heard the sharp intake of his breath. She felt the breath as it entered his rigid body that she pressed against. He moved so quickly away from her that she had to catch hold of the edge of the sideboard to keep herself righted.

"It's Asquith back of this!" he said. "He'll answer to me! He's carried his tricks too far!"

Elizabeth moved near him again, bringing the softness of her thighs, the softness of her breasts to touch and press his thighs, his chest. "It was only as a favor that he did it," she said. "I begged him. I wanted so much . . ." She turned her face up to his and looked into his stony eyes. She almost lost the pliant softness of body that she was working so hard to keep—his eyes were so cold and unreceptive—but she controlled the feelings against him that rose in her and stayed soft and pliant against him. ". . . I wanted so much just to be with you . . . I wanted . . ."

He brought his hand up behind her back and grasped her hair at the nape of her neck. His fingers were cruel, tightening on her hair as if he would rip it from her head at its roots.

"Wanted what!"

"You . . ." she breathed, shuddering at the pain, shuddering at the feeling inside her brought on by the nearness of him, by the fact that it was *he* who was so close to her, *he* who was holding her so tightly grasped.

He threw her from him and she fell against the sofa. She was on the floor, her elbows grotesquely on the seat of the sofa behind her, supporting her sprawled body. She could see herself in her mind's eye. What a fool she must look—what an ignominious fool!

"Get yourself up and get your own clothes on!" the Lord of Polreath gritted between his teeth. "I've had more than enough of this masquerade! I'll call for the carriage. You have five minutes!—no more!"

Elizabeth turned and put her face on the cushion of the sofa and started to cry. She hadn't intended to. She had meant to be as strong as he was . . . stronger. But she turned her face from him, and hid it from him, and cried.

"Don't cry! For God's sake!" he roared. "Crying has never yet wheedled me into anything. It won't stand in good stead for you now."

Elizabeth couldn't stop crying. She expected to hear him leave, to call for the carriage. But he didn't leave. He came to where she was on the floor, her arms on the sofa and her face buried in her arms.

". . . Elizabeth . . ."

He knelt down beside her.

". . . Elizabeth . . ." He put his hand on her arm.

"Leave me alone!" she sniffled. "Get out of here and leave me alone! That's all you've ever wanted to do, so do it."

"Elizabeth, I know you've got yourself into something you didn't really mean to get yourself into. I know that it would not have come about, left to you. I know that . . ."

Elizabeth jerked herself away from his touch. She got unsteadily to her feet. She was standing on the cape, and when she rose to her feet, the clasp was jerked open and the cape fell from around her. She heard the still-kneeling man gasp. She bent down to retrieve the cape, and when she did, her half-exposed breasts were so close to his face that she felt his breath on them. When she moved to stand upright again, abandoning all thought of the cape, she felt her swelling breasts brush against his mouth. She hadn't done it on purpose. She would have sworn to the Holy Mother that she hadn't done it on purpose. She felt arms of steel encircle her. She felt him rise to his feet and pull her upright as he rose.

"We'll have that brandy," he said.

"No!" Elizabeth said. "No!"

"You offered me brandy, did you not?"

He half-carried, half-propelled her to the sideboard. His arms were still a vise around her. When they were at the sideboard, he did not release her. He held her, backed up against the sideboard, imprisoned by it and his hard body—she could feel the pistollike hardness of his organ against her abdomen. "I am going to have a brandy," he said, in imitation of her earlier invitation. He turned his face down to her. He smiled at her and tilted his head in facetious, ridiculing imitation. "Will you join me?"

"No!" she gasped. "No! I don't want brandy! Let me go!"

His hands behind her had been lifting the top from the decanter of brandy, had been bringing the goblets near it for pouring. Now they left the crystal of the goblets and the decanter. With both hands against the edge of the sideboard, he pushed himself away from her. "My God!" he said. "What am I doing?" He looked down at Elizabeth. She was visibly trembling, her eyes dark pools of fear. "Don't be afraid," he said. "It's passed. It's over."

Elizabeth had never seen such stark regret on anyone's face. He was looking at her as if she were dead, and he had murdered her. He looked as if he were branded for life by some unforgivable crime that he had committed. . . . He hadn't done anything except something she had driven him to. When he took his hands from the sideboard and turned away, she put her hand on his arm. "It wasn't your fault," she whispered.

"Don't, Elizabeth!" he said, his voice harsh. He tried to move from her touch, but she kept her fingers pressed on his arm and moved closer to him, having to speak to his back. "It wasn't your fault," she whispered again.

Suddenly he had turned to her. A groan came from him as his arms encircled and imprisoned her. "I am not strong enough," he said. His voice was a strangled whisper against her hair. He picked her up in his arms.

He held her cradled in his arms and was moving toward the drapes that enclosed the bed.

"No!" Elizabeth said, struggling to get away from him. "No! I didn't mean . . ." Fires were raging within her. She had to struggle against them as much as she had to struggle against the man who caused them. "Let me go! Please! I didn't mean . . ."

They were inside the drapes. He was climbing the three steps to the bed.

"No!" Elizabeth cried, gasping and twisting in his arms. "No!"

He laid her on the bed. He held her as if impaled upon it with his hands on her shoulders pinning her down. "I will have you, Elizabeth."

"No!"

He held her imprisoned upon the downy softness of the bed.

"Yes, Elizabeth. I will have you."

Elizabeth couldn't stop her convulsive, panting

breathing, though she knew that each heaving breath
thrust her breasts farther above the neckline of the
peignoir. She arched her body upward to try to break
his grasp and the threads that held the buttons closing
the peignoir strained and burst. The peignoir opened.
Her breasts were exposed to him under the thin
transparency of the nightshift that she wore. "Oh,
God!" she heard him breathe. "Oh God!" His mouth
came down on her nipple. He nursed it and teased it
with his mouth and teeth and tongue through the
gossamer fabric. All the while his hands were tearing
the nightshift from her. He slid his hands under her
shoulders and slid the peignoir and the nightshift down
her back and along her arms and pulled them from
under and around her and threw them onto the steps
beside the bed. His arms moved swiftly back and imprisoned her again. His mouth took one breast greedily
and then the other. His hands moved over her body,
rough with the fever that was in him. "Forgive me,"
he said, and repeated it. "Forgive me!"

Elizabeth found herself fumbling with his neck-
cloth. She didn't know how to get his clothes off him,
but she wanted him to be as naked as she was. She
was in a fever as much as he was. There was a rising,
wanting, demanding fever of desire in her. She didn't
know what it was that she was feeling, but she knew
that every intention that she had had when she had
been waiting for him to come to Madame Labouille's
had left her. There was something in her that pulled
her toward his body, pulled her own body toward his
body. It was stronger than any wish or any intention
that she had ever had. She felt him pull himself away
from her, and she threw her arms around him to hold
him to her. "My clothes, Elizabeth," he whispered. He
was kissing her cheeks, her throat, her shoulders. "Let
me get out of my clothes." He was lying on top of her,

and her arms were around him. She wouldn't release him. He had to struggle out of his clothes the best way he could, bracing himself a little away from her on an elbow or a knee.

Finally it was done, and he was upon her in all his naked maleness. His arms went around her and his mouth came down on hers. Elizabeth's mouth parted under his. She felt the sweetness of his probing, searching tongue. A thrill flamed through the whole length of her when hers came together with his. She felt the length of his legs on her, the strong hardness of them. She felt the hardness of his loins. She felt the breathing heaviness of his chest against the softness of her breasts. She felt his knee between her legs, spreading them. She felt a tearing pain when he entered her and she screamed. "Forgive me!" he whispered. "Forgive me!" He started to move in her and continued to move in her, hurting her, tearing her.

Elizabeth felt his heat explode within her. She heard him groan and felt the full heaviness of his body come down on hers and relax upon her. "Don't stop!" she begged frantically. "Don't stop!"

"Elizabeth . . ."

She felt him shrinking inside her, beginning to slip from her. "Please don't stop!" She strained her body under his. "Please!" She felt him grow and harden within her. She felt him begin to move again upon her. This time she moved with him. What had been all pain and a desperate wanting for she knew not what before, was awakening an ecstasy within her now, was taking her to fulfillment. She abandoned herself to it and to him, and she felt an abandonment in him that hadn't been there before, and a giving of himself to her. A sweetness she had never known existed spread throughout her and burst within her and flooded her. It left her dazed and panting, fulfilled, still tingling from the spasm that had released the tension of every nerve in her body.

Elizabeth heard her sobs, but she couldn't stop them. She held her lover to her. There would never be another! Never! She held him pinioned to her and sobbed against him.

"Elizabeth . . ." His hand caressed her hair. He kissed her streaming cheeks. ". . . my Elizabeth . . ." She had never heard a voice so tender. &

11

Elizabeth was back in Lady Margaret's mansion. The Lord of Polreath had left. She hadn't seen him since she had gone to sleep in the circle of his arms on the silken sheets of the bed in Madame Labouille's house. She had heard his voice, but she had not seen him. Before he left he had quarreled again with Lady Margaret—or had caused her to quarrel.

"It's so awkward, John!" Elizabeth had heard Lady Margaret storm. "One doesn't take a *nobody* to court!"

"I'm sure you'll find a way. You're clever in things like that."

"Who am I going to say she *is*?"

"Mystify them, Margaret," his voice drawled, as if he were bored with the conversation. "Everyone loves intrigue. Be purposely mysterious."

"But who *is* she?"

"She is not gutter-born. That is obvious. You've no need to know more than that."

"If you were ten years older, I'd swear she was yours!"

"Five minutes ago, you were swearing that I'd seduced her." Elizabeth could see—without seeing it—

the condescending smile that came over his face. "But there's your solution. Pretend that she's the bastard of someone highly placed. When someone asks about her origins—and they all will—throw cautious glances toward someone, anyone. . . . How about the old duke . . ."

"The Duke of Wellington? You're mad!"

"The king then. . . ?"

"And have myself barred from court!"

"Really, Margaret . . ." There was a yawn in his voice. "It's your problem."

Elizabeth's face went cold and hot by turns as she listened. He spoke of her as if she were nothing to him —and never had been anything to him. What had happened between them that she had thought had irrevocably bound them, that she had thought had proved to them that they had been predestined to be irrevocably bound, had been nothing more to him than another night of venting his lust on a female body in a bawdyhouse in the Haymarket!

If she had had a score to settle with the Lord of Polreath before, she had double the score to settle with him now. He had used her and abandoned her. He had taken her to glorious heights and let her drop from them. He had made her own body betray her, and continue to betray her, for every traitorous, treacherous muscle and quivering nerve in her begged for him and ached for him . . . and he cared not a fig for any of what she felt, for he felt nothing.

She hated him—how she hated him! She would pay him back!

"Have you ever met royalty, Miss Stewart?" Lady Margaret asked. She and Elizabeth were in the small salon.

Elizabeth's head lifted. She didn't realize that the

look on her face—which she had meant to be one of casual, polite interest—was one of hauteur. All she knew was that she was not going to let Lady Margaret know how she bridled inside every time her unwilling hostess addressed her, even when Lady Margaret was making an effort to be cordial. This time Lady Margaret was not trying to be cordial; her attitude was superior.

"No, Lady Margaret." Elizabeth's voice was cool.

"I thought not. You will have a lesson in court manners this afternoon. Lady Stilton, lady-in-waiting to Her Majesty, is coming to tea. I've asked her to instruct you on what is expected of one on meeting royalty, and on how one should behave in the presence of royalty. I'm having a small soirée Thursday next. Prince George of Colstonwood will attend, and several other notables. I would not wish to have my position in society damaged by introducing someone to them as my house guest who proved gauche in their presence."

Elizabeth covered her resentment at Lady Margaret's attitude, both then and during tea that afternoon. She hated every moment of listening to Lady Stilton while Lady Margaret sat by, a supercilious smile on her face. She hated practicing the curtsy in its varying degrees, depending upon whom it was she was supposed to be curtsying to. But she gritted her teeth and bore it, and she learned her lesson well. It was much more important to her that she not appear gauche than it was to Lady Margaret. She would need friends in high places, for she was determined that she would meet in contest with the mighty Lord of Polreath on his own level! The soirée was not going to end without her having received at least one invitation to a great house, perhaps the palace itself!

Elizabeth was not disappointed. As a result of Lady Margaret's brilliant soirée, she was launched.

Lady Margaret proved to be as clever as Lord John had said she was. She carried off the ruse that he had suggested to perfection. She was vague when the question of Elizabeth's background came up, always with the impression that she knew it in all its details, but that it was knowledge to be kept private.

Elizabeth was equal to her own part. She would say only that she had not spent all of her life in England, and that she had really not planned to come to London just now, but . . .

Everyone assumed that Elizabeth was the natural daughter of some member of the court, someone old who wanted his daughter near him in his declining years. The speculations included the Duke of Wellington. He could have sired her almost anywhere on the globe. It wasn't likely the king, the whispers went . . . but it was possible. The king had visited in America. When had that been? Some years ago, about the time she must have been born. There was something about her that could be the American influence, a self-assurance. And she had a hauteur and an arrogance that was inborn. Yes, it might be the king. Lady Margaret was a close friend of Miss Wykeham, the king's great love. Could Miss Wykeham have had a child by the king? God knows he was prolific. He'd sired ten bastards on Mrs. Jordan!

Elizabeth was a great success, was invited everywhere. If she had been the dowdiest female in all of London, she would have been, because no one dared take the chance of offending whoever her father was. But she was far from dowdy. Lord John had opened his credit for her use. She could buy anything anywhere in the city and ask that bills be sent to him. She was dressed in the latest fashion and seldom wore the same costume twice. She had jewels befitting the clothes she wore. She spent as she pleased, and overspent.

Lord John had sent for Lady Margaret to meet him at his house in St. John's Wood. He had not been back to her house in London, nor to his, nor in fact to London itself, since the trip to London when he had last seen Elizabeth. He felt that he could not bear to have his eyes so much as fall upon her if he could not be with her then as he had been with her last. More than ever, he had to stay away from her now. He would not ruin her life—her sweet life. He *would* not! If he were near her for any length of time, he would lose that resolve and he knew it, for what drew him to her—whatever it was in him that hungered so for her— would sweep all resolve before it. If he were free . . . Oh, God, if he were only free. . . .

He had sent for Lady Margaret on the pretext that he wanted to see her, but what he wanted was a report on Elizabeth, and she was not deceived.

"You're a fool, John!" Lady Margaret raged. "Do you know how that girl is spending money?"

"I wasn't aware that you had such concern for my purse, Margaret."

"Do you know what she's using your money for? To elevate herself!"

"When did it become an undesirable trait for one to wish to better himself?"

"If you saw how she flaunts herself, you would not be so complacent! She has half the bloods in London panting after her!"

A blank, noncommittal look closed over Lord John's face. He did not answer her. She knew that she had gotten to him. "Come to London and see for yourself," she said, thrusting the knife deeper. "The Gilt and Buckles Ball is Tuesday next. Why don't you come? You're always expected at the palace. Hide yourself in an alcove and watch. You'll find yourself much enlightened, I think!"

He turned his back to her and went to stand at the window. He stayed there, staring moodily out, as if he were alone. Margaret tossed her head and left the room. She went upstairs to the dressing room that she used when she was there and called for her maid. She had herself changed into a long, flowing robe. She wore nothing under it. When John was in the mood he was now, he suddenly and abruptly wanted lovemaking. He was more violent in his lovemaking than he had ever been. She tried to make herself think that it was desire for her, but she knew that it was not. There was something in him that had to be released. It had to do with the girl. Goddamn her!

Margaret knew that John was using her—using her body—but she couldn't have refused him if she had wanted to. Her need for him was greater than her pride. Even having him the way she had to take him was better than not having him at all. He would not be kind nor gentle, she knew. He would push her roughly on the bed, stripping the robe from her, and take her, roughly, without love. He would not be gentle with her afterward. He would not stay to be gentle nor otherwise. He would stride out of the house, angry bootsteps ringing, fling himself on his horse, and ride at a mad gallop until he had exhausted himself. Only then would he be able to fall into bed and lose himself in fitful sleep.

To his utter disgust with himself, Lord John did exactly what Margaret had suggested that he do. He went to the palace on the night of the Gilt and

Buckles Ball and concealed himself in an alcove from which he could watch Elizabeth in the ballroom. He left there the more disgusted with himself, disgusted with Elizabeth, and more sick at heart than he had ever been. The sight of the dandies gawking after Elizabeth, clustering around her, fairly drooling . . . And she—she was worse than they! Leading them on! Flirting! Smiling one moment, eyelashes batting. Pouting the next with that petulant mouth! She'd find herself in trouble, playing one against the other! He ought to send her from London before she disgraced herself! That idiot, Prince George of Coltonswood, barely old enough to be in pants, followed her around like a lovesick puppy! Spoiled and pampered brat that he was, he wasn't going to be content for long with smiles and batting eyelashes and pouts!

Lady Margaret knew when Lord John came to the palace and knew when he left. She put away from her the hurt that she felt that he had not so much as bid her good evening. Her time would come. She had a plan. She'd be rid of Elizabeth Stewart, and soon! Her hatred for the girl was no less than the girl's for her, and she knew it. She'd take the first opportunity offered to get out of Margaret's house—the first that offered her a greater house. Margaret had one in mind—the House of Hanover.

The challenge before her wasn't even great. All she had to do was find a way to snap Prince George out of his lily-livered youthfulness and make him man enough to make the proposition to Elizabeth that he already wanted to make. He was beginning to come round. She'd hinted to him discreetly on several occasions that Elizabeth was much taken with him. Actually, Elizabeth couldn't bear him near her, but he was so lovesick for her that he believed what Margaret told him.

Lady Margaret smiled to herself thinking how easy it would be to continue slyly and carefully leading the gullible youth into believing that he could have Elizabeth for the asking. She smiled with deeper satisfaction thinking of the day when John would know the girl for what she was—a fortune hunter and an opportunist. He would come back to her then—really back— and things would be between them as they had been before Elizabeth Stewart had come from out of nowhere to blight their lives.

Lady Margaret knew where Elizabeth Stewart had come from. That had been easy enough to guess. What she wanted to know was who she was. It must be something about who she was that caused John to be so unlike himself where she was concerned. He gave all the appearance of a man in bondage, and she knew that he was not a man to be in bondage to any woman.

Lady Margaret put the nagging enigma out of her mind. She wanted a free mind so that she could concentrate on working out the details of her plan. ☙

12

Lady Margaret opened her house in Regency Square in Brighton with a flourish. It was unusual for her to open the house at this time of year. Usually she was there when the court was there, from mid-November to mid-February. She spent part of each summer in the south of France, but no one was going to France just now because of the unrest. Anything might happen at any moment, if the revolution that everyone was so concerned about really came to be. That was the reason she gave out for opening the house. Her private reasons she kept private.

She had invited thirty guests for dinner, and an additional hundred guests for dancing and supper afterward. All was in the grand style. As each guest arrived in a fly, several of the liveried servants who were stationed in double rows outside the house rushed to meet the carriage. Footmen lined the walls of the hall inside. The name of each guest had been passed from one appointed footman to the next, six times in all, by the time the guest arrived at the drawing room to be greeted by Lady Margaret and introduced to Elizabeth if it was someone she had not already met.

The opulence of the house was staggering. There were deepest wool carpetings underfoot, silk hangings and lush upholsteries all around, and massive crystal chandeliers sparkling overhead. Paintings by the best-known contemporary painters and old masters covered the walls. Gold fittings glimmered in the candlelight. The arms of the Litchfield family were engraved everywhere appropriate.

To Elizabeth, dinner lasted an interminable time. Turtle soup was served first, followed by course after course of fish and game and joints of beef and vegetables. Wines were served with every course, champagne for those who preferred it. Jellied fruits and stewed fruits, tarts and cakes and puddings were served afterward with claret and champagne.

Prince George was to Elizabeth's left, and the Duke of St. Albans to her right. The two were friends, and delighted to see each other. They were not too far apart in age. Elizabeth guessed the duke to be not much more than twenty-one, though his notorious wife was near fifty!

Elizabeth had heard of the Duchess of St. Albans. There was always gossip about her, most of it malicious. She was Harriet Mellon, the illegitimate daughter of a onetime wardrobe keeper of an Irish theatrical company. She'd become a successful actress, had married a man forty-two years older than she, a rich banker named Coutts who had left her the richest woman in England when he died. Everyone had toadied to her. Many men had wanted to marry her. She'd chosen the young duke, and it was said to be a love match—at least, on his part!

Not a few of the guests had been surprised to see

that the Duke and Duchess of St. Albans had been
invited. To invite them took no small daring on the
part of the partygiver. The Duchess of St. Albans was
no longer acceptable at court. As long as George IV,
that rakehell, had been king, she'd had as much free-
dom of the court as almost anyone, but once William
IV was king and the prerogative Queen Adelaide's,
the queen had declared the duchess unacceptable. All
who enjoyed the queen's favor were expected to adopt
her attitude toward the duchess, and most did.

The prince and the duke talked all through dinner
of hawking, the prince explaining to Elizabeth that
the duke was Hereditary Grand Falconer of England,
that he owned the finest hawks in all of England, and
that he was famous for his hawking parties. The duke
effused about how perfect the Downs near Brighton
were for flying his birds, elaborated upon the problems
of bringing to Brighton his highly trained hawks and
all the attendants and horses necessary for flying them.
He enthusiastically described to the prince and Elizabeth the extensive stables that were attached to his
own house in Regency Square, which he had acquired
only that summer.

"By George!" the prince exclaimed—it was his favorite expression and his ultimate compliment. "You
must invite me! You're having hawking parties already,
I've heard. I can't let the summer pass without seeing
your birds fly!"

The duke laughed, glancing toward his wife. She
was engrossed in conversation with a young dandy to
her left, on the opposite side of the table, looking away
from their direction. "You're welcome anytime, as you
know. . . . But will Her Majesty allow you bed in the
palace after?"

Elizabeth saw the duchess stiffen. Old Mother St.

Albans was listening, much as she was pretending that she was not.

"If you want to enjoy my company," the ebullient duke was continuing, "you should cultivate Miss Wykeham! Or should I say the Baroness Wenman? King Billy still pines after her, half-crazy though she always was, and becoming the more so every day, or so they say!"

"By George!" The prince had entirely missed any facetiousness on the part of the duke. "I'll have Lady Margaret introduce me! Deuced clever, Lady Margaret, is she not? She likes your company, and so what does she do? She comes to Brighton when you are here and the court is not, so not to embarrass either! Deuced clever, by George!"

It was three hours before the ladies left the dining room. Elizabeth hoped that the men would stay at their port and cognac forever. However, it was not much more than an hour before coffee was announced. When the prince came to claim her company, he was full of plans for attending the duke's hawking parties, beginning the following morning. He gave Lady Margaret all the credit for making it possible. His youthful enthusiasm was so great that he was even talking of sending for his own birds to put them in contest against those of the duke.

As the prince babbled on, he glanced toward Lady Margaret from time to time. She returned his open grins with sly smiles. Elizabeth caught a gleam of triumph in Lady Margaret's glittering blue eyes—she was up to something! She hadn't opened her house and brought the duke and the prince together just so the prince could attend the hawking parties he loved so much. There was something more she wanted out of all of this.

There was. Lady Margaret told the prince, privately

and with shows of great regret, that she had just received some very distressing news from London, and that she must return to London within a few days. She was so terribly sorry, she said, to have to ruin all his lovely plans. But . . . A smile shone on her face. Why should not the prince stay on? Her house was his. She insisted, overruling his not very strong protests.

Lady Margaret gave a garden party on her last day in Brighton. The prince was downcast. He couldn't make up his mind to stay, since Elizabeth would be leaving. Lady Margaret took him for a walk on a path out of the sight and hearing of the others. "I know how fond you are of my young protégée," she said to him, "and I've told you how she dotes on you." She leaned toward him, smiling as she took the arm he offered her. "I wish you to know," she said, looking away from him, "that I would not take it amiss if you persuaded her to stay on with you here." She felt the prince stiffen slightly and gritted her teeth at his calflike prudishness, but she kept a serene, thoughtful expression on her face. "It would be such a shame," she went on, "for Elizabeth to miss the rest of the summer in Brighton. I do hate the thought of dragging her back with me to London. The city is so stifling in the summer! And her health . . ." She looked at him, eyes shaded with worry, and sighed. "Her health . . . I'm afraid her constitution is not as strong as one could wish . . ."

"She is not well?" The prince was immediately concerned.

"Oh, it's nothing serious, I assure you, my dear prince! It's only . . . well, she *is* delicate. Surely you've noticed."

The prince had noticed nothing of the sort. He had found Elizabeth stronger and more resilient than himself. She could outride and outhunt him any day in

the week, and be as fresh in the evening as if she had
rested all day. However, he let himself be persuaded.
He became the great protector. "I shan't let her return!" he declared.

"You can imagine what a great relief that is for me."
Lady Margaret turned their steps so that they were
headed back toward the others, and Elizabeth. She
didn't want the prince's determination to have time to
waver and dissolve. "I should hate to answer for the
state in which you would find her health after a summer in the heat of the city." She pressed the prince's
arm consolingly as if sympathizing with him for the
sad state in which he would find Elizabeth. "Actually,
England has not the best climate for her . . ." Lady
Margaret's plan had advanced a step. She was confident that she had contrived to have him take Elizabeth
off her hands for the summer. Now she wanted him
to take her out of the country altogether, back with
him to Hanover!

Lady Margaret and Prince George returned to join
the others to find a newcomer to the party—the Lord
of Polreath. Margaret trembled when she saw him.
She always did, but this time there was fear mixed
with the physical excitement that sent her blood racing. What if he got onto her plan? "Speak to Elizabeth
now!" she smiled brightly and encouragingly at the
prince and pressed his arm, hoping he would take the
urgency in her voice to be caused by concern for Elizabeth. She gave the prince a slight push in Elizabeth's
direction, and turned with a bright smile of welcome
toward the Lord of Polreath.

"My Lord Polreath!" the Duchess of St. Albans was
exclaiming. The duchess insisted on using Polreath,
though all who knew him were well aware that he
preferred the given name for both himself and Lady
Sarah. "One so seldom sees you in company anymore!"

"His lordship is always pressed by business!" Margaret said, smiling, coming up to him to take his arm possessively. "Welcome, my lord. Did you come today from London?"

"I came from Harwich." His answer was preoccupied, his gray eyes wandering over the crowd, growing icy as they roved.

"He could come from anywhere!" Margaret said to the duchess. "His interests include everything, you know. If he's from Harwich, or any port city, it's shipping that's kept him from me. But he might come from his mines in Cornwall, or his farms and fields anywhere and everywhere. He's into everything!"

"Everything except politics, I gather," the duchess returned.

"My boroughs are never without representation," the Lord of Polreath stated distantly. "However, it is a policy of mine not to discuss my political faiths. . . . If you ladies will excuse me." He bowed stiffly and turned toward the house.

"Touchy, aren't we!" the duchess sniffed.

"You must forgive him. His mind is always occupied with business."

"It wasn't *business* that went inside the house just now on Prince George's arm! That puppy! . . . I will say, Margaret, that your house guest lives up to her reputation! She quite overwhelms one! Looks as soft as a kitten, but don't let it fool you! She'll not take the prince unless she wants him, and I doubt she does. It's obvious the poor dolt thinks she does, but I say she's using him. Her eye is out for someone else. . . ." Her expression became bemused. "I haven't discovered who, as yet . . ."

The old reprobate! Margaret was furious—because the old duchess was probably right. Who, better than she, would recognize a woman on the make for someone. Margaret's light laugh was brittle. "My dear duchess, how you love intrigue!"

The prince had led Elizabeth into the drawing room. They stood at a tall window, looking out on the party a distance away. "The Dowager Lady Wexford, my godmother, will come if I ask her . . ." The prince slipped his arm about Elizabeth's waist. "It will be most circumspect." His arm tightened, belying his words. "Oh, Miss Stewart, please say you'll stay!"

Elizabeth was at the point of jerking away from him and turning to laugh in his face when a drawling voice came from the door behind them. "I suggest that perhaps the Dowager Lady Wexford should be here present now. I think it would amuse her, the sight of her unfledged pup playing at making love."

Elizabeth whirled around. The Lord of Polreath was in the open doorway, his long, thin figure relaxed languidly against the frame. One eyebrow was raised in a smirk. A scornful smile played on his mouth. His eyes were like ice, not touched by any expression.

"How dare you spy on me!" Elizabeth could have bitten out her tongue at the same time the words were hissing from her mouth. Why did her quick temper always have to give her away? Why couldn't she be as cold, as nasty, as *untouched* as he?

The raised black eyebrow rose higher in a point. "Spy, Miss Stewart? Were you hiding, then?"

The prince, red-faced and spluttering, was trying to explain. "Lady Margaret has to return unexpectedly to London," he said. "She was disturbed and worried at the prospect of a summer in the city for Miss Stewart . . . Miss Stewart's delicate health . . ."

"Ha!" came from the doorway. The harsh, scoffing syllable was followed by a scornful, sneering chuckle.

". . . Sir . . . ?" The prince's confusion was plain.

"How dare you laugh at the prince!" Elizabeth kept

her voice low, but she wanted to yell and scream,
wanted to attack the languid, scoffing man!

The figure in the doorway stood upright. "I dare to
laugh at kings, Miss Stewart. . . . But was I laughing
at the prince?"

"Oh!" Elizabeth wanted more than ever to scream
at him, to lash out at him that she knew he wasn't
laughing at the prince, that she knew he was laughing
at her, that he never did less than laugh at her, sneer at
her, scoff at her. It was hard for her to gain control.
But she did. She turned back to the prince. "Shall we
walk in the garden, George? I feel the need of fresh
air."

The prince blushed with more than pleasure . . . triumph. It was the first time that Miss Stewart—Elizabeth—had made him such an offer.

He offered his arm and the two crossed the room
and swept past the man in the doorway.

Elizabeth, head high, had never been more miserable in her life. The Lord of Polreath hadn't even
turned to watch her leave him. Her show of victory
was no victory at all; he didn't care.

The party wore on to its close. Lady Margaret was
everywhere among her guests, seeing that all were
entertained, but there was a feverishness in her too
quick and flashing smiles and in the brilliance of her
eyes. Often her eyes darted about the crowd, looking
for the tall figure of the Lord of Polreath, the noble
head with its white hair fringed with black that stood
out in any gathering. But the Lord of Polreath was
nowhere to be seen. Elizabeth and Prince George
were always in evidence, she leaning on his arm and
he with head inclined toward her. They gave every
impression of being two lovers who wanted to be left
alone, and so they were.

It was late by the time the last guest had supped and left. Lady Margaret rushed to her rooms. Lord John was not in her sitting room. She threw open the door of the bedroom and rushed inside. "John! Are you there, John?"

His hand lashed out and smashed her across the face and sent her reeling to the bed. She sprawled across it, whimpering. She pushed herself up on one elbow. "What is the matter, John? Darling! What have I done?"

"I didn't enlist your services to play matchmaker!"

"Darling! Whatever do you mean?" She pushed herself to her feet and moved toward him.

"I suggest you keep your distance," he said.

His voice, always cold lately, was even more so. Lady Margaret's hand went involuntarily to her bruised face. She stopped. "I would never wittingly do anything to displease you. You know that! How could I wish to displease you when I love . . ."

"When you leave tomorrow . . . The information that came to me in Harwich was that it is your plan to cut short your stay in Brighton and return to London tomorrow. When you *do* leave, Miss Stewart leaves with you!"

Lady Margaret backed away, out of his reach, before she spoke. "You're *jealous!* You're jealous of that little *snit!* You're *in love* with her!"

"You're not being clever, Margaret." With that, the Lord of Polreath turned on his heel and walked toward the door.

"I can't control her!" she screamed after him. "She's out of my control! She's been making a play for the prince since we came here. You think it's my doing. It's not—it's hers! Even the Duchess of St. Albans noticed the play that she's been making for the prince!"

Margaret saw a break in the man's stride. "Yes! I tell you she's out to better herself. She's beguiled a mere youth!"

The Lord of Polreath's hand was on the knob of the door. Lady Margaret's voice rose to a shriek. "I'm not going to play the madam for you any longer!" she screamed.

The man at the door stopped and turned. "Nor the procurer for Prince George of Coltonswood!" he said. He went out the door and closed it behind him. ᘓ

13

Oxford had been muttering to himself all morning. Tremblay, his new helper in the coach house who had been brought in after the deaths of Dax and Jax, didn't know whether to answer his mutterings or to keep still. And Ross, also new to the coach house but long in service at Polreath and closely acquainted with Oxford, wasn't there to answer him. Oxford had sent Ross to watch for the arrival of a hired wagon that would be bringing two puppies to the manor. All of Oxford's mutterings had to do with her ladyship. Tremblay would not have dared even think thoughts about such an exalted person.

". . . Her ladyship havin' dogs brought here, and herself in mortal fear on 'em . . ." Oxford muttered, "Don't set right . . . Pets for the little girls, she says . . . Even at that, don't set right . . ." He raised his voice. ". . . Me not sent for to fetch 'em neither! What do ye make of that, Tremblay?"

Tremblay busied himself with the traces he was mending, not knowing what to answer, nor whether he was expected to answer.

"It's a pure disgrace, it is!" Oxford went on. "Her

ladyship hiring a public wagon when we got . . . just
look!" He waved his arm around the coach house.
There were nine vehicles of various kinds housed
within.

"Maybe her thought as how her couldn't spare you
from the manor," Tremblay said hesitantly, trying to
be placating, thinking that perhaps Oxford felt rebuffed by her ladyship.

"Not a minute of it! I wouldn't've gone meself, and
her knows it. I'd've sent Ross." He didn't notice that
he was reversing himself. "Could've sent yourself if
you knew the way to Lord Moulton's place, Baloorin.
It's nothing such a much to cart two dogs!"

Ross came running in. "It's comin' up to the manor
now." He was out of breath from running.

Oxford stood up from a leather seat he'd been
checking for splits in the seaming. "Keep an eye on
things here, Ross, and on the boy's work," he said,
indicating Tremblay, " 'til I comes back. I be going
up to the manor."

Oxford didn't go straight to the manor. He went out
of his way to a cottage off the lane that led to the
near woods. "Be ye there, Hawkins?" he called through
the closed door, rapping on it the while.

A sleepy voice answered. "I be here. Who's waking
me in the middle o' the day?"

"Ye'll do your sleeping later! Bring your gun and
come with me. Something wrong up at the manor. I
got a feeling on it."

"I can't watch the fields o' nights without'n I sleeps
days."

"Ye'll come with me or ye'll answer to his lordship
if you was needed and wasn't there! You're the best
marksman on the place. Come!"

There was a rustling and stumbling about inside the

cottage and Hawkins came out, buttoning the lappet
of his pants at the waist with one hand. In the other
hand he carried a long-barreled shotgun.

The two arrived at the Manor to see a strange conveyance—part cab, part wagon—pulled up on one side
of the lawn. Two slatted crates were being taken from
it. There was a crowd of Polreath's people gathered to
watch. Lady Sarah stood to one side with Nonna, her
mannish-looking maid. She had each of her wards by
the hand, holding the little girls close beside her.
There were servants from the house and workmen
from the fields and grounds. Daly was directing the
men who were unloading the crates. The boy, Colin,
was in his shadow in every move he made. Oxford
stopped at the rear of the crowd out of sight of Lady
Sarah. He motioned to Hawkins to stop beside him.

Once out of their crates the puppies stood trembling
and looking cautiously about, obviously frightened at
the strangeness of their surroundings. They were handsome puppies—collies—one of richest brown with
white markings on its face and breast and forelegs.
The other had a coat of purest white.

Daly and Colin stayed near the puppies but made
no attempt to touch them. They spoke to them in soft
voices, Colin's boyish treble tones alternating with
Daly's full ones.

A kennel had been built for each of the puppies
and they were brought and placed inside a fenced-in
area, well to the back of it so that there was a large
space for the puppies to exercise. Colin moved toward
the pen, coaxing and cajoling. The white puppy followed, then stopped, then followed again. The brown
puppy was on the tail of the first. When both puppies
were finally inside the fence of the pen, Colin set about
attaching one to a kennel by a long rope. Daly went

to the gate of the pen, but he stayed there, leaving the handling of the puppies to Colin.

"I don't want them tied up!" Hope, the younger of Lady Sarah's wards, shrieked. "How can we play with them if they're all tied up?"

"Of course you're right, sweetness." Lady Sarah smiled down on the child. "Of course you are." She called to Daly. "The puppies are not to be tied!"

Daly turned to face her. "We don't yet know the nature of the pups, ma'am," he said.

"Exactly as you say." Lady Sarah exclaimed. "And how will we come to know their natures if they're tied?"

Daly turned from her and spoke a few words in lowered tones to Colin. The boy stiffened but said nothing. He untied the knot that he had tied, rose, and without a look toward anyone, walked out of the pen and disappeared in the direction of the gatehouse.

"Where is he going?" Lady Sarah's voice was sharp with anger. "Call him back!"

When the small, slight, straight figure had gone beyond their view, Daly turned toward Lady Sarah. "You promised Master Colin, madam, that he would have the care of the puppies."

"So I did. And so he shall. Call him back!"

"His care would be to tie them, madam."

Lady Sarah laughed offhandedly. "Tie little puppies? Why would he want to tie them?" Her voice became steely. "Send for him to come back immediately. He's to stay inside and tend the dogs. The girls can watch from outside." She turned and went toward the manor. Nonna followed closely after her. Before she rounded the tower, which would have blocked her from Daly's view, Lady Sarah turned back to face him. "Call that boy back!" she ordered. "Put him inside that pen to tend those dogs!"

Once she was out of sight, the little girls ran toward the fence of the pen.

"The brown one is mine!" Patience declared.

"I was going to choose the white one anyway." Hope shrilled. "He's my favorite!"

"I'm going to name mine Lochinvar!"

"It's a female, Miss Patience," Daly said flatly, walking in the wake of the little girls' running figures.

"Then I'll call her Guinevere!"

"I'm going to name mine Silver King!" Hope shouted.

"That's apt."

Hope had raced ahead. She unlatched the gate and ran inside, Patience after her.

"You're not to go inside!" Daly rushed in to collar them and send them out.

"Just for a minute, Daly! We'll be good—we promise!" Hope pleaded.

Daily looked back and forth at the puppies, no longer cowering, tails wagging now. "All right, but not for long," he said. "But you'll not tease them and you'll not be rough with them, and you'll go along when I tell you."

Each puppy seemed to recognize the little girl that it belonged to. Guinevere contented herself to jump up on Patience and stand braced against her, forefeet on her shoulders and almost as tall as she, while Patience ruffled her handsome, not yet sleek, puppy coat and smoothed it back flat again. Silver King was playful, nipping at Hope's hand when she—forgetting Daly's admonition about teasing—held her hand out to him and then, before he could catch it between his snapping teeth, quickly withdrew it. He would spring away and then spring back, nipping at her when he failed to catch her hand, and jump away again. Daly cautioned her.

"He likes it, Daly! He does! See?"

Daly stood beside her for a moment, watching the playful pup. Then he went to inspect the hastily erected fence.

Silver King continued playful and frisky for a few minutes longer. Then he became quiet and retreated a few feet from Hope and lay down, panting as if from exhaustion. He showed no interest in Hope's attempts to coax him back to their play.

Daly glanced around. He stopped what he was doing and headed toward the girls. "You'll have to come out now, misses!" he said sharply. "Come on! Come out!"

"Just a few minutes more, Daly." Hope begged in her high voice. "Just let me get him to play one more time!"

At Hope's trilling voice, Silver King stood up in wobbly, drunken lurches and backed into the farthest corner of the pen.

"He's tired, as you can see, Miss Hope!"

Suddenly Daly quickened his stride and reached the little girls. He took them by the shoulder and propelled them through the gate. "Out! Both of you! Now!" He called to their governess, Miss Wells. "To the house with them—quick about it!"

The children's governess, indignant at being ordered about by Daly, was slow to respond to his order.

"Get the other dog out!" someone from the gathered crowd of watchers yelled. "Get the other dog out!"

But there was no time for that. Daly gave the little girls a sharp push in the direction of Miss Wells and turned and slammed the gate of the pen shut and secured it.

Silver King was out of his corner and was running in crazy, broken circles around and around the edges of the enclosure. He was running next to the fence. He ran so close to the fence that his body brushed

against it. At intervals he lifted his head and bayed
with wide-open mouth in a baleful, pain-wracked
moan.

"What's the matter with him?" Hope screamed.

Miss Wells ran to her and grabbed her by the arm,
grabbing Patience at the same time. She started with
them toward the manor.

"What's the matter with him?" Hope screamed.
again, looking back and trying to pull away from Miss
Wells.

Silver King continued his mad chase. Froth began
to show on his livid, open mouth. At times he would
suddenly stop his forward plunging and back up, hind
legs curled under him. The watchers stood as if
hypnotized, gripped in fascination at the sight before
them.

"He's hurting!" Hope screamed. "Daly! Do something! He's hurting!"

The puppy was running back and forth the length
of the pen now instead of making circles around its
outer limits. His eyes had taken on a blazing red
gleam. He stopped only to howl and moan, and then
plunged on. Suddenly he bolted wildly, on buckling
legs, to the far corner of the pen and fell prone. The
frame of his rib cage rose and fell with each labored
breath.

The girls' nurses, Rosie and Leah, came rushing from
the house. With their help, Miss Wells managed to
get the girls inside. Lady Sarah came swiftly down the
wide stairs as they entered the gallery, Nonna in her
wake. "What is the meaning of this disturbance!" she
demanded. She made straight for Miss Wells and the
weeping Hope in her arms. "What has happened to
the child?" Her voice was sharp with fear and full of
accusation.

"She's all right, ma'am," Miss Wells said hastily. "She's not hurt."

"She didn't get bitten, did she?" Lady Sarah's eyes were anxious as well as accusing.

"No, ma'am. There's nothing wrong with her. She's all right."

"It appears that she is *not* all right, Miss Wells!" Lady Sarah reached to take Hope from the governess. Before she could take her, a high-pitched scream struck all their ears. It had come through the open door of the library. Lady Sarah and the others wheeled and ran in the direction of the sound.

Patience was at the window overlooking the lawn. It was she who had shrieked. "He's out! He's out!" she screamed.

"What's going on out there?" There was a grating quality and yet a slight rising of hysteria in Lady Sarah's voice. She brushed aside Nonna's attempts to restrain her and ran across the library and to the window. The others crowded around her.

Silver King was out of the pen and running free on the lawn in the same pattern of jagged circles that his maddened, driven feet had etched earlier inside the pen. Guinevere crouched huddled in the pen, squeezed against the wall of her kennel, muzzle pressed hard into the short grass, her liquid brown eyes moving as they followed Silver King.

A tall husky man dressed in the sturdy brown cords of a fieldkeeper forced his way through the frozen crowd of onlookers and strode beyond them and stopped just before them, between them and the mad puppy. He carried a heavy shotgun. He pointed the gun in Silver King's direction, but, not able to take certain aim because of the unpredictable movements of the puppy, could only follow its movements as best he could with the pointing barrel of the gun.

"He's going to shoot my puppy!" Hope screamed. "Hawkins is going to shoot my puppy!"

"Where's the brat?" Lady Sarah hissed. "He's supposed to mind the dogs! Where is he?"

"The little dog is mad, ma'am," Nonna said. "You'd not want the lad near him."

"Don't cross me, Nonna! I gave him the care of the dogs because he dotes on animals so! Where is he? Call Daly in to me! I'll find out why my orders . . ."

"Don't let him shoot my puppy!" Hope screamed wildly, struggling against Miss Wells's holding arms. "Ma'am! Don't let Hawkins shoot my puppy!" Her voice ended in a keening wail.

Lady Sarah turned on the governess. "Do you wish to make the child ill, Miss Wells?" she screeched. She snatched the weeping, wailing child roughly from her. She leaned farther into the window, cuddling Hope in her arms, crooning into her hair. "Oh, my sweetness! My poor sweetness!"

"He's not running now," Patience said.

Silver King was almost out of sight of those in the window. He was toward the front of the lawn. He had stopped running, had stopped all movement. He was standing in his tracks, his head hanging, his tail limp and curled between his legs. He seemed totally without spirit or life. His breathing could not be seen in any movement of his ribs.

It was very still overall. The very atmosphere was still. The light was very clear. It was the kind of late-day airless light that said that a night storm was coming. It was too bright for the time of day. It was too still.

Hawkins shifted his stance, planting his feet firmly and sighting carefully, making sure his aim was true. His finger was poised on the trigger, his muscles tensed for the recoil of the explosion when he pressed the trigger.

The small figure of Colin bolted from the crowd. "No!" he screamed. "No!" He ran past Hawkins. He ran directly in the path of the deadly aim of the gun, arms outflung to ward off the shot from the puppy.

14

It had been Lord John's intention to return directly to Harwich, to finish the business that he had interrupted to go down to Brighton. But he was bumping over dried ruts and potholes on the hard wooden seat of a fast mail coach, the fastest conveyance on the road, headed toward Cornwall and Polreath. He had made up his mind to take up the matter of Elizabeth Stewart with Sarah. The girl must be returned to her guardian, to wherever home was for her. Her guardian must be wondering already why news from her was so long coming.

Lord John had made up his mind to do now what he should have done in the first place, instead of kidnapping the girl. For wasn't that what he had done? What kind of hooks had she got into him in the space of an interview of no more than fifteen minutes' duration that had sent him reeling into a craziness that had made him think that the only thing to do was to grab her up and fly away with her? He'd had to get her out of Sarah's reach—that much was true. But he hadn't had to keep her within his.

And she herself. Why had she not demanded to be

151

taken home? Or sent home? Was she afraid to face her
guardian? Was he so ambitious for himself, by way of
her? Would he hold her at fault for not having had the
successful—and productive—introduction into society
that he had expected her to have under the sponsor-
ship of the Lady of Polreath? Lord John tried to find
excuse for himself. Perhaps he had been trying to make
up for what Elizabeth had been promised by Sarah—
and then denied—when he had demanded that Margaret sponsor her.

Elizabeth's face and form had been before him
throughout the long predawn hours and the even
longer hours of the day. He could not rid himself of
the remembered sight of her and the feelings that the
sight of her had brought to him. He had wanted to
snatch her from the prince's arm and to shake her
senseless when she had sailed so arrogantly past him
in the doorway of the drawing room at Margaret's
house in Brighton. He had wanted to pound the
prince's blissful face into pulp!

What right had he? He cursed himself for the
thousandth time for having feelings as adolescent as
those of the stripling prince—and less control! He
should not have gone to Brighton. He had gone for
only one reason. To break things up between Elizabeth and the prince. Why couldn't he be strong enough
to let her go?

He *was* going to let her go. He had no right to hold
her, nor to try to. He was going to find out who her
guardian was and where he lived and send her home to
him. He would make it as easy as he could for her to
face him. He would assure her and her guardian that
she was being returned home before the end of the
season—or even the beginning, he reminded himself—
because Lady Sarah was in ill health and not for any
reason of failure on Elizabeth's part.

Every sight that Lord John had ever had of Elizabeth repeated itself over and over in his mind. The only ones that he could bear with any equanimity were the first ones—when she'd been out of her mind from fright because of having been alone in the darkness of the dungeon. He could even smile a little when he thought of that. What a spitfire she had been! And what an imagination she had! She really believed the tales she had told him about Hurford. Her hallucinations—or nightmares—had been so vivid to her that she had thought they had really happened. . . . Hurford . . . staid, sobersides Hurford. . . . One had to smile to think of his taking sadistic pleasure from tormenting a girl with a whip!

Elizabeth . . . What did she think about when she thought of him? . . . What kind of feelings did her thoughts of him bring to her? . . . If she ever thought of him. Why hadn't their night meant to her what it had meant to him? . . . He had lost himself—his lover's self, his lover's heart and soul—that night, had surrendered all to her. And he had thought that she had surrendered herself to him in equal measure, only to learn when he saw her next that her heart was as carefree and as untouched by him as if their night had never happened. She cared for nothing but the conquests she was making.

He could have understood that. Perhaps he could have learned to bear it. It was only natural that she would enjoy the taste of victory, the coming into her own. There wasn't the woman born who didn't, at some point in her life, bring every man she could to her feet and savor the thrill of conquest. But then he had learned that it wasn't a simple flirtation that was going on between her and the prince. Asquith, so deep in his cups after a hunt that he didn't know where he was, much less what he was saying, had admitted it to him. Margaret had been too proud of her match-making skills to keep them to herself and she had crowed to Asquith about the royal liaison that she'd soon have to her credit. It was Asquith who had sent him word that Margaret was cutting short her stay in Brighton. Asquith. Asquith would plumb any depths in his quest for Margaret. He had used to think him the worst kind of besotted fool, and perhaps he was, but he himself would be no less besotted a fool if he were free to fight to have Elizabeth for his own.

... Elizabeth ... Her soft arms around him, as tight as iron, but soft as only love can make arms soft ...

Suddenly Elizabeth's image was replaced by that of Colin.

Lord John abruptly sat up straight, jolted out of his half-sleep and from his reverie. "Where are we?" he demanded of the driver. "Quick, man! Where?"

"Just closin' on Plymouth, sir."

"I'll want a horse at Plymouth!"

"I'll be goin' on, your lordship. All the way to Penzance I goes."

"I'll want a horse. Take the north road above Plymouth and take me to Badilly's horse farm!"

The driver hesitated, afraid to speak out, but afraid also to go so far off his route. Finally, "It's long off the way I'm s'posed to go, sir, Badilly's," he said.

"Take me to Badilly's!"

"Yes, sir!" the driver said hastily. He touched his hat with a respectful finger. "Yes, sir!"

At Badilly's stud farm, Lord John found a horse equal to the ride he intended to put him to. He stopped there only long enough to choose the mount. He was too anxious to stop long enough to take nourishment or to rest. He set off at a gallop, riding hard across the breadth of Cornwall. Colin's image, coming to him so sharply and so vividly out of nowhere, had thrown him into an anxiety that was close to panic. He spurred the horse on, taking every short-cut he knew, riding forward over the saddle like a jockey.

He rode onto Polreath lands through the east woods. The nearer he came to home, the more his anxiety choked him. He thundered up a long incline. From the top he could see the rising towers of the manor house and the spire of the chapel. Then he could see the low outbuildings between him and the manor house—the barns and stables and the coach house. And then he was riding past them. He saw the crowd and he saw Hawkins before them, gun raised and aimed. He saw Colin running before Hawkins, saw his small straight back and his outflung arms.

"Hawkins!" he roared. He was off the horse and bolting toward Hawkins when he saw the puppy. "Colin!" he yelled. "Come back, Colin!" He veered around Hawkins and raced after Colin. "Shoot the dog, Hawkins!" His voice was a thundered order. "Shoot the dog!"

Colin heard the order to Hawkins. He wheeled about and darted back and past his father, running toward Hawkins, again directly in the path of the deadly aim of the gun, arms again flung wide. Lord John swerved and lunged for him. He caught him as he threw himself on Hawkins. The force of the colliding bodies sent them all sprawling. Lord John grabbed Colin and rolled away. The gun flew out of Hawkins's hands, arcing a half-turn in the air before falling heavily back upon him. It went off with a burst-ing explosion of sound.

Lord John was on his feet with Colin in his arms. He held Colin's face to his breast to shield him from the sight of Hawkins. The blast from the gun had hit Hawkins full in the face.

The people in the crowd shrieked and gasped and backed away. Where Hawkins's face had been there was a bloody red hole. His throat and the upper part of his clothing were saturated with his blood.

Oxford came forward from the crowd. "See to him, Oxford," Lord John said, indicating Hawkins. "I'm sorry," he said.

Oxford touched his cap. "I be the one brought him here, your lordship, sir," he said. Oxford tried to keep his face impassive and noncommittal, but there was anger and accusation in it as well as grief. He tried to avoid looking toward the manor, but he couldn't help himself, and his eyes went to it.

Lord John turned deliberately toward the manor. His eyes found the window where those inside were gathered. He stared at it for a long moment and then pressed Colin more tightly to himself and turned and strode off with him in the direction of the gatehouse.

Silver King, dried froth masking the blackness of his muzzle so that it was one in color with the silver whiteness of the rest of him, went slinking, sidling, to the pen. He went again to the far corner and stood there in his forlorn, spiritless stance, muzzle down, limp tail curled between his legs.

Daly went to the pen and inside. He brought out the frightened, quivering Guinevere and locked and secured the gate. He strode off after Lord John and Colin, carrying Guinevere with him.

Oxford picked up Hawkins's gun, loaded it, and, from where he stood, shot the small white puppy. Tears were in his eyes when he put the gun down and turned to the body of the dead fieldkeeper. "Help here!" he shouted angrily to the crowd. "I need some help here!" ๛

15

Lord John, his tall frame leaning into the rising wind of the gathering storm, held his son close against his heart. Colin huddled in his arms, crying in heartbroken sobs.

"They didn't have to kill him," he sobbed.

"Yes, my son, they had to. They had no choice. The pup was mad. If he had bitten you, you would have died of rabies." His arms tightened around Colin. He almost staggered, thinking of how close Colin had come to being bitten by the mad puppy. "It's a horrible death—rabies—and would have been for the pup as well. Much better for him to die quickly from a clean shot. Otherwise his sufferings would have been long drawn out and terrible. Remember that when you remember your own sadness over the loss of the puppy."

Daly came up alongside them. Colin stopped crying when he saw the puppy Guinevere that Daly was carrying. Lord John's eyes questioned Daly.

"She's all right. Seems to be," Daly said.

Lord John put Colin down and Daly handed him Guinevere. They continued the walk to the gatehouse,

Colin between the two men, cuddling the puppy in his arms.

Lord John, looking down at Colin's head bent over the little puppy, relived another time of panic when he had almost lost his son.

Lady Sarah had arranged a picnic at the summerhouse on the cliffs. Lord John was from home at one of his mines. The little girls—her wards—were hardly more than babies; one was two and the other three. But if anyone thought it odd that she proposed a picnic as entertainment for children so small, nothing was said for it was not the privilege of any to question her ladyship's wishes. She had invited Colin "as company for the girls."

It was a lovely day, one of those sunlit, balmy days of spring that promised the best of Cornish weather. Not a rain cloud was in sight. The weather would hold clear throughout the day.

Daly also was away from home. He had gone early that morning to Truro on business to do with taxes. He was bailiff of the Polreath estates now, and had been for some years since soon after he and the present Lord of Polreath had returned from India, where he had gone as valet. Daly was not expected back at the manor until early afternoon. If he had been there it was not likely that he would have allowed Colin to go to the summerhouse without him for the picnic. When Lord John was not at home, Daly kept Colin near him.

There were not many included in the party. There were Lady Sarah, the two little girls, their two nurses —Rosie and Leah—and Colin. And, of course, several footmen and Lady Sarah's maid, Nonna.

The footmen placed the picnic table under the trees within the stone wall that girded the summerhouse.

They spread the cloth and set the table and served the food.

Lady Sarah was in very gay spirits. After the picnic lunch she suggested that she teach the children the game of Witches' Hunt. She busied herself out of the sight of the others, hiding various articles for the children to find. All of them were things that they had seen that very day, she said; one of them, she had been wearing.

The girls quickly tired of the game, but Colin, being an eager and energetic little boy of five, continued rushing about everywhere searching for the things that hadn't been found yet. Lady Sarah allowed him to go beyond the gate of the stone wall. When Leah, the older of the nurses started to go after him, to watch him, since there was no fence along the edge of the cliffs, nor other protection from the sheer drops from them, Lady Sarah stopped her, saying that she would go along behind him to watch him himself. Colin soon disappeared from the sight of those at the summerhouse, and Lady Sarah disappeared after him.

After a while, Lady Sarah was heard calling, 'Come, Rosie! Come, Leah! Come help me find him! The naughty boy has got away from me!" And when they came up to her. "Where do you think the child could have got off to? He was right under my eye!"

Far below on the beach, Colin heard Lady Sarah's exclamations. He held his hand over his mouth to keep himself from laughing aloud and giving away where he was. He and Lady Sarah were playing a joke on the others. It had been Lady Sarah's idea. She had shown him a hidden path down the cliffs to the small cove below and the small beach that edged it. She had gone partway down with him and had shown him how to get down the rest of the way by himself. The most important of the things she had hidden was

down there, she had said. He had started on down and
had found a gold disc that Lady Sarah had been wearing on a chain around her neck that morning. "I found
it! I found it!" He had turned back to show the
Witches' Treasure, holding it up for her to see. But
Lady Sarah hadn't been behind him up the path. He
had expected that she would wait there to see him
safely down. Then he heard her calling to the others
to come and help her find him. Colin scrambled the
rest of the way down the path to the beach as she had
said he should. He stood there now, hand over mouth,
eyes sparkling with the fun of it, listening to those
above call his name. Soon there were male voices also
calling. The footmen had joined the search for him.

Colin soon became more interested in the gleaming
white sand of the beach and the shallow clear water
of the cove than in the hiding game. The waves were
lapping gently in, ever nearer his feet on the sand. He
heard a voice directly above him calling his name. He
looked up, thinking he had been discovered. He could
see no one for the cliff was overhanging. He heard
Lady Sarah call out, "You won't find him in that direction! He went the other way. That mischievous child!
He's probably back at the manor by now!" Colin knew
that she had kept someone from coming too close to
the hidden path. He hugged himself with glee and
then forgot about the searchers. It was the first time he
had ever been on an isolated, walled-in beach all
by himself. The sea, the rock walls, the white sands
of the beach . . . all were his domain.

Soon Colin couldn't hear voices any more. The water
was crashing on the rocks beyond him, but not on the
beach of the protected cove where he was. The roar
was only louder because the tide was coming in and
breaking on the rocks. He tucked the treasure he had

found in his shoe and played happily in the sea water
that covered almost half the beach now.

Lord John had been surprised, on walking out of the
counting shed at Wheal Maiden, to see Oxford tearing up the narrow mine road in the gig. "Your lordship!
Your lordship!" he called. The horse was going at such
a clip that he had to stand up on his feet to get the
leverage to pull him into a stop. "The boy, sir! He's
lost on the cliffs by the summerhouse!"

Lord John's head jerked up. He asked no further
information. He wheeled from Oxford and ran to the
post where his horse was tethered. He snapped up the
reins and jumped into the saddle and raced toward
home, Oxford following in the gig. Wheal Maiden
was the nearest to the manor of all his mines, but it
was still a hard twenty minutes' ride. He took the back
lane once he reached the grounds, forcing the last
wind from the horse in his race toward the summerhouse.

"Why, what's brought you home?" Lady Sarah exclaimed when he flung himself from the horse and ran
toward the scattered group. One of the footmen ran
toward him. "We've searched all the cliffs, sir! We've
searched and searched . . ." He was white-faced with
fear. If harm came to his lordship's son, there was no
knowing what his anger would bring on all of them.

"I'm sure we'll find the naughty boy at home, laughing about all the trouble he's caused us!" Lady Sarah
exclaimed. "The last sight I had of him was in the direction yonder!" She gestured toward the path that led
back toward the manor house.

The seas were crashing heavily, breaking into the
sounds of the excited voices. Lord John ignored Lady
Sarah. He hadn't even glanced at her. He ran toward
the edge of the cliff, calling, shouting, "Colin! Colin!"

The wind blew his shouted calls back at him. Even if not so, it was doubtful that they could have been heard by the child over the crashing of the incoming seas. He raced along the cliff, shouting for Colin. He called back to the others. "Fan out in all directions!"

Oxford and a large party of men that he had collected from the fields and grounds came on the run to help in the search. Lord John had disappeared by the time they got there, but Daly had arrived by then. He'd heard what had happened before he'd gotten through the main gate when he'd returned from Truro.

"The child wouldn't have been allowed so close to the edge of the cliffs that he might have fallen, would he, madam?" he asked Lady Sarah.

"Indeed he would not! I told his lordship that the last time I saw him he was headed toward home. He's home at this moment, safe as can be, laughing at us!"

"Perhaps you'd like to help us in the search by looking for him there," Daly said.

"I shall return home, but not to search! I'm not one to be taken in by a child's tricks!" Lady Sarah returned. She called the little girls and their nurses to her and they climbed into the straw cart to be driven back to the manor.

Lord John was on the hidden path that Lady Sarah had shown to Colin. The path was safe enough if one took due care. The cove at the bottom was safe when the tide was out. But when the tide came in, it filled the cove to a height of six feet sometimes. The beach disappeared altogether, and the water in the cove was walled by towering rock. There were no deep recesses in the rock, and unless one could swim and could find the entrance to the path, he would drown. Colin was a good little swimmer—he'd had him used to water almost before he could walk—but he was only a child

and might easily panic finding himself in water over
his head and water still coming in. One could watch
the slow, steady rise of the water level up the rocks
when the cove started to fill. The most deadly of the
dangers was the fact that the path up from the cove
took on an altogether different look after the cove
was filled with water, and his real fear was that Colin
would not be able to find it. He lost his footing several
times in his haste and slid as much as scrambled down
the path. He continued to call to Colin. "I'm coming;
Colin! You'll be all right! I'm coming!" He knew that
Colin was in the cove. Every instinct in him told him
that he was. And told him how he had come to be
there.

When Lord John was at the point on the path where
the water level reached it, he heard—or thought he
did—faint sounds of muffled crying. He strained hard
to hear the sounds clearly, to give him the direction
in which to go. His heart was pounding so hard that
it interfered with his hearing. He was on the floor of
the cove. The water was up to his knees, and rising.
He couldn't see Colin. He wasn't sure that the sounds
he had heard were sounds of crying. He shouted
Colin's name again and again and waded out into the
cove. He strained everything in him, trying to hear
the sounds again. He thought he did, coming from his
left. . . . If he could get to him soon enough. . . . If
Colin didn't panic and he could get to him soon
enough!

He waded out into the cove, headed to his left,
searching the rock wall. Around a bend in the slippery wall he saw him. Colin was clinging to a narrow
ridge that was just deep enough to give him a finger-
hold. He was afraid to let go, afraid even to turn his
head toward the sound of his father's voice or even to
call back to him. His arms were stretched high above

his head, his fingers hooked over the edge of the ridge, his cheek pressed against the rock, his face turned away from the direction of his father.

The water in that spot was deeper than in some. It was almost up to his shoulders. At any moment its weight might drag the slender weight of the child down.

Lord John pushed his way through water over his knees now. "I'm coming, Colin," he said gently, trying to soothe him so that he wouldn't panic and let go of the ledge. "Hold on, my son. I'm coming. Don't let go."

Colin turned his head toward him, and when he did, his fingers lost their hold on the rim of the ledge and he went under. Lord John dove under the shallow water toward the spot where Colin had gone under. He reached him on the first dive and brought him up. Colin hadn't inhaled or swallowed enough water to harm him. If he hadn't been gulping and crying, he probably wouldn't have swallowed any. He choked and sputtered and gasped, ejecting the seawater, still crying, but now clinging to his father's neck and crying shuddering sobs of relief instead of mewing sobs of fright.

Lord John held him close and soothed him, sloshing back toward the path. The water was up to his hips by the time he reached it. If he had not gotten to Colin when he did, the water would have been well over his head by now.

"The path is gone," Colin said, his voice catching on sobs. "I couldn't find the path when the water came up."

"I've found it!" Lord John made his voice cheerfully gay, as if they were playing a game. "Here we are! Look, Colin!" He had to release one arm from around Colin to pull them up on the slippery rock of the path. It frightened Colin, and his arms tightened convulsive-

ly around his father's neck. "We're on the path, Colin!"
Both his arms were back around Colin now. "Look!"

Colin hadn't lifted his face from the curve of his
father's neck and shoulders where he had buried it
when his father had brought him up from the water.
Now he lifted it fearfully and turned to look. He
turned his face back and buried it again. His arms relaxed their convulsive clinging, but they were still
tight around his neck. "I knew you would come," he
said. "I knew you would. But the water kept coming
in. I was afraid you wouldn't come before the water
got over me." He started to cry again, weak, trembling
cries brought on by remembered fright.

Lord John kissed his wet hair and rested his cheek
against it. He couldn't speak. He was crying also,
and he didn't want Colin to know that he was. He
didn't want Colin to know how afraid he had been. He
didn't want him to know by what a narrow thread
he had been saved from drowning. He didn't want
Colin to become fearful of things and lose the bright,
strong confidence that he had in himself and in the
world around him.

Lord John did not take Colin back to the manor
house. He took him to the gatehouse where Daly and
Mrs. Daly lived. And where Jason lived. He stayed
with him until he was bathed and warmly dressed
and content to be in a bed upstairs in the gatehouse
in the room with his friend Jason. From that day on,
Colin lived there.

When Lord John left the gatehouse, he went to the
manor-house and to Lady Sarah. He forbid her to have
any further contact with Colin. He threatened that if
she did he would expose himself and her. It was not
his way to make threats—it went against his princi-
ples. But he cared more for Colin than he did for any
principle.

* * *

Now, looking down at Colin's head bent over the puppy, Lord John knew that he had to remove Colin from Lady Sarah. He had known before that he must, had known that sooner or later he would be forced to. But he had wanted Colin near him. That selfishness on his part had almost cost Colin his life again. He could not let it happen a third time. That time Sarah might be successful. &

16

Lord John planned to take Colin on a long, hard ride that morning—perhaps across the hunting fields —but at any rate, well away from any view of the grounds of the manor, particularly the spire of the chapel. Hawkins's funeral would be held that day and he didn't want Colin to see any part of it nor any part of the preparations for it. He had excused his own attendance at the funeral with a reason fully acceptable to his people of Polreath. He could do nothing for the dead, except make a show of respect. He had shown his respect for Hawkins during Hawkins's lifetime. He had recognized his qualities and had elevated him steadily all during his service. Hawkins would have been gamekeeper when old Barnely was retired a year hence. Now Lord John must care for the living, and Colin needed him.

Lord John had to change his mind about the ride, but for a reason that pleased him. He had bought a new horse for Colin, and the horse had arrived early that morning. He wouldn't take the chance on taking Colin out on a long, hard trek on a horse that he didn't know.

The arrival time of the horse couldn't have been more propitious. Between the puppy Guinevere and the new horse, Colin would be too preoccupied to mourn the fate of the other puppy. Colin was extremely sensitive where animals were concerned, especially horses and dogs. He had been much affected by what had happened to the unfortunate puppy.

Colin was a fine little rider. He had the makings to be topnotch, and Lord John intended to see that he was the best. He took him in hand himself as often as he could. When he was home, they rode together every day. Colin had absolutely no fear of horses, but he would sometimes hesitate to force control. He didn't seem to want to bend their will. He was afraid he would break their spirit. He hadn't learned yet that they preferred a strong discipline. The new horse would be a lot for Colin to handle, but he was up to it. He had a good little Welsh mountain pony, Dusty, but he and Dusty were too accustomed to each other. Colin wasn't advancing—and couldn't advance—on the pony. The pony wasn't horse enough for him now. He was ready for more horse under him.

Lord John was on his way to the stables to see how the new horse had stood the trip to Polreath. He detoured on his way to stop by the coach house to speak a few words of reassurance to Oxford. Oxford was a favorite with him and always had been. From the time he was a child there had been a bond between them. He knew that Oxford was taking Hawkins's death hard, and blaming himself when blame was not his.

As Lord John passed the shed attached to the coach house where the coachmen and their apprentices took their ease, he heard voices of men raised in argument. He stopped when he realized what the argument—if such it was—was about.

"Thanks God it happened master was as close to home as he was!" he heard.

"It was a providence, as you might say. He could've been anywheres in the whole of England!"

"Anywheres in the whole of the world, more like!"

"Aye, that's true. Like I says it'uz a providence."

"A man lies dead—where's the providence in that?"

"Aye, an' I wasn't thinkin' on Hawkins when I said it. Aye, an' there's no providence there. Hawkins was a good man."

"That he was. God rest his soul. Worser couldn't've happened."

"It could've been the boy lying dead! There's a worse of it!"

"That's God's truth!"

"The worse of it isn't yet come. But it be comin'. It be comin'."

"And so I believe meself. Since the boy came it's been bad times on us. Mark what I say. Until the day he goes . . ."

The speaker was interrupted. "For myself"—Lord John recognized the voice as that of Ross—"I want it known and clear, I've nothing said against the lad!"

"I wasn't speakin' against the lad."

"It's to speak *for* him we should—and not against—for what has the lad ever done to her? What she did to him this yesterday past was the lowest sort of wickedness! Letting him think he was going to have the trainin' of pups when she knew there'd be no trainin' of them. She knew one of 'em was mad, and mayhap both! God ought to'uv cut her down where she stood!"

"Mind, Ross!" That was Oxford's voice. It was the first time Lord John had heard him speak.

"It's true—he ought! She almost got the lad killed, and I vow that's what she was after! I tell you that

woman is out to revenge herself for something. A bein'
wouldn't do the things she does except to revenge hisself. Why she don't even want the child called 'Master.'
Could just that little bit of deference paid him make
her hate him so much? He's due his due the same as
any. He's due respects to be paid him. His mother
was a princess . . ."

"Now where'd ye be hearin' such nonsense?" Oxford
asked.

"She was a high-ranking lady at the very least!"

"Ye've been listenin' to the house servants. Listen
long enough to their tales and ye'll begin to believe
anything."

"He's got the look of blood! And not to my eye
only!"

"It's the look of Polreath blood he's got."

"Reckon why his lordship don't take a stand," a new
voice put in. "He can't be blind to her doin's."

"He will. You'll see. She's come too close this time
to doin' hurt to the lad couldn't be undone. What say
you, Oxford? Will he take a stand or no?"

Oxford didn't answer the question. "It's not bein'
able to anticipate her keeps me discomfortable in meself more'n what she does," he said. "I shoulda took
steps afore them puppies was brought . . ."

"None of the fault of it lies with you. I put it to that
maid Nonna of hers! She don't do the job of watchin'
that she should do. The master ought to dismiss her
from service out of hand and get somebody . . ."

"Now ye be presumin' to instruct the master, be
ye?"

"Well, that Nonna of her'n's not doin' her job! She's
not watchin' her careful!"

"No more then ye be watchin' your tongue careful!"
Oxford said. "Where's your loyalty?"

"I've no loyalty to her, and I'll say it out! For his lordship, yes! And enough to match your own!"

A pause followed, and then a quiet voice at some distance from the ones who had been speaking said, "Her spelled them pups."

"What would her ladyship be havin' to do wi' spells? It's craziness you're talkin'!" Ross retorted.

"There's some as thinks her spelled them pups," another voice from the more distant group said.

"Fool's talk!"

"Her's able of it, some say, time them fits of her'n comes on her."

"Fits? What fits? It's gentry you're talkin' on! Gentry ain't like we'uns. They ain't come on by fits."

"The devil visits in her! It's a fact!"

Apparently there were two camps within the group.

"Recall the time a fit come on her and she spooked Juniper? Near to killed Davey, Juniper did. And he was right as rain 'til her come in the stall next his."

"I seen her in a fit onct. Seen it meself. Damn me for a liar if you want, but I know what I seen."

"Faugh!"

"That's enough of talk!" Oxford said. "What's the good of talk? What's done's done."

Lord John had known that there must be talk among his people about Lady Sarah, but he had thought it confined to the servants in the house. He hadn't expected that it was so rampant among the people, nor that it was of as strong a nature as it was. He passed on by the coach house without stopping in to speak to Oxford. His sudden appearance in the midst of such talk would throw a scare into every man and boy in the shed. He continued his way to the stables.

Heller had the new horse in the paddock putting him through the paces. He was a fine bay gelding.

Lord John stood at the rail fence and watched. The more he saw of the horse, the more he liked him and thought him suitable. But it wasn't his opinion of the horse that counted, it was Colin's.

"Has Master Colin seen him?" he asked Heller.

"Yes, sir. No sooner was this one come than Master Colin was here to the stables. It was like he'd sensed the horse had come."

Lord John didn't ask him about Colin's reaction to the horse, and Heller didn't volunteer any information about it. Heller knew that his lordship didn't want his interpretation of it. He could gauge it better if he had it straight from Colin.

A shrill impatient whinny came from within the stable.

"Juniper heard you," Heller said, gesturing with his head toward the sound.

"So it seems," Lord John said. He started toward the stable door to go inside to soothe the jealous Juniper. "We'll not be riding today," he called back to Heller.

Lord John and Colin were walking toward the summerhouse. Lord John had decided that they would picnic there instead of taking the ride he had planned. He'd sent a footman ahead with a picnic basket of lunch to leave there for them. The footman would return to the manor to attend the funeral.

Colin was much more recovered from his low spirits than Lord John had expected him to be. From time to time he would grasp his father's hand and hang onto it as he jumped and skipped about over jutting rocks and tiny springs that were on the path.

"I understand you've seen the new bay that arrived this morning," Lord John said.

"Yes, sir."

"Were you up?"

"No, sir. Heller said it's too soon."

"I expect that's true, but I don't want him used to someone else before he's used to you."

"He won't be, sir. Heller is going to put the stable-boys up in turn, Davey, and Jude, and the others with the best hands, so he won't get used to anybody special until he's ready for me. And I'm to be the only one allowed in his stall except for Davey and Heller."

"Intend to make a Juniper out of him, do you?"

"Yes, sir. I want him to be toward me like Juniper is toward you."

Juniper was a one-man horse. He even seemed to be of a mind with Lord John. But it took a strong control to handle him. Even the stableboy Davey who, according to Heller, could ride the devil's own mare, couldn't control him. He would allow only two people to sit him —Lord John and Heller.

"Don't look for too much until you see how he's bent," Lord John said to Colin. "He may not be of a disposition to turn out like Juniper. I wouldn't want you to be disappointed."

"He won't disappoint me."

"I hope not. What do you think of him as horse?"

"He's big."

Lord John laughed. "Hardly a judgment of horse-flesh," he said. "Have you named him?"

"His name came right to me! The minute I saw him!"

"That's the best way to come on a name. What was it?"

"Commander!"

Lord John smiled down at Colin and ruffled his hair. "Let's hope it's you who will be."

"Sir . . . ?"

"It's a good name, Colin."

"Do you really like it?"

"I think he looks every inch the name."

"It's a better name than Juniper. That's not a name for a horse. Why did you name him that?"

Lord John laughed again. "Because the first time I put a leg on him, he threw me into a juniper bush."

Colin stopped and looked up at him, his eyes incredulous and astonished. "He *threw* you!"

"He certainly did."

"I didn't think *any* horse could throw you!"

"Any horse can throw any man. And don't you ever forget it!"

At midday Lord John and Colin took the picnic basket to a spot that they had found by accident one day while on a meandering walk along the cliffs. It was a crevice between two leaning rocks. The rocks seemed to overhang the cliff, but on inspection they had proved quite safe. And there was some protection from the ever-blowing wind in the space between them.

After lunch they stayed where they were, in no hurry to leave. Lord John was leaning against the leaning wall of rock and Colin was leaning against him, his head nodding, almost asleep.

Of a sudden the atmosphere stilled. The winds had hushed. The sun was still shining, but the strong burning strength of its glare was missing.

Colin sensed the change and roused. He was wide awake now.

"Sir?"

"Yes, Colin?"

"Look, sir. Look how the sea is capping. And there's no wind."

Lord John sat up a bit reluctantly. He had been thinking of Elizabeth, imagining her there with him and Colin. The feeling of the three of them together

had a naturalness and peace about it. He was reluctant
to give up his reverie. He looked over Colin's head
at the sea below and beyond them. He stood up, bringing Colin to his feet also. "It seems we might be in for
weather," he said. He sighed, but tried to make his
voice light. "Let's hie away home. This is no place to
be caught in a blow."

He looked around. Elizabeth had been so strongly
with him in his thoughts that he almost felt that he
was looking around for her to bid her come along
home. He felt the emptiness come back inside him
that always came with thoughts of Elizabeth. It was
the emptiness of wanting something he could never
have. He wanted Elizabeth to share with him and
Colin the quiet, trusting times, like the moments that
he and Colin had just shared, that came from simply
being together and away from all others. He wanted
Elizabeth and Colin with him at Polreath, and all
others away. . . . He could never have that. ☙

17

When Lord John and Colin were partway home, Heller came around a curve in the path leading Juniper and Commander.

"Juniper was acting up to come after you, your lordship." Heller said, "so I walked him out to meet you. Smells weather, I think he does."

Lord John took the lead rope from him and reached to rub his hand along Juniper's face, his usual gesture of greeting. Juniper tossed his head and wouldn't accept the caress. Heller laughed. "That's another thing," he said. "He thinks this one is for you."

Colin was practically up under Commander's neck, so he could pat both sides of it at once. Heller gave him the lead rope. "See, Juniper," he said, "I told you this one was Master Colin's."

"The trouble with Juniper is that you and your stableboys give him too much credit for sense," Lord John said. He took hold of Juniper just below his withers and hoisted himself up on his back. "Put Master Colin up," he said.

Heller chuckled as he lifted Colin up on Commander. Nobody gave Juniper more credit for sense that his lordship did, and nobody spoiled him more. What was he doing now if not spoiling him? He was going to ride him home bareback just to get his nose back in joint. Heller stood on the path and watched the two ride off and then smiled and shook his head and trudged after them.

From a distance, as they rode up, Lord John and Colin could see a carriage that didn't belong to Polreath standing before the coachhouse. The driver was off to one side talking to Oxford. Two postillions were by the horses. Two of the Polreath stableboys were idling with the postillions. They had empty water buckets in their hands. They had already watered the horses. The uniforms of the three strangers were of forest green and buff.

"Someone's come," Colin said.

"So I see."

"You didn't tell me someone was coming!" Colin said angrily. He was quick to peeve sometimes, and he was quick to show jealousy when visitors came to stay and his father gave time to them that he could have spent with him.

"You are quick to anger, my son. I was not expecting anyone. Had I been, I would have told you."

"Who is it?"

"The driver and his boys are wearing the Clarwicke colors. It must be Lord Moulton who's come."

"I wonder what he had to say!" Colin exclaimed, excited. "I wonder if she told him!"

"Told him what? Who?"

"Lady Sarah! Told him about the puppy! That's where the puppies came from—from Lord Moulton's kennels at Baloorin."

Lord John's eyes narrowed in a frown. "Are you sure, Colin? I can't imagine that Lord Moulton would let pups from his kennels that he wasn't sure of."

"He wasn't there when she got them!"

"When *she* got them?"

"Lady Sarah! She went herself to pick them out. But she didn't bring them. She hired them brought."

Lord John's frown deepened. "*Hired* them brought?"

"Yes, sir. By somebody close by Baloorin with a cart for hire. She almost didn't get to have them brought. Lord Moulton's kennelman didn't want her to have them. She had to take a hand with him."

His father turned to regard him. "How do you know all of this?"

"I heard them talking at the stables this morning. They said Lord Moulton would lay on his kennelman with a cane when he found out he'd let the puppies go. He suspected the white one, and he ordered his man to keep him close penned and watched and destroy him at the first sign. But they said the kennelman didn't dare cross Lady Sarah because she's a Howard, the same as Lord Moulton himself. They said the Howards were powerful across the whole kingdom. Is that true, sir?"

Lord John's mind wasn't on Colin's question. He was concerned with that he'd said about the puppies. ". . . There was a time," he answered absently.

"They said the Howards were known to have a strange one in their stock every so often in their generations, and that Lady Sarah was one of the strange ones. What did they mean by that?"

They had come to a stop at the stable door now. Lord John was looking toward the manor. He didn't answer Colin. "I think I'd better go in," he said. He slid off Juniper and turned to watch Heller who was jogging toward them. When Heller got up to them, he handed him Juniper's lead rope. "Have Davey ride with Master Colin to the gatehouse," he said. "He's to see him in Daly's hands before he leaves him."

Davey came out of the stable, bareback on a chestnut mare.

"You heard me, Davey?"

Davey tugged at his forelock. "Yes, your lordship."

"I want to stall Commander!" Colin said. He drew his leg over to dismount. Lord John walked over to him and placed him firmly back on the horse. "Go with Davey," he said. He knew that Colin's pride was such that he could not bear to be reprimanded in front of others, and he seldom reprimanded him or crossed him except in private, but he was worried about what was going on in the house and he wanted Colin safely away and in the gatehouse with Daly. "I ask you to do this," he said. "I do not order you."

The black frown that had clouded Colin's face lightened somewhat. But he wanted further concession. "Will you come for supper?" he asked.

"If at all possible. As always."

All shades of anger and offended pride left Colin's face. "I'll wait," he said. "I won't be hungry until you come." He put his hand on his father's shoulder. "However late you have to be, sir, may I wait?"

"Yes, my son. You may wait."

Lord John heard sounds of screaming when he entered the manor. He ran toward the library where it seemed the screams were coming from. A maid was standing in the doorway, her hands over her mouth, her eyes bulging with terror. It was she who was screaming. The sounds of a struggle came from inside the library. Lord John ran past the maid and into the room. Nonna was struggling with Lady Sarah, trying to subdue her. Lady Sarah clutched a bloody poker in one hand, waving it wildly, trying to free herself, trying to strike again with the poker. Lord Moulton lay on the hearth, blood streaming from his head.

Lord John jerked the poker from Lady Sarah's hand. "Take her to her apartments!" he said to Nonna. He knelt down beside Lord Moulton while Nonna hauled Lady Sarah bodily from the room. The butler, Andrews, came running in. "Have someone ride for Dr. Jervis!" Lord John ordered. "Quick about it!"

Andrews ran out again. As he ran out, Mrs. Hill, the housekeeper, was coming hurriedly down the wide hall. When she reached the screaming maid, she slapped her across the face to stop her hysterics and caught her by the arms and pushed her in the direction of the back stairs. "Belowstairs!" she said. "Get yourself belowstairs!" As the maid stumbled off sobbing, Mrs. Hill called out, "Louisa!" A tall elderly maid appeared. "Go after Mercy and quiet her talk!" Mrs. Hill said, "And keep all the servants belowstairs! Not one of them's to come up unless sent for!"

"Yes, ma'am." Louisa turned to follow the younger maid.

Mrs. Hill went into the library and closed the door firmly behind her.

Lord Moulton was not dead, but his condition was grave. He'd lost much blood. Dr. Jervis had dressed the wounds on his head and face—he'd been struck four times—and sutured the gaping cuts. He was abed now in one of the guest rooms of the manor. Old Mrs. Vellin had been called in to sit beside his bed until the nurse that Dr. Jervis was to send would arrive. Lady Sarah was deep in sleep, sedated with a strong dose of laudanum.

Lord John had Nonna sent to him.

"Well, Nonna? What explanation have you?"

"He threatened to take the girls from her, sir. That's
what brought it on. For their own safety's sake, he
said, he felt that he should take them. He came home
this morning to Baloorin from Bath and he found out
ma'am had forced the puppies from his kennelman in
spite of all his orders, and he came straightaway here.
He said to ma'am that one of the little girls—or both—
could be dying this moment of rabies. He was beside
himself about it. He said as godfather to the girls he
had a responsibility for their welfare. He's afeard if he
don't do his duty by them, his own Rosamond will be
neglected in the same degree he neglects the girls.
Ma'am told him she'd have him in Magistrate's Court
for kidnapping if he took the little girls from Polreath. Oh, sir, it would have been scarifying for anybody but me! Screaming at each other, they were!
Lord Moulton, when he saw he wasn't going to win in
argument with her ladyship, threatened to cut her off
from what's rightly hers. He reminded her it's him
controls the Clarwicke holdings and that she can't inherit except from him. That's when she grabbed the
poker and went at him with it. I tried to get to her before she did damage, sir, but she was too fast. I was
across the room from them as it was only fitting I
should be. And her ladyship can be fast as quicksilver,
as you know for yourself, sir, when—"

Lord John raised his hand to silence her. He had
all the information from her that he wanted.

"Lord Moulton will have to remain here for the time
being," he said. "He's in no condition to be moved. It
would be better, I think, if her ladyship were not here.
Perhaps she could be persuaded to go to Scotland early
this year . . ." He paused.

"Her ladyship has been talking of going up to London, sir," Nonna said.

"To London? There would be little for her amuse-

ment. The city will be empty this summer. Court will
not be in residence. The king's health has taken him
to the country."

"It would seem, sir, that all the same, she has her
heart set on going."

Alarm filled Lord John. Did Sarah know that Elizabeth was in London? Had gossip about the latest favorite of society and the court spread as far as Cornwall? And how could he stop Sarah from going? Short
of putting her in chains, there would be no way of
stopping her if she were determined to go.

Lord John dismissed Nonna and sent for Mr. Hurford.

"The young lady who was here from the school,
Hurford . . . Miss Stewart . . . I want her background."

"I believe she has none, your lordship."

Lord John's eyebrows shot up. "No background?
And her ladyship took her under her protection?
Come, Hurford!"

"Her ladyship has looked upon Miss Stewart kindly, sir, since the time she came to the school as a
child. It was the same year her ladyship offered her
patronage to the school."

"Came to the school from where?"

"From India, sir. Her parents had died there, but
they'd arranged for her upbringing at Miss Holybrook's in the happenstance they should be separated
from her by death. It was in the time of an outbreak
of cholera there. They were both taken by it. The
child was sent home to England and monies put in
trust in King's Bank in London for her schooling."

Lord John pondered that. Then he said, "She must
have relatives. There must be kin."

"If so, her parents wanted her kept from them."

Lord John frowned. "Most strange," he said, "that

her parents would wish to make her more of orphan than she was."

"Very strange, sir."

Lord John was suddenly overcome with impatience. "Trace her through the name, then! I want to know who she is."

"Stewart is the name she came to the school under, but it is not her true name. Even the trustees for her money don't know the true name of her parents."

Lord John was struck by the intimacy of Hurford's knowledge of things to do with Elizabeth. He turned to face him squarely.

"How did you come by your information, Hurford?"

Mr. Hurford backed an obsequious half-step away. "Her ladyship had me make inquiry, sir, when she first became interested in Miss Stewart's welfare."

"And that time was . . . ?"

"As I said, sir. When Miss Stewart first came to the school. Her ladyship was much taken by her, being she was, as one might say, stranded."

Impatience was on Lord John again, and frustration. "Someone—somewhere—knows who she is!"

"I daresay you're right, sir," Mr. Hurford said. "Perhaps the young lady herself. Though, if she does, she has never divulged the truth to anyone."

Lord John paced the floor. "She has monies in trust in London? She is not a pauper then?"

"I believe her board at the school, and her schooling, have depleted the funds."

"And she has no resource to more?"

"Not that I know of, sir."

Lord John continued his pacing. "At least her parents assured that she would have the best in education that England has to offer," he said.

"Yes sir, they saw to that. The monies in trust were to go to Miss Holybrook's only."

". . . So they must have been acquainted with the
school . . . That might be a start in trying to trace her
parentage. Perhaps her mother had been a student
there . . ." Lord John stopped before a window, looking out, his back to Hurford. "There must be some way
to find out who she is!"

"I'm afraid you'll only be disappointed if you try
to trace her parentage, sir. Her ladyship has exhausted
every avenue of inquiry about it."

Lord John sighed. "Since her ladyship was interested, I'm sure she has," he said. "Her ladyship can be
most thorough."

"Yes, sir. And in that she was."

"What else can you tell me about Miss Stewart, Hurford? Anything more at all?"

"I'm sorry, sir. All I know of her I've said."

Lord John dismissed Hurford. But before Hurford
got to the door, he turned and addressed him. "I suppose it was foregone that when Miss Stewart graduated from Miss Holybrook's, she would be the one
from the graduating class selected to join her ladyship for the social seasons?" He made it a question.

"Yes, sir. It was not likely that her ladyship would
have passed Miss Stewart over, having taken such an
interest in her in all the years between."

"As you say, it was not likely," Lord John said. He
turned back to the window. "Good night, Hurford."

Lord John paced the floor until nightfall, and past,
turning things over in his mind.

He remembered well when Sarah had decided to
become a patroness of Miss Holybrook's School for
Young Ladies. It was immediately after they were
married. He had encouraged Sarah in her decision. It
was well and meet that the Lady of Polreath take on
such responsibilities. That was one of the obligations

of position. Miss Holybrook's school had been a natural
choice for Sarah. She had had her own schooling
there.

Lord John tried to remember whether he had ever
heard Sarah mention Elizabeth—or any other student
in the school that she had a particular interest in. He
was sure that he had not. He tried to remember
whether any hint of Hurford's involvement in the in-
quiries into Elizabeth's—or any other student's—background and state of finances had ever come to his attention. He couldn't remember that any had—but if
any had, he would have thought nothing of it and
would not have marked it. Hurford's duties as business
manager for the Polreath affairs included the handling
of Sarah's various charities and other largesses.

Lord John's mind turned from that to other things.
What had made Sarah turn on Elizabeth, he wondered.
But it was a waste of time to speculate on that. It
could have been anything, or it could have been nothing. He knew how Sarah had gotten Elizabeth down
to the dungeon—or his suspicion was strong enough
to pass for knowledge. Sarah had put a draught in
Elizabeth's tea. And then she had taken her on a "tour"
of the manor house. Elizabeth had been too much
under the influence of the drug to know where she
was. And when she had awakened, everything that
had happened from the moment she had swallowed
the drug had been blanked from her mind, for that
was the effect the drug had. Sarah had once imprisoned Margaret in such a manner.

Hurford was innocent of any wrongdoing where
Elizabeth was concerned—and Lord John had never
suspected that he was guilty of any. After Oxford had,
with much deliberation, "spilled" to him that morning at the paddock that there was a Miss Stewart at the
manor, he had questioned Hurford. Hurford had

readily backed up Oxford. They had brought Miss
Stewart to Polreath on the night of the day that he
had returned from his hospitalization in London, Hurford had said. He had said, further, that he had not
thought it of sufficient interest to his lordship to mention anything about the young lady from the school
in view of the pressing interests to his lordship to do
with the tinners and the deaths of Dax and Jax.

He had assumed, Hurford had said, that the journey
from Launceton and the frightening experience with
the tinners had exhausted Miss Stewart to the point of
illness and that she was keeping to her bed.

That was a natural assumption, and one that Lord
John would have made himself, except for the fact that
no mention at all had been made of a Miss Stewart
but for that made by Oxford. And, for some reason
that he did not know himself, he had remembered
the time that Sarah had imprisoned Margaret. He had
been compelled to go to the dungeon. Not because of
Margaret's short imprisonment there—that had been
a laughable joke between them. . . . No . . . His going
to the dungeon had not had to do with Margaret. It
had had to do only with Elizabeth.

Lord John shook himself. This was no time for
adolescent mooning. Much as he wanted to let himself
believe that destiny had brought Elizabeth to him and
that they were destined for each other, he must recognize that that was only his hopeful wanting. He shook
his head to clear it of his dreamings. He reminded
himself that the purpose of this trip home—which had
so fortunately brought him home at just the time it
did—had been to find out who Elizabeth was and to
send her home. That was still his resolve, but he
would have to find what he wanted to know from
Elizabeth.

It was not likely, he told himself, and realized it for the truth, that Sarah's wanting to go to London had anything to do with Elizabeth. He had been alarmed unnecessarily on that score. Once Sarah ridded herself of something she wanted to be rid of, she forgot about it as if it had never existed. That was one of the symptoms of her illness. Once she had imprisoned Elizabeth, she had thought herself rid of her. As long as the fact of her existence was not brought back to Sarah, Elizabeth was safe from Sarah. Gossip about Elizabeth had not reached Sarah. If it had, Sarah would have been in London long since.

If Sarah went to London, Colin would be safe from her. He could continue here at Polreath—where he was happy and where he was home—at least as long as Sarah was in London. And surely Sarah would go to Scotland from London.

So . . . Lord John decided, Sarah would go to London. He would encourage her to do so. He would even accompany her there. Elizabeth would be safer from Sarah with the two of them in London than she was with Sarah at Polreath. No hostess in London nor in Brighton, including Queen Adelaide herself, invited Lady Sarah and Lady Margaret to the same affair. And no one dared mention Lady Margaret's name in the presence of Lady Sarah, and therefore would not dare to mention the name of Lady Margaret's house guest. He chuckled to himself. Besides, there was not a hostess of Lady Sarah's acquaintance in London at the moment.

Lord John became aware that night had fallen. He put his thoughts and speculations away from him. He must hurry to the gatehouse. Colin was expecting him for supper.

As he hurried to the gatehouse, longing for Elizabeth was strong in Lord John. He wished that she were with him and that the two of them were going together to Colin. The feeling of emptiness returned within him. There would never be the day when he would be together with the two beloved by him. ❧

BOOK III

A Royal Courtship

❧

18

"The flag is up in Piccadilly," Ronald Asquith said. His attitude was deliberately casual.

Elizabeth simply looked at him. She didn't know what he was talking about, but Lady Margaret reacted with anger.

"I'm not in the mood for jokes, Ronnie!"

The three were having lunch under the trees in the garden of Lady Margaret's house in London. A table had been set up there. It was laid with white damask and set with Irish crystal, heavy English silver, and French Limoges. There was sometimes a breeze in the garden, and it was always cooler there than it was inside the house even when every door and window were open to catch any movement of air. It was stifling in the city.

"I assure you, my dear Margaret, I do not joke."

Lady Margaret's eyes narrowed on him. She regarded him silently for a moment before she spoke. Then, "How do you know?" she asked.

"Anyone who was abroad in Piccadilly this morning could not help but know. A regular caravan arrived. It would seem that she's come for a stay of some length. She had her two wards with her, and her personal staff."

"I take it you were *abroad*"—Lady Margaret stressed the word—"in Piccadilly this morning."

"My dear, why wouldn't I be? I live in Piccadilly." He turned his head to Elizabeth. "I have apartments at the Albany," he said. "Poor bachelor's digs." He leaned back in his chair and smiled and became expansive. He could get away with jibing Margaret now, and he knew it, because he knew that she would want to know every detail that he could tell her. "I was cantering along, on my way to Hyde Park and Rotten Row, with not a thing on my mind except that I'd probably have to enjoy my ride in solitary contemplation, since not a soul of my acquaintance—except of course you, my dear Margaret, and you, Miss Stewart" —he inclined his head to each in turn—"has chosen to remain in London this summer since the court is absent, when, lo and behold—"

"Get on with it, Ronnie!" Lady Margaret snapped.

"—when, lo and behold"—he continued slowly and deliberately—"what do I see but a caravan approaching up Piccadilly!"

Elizabeth's heart began to beat faster. The Polreath mansion was in Piccadilly. She had never been inside it, nor even inside the walls that secluded it from the street, but she had seen the upper floors that rose from the rear of the wide court that was between it and the wall. It was near the Albany, which the people of Lady Margaret's acquaintance—except for Ronald Asquith—and he had said *poor,* not meaning that he lived in poor quarters, being deprived of funds, but lived in poor bachelorhood, being deprived of wife—still called York House. That had been its name when Frederick, the Duke of York, favorite of his father, King George III, had owned it and had lived

in it when he was in London. York House—when it
had been York House instead of the Albany—had not
overshadowed Polreath House. Polreath House was
one of the most famous architectural triumphs in
London. It had been done, inside and out, by Wyatts,
uncles and nephews. Nothing by the Adams could
challenge it.

Lady Margaret sipped her wine to steady herself.
Elizabeth did the same.

"You spoke to her?" Lady Margaret asked.

"Indeed I stopped and made obeisance," Ronald
Asquith said. He paused. "But the party of arriving
travelers was not in the mood for chatter. They passed
me by."

"They?"

"They."

"Answer me, Ronnie!"

"Ah, but I thought I did," Ronald Asquith said. He
looked at Lady Margaret. "Yes, Margaret," he said,
"the Lord of Polreath was with his lady."

Elizabeths' hand shook so hard that she had to put
down her wineglass.

Lady Margaret rose abruptly and left the table.
Ronald Asquith got to his feet and remained standing
until she had disappeared inside the house. He sat
down again, his eyes on Elizabeth. "That was more or
less what I expected from Lady Margaret at the staggering news," he said, "but I had thought to see more
of welcome in your expression for your newly arrived
friend, Miss Stewart."

"He is not—" Elizabeth began angrily, but he cut
her off.

A mocking smile widened his lips. "I was speaking
of Lady Sarah," he said.

"I don't believe that I described her to you as a
friend," Elizabeth said. She felt that she had been

caught in a lie. It was the mocking smile on his mouth and the mocking light in his eyes that made her feel so. "I said that my connection to Polreath was through her."

"Yes, so you did," he said lazily. "And then, too, one's affections can take a turn, can they not?"

Elizabeth bridled. "I don't know what you're talking about!" she said heatedly.

Ronald Asquith spread his already spread napkin over his knees. He spoke, looking down at what he was doing. "I seem to be in the company of two very dense ladies today," he said. "One's every utterance must be spelled out for them. What I meant was—"

"I know what you meant! But you're mistaken by a wide margin if you think that I have any feelings for—for *him* that would in any way change my regard for Lady Sarah! I've had a speaking acquaintance with her since I came to England as a child. She's the patroness of the school I attended for ten years. She has never been less than gracious and kind to me!"

As much as Elizabeth was vehement, Ronald Asquith was calm.

He said, "And you would certainly not do anything to disrupt that kind and gracious lady's marriage."

"Certainly not!"

Ronald Asquith leaned back in his chair again, and took a time to speak. When he did speak it was in a voice of great patience, as if he were instructing her in something that she was having difficulty grasping. "My dear Miss Stewart," he said, "you distress yourself unduly to think you might. There is no marriage there. Surely you must know by now that the Lord and Lady of Polreath have arrived at what is politely termed, 'an arrangement.' And if I must spell that out"—he glanced toward the door that Lady Margaret had disappeared through—"it was Lady Sarah who brought the two together. Were you aware of that?"

"No, I was not! And I don't believe you! What you imply is unthinkable. Furthermore, their business is theirs and not mine. I . . ."

Ronald Asquith allowed a look of slight puzzlement to come to his face. "Perhaps I have been mistaken all this while," he said. "I thought you had a—shall we say *vested* interest. . . ."

Elizabeth knew what he meant. He was telling her that he knew that she had been living—and still was —on the Lord of Polreath's benevolence.

She stood up from the table. She would not listen to more of Ronald Asquith's affrontery. "I have no interest in him, vested nor otherwise!" she said. "If you'll excuse me . . ."

Ronald Asquith rose languidly to his feet. "I seem to have offended you," he said.

"You've disgusted me!"

"Entirely unintentional, I assure you." He became the correct, solicitous gentleman. "Shall I give Lady Sarah your greetings when I see her," he asked. "I'm one of the few who straddle the fence. Her ladyship won't be calling at Belgravia, as I'm sure you expect that she won't. And," he added, his eyes knowingly on Elizabeth, "nor does his lordship lately. So, if you wish now, or at any time, to call upon my services as emissary . . ."

"I have no need for you as emissary. I can handle my own affairs."

Ronald Asquith inclined his head. "As you wish," he said. "But . . . if you should change your mind . . ."

"Excuse me," Elizabeth said. She went toward the house. She wanted to run, but she kept a dignified pace until she was out of his sight. Once inside the house she ran all the way to her room.

Lizzie came immediately in from the dressing room, all agog.

"You'll never guess what's happened, Miss Stewart! They're all talking about it belowstairs" she said breathlessly. "Guess who's come to London!"

"I know who's come to London, Lizzie," Elizabeth said. She sighed as she spoke. She felt a tiredness on her, an overwhelming desolation of spirit.

"What do you think's brought her?" Lizzie was unduly nervous and excited over the news, it seemed to Elizabeth. "Do you think she found out . . ."

"Leave me alone about it, Lizzie."

Lizzie felt rebuffed and became instantly subdued. "Yes, mum," she said. "Beg your pardon for speaking, mum." Her voice was sulky, and her use of *mum* was a way of showing defiance, but most of all her feelings were hurt.

"Don't pay any attention to my mood, Lizzie. I'm not angry with you."

In spite of the tiredness of spirit that Elizabeth felt, an excitement was throughout her that grew with every breath she took. *He* was in London! He was in his house in Piccadilly that very moment! She felt a stab of jealousy toward Ronald Asquith. He had seen him. Just by chance, because he'd happened to be in Piccadilly. Anyone walking along Piccadilly might see him entering or coming out of the gate of the wall in front of his house. If she were walking along Piccadilly, she might see him. One part of her wanted to run there that moment on the chance of it. But another part of her sneered at her for wanting to. That was the only way that she would see him, that part of her told her, for he would not come to Belgravia. He would not come because she was there. He would give her free rein with his credit, and he would force Lady Margaret to continue to sponsor her in society—all to make up

for having used her as a decoy to save himself from
Mr. Calvin and the tinners—but he would not come
near where he might see her. He couldn't bear the
sight of her.

Elizabeth kept to her room the rest of the day and
the evening. Every sense in her was alerted to the
sounds on the street and those in the house, in the
event he might come. But he did not.

It was late before she gave up and made herself go
to bed, and later still before she finally drifted into
sleep. It was a sleep of exhaustion.

She awoke in the night sobbing and beating at her
pillow with her fists. "I hate him!" she sobbed, "I
hate him! I hate him!"

Lizzie was quickly beside her bed. "Don't upset
yourself so, miss," she said. She paused Elizabeth's
damp hair from her forehead and bathed her face with
a cool, freshly wet cloth. She was always prepared for
Elizabeth's wakefulness in the night. Her mistress was
prone to bad dreams and nightmares. "You don't hate
him. That's your trouble, and his the same. Only
thing can hide love is pretense of hate. You two keep
it up the way you're going, and one of you will convince the other one day. Then'll be the time to cry."

"He wants rid of me!"

"No, miss. Surely he doesn't."

"He wants rid of me, I tell you! He wants me away
from here so he can come!"

"If he did, Miss Stewart, you can be sure you would
be away. What would there be to stop him from sending you?"

"I'll not wait to be sent!" Elizabeth sat up in the
bed. "I'll not be shuttled about by him like a piece
of his chattel!"

A thought had come to Elizabeth—and with it an
instant decision. She scrambled out of the bed and

took up from her bedside table the lighted candle that
Lizzie had put there and went to her writing desk. She
scribbled a note hurriedly.

"Go down and tell Thomas to saddle his horse!" she
ordered Lizzie. "He's to ride to Brighton—now! This
instant! He's to take this message to Prince George!
He's to deliver it to the prince's hand only!"

Lizzie drew back from the folded, sealed paper
that Elizabeth thrust toward her.

"Take it! Do as I say!"

Lizzie made no move to take the note. "Wouldn't
you like to wait 'til the morning, Miss Stewart? Things
always look different in the morning. It's dark of night
itself makes things seem bad sometimes."

"Take this to Thomas! And tell him what I told you
to tell him!"

"No good ever comes from something done in spite,"
Lizzie said. "Please, Miss Stewart . . ."

Elizabeth slapped Lizzie across the face. "Don't
preach to me! Do as I say!"

Tears gushing from her eyes, Lizzie took the note
and fled from the room to go to the stableyard and find
Thomas.

Elizabeth flung herself across the bed and wept.

By the time Thomas arrived back at Belgravia the
following day—not on his horse but in a landau supplied by the prince—Lizzie had packed Elizabeth's
things and her own—in silent protest following the instructions that a tight-faced Elizabeth gave her.

Only the servants saw Elizabeth's departure. Lady
Margaret was not at home. She was at her dressmaker,
Mrs. Porter, in Regent Street, having fittings for some
gowns she had ordered. Elizabeth left a note for her,
thanking her for having kept her as guest for so long

and for the favors of introductions. She did not say in the note where she was going.

The prince had sent Elizabeth a rapturous note. He had taken accommodations, separate suites for himself and her, in the Bedford Hotel. He wrote the note on Bedford Hotel stationery by way of proof. One of the conditions of Elizabeth's coming had been that they not stay in Lady Margaret's house. Come quickly, he begged, he was dying of loneliness for her.

It was well into night when the landau drew up before the lighted entrance of the hotel. Elizabeth saw it with dread. She didn't want to pass through it. But she would. She had the strength to do it. Her hatred of the Lord of Polreath gave her the strength, her wish to be free of dependence upon his purse. Conscience money was what it was. He gave freely of something that he had in abundance in order to salve his conscience. She wanted no more of it! That was why she had taken the step she had. If she had resources of her own she would not have taken it. But she had none.

Elizabeth's resolve wavered when she saw the prince. An eager smile spread his face from ear to ear. He bounded through the door and toward the landau. When he reached it—a path having been opened for him by the attendants crowded around it —he reached forth both arms in welcome to help her to alight. Elizabeth shuddered inside herself, but she smiled brightly down at the prince. What she would receive from him would be given her because of love for her. She gave him both her hands as she stepped down, and then took the arm he offered. When he closed his other hand over hers on his arm, she smiled the more brightly into his eyes. She knew that if she didn't immerse herself totally in the role that she had taken on she would turn and run. She passed through the portals on the prince's arm, her head high, her countenance assured. She was the envy of every eye that beheld her. ❧

19

The prince's suite adjoined Elizabeth's. She had been prepared for that. The rooms that he had taken for Lizzie and Thomas were on another floor reserved for servants. Elizabeth was accustomed to having Lizzie with her to help her prepare for bed, but she could not protest when the prince dismissed her when they were ready to sit down to the supper that had been set out for them in the sitting room of his suite. The prince was gay and talkative all through supper. Elizabeth was quiet. He attributed her quietness to the fact that she must be tired after the long drive. He was too eager for supper to be over and to be alone with her in her bedroom to have much care for anything else.

The prince was as clumsy as a colt in his lovemaking. His hands were all fists and no fingers, it seemed to Elizabeth. Could this be his first time? It seemed impossible that it was. A prince? Thousands of willing bodies must have been available for his use since his puberty.

He wanted to undress her himself, and she allowed

him. He relished the removal of each garment, unbuttoning each button and unhooking each hook and untying each ribbon with slow deliberation and growing pleasure. He handled each garment lovingly as he took it from her body and placed it on a nearby chair. It seemed that he would drag out the process forever. He finally had all of her clothes off of her, but he stayed fully dressed. He drew her to stand before the fireplace. The light of the muted fireglow was on her naked body, and the light from the candles in the sconces on the walls played over it.

The prince was in raptures. He loosed her hair and let it fall, spreading it with his hands so that he could see the flickering lights play on it and through it. He would stand near her, to look at a part of her close up —her shoulder blades, her ear, the nape of her neck, lifting her hair from it—and then he would stand away to have the full view of her body—from the front, from the back and from both sides. Elizabeth could barely restrain herself from shouting at him to get on with it and get it over with!

After his visual inspection, he inspected her with his hands, every intimate inch of her, passing his hands in his clumsy fashion over her throat and shoulders, her breasts and arms, her waist and abdomen and buttocks, her thighs and knees and calves and ankles and feet. He was kneeling before her to caress her legs and feet. He bent downward suddenly and began to kiss her feet. His kisses were dry pecks at first, but he began to breathe in panting gasps and his kisses became feverish and wet. Elizabeth stood there in extreme embarrassment for him. She wanted to take him by his shoulders and raise him forcibly upright. She was afraid that he intended to cover her whole body with his kisses as he had with his hands and his eyes.

She didn't think she could stand it if he did. Why wouldn't he take his satisfaction and have done with it!

He stayed so long at her feet that she began to wonder whether that was how he took his pleasure. He was grunting like an animal.

Elizabeth almost fainted when a wave of remembrance came over her, brought on by his animal grunts and pantings. She was seven years old again, and in search of her parents. She had slipped so quietly from her own bed that her nanny, sleeping on a coat beside her bed in the nursery had not awakened. Soldiers had come to the house, sent by the East India Company, and had carried her mother and father away. It was feared that an outbreak of cholera threatened. In an effort to avert it the company was having every house in the district searched and everyone ill of the slightest symptoms of cholera taken to a barracks and quarantined there. Elizabeth's mother and father were both ill abed with fever and they were taken. Elizabeth had screamed and cried, overcome by panic. She would never see them again if they were taken away! They would be forever lost to her as her other parents had been.

Elizabeth had tried to go running after the soldiers taking her mother and father away, but Nanny had caught her and held her and carried her kicking and struggling back into the house. She kept Elizabeth close by her all the rest of the day and went to sleep close by her that night.

Elizabeth couldn't sleep because of the panic that was on her. Since the time they had told her about her real parents, she had been afraid that she was destined to lose the two who had been parents to her since she could remember. She had been orphaned when the ship on which she was sailing to India with her real parents went down at sea. Somehow, in the midst of

the holocaust, she had been saved. She was discovered
lying wrapped in a piece of tarpaulin in the bottom of
a lifeboat. Several from the ship had clung to the sides
of the lifeboat until torn away from it by the rushing
force of the waves, or until the strength of their arms
failed them. It was probable that her parents—or one
of them—had been among those clinging to the slender
hope of life that the little boat afforded.

Elizabeth couldn't remember the shipwreck in her
conscious mind, but something of it was forever lodged
in her memory. Since the time of hearing the story,
she had had nightmares that were filled with the sound
and fury of winds and waters, with the tortured groan-
ings and creakings of a ship at the mercy of the ele-
ments. She could hear the breaking up of the timbers
of the ship, could see the waterlogged sails thrashing
in the winds, see them smash upon the deck of the
ship. She could see bodies floating in angry roiling
black waters, and could see the waters washing over
the deck of the ship and washing into the sea the blood
of the bodies that lay mangled on the deck held down
by the weight of the fallen spars.

She would have no nightmares that night for she
could not—and would not if she could—sleep. She was
going to find her parents. When she was sure—because
of her gentle snoring—that Nanny was asleep she crept
out of her bed and out of the house. She knew the direction of the barracks, the edge of town where all the
soldiers lived. She ran on bare feet through the dark
streets. It was a chilly night with a feeling still in the
air of the rain just ceased. She splashed through pud-
dles of water and slipped on the slimy mud. She was
dressed only in her nightgown, but she didn't mind
the chill of the air that she rushed through. It felt good
on the burning hotness of her face and body that was
brought on by the panic she was gripped in.

When she reached the barracks grounds she ran into the first tent that she came to.

"Well, hello! That's this?"

A young man in the uniform of a lieutenant who had been sitting on a canvas camp chair at a table covered with papers stood up.

"What's this?" he repeated.

Elizabeth was out of breath and couldn't speak. She stood gasping, cold now and shivering. She was in the wrong place. This wasn't the place she wanted. This was just a little tent. There was just room enough in it for the table and the chair and the bun along one wall. She turned to run out again. She had seen some long wooden buildings farther inside the campgrounds. That would be where they had taken her mother and father. The man lunged around the table and caught her arm before she got through the open flap of the tent.

"Hold up!" he said. "Let's have an explanation here!" He pulled her back inside the tent and stood between her and the opening. "You ran from the hospital barracks, did you?"

Elizabeth shook her head.

"Come, now . . ." His voice was not unkind. "You were trying to run away? You wanted to go back home? They'll let you go back home when you're well enough. But I'm afraid that until then—"

"I want my mother and father!" Elizabeth burst out. "I want to go where my mother and father are!"

"Your mother and father?"

"They came and took them! Soldiers did! You tell me where they are! I know they're here somewhere! I came to find them!"

"Poor child," the man said. "Poor child." He leaned down to her and took one shoulder in his hand and laid his other hand on her forehead. "You don't seem to have fever," he said.

"It's not me who has the fever! It's my parents! I want to go where they took them!" She kept darting her eyes past him toward the open flap, waiting for the moment when she could run past him and out of the tent and to the wooden buildings that she had seen.

The man reached behind him and closed the flap. "I can't let you go there, child. It's a regular pest-house."

"I don't care!" Elizabeth's voice rose to a shriek. "I don't care! I want my mother and father!"

"What's your name, little girl? Where do you live? I'll send for my orderly to take you home. You shouldn't be abroad in the night air when there's pestilence about." He said again in a very gentle voice. "Tell me where you live so I can have you taken home."

"I won't tell you! I won't tell you anything!"

The man looked around himself as if he didn't know what to do next. Elizabeth knew that if she wouldn't tell him where she lived he couldn't send her home. She thought that when he realized she wasn't going to tell him, he would have to let her go to her mother and father. "I won't tell you anything!" she repeated as forcefully as she could.

"Come. Sit down. Let's talk about it," the man said. He led her over to the bunk and sat down and sat her down beside him. "Do you understand why your mother and father were brought here?" he asked.

"Because they're sick." She almost started to cry when she said it, but she wouldn't let herself.

"No," the man said, "not because they're sick, but because they might make others sick. Do you understand what I mean?"

"But they didn't! They didn't make anybody else sick! Not me! Not Nanny! Not any of the servants!"

"It takes a while sometimes before you know whether somebody's been infected."

"They didn't make anybody sick!"

The man took a deep breath. "Perhaps they didn't," he said. "But where they are now, there are patients who *would* make others sick—would make you sick if you went there. That's why I can't let you go."

"I don't care if I get sick." Elizabeth started to cry. "Please let me go where they are. Please let me."

He patted her shoulder. "As soon as they're well they'll be home again," he said. "They were brought here because there are doctors and nurses who can make them well. You want them to get well, don't you?"

Elizabeth cried piteously. "I want to go where they are."

He passed his hand up and down her back. "There, there now. Crying's no good. You wouldn't want them worrying about you, knowing you were crying, would you?" He put his hand on her knee. His other hand continued to rub her back. The hand on her knee started to pass back and forth on her thigh. "I'll tell you what I think they want you to do. Shall I? I think they would like for you to lie down here on the bunk and get your night's sleep. Then, in the morning . . ." He stood up and pulled Elizabeth up and turned back the heavy wool blanket that covered the bunk. "Climb in now."

"If I sleep now, I can see them in the morning?"

"Yes."

"You promise?"

"Yes," he said. He pushed her a little as if he were impatient for her to hurry and do what he said. "I promise. You can see them if you get in the bunk and do what I tell you."

Elizabeth climbed up on the bunk and turned on

her side with her back to him, in the position in which she always went to sleep. He reached down and turned her over on her back. He held her on her back with one hand on her shoulder. "I just want to play with you a little bit," he said. "You be a good girl, now, and let me play with you a little, and in the morning . . ." With the hand that wasn't holding her down, he unbuttoned his pants and took part of himself outside his pants and held it in his hand.

Elizabeth stared in amazement. She didn't know men had things like that on their bodies. She was too surprised to be frightened. She didn't become frightened until he started making panting sounds and grunting. He was grunting like a rooting pig and panting like a dog that had run too hard. He swung one leg over her and reached down and pulled up her nightgown. Then he put his hand between her legs and spread them apart. He did it before she could twist herself away from him. Then she was twisting and screaming, trying to get away from him. He was going to do something to her with that thing he was holding in his hand!

Suddenly the tent flap was thrown back and a man was in the tent. He roared like a bull elephant. He grabbed the man over Elizabeth, pulled him away from her, and smashed the back of his head with a blow that sent him to the floor. He jerked him up to his feet and hit him another powerful blow that sent him reeling across the floor of the tent. He pulled out his sword and lunged toward the reeling man. The other ducked the blow and ran from the tent, trying to button his pants as he ran. The man with the sword ran after him.

Elizabeth had watched, sitting as far back on the bunk as she could get, huddled against the side of the tent, terrified beyond any terror that she had ever felt.

She was still sitting huddled in terror when the man with the sword returned to the tent. His uniform was wet with rain. She had been too frightened to hear anything, even the rain that had started again and was beating on the canvas walls of the tent.

The man—he was in the uniform of a full colonel—put the sword on the table and turned to Elizabeth. "Are you hurt?" he asked.

Elizabeth's eyes were wide with fright, and staring. She shook her head jerkily in answer to the man's question, not taking her staring eyes from him.

"Don't be frightened," the man said. "No further harm is coming to you. Tell me the truth. Did he hurt you?"

"No sir," Elizabeth managed to say. "You got him off of me before he hurt me."

The man's shoulders slumped. "Thank God!" he said. He sank down on the camp chair and put his head in his hands on the table. "Thank God!"

When the man got up and bundled Elizabeth in the heavy blanket to take her home, she made no protest. She wanted the safety of home.

As they passed down the road outside the campgrounds, she saw the man who had tried to hurt her lying in the ditch by the roadside. His uniform was muddy and rain-soaked, blood-soaked.

"Is he dead?" she whispered.

"No," the man said. "He should be," he added bitterly, "and he would be if I had the moral courage that I should have. But I am lacking in it. I could not kill him. He is my son. I could not kill him."

The prince's grunts and pantings stopped suddenly and he stood up.

"So sweet," he said. "That was so sweet, Elizabeth. And the best part still to come." He picked her up

and carried her to the bed and laid her on it. He lay
on the bed beside her, but his head to her feet, and
still fully clothed. He moved on top of her, one slippered foot on either side of her head. He played with
her feet with his hands, kneading them, caressing
them. He started again to kiss them, and then he was
slobbering over them, biting them, painfully biting
them.

"No!" Elizabeth gasped. "No! You're hurting me!"
She tried to get her feet away from him, to move from
him, to move from under him, but she was imprisoned
by his body. "No!" she continued to protest. "No!"
You're hurting me!" Her pleading and writhing under
him spurred him on to worse attacks upon her feet.
She realized it finally and pressed both hands over her
mouth to still her cries. She ceased the writhing of her
body and held still, having to use every force of her
will to do so.

The prince stopped biting her feet and began to
croon over them. And then he was nursing her toes,
one by one, pulling hard on them like a famished
baby at its mother's breast. His body began to jerk and
heave. The heaves and jerkings of his body grew
stronger as the nursing pulls on her toes grew harder.
Of a sudden his buttocks reared in an arc over her.
His whole body convulsed violently and then fell with
all its weight upon her. His face was between her feet,
his body sprawled over hers, his arms outstretched on
the bed. It was some while before he roused himself
and moved from her.

He pulled his feet and legs around and sat up on
the side of the bed. "You know my secret now, Elizabeth," he said. "That makes you mine more than anything else could ever make you mine. From this moment on you belong to me, and exclusively to me. You

had nothing different in mind when you came to me, did you?"

Elizabeth didn't answer him.

He took one of her feet in a savage grip, the nails of his fingers cutting into her flesh. Elizabeth screamed and his nails dug more deeply into her flesh. He turned his face to her. His eyes were murderous and threatening. "Mine!" he said. "Mine! It would not bode well for you to forget it!"

Elizabeth and Lizzie and Thomas left Brighton the next morning while the prince was still asleep. There was no time for any of them to pack. Everything that they had taken there with them was left there except for the clothes they wore, and Elizabeth's jewel case. She pawned a ring and bought three horses, and they rode from Brighton to London, poor Lizzie having the worst of it. She had never ridden, except bareback on the plodding mules at Polreath.

Elizabeth did not return to Lady Margaret's house. She went to the woman who had been kind and gracious to her since she had come to England, and who had been her savior once before—Lady Sarah of Polreath. Let the Lord of Polreath be present in the house! Let him try to prevent her! She would make such an outcry. But there was no need for outcry. The Lord of Polreath was not at home. Elizabeth Stewart's name was taken at the gate and relayed to the lady in the mansion beyond the wall, and the gate was opened to Elizabeth Stewart. She was taken to the presence of Lady Sarah of Polreath.

"My gel!" the lady exclaimed. "My dear gel!" She advanced upon Elizabeth and enfolded her in her arms. "After so long a time and so many tribulations, I have you under my wing at last!"

Elizabeth wept from sheer relief. ᘓ

20

"Have you ever been to Scotland, Elizabeth?"

Lady Sarah was sitting beside Elizabeth's bed. She spent a great part of every day with her, chatting, telling Elizabeth amusing anecdotes, trying to raise her spirits. Elizabeth had been ill and dispirited since she had arrived at the mansion.

"There, there. There's no need for tears," Lady Sarah had soothed her when Elizabeth had broken into tears at her kind and effusive greeting. "You'll be fine soon. You'll have a lovely rest. We'll have a lovely, quiet time of privacy, and we'll become truly acquainted. We have no one to entertain and amuse but ourselves. My husband had to leave quite suddenly this morning for Brighton, so he is not here. And from Brighton he must return to Cornwall. I had to send word after him to go immediately home. Word had come here of an explosion in one of the mines. . . ." She stopped, peering at Elizabeth. "Why my dear gel! You look ready to faint!"

Elizabeth could only stand staring into space. He had gone to Brighton. If she and Lizzie and Thomas had stayed on the main road—which she had been afraid to travel in fear the prince might have sent searchers for her—they would have passed each other. . . . Or perhaps not passed . . .

On the day after her arrival, Lady Sarah had insisted that Elizabeth take to her bed. On that morning, though she had slept as if drugged, Elizabeth was awake to see the first pink light of dawn thin the blackness of the night. She lay in the inviting softness of the big bed and watched as morning advanced. Articles of furniture were at first nothing more than dark blotches against a gray emptiness, then were blurred nonshapes that slowly emerged as bureaus, commodes, chairs, a washstand, a long low chest, and other bedchamber pieces. It was a large room, though not as large as it had seemed the night before when, in her exhaustion, she had seen it in the hazy, shifting candlelight as extending to dusky, unlimited reaches in every direction.

Curtains of a soft transparent white fell from near the ceiling to the floor. The windows were narrow but high, with leaded glass panes. There were two sets of windows, four in each set. The ceiling was high. The bed canopy and curtains, the window drapes, and the furniture upholstery were of a heavy worked silk, a dark rose in color.

Elizabeth listened to the sounds of awakening morning. Her room must be on the court, for she heard horses neighing and snorting in the dewy freshness of morning. She heard pails clinking empty echoes as they were plunked down on the cobbles under a pump. They wouldn't clink so emptily when they were set, filled to the brim with water, on the stone floor of a stall. She strained to hear the sound of that, but she couldn't. Elizabeth loved horses and everything to do with them. It pleased her to know that three of her own were among those being attended.

A gong sounded. It was a muffled, blunted resonance at some remove from her, but somewhere within the house. It was a sound that would be made if the face of the gong were covered with a small rug or a tapestry. Probably it was, so not to disturb those who needn't be about so early.

Elizabeth was at the point of leaving her bed when a light rap sounded on the door and Lizzie came in. She carried a small tray in one hand and articles of clothing over one arm.

"I've brought your morning tea, Miss Stewart. And ma'am has sent a dress of her own for you to wear. She's sent your dress and things to her dressmaker to have clothes done up for you in your own size, but this will serve for now, she said. She's evermore solicitous of your welfare, seems . . ." Lizzie chirped on and on. She was in overgay spirits and had been since they had left Brighton, as if their departure from there had been an escape from some awful fate—and perhaps it had been. "The gong will be sounding for prayers soon," Lizzie said.

Lady Sarah's house was run on quite different lines from those at Lady Margaret's, Elizabeth learned. Lizzie had finished bathing and dressing her and was just finishing arranging her hair when the peremptory command of the gong—unmasked now—rang through the house.

"We'd best make haste, Miss Stewart," Lizzie said. "Her ladyship doesn't countenance lateness for prayers." She opened the door for Elizabeth and then hurried after her.

Something disturbed Elizabeth vaguely. It was the

house itself. It was too quiet. Where were children's voices, murmurings of elders and servants, echoes of the sounds of movement in near and distant rooms? This was a household of several members of family and many servants. And there was not a sound to be heard from inside the house except the ticking of a clock that she could not see.

Andrews, the butler, stood at the bottom of the stairs that Elizabeth and Lizzie descended. He was in livery, his elegant satin tailcoat and knee breeches the same shades of maroon and navy that Elizabeth had first seen in the overlay and lining of Oxford's serviceable driver's mantle. He was of very short height, and slight of build.

Andrews bowed to Elizabeth. "Her ladyship sends you morning's greetings, Miss Stewart," he said. His voice was decorously low-pitched, his manner solemn. His tone was officious. His pride in his position was evidenced in his every inflection. From the top of his small powdered head, to the tips of his polished slippers, he was every inch the rightfully proud representative of a proud house.

Lizzie had ducked her head at the sight of Andrews and skipped past Elizabeth down the stairs and disappeared.

"Her ladyship expects you in the dining room for prayers," Andrews intoned, and he moved off in stately tread along the corridor to the left of the stairs. At the tall, open double doors of the dining room, he stopped. "Miss Stewart," he announced.

Elizabeth could see that the servants were assembled, standing in rows to the rear of the room. Mrs. Hill, the housekeeper, whom she had met the evening before, stood in front, a little separated from the others. The servants were ranged according to their places in the serving hierarchy. This was evident from Mrs. Hill's position, a short space separated from the others, and Lizzie's bright face, now subdued, in one of the rows in the middle. The scullery maids and men and other belowstairs servants were to the rear.

"Have Miss Stewart come in, Andrews!"

The tone of voice was somewhat sharp, but there was a lilt in the words, as if they might be welcoming and cheerful except for the solemnity of the occasion of prayers.

Lady Sarah sat at the head of the table. Two chairs had been placed, facing her, on one side of the table. Two small girls, whom Elizabeth had not met the night before, who looked to be about seven and eight, stood in front of the chairs. There was a single empty chair on the other side of the table. It also faced Lady Sarah. Near the wall in back of Lady Sarah stood a hefty, mannish-looking woman in abigail's uniform. A young woman in gray bombazine, evidently the little girls' governess, stood beside her.

Lady Sarah's head in its lavender taffeta bonnet inclined toward the single empty chair. "Will you sit down, Miss Stewart?"

Elizabeth went to the chair and sat down.

"Patience . . . Hope . . ."

With a minimum of difficulty, the two little girls seated themselves on the chairs rather too high for them.

Andrews closed the double doors and took a standing position to the right of Lady Sarah's chair.

A large Bible lay on the table before Lady Sarah. Andrews opened it to the page indicated by a thick black satin ribbon. From the disproportionate division of the leaves of the opened book Elizabeth judged that they would hear from one of the gospels, probably the Gospel of St. Luke.

Lady Sarah commenced to read. She read in a strong, fervent voice. Andrews turned the pages with such excellence of timing that there was no interruption in the flow of verse.

Elizabeth's mind wandered during the reading. She was far more impressed by the lady reading than by the words she read.

Lady Sarah's face was almost pretty. And might have been pretty except that there was a tight, pinched look about it. Her complexion was youthful in its coloring, but there was no glow in the coloring and many fine lines about the eyes and mouth denied its youthfulness. Her eyes were a bright and stabbing brown. Her hair was a dark brown, and there was an aged quality about it also, as if it had once been a lively darker brown. It was combed a la mode, piled high on the head with curls around the face and dainty tendrils carefully escaping from the base of the Lady's bonnet. Her dress, of a dull grayish lavender, was cut in the latest London fashion. The material was of richest quality silk taffeta. A pin of platinum and onyx was placed high at the throat. She wore a platinum band on her ring finger, and on two fingers of her right hand she wore rings of onyx, pearl and platinum. From her seated position, she looked to be slightly shorter than Elizabeth and slightly more rounded of figure—which Elizabeth hadn't particularly noticed the night before but which she knew her to be from the fit of the dress she herself was wearing.

When Lady Sarah finished reading, Andrews closed the Bible and held her chair. She stood. The two little girls got to their feet and Elizabeth followed suit. Lady Sarah bowed her head and said a short prayer in a strong voice.

"Amen," she finished.

"Amen," Andrews echoed.

Lady Sarah raised her head. "You may open the doors," she said to Andrews.

The servants curtsied and filed from the room. Andrews remained in the doorway.

"Girls!" Lady Sarah said with spirit. "This is Miss Stewart, our friend this year from Miss Holybrook's. You may say good morning." She beamed at the little girls and smiled brightly in Elizabeth's direction. "Patience . . ."

The older of the two girls came to stand in front of Elizabeth. She made a proper curtsy. "Good morning, ma'am."

"Good morning, Patience."

Elizabeth smiled down at the child. The little girl did not return her smile. Timid, thought Elizabeth, although she could see no evidence of that trait in the child's stance or face. She would have patted the small head but instinct told her that the gesture would not be well received.

"Hope . . ."

The ritual was repeated. It was exactly the same as with the other, except that small Hope, for a brief moment, stared up at Elizabeth. It was not a child's curiosity that showed in the narrow, light-colored eyes, however, but a sort of appraisal, or sizing up.

"You're excused, Patience . . . Hope," Lady Sarah said brightly. "Perhaps you may have Miss Stewart all to yourselves for a while after breakfast."

Neither her tone nor her words in any way related to the attitude of the children. If either one of them was animated by the prospect of Elizabeth's company, it was not evident.

Patience, and then Hope, kissed the lady's proferred cheek, curtsied, and left the room—Patience marching purposefully ahead and Hope following, half-running to keep up.

"You look a bit pinched this morning, my dear," Lady Sarah said to Elizabeth. "A good English breakfast is the ticket for you, I think." She took Elizabeth's arm. "I always breakfast in my morning room," she said. "It's so cheerful."

The lady's morning room should have been cheerful. Every attention had been given it to make it so. The sets of windows—tall and narrow, as in Elizabeth's room—faced on the east and were undraped to admit the full light of morning sun. The theme of the decor was daffodils—in both design of fabric and in the painted colors of the furniture. But the room was not cheerful.

A maid and two footmen, busy about a table set for breakfast, stopped what they were doing and stood at attention. Andrews, who had attended Lady Sarah and Elizabeth to the room and opened the door for them, continued in his diminutive but authoritative pomposity to the table to check its fitness for her ladyship.

The hefty, mannish woman whom Elizabeth had seen in the dining room was sitting in an obscure recess in the far corner of the room intent on a book. When she had left the dining room, and when arrived there, Elizabeth could not guess. She rose when they entered.

"My maid Nonna," Lady Sarah said, with a nod in her direction. ". . . And confidante!" she added.

"Good morning, Nonna." Elizabeth smiled, and again felt that a smile was out of place, for Nonna accorded her the barest of nods and curtsies and retreated back to the shadowy recess. Elizabeth wondered why Lady Sarah had introduced her. She must have some reason to want to make the maid feel elevated.

* * *

For the most part, breakfast was had in silence.
Lady Sarah made conversation in fits and starts, and
Elizabeth didn't feel comfortable enough with her to
offer comments or questions to fill the silence. And
she found some trouble in responding suitable to Lady
Sarah's outbursts.

"Daffodils are my favorite flower!" the lady said
once. "Except, of course, for heather! I adore heather!
And violets!" Her words came out in gushes of breath.
"Violets are a great favorite with me! . . . But then,
heather, really, is not a flower! strictly speaking! Is
it?"

She ate with enormous appetite at times, and at
others ignored her plate completely to stare out the
windows or to watch Elizabeth with speculative eyes—
smiling suddenly and brightly when Elizabeth met her
gaze.

Elizabeth spoke very little and ate very little. Her
fork and knife felt heavy in her hands. It took too
much effort to lift the fork to her mouth. She sighed
often, though she tried not to.

Lady Sarah took sudden notice of Elizabeth's condition. "But my dear gell You're not at all well! You've
let me sit chattering like a foolish magpie when you
can scarcely sit straight in your chair! Come." She
rose. "It's to bed with you! Bed is where you belong!"

Elizabeth had been in bed for almost a week. She
was still as dispirited as she had been, but the tiredness was less heavy upon her. She was beginning to
feel a restlessness to be out of the bed when Lady
Sarah brought up the subject of Scotland.

"Have you ever been there, Elizabeth?"

"No, ma'am," Elizabeth said.

"It's second home to me," Lady Sarah said. "First

home. It's my childhood home. Or was for the early part. My family has had a seat there for many generations. It's beautiful country. Very wild, and quite rugged in some parts. Quite different from England. And from Cornwall, though similar to Cornwall in some areas."

"I love the country of Cornwall," Elizabeth said.

"Then you will love Scotland."

"Will love . . . ?"

"You need a change of scene, my dear. There is nothing like travel to restore the spirit! The sooner we start, the better for you!"

He's coming home, Elizabeth thought. She wants to get me away before he comes. She's afraid for me.

Why couldn't she feel grateful? Why did resentment toward Lady Sarah surge up in her? She had Lady Sarah to thank for every breath she drew. Why must she always be so torn by conflicting feelings?"

"I expect the summer is the best time to visit Scotland," Elizabeth said, trying to smother all that she was feeling and to show some enthusiasm.

"It is a good time, yes. By far the best! Winter can be very difficult there. It is damp country, as you must know. And in the spring and in the fall . . . Well, but one cannot fault the seasons of spring and fall in Scotland. Nor, for the matter of that, the winter. Summer is choice for some, but as for me . . ."

Was she going to run on and on forever, like Lizzie? What was this need on the part of everybody she had to have around her to talk? It was suddenly all too much for Elizabeth. Tears streamed down her face. "Let's go quickly," she said. "I don't want to stay longer in London." She wanted to go far from any reminder of him, and far from any chance—or hope— that she might see him.

Lady Sarah leaned over Elizabeth and dabbed at her

tears with a linen and lace handkerchief. "All the arrangements have been made," she said. "We leave in the morning."

Elizabeth's treacherous heart flopped over in dismay. "So soon?" She held her breath, her stupid weaker part hoping that Lady Sarah would laugh and say that she had been teasing and that they could not possibly leave so soon.

"Not a moment later than first daybreak tomorrow," Lady Sarah said. "So you must rest especially well today and tonight to fit yourself for the journey."

Elizabeth turned away from Lady Sarah's dabbing fingers and buried her face in the pillow. Lady Sarah patted her shoulder. "There's a good gel," she said. The downy softness of the pillow was soggy with the wetness of Elizabeth's tears before the good lady was out of the room. ☙

21

The party traveled overland to Scotland. It did not make up as large a caravan as that which had arrived in London. Traveling in the party were Lady Sarah, her two wards Patience and Hope, Elizabeth, Nonna, and another maid—Erma, a strong German girl—for Lady Sarah, Lizzie for Elizabeth, the children's governess—Miss Wells, the children's nurses—Rosie and Leah, Victor and Henley—footmen for her ladyship, Thomas for Elizabeth, and the various drivers, postilions and other lackeys. In addition, there were two outriders—to scout the road ahead if necessary, or to ride ahead with messages for those where they would be arriving. There were five vehicles in all: two traveling coaches, two landaus and a luggage dray.

Elizabeth had hoped that Oxford would be one of the drivers, but she learned from Lizzie that Oxford had not come to London from Polreath. Andrews and Mrs. Hill and the rest of the staff who had been brought from Polreath remained in London to be at the service of his lordship, when he should be there, until all would return home to Cornwall.

The travelers proceeded in leisurely fashion up the

back of England. Lady Sarah had friends everywhere,
it seemed, and they spent few nights at inns. Their
last visit in England was with Lord Mowbray, the
father of Ronald Asquith, and Lady Mowbray. The
gentleman did not once mention his son's name. From
there they went to Edinburgh, and then to Stirling and
on to Inverlore Castle, which was to be their last stop
before continuing to Oban. They rested with their
host and hostess at Inverlore and were entertained
there until they were refreshed and ready to start on
the last lap of their overland travels northward. At
Oban they would cross the Firth of Lorne to the island
of Mull. The object of the visit to Mull was, as Lady
Sarah expressed it, to immerse themselves in the re-
ligious atmosphere among the relics that abounded
there. From Mull they would return to Oban and retrace their way back across Argyll, and so on to Dunmavern and the Clarwicke seat where Lady Sarah had
been born and had spent so much of her childhood, as
she had explained to Elizabeth, explaining further that
she had reserved that stop for the return trip so that
they would not be under the compulsion to "push on"
from there, but could remain as long as they liked.

Oban was a bustling little waterfront town, not a
port city like Penzance or Plymouth. It was scarcely
more than a village. But Elizabeth was immediately
charmed by it. Lady Sarah had sent an outrider ahead
to engage rooms at the Caledonian, a rambling wooden
hotel two streets away from the harbor, but on an
elevation so that it gave on a fine view of the waterfront. Lady Sarah pointed out the ferry, that was just
then sailing into the harbor, that would take them
across to Mull the following morning.

By the time they were settled in their quarters in

the Caledonian, it was getting toward late afternoon.
From the windows of the hotel the fishing boats could
be seen coming in with the day's catch. The little
girls were clamoring to go down to the pier for a closer
look. Elizabeth wanted to go herself, so when Lady
Sarah gave her consent to the children, she went along
with them and Miss Wells, Thomas and Henley trailing
behind.

The little group stood on the pier directly above
where the boats came in and the captains tied up. They
watched as the fish were transferred from the nets to
casks and packed with broken ice. Great hosts of gulls,
with great noise of flapping wings and piercing cries,
met the boats at some distance out and escorted them
—wheeling in wide, swooping circles, and screaming
in loud and raucous caws—to the very dock, where
they continued to circle and scream and swoop. The
fishermen trimmed the heads and fins from the fish—
or from certain ones of them—and rid them of
viscera when they took them from the nets prior to
packing them in the ice. The trimmings and viscera
were thrown piecemeal high into the air, in game
with the gulls, or accumulated in baskets and dumped
in a mass from the baskets into the water alongside
the boats. The gulls caught the thrown pieces high
in midair, and they were on the dumped pieces before
they could sink from sight in the water.

Lady Sarah and Nonna joined Elizabeth and the
others on the pier. The enlarged group enjoyed a
pleasant walk about the streets of the village. They
were relaxed and enjoying their holiday. Elizabeth
had never seen Lady Sarah so placid. After the walk
they returned to the Caledonian for tea and retired
to bed early.

The next morning there was no bustle of packing.

They would return for another night in Oban after their trip to Mull. The peaceful mood of the evening before was still upon them.

The day was fair and full of sunshine. There was wind for headway, but there was no hint that they might encounter weather.

"Best time of year for these waters," a gentleman of acquaintance said to Lady Sarah. He made the trip regularly, he said. "One misses the spring turbulence and avoids the later summer lulls. It's the time of hiatus for weather."

They were among the first passengers aboard the ferry, which plied daily back and forth between the island and the mainland. They watched from the rail, down the steep sides, as wagons, carts, carriages and traps were driven into the depths of the hold. The harnessed horses must have been accustomed to the dark airless hold, Elizabeth thought. None of them seemed more than ordinarily skittish about entering it. Some of the vehicles carried their owners and drivers into the hold. Some carried only drivers, as owners and passengers preferred to ride topside and alighted from the vehicles and ascended the gangplank.

Lady Sarah had selected the most advantageous spot along the rail from which to watch the proceedings below. From where they were, they could also watch the anchor being weighed.

Lady Sarah pointed out the lighthouse to the right of their passage. It was high on a narrow, jutting promontory, with steep cliffs on three sides of it. Elizabeth's attention focused from time to time on the lighthouse, strangely arrested by the sight of it so very high on the narrow peninsula of rock standing out of the gray water. How could boats in a thick fog see the light, no matter how strong its brightness, at such a height?

The gulls had been leaving them alone, circling and diving about other boats, but they seemed to realize when it was time for the ferry to leave the dock and began to circle around over it, screaming out their ragged sharp caws. Patience had remembered her sketch pad. His lordship had asked for a sketch as a present for his next birthday, she had said. She was going to surprise him with one of Hope feeding the gulls. Rosie had the pad and crayons in readiness for when Patience would want them. Hope had been provided with biscuits with which to tempt the gulls near.

Elizabeth felt the first sharp pull on the boat when the sails took full wind. It startled her. She hadn't realized that they were underway.

The party took places now at the stern. Hope was lifted up to sit on a capstan, with Rosie holding her securely there while she broke off pieces of the biscuits and held them toward the gulls. At first, she would quickly snatch her hand back when a swift, white-feathered shrieking bird dived for the crumb, but she was soon persuaded that she would not be hurt, and allowed them to peck the pieces from her fingers. Patience sat near on the end of one of the long benches stretched along the center of the deck and drew busily. A great host of gulls was flying about now, making a blanket of white and gray feathers between the boat and the sky. Other passengers about the rails were also tempting them.

The bulls at first seemed voracious in their snatching at the crumbs. But suddenly something distracted them from the offered food. Their screams became louder, more piercing and raucous. They circled and swooped where they were, allowing the ferry to pull away from them, not following after it.

A cloud drifted over the face of the sun, dimming its brightness temporarily.

Elizabeth didn't know where Lizzie was. Everywhere at once, as usual, she expected. Since they'd come aboard she had been flitting about, examining every nook and corner, exclaiming over everything including the clouds in the sky, breathless over all of it.

"Never mind about the gulls, children," Lady Sarah said. "They will soon come following again."

"Is it going to rain?" Hope asked.

Lady Sarah laughed lightly and easily. "No, I don't think so. That's only a cloud passing between us and the sun. But whims of weather are not unusual here. It may sprinkle a bit."

The atmosphere, without the bright sun, was damp and gray, but the smell of water in it was of salt sea water and not of fresh rain. Elizabeth felt a twinge of fear. But because of Lady Sarah's placid calm, she was able to overcome it.

Lady Sarah chatted amiably with them, and with some of the passengers near them—a most unusual thing for her to do. She was usually very strict on form.

A mist was beginning to settle upon the boat and the water. Some of the other passengers went inside the salon, expecting rain. Lady Sarah and her entourage remained on deck.

Elizabeth watched the lighthouse, remarking on it to Rosie and the children. She was hoping not to lose sight of it in the mist. She noticed the absence of the cries of the gulls. There were none at all that she could see circling about now, even in the distance.

Suddenly all sunshine was obliterated by a heavy dense fog that was above and all about them. The lighthouse was swallowed up by it, and no light from the lighthouse pierced it.

"His lordship will be disappointed in me, ma'am," Patience said. "I didn't finish my drawing."

Lady Sarah didn't answer.

Elizabeth said, "I'm sure his lordship will not hold you at fault, Patience. And there will be many other occasions when you can draw . . ."

"Ma'am . . . ?"

Elizabeth heard Nonna, but her mind was on the children.

"Rosie, hadn't you better take Hope down from there?" she asked. "I can scarcely see my hands before me in this fog. I think perhaps we should go inside. Come, Patience. We wouldn't want to lose you in this pea soup. Is that what they call it?" Elizabeth was on friendly—almost family—terms with the little girls by now, having been living so closely with them for several weeks. She tried to make her voice light and teasing, but she was becoming anxious. She kept telling herself that they were not on open sea and that there was absolutely no cause for alarm, but she had lived too long with the fear of water to be able to put down her fear easily. She took Patience by the hand.

The fog all about them was making even near visibility difficult.

A hand caught Elizabeth's arm is a hard grip.

"Give Miss Patience over to Rosie, Miss Stewart, please!" It was Nonna's voice, harsh and anxious in Elizabeth's ear. "Quickly!"

"Take the girls inside, Rosie!" Elizabeth said, giving Patience's hand to her. "This minute! Take them inside!"

When the others were out of earshot, Nonna said, "Her ladyship's nowhere here, Miss Stewart! Will you help me find her?" Elizabeth had never known Nonna to become agitated, no matter what stress she was under.

"But she was right here, Nonna. Not a moment ago."

"She's not now! Please, Miss Stewart! We've got to find her!"

"Call the others! Get Henley and—"

"I don't want to make a fuss about it! She wouldn't like it. It will be better if we two can find her. You go that side, I'll take this. Don't be asking for her, please, Miss Stewart! Just look!"

Elizabeth groped her way to the rail on the right hand side of the boat that Nonna had indicated and groped her way along it, peering about, trying to see in the fog, calling—but trying to make her tone sound conversational. "Lady Sarah . . . ma'am . . . We thought we'd go inside now. Ma'am . . ."

She made her way along the narrow aisle between the railing and the wall of the salon. If Lady Sarah had been anywhere along the length of the aisle, she would have had to walk into her. There was not room for two to walk abreast, or to pass except by squeezing against the rail and the wall of the salon.

She reached the end of the aisle without encountering Lady Sarah, and groped along the rail toward the raised section of the deck, the wheel deck. When she was at the steps leading up, she bumped into someone.

"Oh, excuse me . . ." she said hastily. And then the scent that Lady Sarah always wore came to her, permeating the mist that filled her nostrils.

"My lady! Thank goodness I found you! Nonna is very worried!"

Lady Sarah did not answer. Elizabeth could see flickering bright glints in her eyes, even through the fog. Lady Sarah was looking straight at her. She must have heard her. Why didn't she answer her? She could feel the sharp brown eyes stabbing into her own. But the woman made no sign of recognition of her presence, nor of her hands holding one of her arms. Was she in some kind of shock?

"I've sent the girls inside, Lady Sarah," Elizabeth said gently, speaking as one might speak to a deranged person. "Won't you come inside and have tea with us? At least, come inside until this fog blows over."

She prayed for Nonna to come—and quickly! Something was badly wrong!

Lady Sarah suddenly wrenched her arm free from Elizabeth's grasp. She whirled away and started to climb the steps to the wheel deck.

Elizabeth knew that she had to get Lady Sarah off the steps. The steps were inset in the platform of the wheel deck, the rail of the boat serving as one side of the inset. At the point near the top of the steps where the rail formed a right angle upward to become the raised rail of the wheel deck, the railing was of no more than knee height. It would be easy to fall from that point into the water below even if one could see his way clearly. And in the fog . . .

Elizabeth lunged after Lady Sarah and managed to catch her around the waist. She dragged her own weight against the straining, determined weight of the woman she held as hard as she could, but Lady Sarah was on the top step before she was able to halt her progress. The woman twisted in her grip and caught Elizabeth's arms in a savage grip of her own. She broke Elizabeth's desperate hold on her waist and shook her violently, but did not let go of her. Elizabeth caught at the railing to keep from toppling backward down the steps and taking Lady Sarah with her. The woman still did not utter a word. Nor any sound, not even that of catching breath. She hung onto Elizabeth with maniacal determination and jerked her

back upright and gave her a savage thrust against the
low rail of the boat as if she would hurl her overboard. Elizabeth had had to help to catch herself from
falling backward earlier by stepping quickly down one
step with one foot. She was braced now with one foot
on one step and the other foot on the step above. Lady
Sarah was on the top step, bending over her. She tried
again to twist Elizabeth off balance and over the
side. Elizabeth had the dizzying sensation that the
black and murky water far below was reaching for
her, pulling at her, lending strength to Lady Sarah's
strength. She grabbed frantically for anything solid
and caught Lady Sarah's legs. The woman shrieked
and kicked, breaking Elizabeth's hold by kicking the
breath out of her lungs. Elizabeth fell to the deck. She
crouched huddled over herself trying to get air back
into her lungs. She was paralyzed without breath.

Footsteps were pounding in her ears. Everything
was black before her. She could not see. A blinding
light flashed before her staring eyes and then was
gone.

"Man overboard!" Elizabeth heard. It was from
just above her head that the sound came.

The cry was picked up and repeated by a chain of
voices.

"Man overboard! Man overboard!"

The boat was stopped dead in the water. Pounding
activity was everywhere and she was in the middle of
it. She could hear it, but she could not see it.

Voices were screaming orders over her head, but
she did not hear what they were. "Man overboard!"
were the words still echoing in her brain. It was Lady
Sarah who was overboard!

She got hold of the rail and pulled herself up,
breathing in painful gulps now, but not able to stand.

"Go back inside, ma'am, please!" a man's voice said in her ear. "You can't be of help here!"

Someone loosed her hands from their grip on the rail. "Go back inside, please, ma'am!"

"God preserve me! Don't let it be!" That was Nonna's voice. Elizabeth stumbled blindly toward the sound of it. Strong, muscular hands gripped her arm like a vise. "Is it her?"

"Yes!" Elizabeth screamed. "It's Lady Sarah! She's overboard!"

"God preserve me!" Nonna let go of Elizabeth's arm and pushed her roughly aside. The sharp pain in Elizabeth's chest where she had been kicked was threatening to choke the breath from her. She gasped and clutched again at Nonna. Nonna brushed aside her clutching hands and disappeared.

Fog lamps had been lit and were piercing the mist all around, swaying back and forth, throwing light about the deck, streaking long paths of yellow light on the water.

A stern, commanding voice rang out. "You there! Does this lady belong to your party? Get her off the deck!" It was to Victor and Henley that the commanding voice spoke. They had come running up. Lizzie and Thomas ran up behind them.

"Come, Miss Stewart. Come now!" Lizzie was pulling at her. "Come inside now, like he says."

Elizabeth would not move. She had to see what was happening down there in the water.

"This one!" the same stern voice called out. "This one, too! Take them both inside!"

Victor and Henley took hold of Nonna by the arms. She was a strong woman, and it was not with ease that they pried her loose from the rail.

Seeing Nonna being pulled away, Elizabeth allowed

Lizzie and Thomas to lead her as far as the door of the salon, but she would not go inside. The door was closed from inside the salon. The stewards were trying to calm the passengers and to assure them that there was no danger to the boat.

The fog lifted. There was less warning of its leaving than there had been of its coming. The sun was bright in the blue sky.

Elizabeth watched the scene before her as if she were dreaming it. The captain was at the rail. He was shouting orders, but Elizabeth did not know sailors' language and she did not know what they meant. But they were being obeyed. Sailors were scurrying in every direction, in what seemed to her disordered confusion and haste, but was not. Lengths of line snaked and twisted in angles across the deck. Two boats were lowered and a ladder was dropped. Sailors scrambled nimbly over the side of the boat and disappeared down the ladder.

The shouting of orders from above continued, and there were shouted answers from below. Then there came a silence and a muted splashing of oars, and the faint slap of water. Out of the silence came a single cry from below, but the sound was too muffled for Elizabeth to make out the words.

The captain shouted orders with even greater urgency than before.

Sailors on deck scurried about, reversing the order of the earlier confusion. Lines were cranked up, wriggling and snaking back along and across the deck in the directions from which they had come. A boat was hauled out of the water and up to the rail. The sailors in it jumped out and joined in the mad scramble to bring up the second one. It was hauled up and secured.

Elizabeth saw Lady Sarah lying in the boat.

The incongruous impression of Lady Sarah that stayed strongest in Elizabeth's mind was that Lady Sarah was still wearing her bonnet. She was lying on her stomach, her midsection making a hump over the board across the middle of the boat. The sun shone down, sparkling on her streaming clothing and her streaming mouth and nose.

"Is she alive?" The captain's voice was anxious.

"Can't say, sir. Looks chancy. But might be."

Lady Sarah was lifted from the lifeboat and held upended. A huge stream of seawater gushed from her mouth and her nose. Elizabeth did not believe that she could have stayed alive with all that water in her. They laid her on the deck on her stomach, and a man in a frock coat knelt down beside her.

Elizabeth felt herself thrust forward by the door behind her. She saw Nonna hurtle from the doorway and run to Lady Sarah. With all the force of her large frame she pushed the kneeling man aside and took his place. She turned Lady Sarah over on her back and leaned over her and put her mouth over hers. One of the officers made to push her away but the man in the frock coat—who must be a doctor, Elizabeth thought—stopped him with a gesture. He gave a shrug of his shoulders and grimaced toward the captain as much to say that it was too late anyway and no harm done if the woman wanted to try.

"Mr. Jordan!" the Captain called out. An officer standing on the platform above answered, "Aye, sir!"

"We'll return to port! Raise the signal!"

"Aye, sir!"

Mr. Jordan shouted orders. A piercing blast from the boat's horn split the air. At the same time a rocket went off. The sailors catapulted themselves into activity again. The sails began to fill, and Elizabeth felt a jerk again as the wind took the boat.

Nonna paid no heed to what was going on around her. She worked on over the body of Lady Sarah.

Suddenly the body on the deck moved in a slight jerk. A horrible croaking strangling sound came from the throat. A small jet of water spewed out of the mouth. And the woman was breathing on her own in convulsive gulps of gurgling air.

"The Lord be praised!" Elizabeth heard some exclaim hoarsely. "The Lord Almighty be praised!"

She looked around. It was the captain who had spoken.

Elizabeth wondered at the depth and abandon of his gratitude. And then she realized the reason for it. There would not have to be a death from drowning written up in his ship's log for that day. ℞

BOOK IV

Reunion with Lord John

એ

22

Elizabeth sat before the empty fireplace in her room at the gracious Caledonian that had charmed them all so much when they had first seen it. That was more than a week ago. It seemed like a hundred years. She had not seen Lady Sarah since the "accident." She dreaded the moment when she would. No one had been allowed to see her, of their party, except Nonna —and Erma, who spelled Nonna in the vigil at the bedside.

The acquaintance, Mr. Leighton, whom Lady Sarah had met unexpectedly on board the ferry, had been very helpful. He had brought in a physician whom he felt confident to recommend to attend Lady Sarah. He saw to arranging for a relay of fast horses, and sent one of the outriders post haste to Polreath with word of what had happened. And, though he was a bachelor, he took over charge of the entire party, much as if he were an experienced head of family.

The little girls had been assured that Lady Sarah would be all right, that she was not fatally harmed, and that seemed to be all they needed to know. They did not beg to see her. Elizabeth felt that it would be

better for the girls if they would pester everyone to
death with questions rather than hold within themselves whatever they were thinking and feeling. But
they did not. They did not ask to go for walks, pre-
ferring to stay in their room, even wanting to have
their meals in the room rather than go down to the
dining room. Elizabeth felt that they were suffering
from embarrassment from the notice they had received
from strangers. Patience spent most of the time at the
window with her drawing pad, sketching scenes of
the harbor in the distance. Hope played with the dolls
that Mr. Leighton had brought to her. When he had
asked what she would like to have for amusement, she
had had no suggestion to make, but her nurse had told
him of her love for dolls. Miss Wells had made several
poor attempts at maintaining a schedule of lessons,
but had finally abandoned the effort.

As the days dragged on, Elizabeth grew more depressed. What would she say to him when he came?
How much reveal to him? Only she and Lady Sarah
knew what had happened on the steps of the wheel
deck. Only the two knew that Elizabeth had been
close to her when she fell. Everyone else accepted the
most obvious conclusion as the answer—that her ladyship had gotten separated from the others in her party
in the fog and, in trying to find them, had somehow
made her way to the steps up to the wheel deck and,
in her confusion, had climbed them and had lost her
footing and had fallen overboard.

A million questions, to which there were no answers
to be drawn from Elizabeth's brain, chased each other
around and around in her head. She had not had an
instant's peace from them. Had Lady Sarah really
tried to push her overboard? Or, in her fright, had
she only imagined it? If she had tried to . . . why? If
it had been Nonna who had found her instead of Eliz-

abeth, would she have tried to push Nonna over the
rail? Would Lady Sarah realize that Elizabeth had
grabbed her legs in a frenzied effort to save herself
from falling, and not with any intention of throwing
Lady Sarah off balance? . . . That question caused a
panic in Elizabeth. But there were others that caused
a greater and different kind of panic. Why did she
grab in the direction she did when she knew there
was only Lady Sarah there? Why didn't she grab the
rail itself? . . . The worst questions of all. Could she
have prevented Lady Sarah from falling? Would she
have prevented her from falling if she could have?

"I can see you're worrying yourself into a state, Miss
Stewart," Lizzie said one late afternoon on a day when
Elizabeth had scarcely left her chair before the empty
fireplace.

"I'll try to do better, Lizzie."

"If it's his lordship that you're worried for, he can't
be too surprised when he hears of it. It's happened
before."

"What are you talking about, Lizzie?"

"Ma'am's tried twice before this to kill herself. Or to
make it look like she did."

"Lizzie, surely you're not suggesting that Lady Sarah
deliberately tried to drown herself!"

"No, ma'am. I'm saying she tried to make it *look like*
she tried to drown herself! Twice it's happened before
this time. Once—the first time—she set her horse to
galloping, as if it was running away with her, and she
threw herself off. Not that she meant to be dead from
the fall. Where she went off was down a rolling slope
of heavy grass, and she just rolled down it easy as if it
was a feather mattress she rolled on. It was clear as
anything, Oxford said, what she did, because she had
to pitch herself over the high side of the horse to fall

off on that side. And there were marks on the mare's
flank to show what her ladyship had been up to. That
she had spurred the mare on. And not a cut nor a
scratch on the horse's mouth anywhere to show that
she had tried to pull her in. And a sharp burr in her
rump that could only have got there by ma'am sticking
it there. And Oxford said she did that when she threw
herself off to cause the mare to bolt and keep running."

"Lizzie!" Elizabeth stared at her in shocked amazement, aghast at the temerity of the girl. "Do you realize
what you're accusing Lady Sarah of? Do you realize how dangerous it is for you to say such things
aloud?"

"It's all true, Miss Stewart. I wouldn't be telling you
except for the way you're taking what happened,"
Lizzie said. All of Lizzie's flightiness was gone. She
spoke more earnestly than Elizabeth had ever heard
her speak. "Everything I'm telling you is true."

"Even if it is, I don't want to hear such, Lizzie."

"I know you don't, miss, and I've worried myself
ragged in my nerves wondering if I should tell you.
But I can't bring myself to think anything but that I
owe it to you to tell you, for your own sake and safety
and peace of mind, so I've made up my mind to speak."

Elizabeth looked at Lizzie in silence for a moment
and then turned back to the fireplace, tacitly giving
her permission to continue.

"The next time," Lizzie said, "she threw herself off
the widow's walk. Not meaning to kill herself that time
any more than she had meant to the first time. She
landed on the roof no more than ten feet below and
did no more harm to herself than to get the breath
knocked out of her. It's scarce ten feet to the roof,
even climbing to the top of the balustrade round the
walk. And you haven't been up on the west garden
roof of the manor to see, but on the court side, the roof

goes down at a sharp slant. And if she had fallen off
on that side, she would have rolled down before she
could stop herself and she would have landed on the
flagstones in the inner courtyard four stories down
and would have killed herself for sure. But she was
careful not to fall on that side."

"I find it difficult to credit all this, Lizzie," Elizabeth
said, shaking her head slowly. She couldn't picture
any of it in her mind. She couldn't imagine Lady Sarah
doing those things.

"That time, she was alone with Genevieve," Lizzie
went on. "Genevieve was nurse to her before Nonna.
That's what Nonna is to her. Nurse. And guard. She's
no more abigail to her than Thomas is. Genevieve had
scratches and fingernail marks all over her arms and
face. She'd tried to hold her back from jumping over.
She could have saved herself the trouble and the scars
because she lost her place anyway. His lordship decided ma'am needed somebody who was stronger than
Genevieve. And Genevieve had to leave. And since
then ma'am's had Nonna."

Lizzie let some time of silence pass.

Then she said, with deliberately spaced words, her
voice laden with meaning, "As for any danger of
her ladyship drowning, Miss Stewart, I've heard them
that have seen her do it say that she can float on her
back for ten minutes at a time in the sea off the cliffs
at Polreath, and that water is rougher than any you're
likely to see in any firth in Scotland."

Lizzie looked Elizabeth in the eyes until Elizabeth
looked up at her. "So you've no cause for blaming
yourself," she said.

Elizabeth's eyes on Lizzie grew wide. Lizzie knew!

"How did you know that I was with her ladyship
when she fell, Lizzie?" she asked. If it had been anyone else, she would have been scared because they'd

guessed, but somehow to have Lizzie know took part of the awful burden of secretly held knowledge off her.

"I know what happened, Miss Stewart, like I was there and saw it. But if I didn't, I'd know it from the way you've been acting."

Elizabeth sighed. "I know you're trying to help me, Lizzie. Thank you for telling me all you did. It helps, knowing it."

"You don't owe me thanks, Miss Stewart." Lizzie brightened and was more like herself. "Why, look what all's come to me on your account! Haven't I seen Londontown? And Brighton? And all the length of England? And where are my feet standing this minute if not in far-off Scotland!"

Elizabeth felt better for a while after her talk with Lizzie—or Lizzie's talk with her—but all of the questions that nagged at her conscience had not been answered and her frame of mind was soon dragged down again by them.

"Why doesn't he come, Lizzie?"

That was what mattered to Elizabeth more than anything else, and she wasn't surprised when she heard herself come out with it.

"He will, Miss Stewart. He's as impatient to be here as you are to have him here. But he wasn't to home in Polreath when the rider got there. Word had to be sent on to him from there to whichever mine he was at. He's on his way by now, and maybe has been these several days past. Why, he may be here this very night!" Her eyes twinkled. She was the true Lizzie again. "I've water warming now to wash your hair, just on the chance of it!" she said—and giggled.

He did arrive that night. He had ridden all the way. Oxford arrived some time after, driving Polreath's

heaviest traveling coach, two teams of his sturdiest
runners in the traces. Dr. Jervis was with him.

Elizabeth was sitting before the fireplace, as usual,
but she had allowed Lizzie to light a fire and it was
glowing with gentle flames. She had allowed Lizzie
to bathe her and to rub her body with scented oils and
to wash her hair and brush and dress it. She wore a
simple gown of spring-green silk and wore green ribbons in her hair. A shawl of lightest cashmere worked
in the Chantilly pattern was over her shoulders. She
heard a light rap on her door and heard the door open,
but she thought that it was Lizzie. In the second's
silence that followed she knew that it was not. She
stood up and turned, trembling in every part of her
body. Her hand went to her throat when she saw him.
She gasped, shocked at the sight of him. It wasn't his
dusty clothing, nor the weary tiredness of his form
that shocked her. It was the haggard lines of his face,
and the haunted expression in his sunken eyes.

He closed the door behind him. The two stood
speechless, eyes locked. Without his willing it, his arms
went out to her, and without her willing it, she ran
to him. His arms closed about her so tightly that they
hurt her. She clung to him with all her strength. "I was
afraid for you, Elizabeth," he said. His arms tightened.
"I was so afraid!" He held her away from him, his eyes
searching her face. "You're all right?"

"Now I am! Now that you're here, I am!" There was
such urgency in his voice that she answered him with
urgency.

"Nothing has happened to you? You're sure?"

"No!" She touched his face. "Nothing," she whispered. Her face was turned up to his, her voice a
whisper because the nearness of him had caused all
breath to leave her. His eyes searched hers still for a

moment. "If anything had happened to you, Elizabeth!" His voice was choked. He gazed into her eyes as if he wanted to lose himself in them. Tears came into his eyes, and into Elizabeth's. He crushed her to him and his mouth came down on hers. It claimed her as much—more so—than it had once before. And Elizabeth gave her mouth to him as willingly—and more willingly—than she had once before. They stood a long time locked in embrace, their lips and mouths and arms hungrily trying to make up for all the emptiness and hurt and yearnings that each had suffered because of the other. The love that flowed between them was so strong that it was like a physical force. It bound them as one. It engulfed them.

"How could I have doubted you, my Elizabeth?" he whispered, "Or you me?"

"I never will again," she swore. "I never will!"

When sanity returned to him, he said, "I should not be doing this, Elizabeth. It was not my intention to do this when I came to you. I swore to myself that I would only assure myself that you were safe and that no harm had come to you. But when I saw you—"

"I would have come to you if you had not reached for me! If you had gone away from me, I would have run after you!"

He smiled at her, but tears were in his eyes again. "I believe you would have," he said.

"I would!" she said fiercely. "And always, from now, I will!"

He tried to put her away from him, but she would not let him. He rubbed her cheek gently with the back of one finger, keeping his touch light. "We must have a talk, my beloved."

"Then we will talk while you hold me! I won't have you put me away from you!"

"My Elizabeth is strong to have her own way, it seems."

"In things to do with what is mine, I am!"

"And I am yours? You would want me for your own?"

"Until we both are dead, and after!"

His arms were hard around her again. "Do you doubt that I am yours, Elizabeth?"

"I want to hear you swear it!"

"I have sworn it with every look and every touch since the moment—"

"I want to hear you swear it!"

"My heart and soul are yours, Elizabeth. I swear it."

She stiffened. "But not your arms to hold me!" She pushed herself away from him. "Not your body to love me!"

"There is nothing in the world that I want more. If I could make it so . . ." He caught her arm and made her face him. "Elizabeth, don't send us both back to the hell that we've come from. If you can bear it, then you are stronger than I am, for I cannot. I cannot be parted from you thinking that you hate me and scorn me and despise me. If your love were as strong as mine—"

She flung herself upon him. "Don't doubt me!" she cried. "Never again doubt me!"

He caressed her hair, gentling her, soothing her. "Let us talk, Elizabeth." She nodded, her face buried against his breast. He picked her up and carried her to the deep armchair before the fireplace and sat down with her, holding her on his lap, her body cuddled against him, his reassuring arms around her.

"My plans are these, Elizabeth. I will send Lady Sarah to her childhood home in Dunmavern as soon as she is well enough to travel. She will recuperate more easily and more quickly there. The girls, her wards, will go with her, and her attendants and theirs. I will take you back with me to Polreath. I cannot allow you to return to London." A grimness came into his voice. "I know about your . . . elopement to join the prince. I went to Brighton as soon as I learned of it, but you had already gone when I got there. I am not blaming you for what you did. I think I can understand why you did it. At least, I am trying to . . ."

"He means nothing to me!" Elizabeth raised herself. She had meant to look into his eyes, but she could not. She shuddered, remembering the awful night with the prince. She hid her face again against his breast. "He's depraved! He's an animal! He could never mean anything to me."

"I believe you, Elizabeth. Still, I wish—"

"I didn't give myself to him! He didn't make love to me! I swear it!" She shuddered again.

"Something happened, Elizabeth, or you would not shudder so at the remembrance of it."

"I can't talk about it. Please don't make me talk about it. Please!"

"I won't, Elizabeth. Put it out of your mind. Try to forget it. I can see how miserable the thought of it makes you. I'm not surprised if the fact is that the pup is perverted. I suspected as much when I learned that you had run away from him after the first night with him. But that's in the past. You will forget it, and I will try to do the same."

"It won't make you love me less?" she asked fearfully.

"If I had had the right to claim you for my own when I took you for my own, you would not later have been with the prince. Blame for it is more mine than yours."

Elizabeth was overcome with weeping. "I thought

our night meant nothing to you," she sobbed. "I thought you hated me. I thought you wanted me gone from Lady Margaret's so that you could come there."

"I realize that now. Don't cry, my sweet, my beloved." He kissed her hair. "We will speak no more of it. It is behind us as if it never happened. . . . You have not told me, Elizabeth, how you feel about returning with me to Polreath."

"I want to go where you go, whether it's to Polreath or to hell!"

"My Elizabeth is reckless," he said, but his arms tightened around her and he kissed her hair again and kissed the wetness of her tears from her eyes. After a moment, he said, "My son is at Polreath. I don't like to be too long from him. That is why I want to go directly there from here."

"The little boy at the gatehouse. . . ? Colin. . . ?"

"Yes. Colin . . ." His voice lingered over the name. Elizabeth wondered at herself that she was not jealous.

"My two most beloved I will have with me," Lord John said. "I had despaired of it." ❧

23

Elizabeth didn't have to travel all the way to Polreath to meet Colin. When the public coach on which she and Lord John and Lizzie and Thomas were traveling reached Launceton—the Polreath coach had been brought to Oban to be converted into a comfortable coach-bed to take Lady Sarah to Dunmavern, and the other Polreath vehicles were left there for her entourage—Colin was there waiting.

Colin was so delighted with the surprise of his being there that he couldn't wait inside the door of the inn, to spring out upon his father as he entered, as he had planned, and he came running out and up the road before the coach turned into the courtyard of the inn. He ran back alongside the coach to the courtyard. "Get out from under the wheels, Colin!" his father kept shouting. There was nothing his father could do to force Colin to obey him from where he was high inside the moving coach, and Colin knew it. He ran along beside the coach laughing in high glee. He was on the landing block, ready to open the high coach door, when the coach came to a stop beside it. He flung the door open and popped his head inside and called out,

"Surprise!" as if that were his father's first sight of him. "I'll surprise you, my lad, the next time you give me such a scare!" his father said, but he ruffled Colin's hair and caught him up like a sack of grain under one arm when he alighted from the coach and turned to assist Elizabeth down. Lizzie and Thomas had been riding on top of the coach. They climbed down and busied themselves seeing to the removal of the luggage from the coach rack.

Lord John put Colin on his feet beside him. His hand was on his shoulder. "May I present my son Colin?" he said formally to Elizabeth.

Elizabeth wanted to smile, but she answered equally formally, "How do you do, Master Colin?"

"Miss Elizabeth Stewart, Colin."

Colin stepped forward and bowed. Elizabeth extended her hand.

"My pleasure, Miss Stewart," Colin said, taking her hand and bowing again before releasing it. The formalities over, he stepped back beside his father and stared frankly up at her. Then he turned his black eyes up to his father, silently questioning him.

"Miss Stewart is a very dear friend to me," his father said, "and so will be to you."

It was an awkward moment, for Colin didn't answer.

Before more could be said Daly came from the doorway of the inn and Heller came around from the side of it leading Juniper.

"He was getting too testy for his own good, sir, Juniper was," Heller said, by way of explanation. "Or for the stables' good. Or some of the stableboys, if I may mention. Every time he cracked his eyes too far to the right or the left, they'd think he knowed of something bad going on with you. He's got them spooked proper."

"I'm glad to see him," Lord John said, smoothing his

hand over the horse's long face. "I've had enough of coach travel."

Elizabeth felt herself tighten. She was remembering the journey to London. Was that behavior on his part going to repeat itself?

"Commander's here, too!" Colin said.

"And we've brought a landau, sir, for the rest of the party," Daly said. "Ross is cleaning it now from the journey coming and readying it for going home again."

"Very good," his Lordship said. "Then we can all be quit of the public coach."

Elizabeth needn't have worried about being consigned to travel in the company of only the servants while Lord John rode ahead, or to the rear—but always out of sight—of the vehicle that she traveled in. When they started out for Polreath, he took her on the saddle before him and, except when she was tired and wanted a rest in the carriage, that was where she rode. "Miss Stewart needs a horse of her own" was Colin's only comment. His attitude toward Elizabeth was reserved.

"He'll come round," Lord John said in Elizabeth's ear in a low voice so Colin wouldn't hear, "once he realizes that you're an addition and not a replacement."

"You make me sound like a piece of goods!"

Lord John laughed. Since the moment he had seen Colin running toward their coach, his spirits had been lighter than Elizabeth had ever seen them. "I sense some high times ahead for myself between the two of you," he chuckled.

Elizabeth was almost overawed by the size and beauty of Polreath Manor. She had seen no more than shadows and a few outlines of the buildings and grounds when she had been there before. This time she was arriving in broad daylight. The gatehouse, where

Daly left the landau, looked to be as large as Lady Margaret's house in London. From there the drive was through open park until they were almost up on the manor house. Its wide lawns stretched mostly to the sides and rear of it. She could scarcely credit her eyes at the size of the house. Lizzie had been right. It truly did look as if the whole of Belgrave Square could be enclosed within its walls.

Elizabeth caught her breath. "It's so beautiful," she breathed. "Stop a minute. Let me look."

Lord John pulled Juniper to a stop just inside the low stone wall. Colin stopped Commander beside them.

"I've never seen anything so beautiful," Elizabeth said.

"It's beautiful to me," Lord John said, "because it's mine, and home, but it's hardly a piece of architectural beauty. It was built to be a fortress as much as a home."

It was a massive spread of gray and mellowed stone, rising four stories in height. There were rounded towers on the four corners rising above the main height. It had the look of a fortress.

"Where we are—where this little wall is—" Colin said, "used to be a moat."

"Yes," Elizabeth said, "I can imagine a moat. It looks as if it would have been surrounded by one."

"We don't need it anymore," Colin said, "so it's filled in."

"Colin can give you the full history of Polreath, should you be interested," Lord John said. "It will, of course, be his one day, so he is well acquainted with all its details."

"I'd love to hear its history."

"That gratifies both Colin and me, being that we're a trifle overproud," Lord John said, and added in light-hearted teasing, "but it will have to be another time. I don't intend to sit this beast of mine another full hour, and if I did, I don't think he would have it." Juniper had been pulling at the bit. He wanted to go to the stables.

They started on. When they were passing the base of the tower on the near corner, Colin pointed to the recess made by the curve of its farther side. "You see that door?" he asked.

Elizabeth shivered and felt Lord John's arms around her tighten. "Yes," she managed.

"That leads down to the dungeon!" Colin said. "We still have the dungeon. You can get to it from inside, too. I'll show it to you one day!"

"Oh, my!" Elizabeth said weakly.

"You won't need to be afraid," Colin said, "I'll be with you."

Lord John reached out his arm and put his hand on Colin's shoulder. He smiled at him and then smiled down at Elizabeth. Colin was coming around.

Elizabeth's rooms in the manor house consisted of a sitting room, bedroom, and dressing room. They were the most beautiful rooms she had ever seen, more beautiful than the ones she had had at Polreath House in London. They were done throughout in a floral print of roses and fern. And they connected, through a stairway concealed behind one of the panels in the dressing room, with Lord John's apartments on the floor above.

Lord John came to Elizabeth that night. It was the first time they had been together, with the whole of the night before them, since their reunion. Elizabeth was dressed for bed in a flowing gown of white batiste with ribbon inserts at the neck and the ruffled cuffs of the sleeves. She wore over it a robe of white challis embroidered overall in satin stitch done in pale green silk, the same shade as the ribbons on her gown. Her hair was loosely tied back with ribbons of the same shade. On her feet were slippers of plaited grosgrain, a darker shade of green. Lord John was covered from shoulders to feet by a dressing gown of dark gray watered silk with deep lapels and deep cuffs of white. His feet were bare, and from the V of his bare chest it was obvious that he wore nothing under his dressing gown. He was the most splendid picture of a man that Elizabeth could imagine. She couldn't take her eyes from him.

He led her to the sitting room, passing through the bedroom to do so. Elizabeth hadn't expected that. When they were in the sitting room, he sat her in a chair and set one to face it and sat down in front of her. He leaned toward her and took her hands in his.

"There are many things that I should tell you, Elizabeth, many things that I should explain to you . . ." He paused.

"I do not ask nor demand explanations of any kind," Elizabeth said.

"But you are due them. I want to be excused from giving them to you now. One day I will have no secrets from you. I swear you that. For now I want to say that I have no marriage with Lady Sarah . . ."

"I know."

"I have no wife but you, and never will."

Elizabeth's lips trembled. He held her fingers tighter. "And never will," he repeated. He looked deeper into her eyes. "Will you be wife to me?"

"Yes," Elizabeth whispered.

"With every duty of a wife to be faithful to me?"

"Yes," she whispered.

"If another man ever touches you, I will kill him."

Elizabeth gasped. There was no doubt that he meant the literal truth of what he was saying.

"None will!"

"And I will never touch another woman. Beginning from now, Elizabeth, we are pledged to each other."

He got to his feet and pulled her to hers. He took her in his arms and kissed her, a marriage kiss. He picked her up in his arms and carried her to the bedroom and to the bed. His breath was hot against her hair. "I have hungered so for you! I have never wanted a woman so! I have never needed a woman so!" He laid her on the bed, loosed the belt of his dressing gown and let it drop to the floor at his feet. He was fully aroused and his hands were hot on her as he took her robe and gown and slippers from her. He came onto the bed beside her, his hands caressing her face and throat and breasts, his mouth following his hands with kisses.

Elizabeth trembled under him. Her breasts tightened and her nipples hardened. She felt the warm wetness of wanting him. She pulled at him to bring him fully on top of her. "I want you!" she whispered urgently. "Now! I want you!" He moved his body downward and between her legs as she spread them. She lifted herself to receive him. The glory that came over her when he entered her was more than she could sustain. It was the same for him. He had no more than entered her when both were in spasms of orgasm. They lay panting, breathing each other's panting breaths, holding each other's hot bodies, she pulsating on him and he growing hard inside her again. And again it was the same. They were barely out of orgasm when they were overcome again. They made love the long night through. No true marriage had ever been more strongly pledged. ℰ

24

There seemed no faintest shadow to mar the happiness of Elizabeth and Lord John and Colin. Lady Sarah would be months—perhaps years—from home. Lord John's various businesses were going along without hitch and he was not called away. Even the shadow of Mr. Hurford's presence was not there. Since Lord John had reopened the mine that had been condemned —Wheal Trawlyn—and had hired Mr. Calvin to be his representative to his miners and theirs to him, Mr. Hurford had been spending all of his time with Mr. Calvin, familiarizing him with the outlying mines that he wasn't already familiar with and with all of the aspects of the conduct of the Polreath mines that had to do with labor.

When they had been coming to Polreath from Oban, Elizabeth had brought up his name. "I won't be likely to see Mr. Hurford, will I?" she had asked.

Lord John had laughed. "Before I came for you, I made sure that you would not," he said. "I don't want any 'dark specters of your past' preying on that imagination of yours. I well remember the attack on my person that brought me once."

Elizabeth had said nothing more. It was of little matter to her now that Lord John thought that she had only imagined Mr. Hurford's vile attacks upon her. And she didn't want discussion of what he had done to cloud their happiness.

Elizabeth was living an idyll, and every simplest event of her life reminded her that she was.

One morning Lizzie had Elizabeth up and dressed and breakfasted unusually early. Master Colin, she said, was waiting for her in his lordship's garden. Colin had free run of the garden now that the menacing presence of Lady Sarah had been removed.

"Wait 'til you see your surprise!" Colin greeted Elizabeth.

"My surprise?"

He took her by the hand and started pulling her toward the far end of the garden path. "My father has a surprise for you! Just wait 'til you see!"

He led her from the garden and toward the stables. He hailed Heller from a distance. "Is everything ready?" he called.

"Ready, Master Colin!"

"But his lordship isn't here," Elizabeth protested. "You said it was his surprise."

"Just wait!"

Lord John came out of the stable door leading a frisky dark bay mare. Elizabeth gasped and stopped in her tracks.

"For me? Is she for me?"

Colin laughed delightedly and pulled her by the hand, urging her toward the animal.

"All your very own!" Lord John said, smiling, as delighted as Colin. "It was Colin's idea, if you remember, when we were riding home from Launceton. Do you find her suitable?"

"She's beautiful! She's just beautiful!" She was a

far cry from the three creatures of unblooded stock that Elizabeth had purchased in Brighton when she had fled from the prince.

"Well, then, come and get acquainted if you like her enough to accept her."

Elizabeth went up to the horse. Immediately the mare's ears flattened.

"Oh!" Elizabeth cried, disappointed. "She doesn't like me!"

Lord John laughed. "She doesn't know your intentions yet. That's all. And further, you're the first female who's approached her since she's been here. She doesn't know what to make of all those skirts."

When Elizabeth hesitated to make a stronger move toward acquaintanceship, Colin piped up, "*You* have to make friends first! *She* won't."

"I should have some sugar . . . or something," Elizabeth said.

"That's not the way we do things around here," Lord John said. "If she doesn't like you for yourself, it's no good."

Elizabeth reached up and tentatively smoothed the long, beautiful face of the animal. The mare threw her head up. Lord John tightened his grip on the bridle, and the mare pawed at the black earth.

Elizabeth stood her ground.

"Good girl!" Lord John said. "But don't get too close under her feet."

"She has a real star!" Elizabeth said, pointing to the white marking on the horse's face. "Isn't that a real star?"

"No, but it's a handsome marking."

Colin laughed. "It would have to be a comet, with that tail!" he said. He ran around to the back of the animal. "But that's the only white marking she has except for this one inside her hock here! And look

how black her socks are!" He was as proud as if he'd
selected the animal for Elizabeth himself.

Elizabeth threw her arms impetuously around the
mare's neck and buried her face against her.

"I love her!" she exclaimed. "She has to love me
back!"

Lord John chuckled. "She must have heard you," he
said. "Her ears are up."

Elizabeth named the mare Sully. She was a sleek
dark bay, almost black along her back and across
her rump and on all four socks. She was part Arabian,
and very tractable once she got used to Elizabeth. But
she was stubborn and skittish enough not to seem
dumb or dull. She was a full fifteen hands, so Elizabeth
didn't feel that she was down in a valley when she
rode between Lord John and Colin, as she had when
she had ridden Colin's pony, Dusty.

Colin delighted in showing Elizabeth the wonders
all around them. From certain heights, on clear days,
they could see the English Channel. He loved for them
to sit their horses high atop a hill where they could see
the ocean on one side and the channel on the other.

The distant sight that most held him in fascination,
though, was that of Bodmin Moor. Elizabeth had shuddered the first time he had pointed it out to her, remembering the terrors she had experienced there. But
her fear of the moor dissipated and vanished and she
became as fascinated by it as Colin—or loved it because he did. He never tired of gazing at the moor.
Even on hazy days, when nothing of it could be seen,
he would stare in its direction, trying to make some
feature clarify itself in the haze. "You see those two
peaks," he had asked the first time they had come into
their view. "That one on the right is Brown Willy.
That's the highest point on the moor! And that one on

the left is Rough Tor. That's the next highest!" He
never spoke without excitement in his voice when he
spoke of Bodmin Moor. It was his dream to visit the
famous moor, and especially the infamous Jamaica
Inn. "They do smuggling there!" he said earnestly. "My
father has promised to take me there one day! Haven't
you, sir?"

"So I have."

"Wouldn't you be frightened if there are smugglers
there?" Elizabeth asked.

"Oh, they wouldn't bother us—if they really are
there. They wouldn't show themselves! They have to
keep in hiding, you know!"

He talked endlessly of the moor and the inn. "Not
very far from Jamaica Inn is Dozmary Pool. That's
where Sir Bedivere threw Excalibur in the lake! It
really is! Isn't it, sir?"

His father smiled and nodded. Colin scarcely noticed. He was running on. "The inn is just about in the
middle of the moor, at Bolventor. You never can see it
from any hill in Polreath, even though it's high itself.
Smugglers may not really still be there, but you can
still see signs of when they were! There are sword
marks and saber marks on things, and bullet holes!
And there's a hole in the ceiling where there used to
be a hook that they hung people on!"

"Colin!" Elizabeth teased. "You sound positively
ghoulish!"

"It's true! There really is! And the wind never does
stop blowing there! Remember you asked me once if
the wind never stopped blowing on the cliffs? Well, it
never does stop blowing at Jamaica Inn!" ❧

25

It was a very special occasion when Lord John and Colin took Elizabeth to the summerhouse for the first time. It was special because the summerhouse was special to Colin. It was already his, in full ownership, and he was very proud of it.

The path to the summerhouse was a double track, used by carts as well as by walkers. It was much overgrown. The vegetation along its borders and on the strip between the tracks sprang lush and abundant from the rich soil. Colin told Elizabeth the names of all the wildlife, picking occasional leaves and blossoms to show her their formations. He seemed particularly to love the yellow folds of the unopened gorse blossoms. "It's like they're holding secrets," he said of them.

From almost the beginning they were climbing to high ground. It was only when one started to climb, Elizabeth learned, that he realized to what heights the hills rose. There was much brownish-green bracken underfoot—the kind that looked dry, but was damp to the touch. The character of the ground and the growth seemed to change greatly with each step of their progress, becoming wilder in character, and bleaker. The growth underfoot changed from proper grass to bracken, and when there was a mixture of other growth with it, the mixture consisted of nettles and dock's foot, so she knew they must be coming close to the sea. After some time they were beyond trees altogether and the higher growths around them changed from leafy bushy plantlife to thorn plants. As they continued the climb, gorse seemed to crowd out all the plantlife, except the sea growth underfoot.

Elizabeth could hear the roar of the sea for some time before they came in sight of it. It came in view with a suddenness that surprised her. Or was she surprised by the distance that it lay below where they were? She had often heard of the wild and rocky coastline of Cornwall's northern reaches. It must have its best and truest representation here.

At the same time she saw the sea, Colin said excitedly, "There it is! See?" He pulled at her sleeve. "There's Eagles' Aerie!"

The house stood on a high cliff, back some twenty yards from the edge, though from where they were the sheer drop to the sea seemed to be directly from its walls. Colin stopped to stand gazing at the house.

"Eagles' Aerie," Elizabeth repeated. "What a perfect name."

"Colin named it," Lord John said, "After it was his. It used to be simply Cliff House."

"It looks as though eagles might really have lived there, or on the cliffs around it," Elizabeth said.

"They did once!" Colin said. "They really did used to nest on these cliffs! Didn't they, sir, when our ancestors first came here?"

The light that came in Lord John's eyes when he looked at Colin sometimes made Elizabeth melt inside and want to cry. Such light was in his eyes now. "Yes, they truly did," he said.

The house was enclosed by a thick stone wall some four feet in height. Parts of the wall were overgrown with ivy and other climbing vines, and the exposed parts were covered with moss and lichen. There was a grilled iron gate at the end of their approach path fastened by a heavy latch. It required the use of both of Colin's small hands to lift it.

The house was a sturdy structure. It was of stone, also much overgrown with vines. There was a stone chimney rising from the roof, which was of slate. The house had been built at the same time as the manor house, and meant to last as long, even exposed as it was to the might of the winds blowing unhampered and unhindered across the wide expanse of open sea.

Colin led the way around to the front of the house. The narrow yard between the house and the wall on all sides was a tangle of tall reeds and trailing ivy and flowering plants. The gate at the front was the same as the one in the rear except that it was a double gate and was decorated with iron scrollwork along the top. From the gate Elizabeth couldn't see the foot of the cliffs, but she could see the huge breakers coming in and breaking on the rocks in the distance to the right and left of them. It seemed that they must break right above the tops of the cliffs, but no spray dashed so high. The roar and crash of the sea were a thundering, continuous noise. They had to shout to hear each other above it.

A picnic basket had been brought for them and left. Colin picked it up when they went inside. It was cool inside, almost chill, because of the stone of the walls. Colin ran to stow the basket somewhere and Elizabeth looked around at the interior of the house.

The ceilings were low. The ground floor was com-

posed of one large room, off the back of which there
was a small kitchen with a pantry—slant-roofed ex-
tensions of the main structure. There were narrow high
windows, two sets of two, on either side of the door
on the seaward front, and two small ones on the back
wall, crowded to the sides of the house by the pantry
and kitchen. On the east side of the large room there
was a massive stone fireplace that made up the most
part of the wall. The west wall was hung with heavy
tapestries and skins. On that wall, backed against the
tapestries and skins, and there was a large and solid
glass-fronted gun cabinet. Firearms were ranged
lengthwise on pegs from top to bottom, and some stood
in braces on the sides. On the low shelf of the cabinet
were hunting knives, the steel blades gleaming like
silvery pewter in the skimpy light. When Colin came
running back, Elizabeth said, "I'd think those blades
would be all rusted, what with the sea air." Colin
explained the calking of the cabinet and the use of the
tapestries and the skins to ward off the damp. The
furniture in the room was of heavy, solid wood. There
was a comfortable leather armchair with a hassock
to one side of the fireplace, a long, low sofa in front of
it and two heavily cushioned stools completing a half-
circle. Cabinets and commodes stood along the walls
on the bare stone floor. The sofa and chair and stools
and the side tables near them were on straw matting
overlaid with skins.

Colin ran about the room, pulling back the drapes,
opening it to air. He was proud of the house. He felt
and showed the pride of ownership. It was his. His
father had given it to him and had forbidden all others
the use of it except on Colin's invitation.

"Come on, I'll show you the upstairs," Colin said.

There was no proper stairway up. They had to go
outside into the pantry and climb some wooden steps—

a sort of ladderlike piece of construction—to the upper floor. There were two bedrooms upstairs, small and cozy under sloping eaves. Each was dominated by a huge bed piled high with quilts and comforts.

Colin wasn't satisfied until they had visited every corner of the house. Every day something in it changed, he claimed, from the effects of wind and weather.

After they had seen the house to Colin's satisfaction, they took a walk along the cliffs. Lord John walked between Elizabeth and Colin, one hand on Elizabeth's waist, the other holding Colin's hand. He felt a contentment and a sense of peace and fulfillment such as he had never known.

They took the picnic basket to the leaning rocks—another of Colin's treasures to introduce Elizabeth to. The wind whipped up more fitfully than usual, but they were protected from it between their leaning sheltering rock walls.

After lunch they rested, Lord John leaning against the rock, Elizabeth in the circle of one arm and Colin in the circle of the other. He remembered when he and Colin had been alone there last and how he had wished for Elizabeth. He drew her closer to him and laid his cheek against her hair. His present happiness was more than he had ever dreamed of having.

The whipping winds died down, and a peaceful lull fell over the little haven between the rocks. In the distance, on the sea, the whitecaps were gamboling in earnest contest with the sea, displaying themselves in ribbons of racing white and lacy froth, only to be swallowed up by overtaking waters that rolled over upon themselves, enveloping the lines of lacy white. Elizabeth thought it strange that the sea was capping when there was no wind.

As they watched, the seawater changed color. The bright green of the water was merged with dark blue shadings that seemed to come spreading up from the depths. The dark blue colorings continued to rise in the water and to spread until all of the ocean that they could see was a deep, dark blue. The blue deepened into black. The ponderous waters became sluggish, and as they did, the color of the waters changed again and became a thick and murky gray. The sluggish movement of the waters became more sluggish. The caps had already ceased to form and play. They had disappeared when the last of the bright green water had turned to blue.

Sluggish though the waters were, movement could be sensed in the depths of them—an unseen, ominous movement of the waters below the surface waters.

They walked back to the house and went inside the gate and stood looking out to sea.

Suddenly the sun was gone. It had not been covered by a passing cloud. There was not a cloud in the sky. A gray, heavy mist had come between the sky and the earth.

With the disappearance of the sun a slight wind began to make itself felt. Elizabeth could not tell which direction it came from. It was not a westerly off the ocean. It seemed to her that it came from the ground under her feet.

"I think we should go inside," Lord John said.

But they hesitated a moment where they were.

In that moment of hesitation, the winds exploded. Not so loud and shrieking were they, but of such a strength that they slammed like broadsides into the three at the gate sending spiking stinging needles of sensation through their skin.

Elizabeth and Colin grabbed onto the spokes of the gate to hold themselves upright against the wind. Lord John steadied himself as best he could and grabbed Colin. "Don't let go of the gate!" he said to Elizabeth, having to yell against the howling of the wind. "Don't try to come by yourself! I'll be back to get you!" He held Colin tightly against him and turned to make his way with him to the house.

Elizabeth, hanging onto the iron fence, watched the struggle of the man to stay upright against the slamming force of the winds. She thanked God that they were where they were. If they had been on the open cliffs, they would have been blown over the edges and sent crashing onto the rocks below. Lord John buckled over. He seemed to be using his head as a ramrod to force his way, staggering sometimes to one side and sometimes to the other when the wind changed dirrection. He made it to the stone step up to the porch. He put Colin down behind the low stone wall that enclosed the porch, close up in the angle formed by the wall and the floor of the porch. He laid him down flat on the floor. "Stay there, Colin! Don't try to sit up or stand up!" The wind brought his words to Elizabeth. "Stay exactly where you are! I'll be back!"

And then, if he had said more, Elizabeth would not have heard it. The wind began a wild, heinous shrieking that was hurtful to the ears and terrorizing in its hellishness. The wind now was from everywhere at once—down from the heavens and up from the waters and across the earth from every direction.

Lord John hung onto the stone pillar supporting the roof of the porch to keep his balance when the winds first attacked. Then he let go and started toward Elizabeth. She didn't think that he would make it to her. She clung for dear life to the gate. It was small defense against the might of the winds. That it was of grillwork and was not solid had disadvantages as well as advantages. Had it been a solid sheet of metal, she and it would have been flattened and scattered at the will of the winds. But the open grillwork, which allowed some of the force of the winds through, offered to her solid self no protection from the buffeting force of the winds.

Lord John was shouting to her but she could not hear him. He was trying to gesture with his arms, but it was impossible to know what he was trying to make her understand. He was partway along the path toward her. His clothes were flattened against his body, his coattails flying sometimes straight out behind him, sometimes to one side and then to the other, and sometimes were wrapped around his thighs and body. His hat had long since blown God knew where.

He reached her finally, and when he did the wind flung him against her with such force that she was afraid the gate would be broken from its hinges.

Lord John was flattened against Elizabeth, his arms around her, his hands on hers on the spokes. "Let go! Let go!" he shouted. He had his mouth next to her ear so that she would hear him. "Let go!"

Elizabeth was afraid to let go. Lord John tried to force her hands loose, but in her panic she gripped even harder. She was frozen by fear to hold onto what had kept her safe so far.

"Let go! For God's sake, Elizabeth! The gate is going to go!"

She clung the harder, trying to shrink within herself to lessen the exposure of her body to the wind. On her back now was the weight of the man as well as the force of the winds."

"Elizabeth! For God's sake! The gate is going to give!"

His hands fastened over the backs of her hands, forming the same curled grip as her palms and fingers beneath them. They tightened like steel traps and she felt a tearing flash of pain when he ripped her fingers by force from the spokes. For a blinding, terror-stricken second, the two were standing freely upright with nothing whatever as defense against the howling, swooping winds that seemed determined to uproot and send them reeling.

"Down!" He yelled in her ear. "Get down!"

He threw them both flat upon the ground. "Crawl to the wall!" he shouted. "To the wall!" He was trying to force her body in the direction of the stone wall of the fence.

Elizabeth finally realized what it was he wanted her to do, and she pulled herself, inching her body awkwardly, to the ground at the base of the wall next the gate. Lord John pulled his own body along, pushing her at the same time.

When they were at the base of the wall, they were protected. The winds were still able to get to them, but they could not buffet them from all sides, and the prone length of their bodies was not the vulnerable target that their upright bodies had been, nor that their prone bodies had been when on the open ground.

"I have to get back to Colin," Lord John said when he got his breath. "Stay here! Don't move! Stay as flat down to the ground and as flat against the wall as you can!"

"No!" She flung her arm around him. The wind was beating like hammer blows on Elizabeth's head and body. "Don't leave me!"

"Colin is frightened! I have to go to him!"

"Don't leave me!"

"You're safe, Elizabeth! As long as you stay where you are, you're safe!"

"No!" She clung to him with a grip that was even stronger and more desperate than that with which she had clung to the gate.

"Elizabeth! You're safe, I tell you! You're safer here than you would be anywhere!"

"No! Don't leave me!"

He hesitated a moment. "I can't leave you. You would try to come after me. We'll both have to go. Now—listen to what I say. We're going to crawl to the porch. Flat on the ground! Stay flat!"

She nodded her head emphatically with each word he said. Whatever he said to do she would do as long as he did not leave her alone in that hideous howling chaos of beating wind.

"We're going to start now." He put his arm across her back and slid his hand and forearm under her, holding her in the tight wedge of his arm. He started to inch himself and her along the ground. Elizabeth helped with her free hand and by pushing with her feet. It was a difficult progress, but it did not take as long as she had thought it would once they were headed in the right direction. The crawl up the low stone step to the porch level was more difficult. They were in a windtrap formed by the front wall of the house and the four feet of wall in back of them. Lord John managed to get his upper body on the step and then his lower body. He pulled her up onto the step as he pulled himself onto the floor of the porch. A thundering, murderous wind, as overpowering and lung-filling as if it had been an onrushing, engulfing water from the sea, swept over her and took her with it, rolling her slight body over Lord John's and slamming her into the front wall of the house. Above the noise of the wind she heard Colin shriek. And then blackness descended on her.

When she regained her senses, the first thing that she recognized was that she was drenched with water and that water was pouring over her in a steady drowning torrent. She had difficulty breathing through it. She had never experienced such rain. She was lying in a strange gray light—which was the next thing she recognized—alongside Colin, who was pressed against the porch wall. Lord John was on the other side of her. He was shaking her shoulder gently. "Elizabeth . . . Elizabeth . . ."

She was lying flat on her stomach with her head turned from him toward Colin. When she opened her eyes again, Colin was watching her anxiously. "She's awake," he said.

"It's over, Elizabeth," Lord John said.

Elizabeth turned her head to him, without lifting her body to do it. She couldn't take in what he was saying. Something was different, but she didn't know what it was.

"It's over," Lord John said again. "The wind has gone." His eyes were worried and anxious. "Do you feel any pain?"

She looked at him, bewildered, and then she remembered the wind hurtling her over him and into the wall. She shook her head. She didn't feel much sensation of any kind in her body. She felt the rain on her—that was all. She shook her head again.

"You don't seem to have any broken bones. I felt for that before I pulled you over here. Nothing hurts? You're sure?"

"I don't feel anything except the rain."

Lord John got to his feet and helped Elizabeth up. Colin scrambled up and clung to her soaked skirts. Lord John herded the two across the porch and inside. He was the last inside, having gently thrust first Colin and then Elizabeth inside before him.

"My God!" Elizabeth heard him exclaim under his breath. "My God!"

PASSION'S PAWN 273

She turned back and looked past him in the direction in which he was staring.

The gate was gone. The gate was gone, and the part of the stone wall where they had been lying and where he had said that she would be safer than anywhere. All of the rest of the wall was standing.

His arm went around her. He pulled her to him and with his free hand held her face against his breast so that she would not see the hideous blank space where the rest of the wall had been. She felt a shudder go through him. Both his arms were around her then, straining her to him. "Oh, my God!" His body jerked with trembling. "Oh, my God!"

Elizabeth's mind wasn't registering. The enormity was too much for her to comprehend. Later there would come to her repeatedly remembrances of the awful blank expanse of ground stretching to the cliffs and nightmare visions of herself rolling and tumbling over it, powerless to help herself, and falling and falling through empty space toward jutting and shelving rock hundreds of feet below.

Colin had been running about. "The shed's gone!" he came running back to tell his father. He caught at his arm to get his attention. "Sir! The kitchen shed's gone! And look! Look what happened in here!"

Lord John was oblivious of Colin. He was still staring ahead at the broken wall, holding Elizabeth as if he feared the winds still might snatch her from him. Elizabeth was first to become aware of Colin. She looked down at him.

"Look, Miss Stewart! Just look!" He tugged hard on his father's sleeve. "Look, sir!"

Lord John turned from the doorway, still holding Elizabeth.

Colin ran to the fireplace, pointing around excitedly

at the area in front of it. There were shards of stone and bits of wood and stone dust strewn everywhere—on the floor and on the pieces of furniture. The mantelpiece had become dislodged and was hanging, one end still attached to the stone above the fireplace and the other slanted down to the floor, making an oblique barrier across the opening of the fireplace. The articles that had been on the mantelpiece were scattered about. Debris and broken bits of china, wood, clay and stone were everywhere. The opening of the fireplace was blocked by pieces of stone and masonry. Wet leaves and pieces of limbs of trees and bushes were lying among the bits and chunks.

"Look what came down the chimney!" Colin hopped about, picking up things to show them. "Look at this! It's part of the roots of—"

Elizabeth started to where Colin was, but Lord John pulled her back and pushed her behind him, barking out as he did so, "Colin!" Before the name was fully uttered, he had snatched Colin up and carried him to the other end of the room, taking Elizabeth's arm as he passed back by her and pulling her along with them.

As they stood at the other end of the room, watching, the ceiling under which Colin had been jumping about slowly sagged down. Above the noise of the rain there was a tearing sound of timbers being torn and ripped, a loud creaking sound like the sound of a wooden ship at sea under stress. Then there was an explosive sound, as if the house itself were a giant human chest expelling a great gust of breath. The ceiling opened in a great gaping hole, the splintered edges of its timbers hanging down into the room. The huge stone ruins of what had been the tall chimney spilled down through the hole upon the debris already on the floor.

The rains came with the ruins through the ceiling, but a great heavy dust rose in spite of the deluging water. And it was as if the crash awakened the winds, for they swooped with a mighty force through the opening in the ceiling, sending every movable thing flying and crashing, and sending the rain to every corner of the room. The front door was sucked open and flung with horrendous force against the wall inside.

There was a last tremendous swooshing whistle from the throat of the storm god. Then the winds were spent and the rain stopped.

The silence was frightening in itself and difficult to take in. The stillness of the house was in such contrast to the former noise that had filled it that it seemed to tremble and shiver in its very stillness.

"All that stuff almost fell on me," Colin said.

The sound of that simple statement of such a huge and monstrous truth hung on the silence.

After a moment, Lord John said, "You stay by me, Colin." He was making an effort to keep his voice steady, but it was not steady. "Don't go running around getting into things."

Colin was more than willing to stay close by him. Where his father moved, he moved, as close as a limpet.

They went outside.

The damage to the summerhouse and the area surrounding it was extensive. All of the kitchen and pantry area that had been added to the original structure had been ripped away from the house. The roof across the whole of the upper floor was either torn away or smashed in. The end of the house where the chimney had stood was in total shambles.

Colin was over the shock now and began to realize his loss. "Can it be fixed, sir?" He started to cry, but he dashed his tears away with a tight fist. He stood with his arms tight along his sides, his fists clenched. "I want it fixed! It's my house! I want it fixed!"

"We will rebuild, my son. We will build it back exactly the way it was."

"The wall, too! I want my wall back! And the gate! That wind blew my gate over the cliff! I want my gate back! I'm going to look for it down on the rocks!"

Lord John took hold of his shoulder. "Don't go near the cliffs," he said. "There may have been damage to them. They may have been undermined. We'll have to have them looked at tomorrow. You'll have a new gate."

"Just like the one I had! I want it just exactly like the one I had!"

"It will be."

The gray mist thinned and vanished. Bright blue sparkling clean sky overspread the freshly washed earth. A strong afternoon shone on them and on all about them. It was an incongruous picture—the drenched and damaged and broken earth and house reflecting brightly in the sun that shone upon them, throwing back glints from the still-clinging drops of water. The three who stood looking about them were wet to the skin and there were tears and rips in their clothing, but unlike all about them, they had come out of it with no harm to themselves.

There was a sound of clumping hoofs and of wooden wheels crunching wetly over sodden earth and fallen leaves and twigs. Davey came around the wall and toward them in the straw cart pulled by a plodding mule.

"There's good news!" Lord John said. "Hello, Davey! And welcome!"

Daved touched his cap. "Begging your pardon, sir, for bringing such as this for you to be riding home in, but it's all I could get through these woods short of horses." He looked about at the devastation. "Oh, my, sir! Ah, more's the pity! Look at that!"

"Never you fret, Davey. We'll have it back as it was in no time, and maybe a few improvements to boot. Eh, Colin?"

"Like it was!" Colin said heatedly. "I want it back just exactly like it was!"

Lord John looked down at him and then at Davey. "He has his own mind for what is his, would you say?"

"So I would, sir."

"His it was, and his it is and will be," Lord John said, "And as he would have it." He looked around once more. "Into the cart, Colin," he said. "Let's away home." He picked Elizabeth up and put her in the cart and then climbed up next to Davey on the board across the front of it that was the driver's seat. Elizabeth put her arms around Colin and held him close to her, to try to warm them both. Their wet clothes were making them cold. Lord John sat with one hand in back of him, sometimes on Colin's head and sometimes on Elizabeth's shoulder.

When they were on the way, Davey said, "Heller would have come and brought you Juniper, sir, but he's acting up bad. I was fearful harm had come to you from the storm, way he was actin' so!"

"He was only alarmed by the weather, Davey."

"No, sir, begging your pardon. He was for comin' out of his stall and comin' after you."

"Has he hurt himself?" Lord John showed alarm. "Heller's with him?"

"Oh, yes, sir! Heller's not left him all this while. No, sir. Juniper's not hurt, but Jude's got his head cut open a good six inches."

"Juniper did that?"

"He did, sir. Not out of meanness, sir. Juniper was

comin' out of his stall, and no Jude wasn't going to
stop him. Time I got there, the stall door was down
and half one wall, and Jude on the floor and bleeding."

"Has Jude been seen to?"

"Heller sent Logan to take him to Dr. Jervis. He'll
sew him together."

"I'm sorry about Jude."

"It'ud have been the worse for him except Heller
had Juniper on the brace."

"That bad, was it?"

The brace was a contraption of plaited leather
thongs that fitted around Juniper, one plait on each
side following the girth line and coming from under
to cross the companion plait at the point of his withers.
The plaits were then attached to heavy metal hooks
on either side of his stall.

"Yes, sir. You not being there, Heller had to use his
own judgment on it, to put him in the brace or not."

"I'm not questioning Heller's judgment."

Colin spoke up, his voice petulant. "You haven't
even mentioned Commander," he said.

"Commander's fine, Master Colin! Nothing bothered
him but Juniper's ruckus. He'll be that glad to see you
though, when you get home. Already he doesn't like
it when you leave from the stables without him. There
wasn't any turning him from looking after you 'til you
was gone out of his sight this mornin'!"

Elizabeth felt Colin sit up a bit beside her, his back
a proud straight line.

When they were nearing home Lord John said, "I
don't suppose there was much damage here from the
storm, Davey. I don't see any."

"No, sir. Being in the valley like we are, we can
take most any weather. . . . Just Juniper's stall," he
added.

They reached the turn-off path beside the stables,

and Davey stopped the cart. Lord John got down from the board seat and lifted Colin and Elizabeth out of the bed of the cart. A loud, high whinnying sound came from the stables. Juniper bolted through the door, headed toward them, plaited thongs flying. He stopped a few feet short of them and waited quietly while Lord John walked up to him.

That night as they lay in the quiet safety of the soft cocoon of Elizabeth's bed, Lord John said, "I fear my happiness is too great, my beloved."

Elizabeth was lying in his arms. She lay a finger on his lips. "It's over now," she whispered. "Don't think about what might have happened. Nothing did happen. We are all safe."

"A fear is on me. I cannot bear to think—"

"Shh, my love . . ." She turned his face to hers and kissed him. "Sleep, my love, my dearest heart. Nothing will ever take me from you, nor Colin. Let what happened today be proof to you of that."

"If I could take it for proof—but I'm afraid of losing what I have . . . . I have so much . . . so much happiness . . . so much joy in every day . . ."

"You will always have it. Sleep, my love." &

26

Because of Colin's wish to go there, when Lord John asked Elizabeth what she would like to do in celebration of her birthday that was coming, she said that she would like to go with Colin to see Jamaica Inn.

He touched her cheek. "My sweet Elizabeth," he said, "Do you know how the things you do and say affect my heart, my beloved? But it is your birthday, not Colin's."

"All the same, that's what I want. I've had so much given to me, and I have so little to give in return."

"Ah, my Elizabeth. You have given me back my life as a man. Do you not realize that?"

Elizabeth insisted, and so they went.

The three left the manor early on a bright sunny morning. "It's going to be a long ride," Lord John warned, "so if either of you starts to feel tired before I stop for a rest, speak up. On a long ride such as this, one must pace himself."

It was a perfect day for riding. There was a nip in the air of the fall that was approaching. Because of it, the horses were more than usually frisky and eager for a run. They had to be held in.

Colin chattered and chattered. Elizabeth had never
seen him so excited. He speculated about pirates and
smugglers, and all the things they would look for when
they got to the famous hideout. "How could it have
been a hideout when everybody knew about it?" he
asked several times.

They took a straightaway cross-country path through
St. Issey and Whitecross and on through Wadebridge.
It was midmorning when they reached the edges of
the moor at Blisland.

Elizabeth learned that there was a great deal more
to the character of the moor than she had seen from
the carriage on the windy dark night when she had
come the first time to Polreath. It was not all charred
gorse, as she had thought then. There were wide
stretches where the moor was dried out and burned
out, but there were also marshes and bogs and springs
and running streams. The moor could be a sunny place,
not always covered with fog and mist and gray gloom.

On the outskirts of the moor they passed some few
hamlets, but once inside, there were only occasional
solitary homesteads, and soon even those were no
more to be seen. An occasional shepherd's hut was the
only sign of habitation.

They rode over marshland and granite slabs, over
hills that were dark on the shadowed side and soft and
grassy where the sun shone on them. There were
shrubs of dry broom, and there was heather. Sometimes stone crumbled under the horses' hoofs.

For all the loveliness of its variety to the eye, it was
not inviting. Tors of forbidding granite rose before
them sometimes, the sheer, unclimbable walls of granite, hot to the touch in the sun, making of them un-
assailable fortresses on the one side, while the other
side, as they passed, beckoned them with its grasses
waving in the wind. Sometimes they passed great

standing slabs of granite leaning at angles to the ground. "How do they stand there?" Elizabeth asked in wonder.

The wind sighed and cried unceasingly. "It's such a sad sound," Elizabeth said. "I don't think I've ever heard such a mournful sound in the wind."

The air stirred by the wind was clean and pure, not perfumed by the scent of flowers, and yet it carried in it a sweetness.

Sometimes they were surprised by curlews—or Elizabeth and Colin were, not really expecting to see bird-life there. Buzzards were spotted sometimes. "And there are ravens," Lord John said. "Though I haven't seen one this morning."

Elizabeth loved the crags hanging over the little running brooks. But she drew back from the weeds and slime that marred the ground around them, hating to put Sully through the brackish places. There were marshes that they had to ride around. "You could get sucked down in those places, and get drowned and smothered to death," Colin said. "Isn't that true, sir?"

"That is true, my son. That's one of the reasons why, as I've told you, if you ever decide to ride on the moor by yourself, you will hear from me in no uncertain terms."

"Are those sheep I see on the tor over there?" Elizabeth asked, to change the subject. Lord John had been a little heavy-handed, and totally without humor where her safety and Colin's was concerned ever since the day of the hurricane.

They reached Jamaica Inn just before midday. When they saw it from the distance, first in view were the tall chimneys rising into the sky, with nothing showing around them on the horizon. Then, as they rode up to a level, the gray slate walls came into view. The inn sat in lonely authority at a high point on the high road that ran from Launceton on the northwest to Bodmin at the south, and was the only road through the moor. "You have traveled this road, Elizabeth," Lord John said. He was not talking about when she and he and Colin had ridden from Launceton to Polreath. They had not come through the moor. His voice had a brooding sound, and a regret in it. He could not take lightly—nor forget—any past hurts to her.

"Yes," Elizabeth said, "and I would make that first journey over this road a thousand times again if I had to, to gain what it has led me to."

"It was well worth, Elizabeth?" His eyes were on her, a mistiness in them. Elizabeth had to blink back tears from her own eyes as she smiled at him over Colin's head.

"Oh, sir!" Colin's low voice, full of wonder, broke the spell that had come over them. Colin had stopped before the low wall that enclosed the courtyard of the inn. "It looks just like I thought it would," he breathed.

Lord John rode up to him. "That speaks well for my descriptive powers," he said. "I think you'd better come in, though. You've been up overlong. Give Commander a drink at the trough."

Elizabeth had already brought Sully to the trough, which was on a grassy elevation in the center of the courtyard. Sully would drink and then sniff the air. She did that several times. "You smell that sweetness, too, don't you, girl?" Elizabeth said, patting her neck.

"I expect she smells the stables," Lord John said.

The innkeeper came out to welcome them. The inn was empty at the moment. The coach that came twice a week was not due until the afternoon.

It was fortunate for Colin that there was no one staying at the inn, for he was allowed to run freely throughout and examine everything. He made a diligent search for hidden rooms and underground pas-

sages and dim cellars even after the innkeeper laughed
and told him that there were none. He decided that
the parlor must be the place of intrigue. "It looks as if
it's never been much used, Colin. Don't you think so?"
Elizabeth asked. "Perhaps the ladies from the coaches
come in here to rest, but I don't think rough men
would have much use for it."

"That room across the passage, then!" He ran across
to it. "This is it! This is where the smugglers met! This
looks just right! They always drink a lot and fight when
they're dividing up the stuff they smuggle! And see?
See those kegs? They're full of ale, I bet! And there
must be rum in those bottles! That's what they drink!
Ale and rum!"

The innkeeper lifted the flap of the bar and let
Colin come behind it to examine the kegs and bottles
and the rows of glasses and mugs. He lifted him up so
that he could see and touch those hanging from the
crossbars overhead. Colin searched the floor for a hidden trapdoor leading to an underground passage to a
dark cave, but there was none.

They were given a midday meal in a corner of the
room. Colin could scarcely eat because of his excitement. He asked question after question.

"Where's the hook that they hung people from? I
see a hole in that beam in the middle up there. See it,
Miss Stewart? . . . Did you ever see any real smugglers?" he asked the innkeeper.

"I think this is the nicest birthday I ever had," Elizabeth said. Colin jumped up and ran around to her and
gave her a noisy smack on the cheek.

Lord John remarked after they had finished the meal
that Colin looked a little tired, and should have a nap.
But Colin would have none of it, and his father gave
in to his pleas not to be made to nap. "It would hardly
benefit you," he said. "You would not sleep."

They walked around the yard of the inn while Colin inspected the stables and the smithy, even the cow-house and barns. Then Lord John ordered the horses brought and they rode to Dozmary Pool.

"It's bigger than I thought," Colin said. "Sir Bedivere couldn't have thrown Excalibur in the middle! It's too big!"

They dismounted and Lord John and Elizabeth sat on a flat stone by the water's edge while Colin walked along the edges of the pool or stood staring at it. Several times he squatted down and put his hands in the water, even washing his face in it and patting it on his forehead. Presently he came and sat down on the stone with Elizabeth and Lord John.

"I think we must start home," Lord John said after a while. "We don't want to be after dark arriving back."

Elizabeth and Lord John were in their saddles, but Colin still was not mounted. Commander was being cranky. His behavior was most peculiar. He would sidestep away each time Colin made to spring up into the saddle. And then he would turn his head and nudge Colin's shoulder. It was his gesture of affection for Colin. But he would not let him mount. Time after time he sidestepped out of reach.

Lord John at first paid no attention, or pretended not to pay attention. He didn't want to embarrass Colin. Elizabeth could not help but watch with some anxiety. She wasn't afraid for Colin. She knew how well he could handle a horse, but she had never seen him have the least trouble with Commander.

Finally Lord John said sharply, "Hold that horse in, Colin!"

Colin shortened the reins until there was no slack and the horse's head was up and pointed straight ahead. Colin was accustomed to grasp a loose rein when mounting, if he held the reins at all. He caught hold of the saddle, back and front, and heaved himself off his feet. Once he was off the ground, Commander stopped moving about and stood absolutely still while Colin wriggled his body up and into the saddle. It was far from his usual springing action.

Lord John said nothing, and Elizabeth, of course, did not. She regretted Lord John's sharp words to Colin, but in this particular—the handling of horses— he was strict. He allowed for no flexibility in a horse- man's command of his animal. She had learned that thoroughly from having heard his sharp words in her own ears.

They moved off at a walk and soon were trotting along. Colin was riding a little to the rear. Elizabeth began to talk about the inn, and the next time they must come to visit it. She remarked on the scenery around them. Lord John was quiet. A slight pucker across his forehead indicated that something was on his mind. He answered politely enough, but he did not really add to the conversation.

They had ridden for some ten or fifteen minutes toward the main road when Elizabeth heard Colin call in a thin, breathy voice, ". . . Sir . . ."

Elizabeth jerked up her head at the sound. Lord John about-faced Juniper in the same space of time in which Elizabeth turned her head.

Colin was sliding out of the saddle.

Lord John was off Juniper and beside him by the time he hit the ground. Commander stood planted be- side him like a statue. Colin was slumped against his hind leg.

Elizabeth jumped down and ran to them.

Colin's face was flushed and wreathed with perspi- ration.

"I'm sorry, sir," he whispered.

"Never mind, my son. Never mind." Lord John lifted Colin in his arms.

"Knot Commander's reins," he said to Elizabeth. She tied them in a slip knot and tucked the knot under the saddle, as she had seen Colin do often when he needed both his hands to demonstrate something to her.

Juniper had walked up to them. Lord John handed Colin to Elizabeth and mounted Juniper and then reached down and took Colin from her.

"Bring Sully up on my right," he said. "I'll give you a leg up."

Elizabeth did so and he leaned down and helped her to mount. They started off, turning in the direction of the inn.

"Shouldn't I lead Commander?" Elizabeth asked.

"He'll come," Lord John said.

The horse did, moving up so that he was on the side next Colin's head. Lord John looked over at him. "You knew more than I did, Commander, didn't you?" He said. "Curse myself for a stubborn fool!" he said to Elizabeth.

"But . . ."

"The horse, not I, knew that Colin wasn't fit to be in the saddle!"

Elizabeth didn't answer. What he said was true.

They rode back to the inn at a walk. Colin made no sound and no movement. He simply lay limp in his father's arms.

Elizabeth remembered Lord John's remark at table that Colin looked tired. And he had been a little flushed, but she had thought that it was from excitement. She remembered his patting the cool water on his forehead and how he had come to sit with them instead of running about. . . . All the signs had been there. She blamed herself for not reading them.

They could see from some distance away that there

was a great bustle and activity in the courtyard of the inn. A coach was standing in the yard, and people were milling about, taking down valises and boxes. The ostler was unhitching the horses and leading them to the stable. Two men were examining the axle where it attached to the coach in front.

As they came nearer they could hear scraps of talk among the people about the coach.

"Could have been a bad accident."

"We could all be lying in a ditch right now!"

"There ought to be a law about hiring out to the public a vehicle in the condition this one's in!"

"We're lucky we made it as far as here. At least we're not stranded back there on the moor somewhere!"

"When will we be able to leave?"

The passengers were crowding around the driver with their clamoring questions. Jamaica Inn was a refreshment stop and a rest stop for the horses. It was few people's destination. The valises and boxes were being taken down because the coach had to be repaired.

"How long will it take to fix it? I've got business waiting me!"

The party of three attracted little attention when they rode up. The people from the disabled coach had their own problems to think about.

When they went inside, there were people crowded about the innkeeper, noisily demanding accommodations. The man had given out all the rooms he had, as he was trying to make understood to them.

Lord John strode through the crowd, shouldering people out of his way. "My son is ill!" he said. "I'll need a room for him—I'll need two rooms. And I'll need someone to ride to Lion's Wood at Polreath for Dr. Jervis. That's Lion's Wood at Polreath! Dr. Jervis!

He's to come immediately! If there's a doctor nearer, fetch him as well! Move, man!"

The innkeeper clutched his hands together in the material of his apron. "Sir, I'm afraid the rooms are all—"

"I'll clear out the rooms I need! You get the doctors here!"

The innkeeper threw his hands up and fled the crowd around him and ran toward the back to send off one of his boys to fetch the doctors.

Lord John had already started up the stairs with Colin.

"Come, Elizabeth! We'll see to the rooms!"

27

It was near midnight of the seventh day of Colin's fever. The inn was quiet. There were no guests other than Colin, Elizabeth, Lord John, and Dr. Jervis. Colin's fever had been diagnosed as typhoid. The people on the midweek coach had been warned when they arrived in the yard of the inn. No one had left the coach, even to walk about in the yard for a few minutes, and the coach had not lingered.

Dr. Jervis was in the room next to Colin's. Lord John insisted that he keep himself as rested as absence from Colin's room would permit, so that he could the better attend him. Lord John and Elizabeth seldom left the room, and never together. Lord John had had a cot brought in, and they took turns during the nights at least lying down and resting, even if they couldn't sleep. Sometimes Elizabeth fell into a deep, conscious-less sleep. It only lasted an hour or so at the most. Lord John got even less rest than she did, and what sleep he got was so fitful that it tired him more than it rested him. He had suggested the first night that she get some sleep in another room while he sat by the bedside. She would not leave him to sit alone in vigil.

She knew that his fear had come back on him. He had not insisted, and he had not suggested since that she leave the room to rest.

Dr. Jervis was worried. He had told Lord John after the third day that he must prepare himself for any eventuality. The fever was intense, and Colin was a slight child. He had expected the fever to reach its crisis on the fifth day, but it had not. The fever was lasting, a very bad indication of its virulence and its hold on the boy, since it did not lessen nor intensify beyond its early strength. And because of its steady, relentless drain on him, Colin's body strength to resist it was being dissipated by the hour.

The strain showed increasingly more with each passing day and hour in Lord John's face and form, and in Elizabeth's as well. At first they tried to hide their fear from each other, but their pretended hopes were so patently unfounded that they gave up the pretense.

Colin lay small and limp in the bed most of the time, his short, light breaths whistling, sharp and soft. At other times he would toss and mumble and throw the covers about. On occasion he would try to get out of the bed. He was never conscious enough to know what he was doing, nor who was with him. In his mumbling, it was always "Sir" to whom he spoke. If he said another name—"Miss Stewart" or "Jason"—it was because he was telling Sir something about one of them. Sometimes he laughed when he was telling something that he thought was funny. The little croak of laughter was terrible to hear.

Lord John and Elizabeth sat and watched and kept him in the bed when he tried to leave it and cooled his little body with cloths dipped in cool water and dried the perspiration that poured from him and soaked through the covers of the bed.

Colin was quiet now. His dark hair lay in lank damp

spikes on his forehead. His dark, straight lashes and eyebrows were black lines on his white face. His lips were parted, showing his small white teeth.

"I want to tell you about Colin, Elizabeth," Lord John said. His voice was quiet, and low, his words slowly said.

There was a long pause.

"I loved his mother very much."

There was another long pause. Elizabeth did not look at the man speaking. She watched Colin. She knew the pain that must be etched on the face that she loved more than life itself. She did not think that she could bear to see it.

"I cannot lose him," the man said. "I cannot."

He stopped speaking. Then he repeated. "I cannot."

He paused again, and then, gazing down upon his son, he told his story.

"I was eighteen when I was sent to India. I was wild as a youth. When I was sent down from Oxford for one of my escapades, my father thought that the discipline of a military experience was the answer. He arranged for a commission as lieutenant for me. I was to go for two years of duty with the King's Lancers and then return to England. . . . I went, and Daly with me. He was valet to me then. . . . The life I led there was no less wild than the one I had led at home in England. Until I met Santha. . . . I don't know how to describe her to you. I can't say that Colin is like her, because he isn't, except in coloring. Everything else about him is from me. He's fine-boned, as she was fine-boned, but she was small . . . and he won't be. He's long of bone, and will be as tall as I am. And he will fill out. I was slight as a child, as he is. . . . Santha was a paradox. Sometimes she was gay, sweet and laughing . . . like a fairy . . . ephemeral. Sometimes she was serious . . . regal. I don't know why she loved

me. But she did. Enough to marry me, according to
English law, and against her father's wishes. Her
father was—is, I suppose—he's still living, as far as I
know—a maharajah—a Maratha prince. He hated all
things British. We had to be married in secret. It was
no easy thing for me to arrange, because of my age
and because I didn't have my father's sanction. But,
with enough outlay of money, I managed. Her parents
knew nothing of the marriage until it was an accomplished fact. Nor did my parents. But mine were
far away, and we felt safe from them. Hers were
there. . . . We thought that we were safe from them.
We thought that her father would disown her, and
that would be the end of it from him. We wished he
would—and mine disown me, if they would not accept
her. We cared for nothing except to be together. . . .
We weren't long together. Her father didn't disown
her. I came home one night and she was gone. I went
to her father's palace. No one was there except a
retinue of servants and guards. They let me search the
palace. They knew how useless the search would be,
for she was not there. I went out of my mind. I stabbed
one of the guards before the others could jump me
and haul me off, trying to force him to tell me where
they had taken her. For days I searched for her. I
went everywhere. Useless places. Places where she
could not possibly be. Then a deputation from her
father called on me. They told me that Santha had
killed herself. They said that I had brought disgrace
upon her and that she had become an outcast in her
father's house and that she had done the honorable
thing and killed herself. . . . I went crazy. I tried to
kill the men who told me. They put me under restraint
in barracks. They kept me there until the day they
came to tell me that passage home had been secured
for me. My father had arranged for my release from

the Lancers. I was not cashiered out, as I should have been. If they had stood me against the wall and shot me, it would have been a favor to me. But six corpsmen were detailed to escort me to the ship and see me on board it and still aboard it when it sailed. Daly was with me, of course. . . . They sat guard in the longboat between the ship and the shore until the ship was so far out that there was no possibility of my jumping overboard and swimming back. . . . I was determined to get to the maharajah and kill him. . . ."

He stood up and brooded over the bed, looking down at the quiet form of Colin.

"I don't know why my son means so much to me. Does a son always hold his father's lifestrings in his hands? I have learned to live without his mother. She is like a dream that I had long years ago. I recognize the feeling that I had for her for what it was . . . part rebellion, part the exhilaration of defying even God for what I wanted. It was a passion of youth. I'm not saying that I didn't truly love her, for I did. . . . But I have learned to live without her. And I'm not sure I could manage that where Colin is concerned. I don't love him the way I do because I loved her so much. The feeling that I have for him is for himself—for his very bones and breath and face and laugh and . . ."

He broke off. He stood gazing down at Colin for a long time. Then he went back to his story.

"For more than a year I believed that Santha was dead. Perhaps it was best in the end. I would never have quit trying to find her if I had thought she was alive. And I would have found her. . . . And then I would have lost her to the epidemic. . . . Sometimes I think I wouldn't have, that I could have kept her alive by my own sheer will. . . . She died in a common pesthouse. She was nursing the sick during an epidemic of cholera—in defiance of her father—nursing the English. . . . She caught the disease, and she died there from it. She had nursed Jason and had saved his life—at least, he believes she did. . . . Jason . . . you don't yet know Jason. Jason was a sailor from one of the Polreath merchantmen. He had fallen ill while in Surat on shore leave and had been carried to the pest-house where Santha nursed him, and where he then nursed her. When she was very ill, Santha talked in her delirium enough for Jason to recognize her as the girl in the tales that had gone around the year before of the Maratha princess who had been kidnapped, first by me, and then from me by her father. She talked about the baby that she had borne me. She was afraid of the treatment it might receive in her father's house after her death because of the Englishman who was its father. . . . But more than that . . . for there was little chance the child would be mistreated. He was a prince of the blood and would be brought up as such. The Marathas are a proud people and jealous of the blood that runs in them. . . . More than that, she wanted our son to be with me if he could not be with her. Jason volunteered to bring the baby to England . . . to me. Santha was dying, and he knew it. She told him how to contact her old amah who would get the baby to him. During the mourning for Santha, when the attention of the household was focused there, the amah smuggled the child out and took him to Jason, to the harbor where his ship was docked. He was able to sneak the child on board the ship, but not the amah. The ship was well out to sea before Colin was discovered. The captain, thinking that the child was Jason's, closed his eyes to the fact of his existence. . . . Colin didn't take well to the change, and he almost died of starvation before Jason discovered that he could digest sea biscuits soaked in goat's milk . . ." He paused. ". . . How many stories

Jason has told me. . . . I have much to be thankful
for." He looked from Colin to Elizabeth. "For I have
had Colin most of his life, and God granting mercy, I
will continue to have him. . . . And now there is
you . . . also come to me from India. It must be destiny, Elizabeth—some great universal pattern—that
scatters human beings from one place, and brings
them together again in another place, and far
away. . ."

"If that is true," Elizabeth said. "If destiny truly
has a plan for us, Colin won't be taken from you."

"I have to believe that. Help me to believe it."

He walked to the window and adjusted the drapes
to close out the brightness of the moonlight that was
coming through a parting in them. The only light then
was from a candle guttering on the mantelpiece. He
returned to his chair next to Elizabeth's and sat down.
He did not continue the story. Perhaps, Elizabeth
thought, it was finished.

Colin stirred. Lord John and Elizabeth were instantly on their feet and leaning over him.

". . . Sir . . ."

They could barely hear the sound. Lord John knelt
beside the bed and put his face close to Colin's.

"Yes, my son. I'm here. I'm here."

Colin's eyelids fluttered briefly.

"I'm thirsty, sir. I want some water."

Elizabeth poured water from the carafe on the
bedside table and handed the glass of it to Lord John,
and then her legs went weak and she sank down into
her chair and buried her face in her hands and gave
way to silent weeping. It was the first time that Colin
had asked for anything since the fever had come upon
him. He was going to get well.

*   *   *

It was not until a week later that Dr. Jervis judged Colin well enough to be taken home. While more than courteous, due to the recompense he had received, the landlord of Jamaica Inn was nonetheless glad to see them go. Having a typhoid patient on the premises had not done anything to increase his business.

Oxford had been sent for, and he arrived in early morning in the carriage. There was a slight chill in the air, but it was a crisp, dry day full of sunshine. Colin reacted well to the crisp, dry air. Some color came into his cheeks that was not the flush of illness and fever. After a while, he wanted to sit up, and his father wrapped his blankets around him and placed him on the seat between himself and Elizabeth. He had been lying on the seat opposite where a bed of comforters and blankets had been made for him. He was quiet, with a question only now and then. Lord John would call it out to Oxford for answer, for all of Colin's questions had to do with things going on at Polreath. He asked about Jason and Commander, who had been taken back to Polreath along with Juniper and Sully, and about the puppy Guinevere.

"Jason has been missing me," Colin said, repeating an answer Oxford had made. "He's lonesome."

"Yes, he's lonesome for you," his father said. "He will be glad when you are home. You are the comfort and reason for his life, as he always says."

"I want to stay where he can see me when I'm home."

"I'll have a bed put in his room for you."

"Then he won't be lonesome anymore."

"No, my son, he won't be lonesome anymore."

"And I won't be by myself."

Lord John took Colin, blankets wrapped around him, and held him on his lap. He lifted his head far back and stared unblinking at the top of the carriage. It was to keep tears from running down his cheeks. It hurt Elizabeth to the quick to see it.

"Would you like to come live in the house with me, Colin?"

"Yes, sir. But you have somebody besides me. Jason doesn't." ☙

the large and small throw pillows that were always piled against it and the headboard. Two of the bed pillows that were stored inside the bolster during the day rolled small enough to fit inside but fluffed out to a height that mounted halfway up the headboard when they were in place at night. Elizabeth slept on the two smaller ones that were placed at the foot of the high ones. One of the pillows that had been inside the bolster had fallen out, and another was partway out.

"Are you trying to undo what you've just done, Lizzie?" Elizabeth asked. She went over to the bed and started to stuff the pillow that had fallen out back inside the bolster

"Don't trouble yourself, Miss Stewart! Don't trouble yourself!"

"What's the matter with you, Lizzie? What's making you so jumpy?" You'd think she was trying to conceal Thomas in the bolster, or behind it, Elizabeth thought. More likely her nervousness was because he was waiting for her in the dressing room. That would be no surprise.

"You go along for your ride, Miss Stewart! It's not for you to be making beds!"

"For goodness' sake, Lizzie!" Elizabeth scolded. She started stuffing the pillow that was partway out back inside the bolster. Suddenly she drew back, staring at the exposed wooden headboard of the bed.

". . . What is that, Lizzie?"

"What, Miss Stewart?" Lizzie quickly put the bolster, with its restored pillows, down against the headboard.

Elizabeth reached over and rolled the bolster away from the headboard. "There. There on the headboard. Is that why you were in such a state? Because you didn't want me to see that?"

The lower part of the headboard—that was concealed by the high pillows at night and by the bolster during the day—on the near side where she slept—was punctured and marked by slashes and gouges. She leaned over and rubbed her hand over the mutilated wood. The surface of the wood had been rubbed and buffed until it was smooth. The damage didn't seem to have been done recently.

Lizzie was standing stock still, not answering.

"How did this come about, Lizzie?"

"I expect it was done in the moving of it, Miss Stewart, when it was brought to the manor house here from London. Such a fine piece as this is came from London, surely!"

"It looks as if someone took an ax and tried to chop up the headboard."

"Oh, no, Miss Stewart! Why, an ax would have gone right through the wood!"

"Well, what then? A knife. . . ? A dagger. . . ?"

"I expect it was done in the moving, when—"

Elizabeth straightened up and looked at Lizzie and cut her off. "I don't think this was done in the moving, Lizzie, and neither do you."

Lizzie tried to face it out, but failed. She lowered her eyes.

"Tell me about it, Lizzie."

"You wouldn't be wanting to listen to servants' gossip, Miss Stewart. How often you've made me hold my tongue from repeating things to you. And it's only servants'—"

"Tell me about it, Lizzie!"

Lizzie looked at her. "You're not going to like what you hear."

"I can see that easily enough from the way you're acting! What do you think provokes me so to want to hear it? I want the story—and I want all of it!"

"You see, you're already getting yourself upset and angry," Lizzie said. She wrung her hands. "Oh why did you have to come in the room just at the wrong time, Miss Stewart? You'll be angry now, and spiteful, and taking spite out on his lordship! That's why I didn't want you ever to see what you just did! So you wouldn't be asking questions and making me answer things and then getting in one of your—"

"Stop that whining, Lizzie! I want to know and I intend to find out! Do you want me to find out from you or from him?"

Lizzie sighed. "From me I guess is better," she said. "That'll give you some time to get over the worst of your temper about it before—"

"Never mind my temper! Go on!"

Lizzie had trouble deciding how to start—or wanting to start.

"It was three years ago, or abouts . . . when . . ." She stopped.

"Am I going to have to drag it out of you, Lizzie?"

" . . . when Lady Margaret was living here . . ."

"What!"

Lizzie tried to soften it. "Lady Margaret was a very dear and close friend of ma'am's, they said. And had been since they were growing up girls together. . . . Now what I'm telling you is gossip that I've heard talked, Miss Stewart, because I wasn't in the house yet when Lady Margaret was here, and I only saw her once or twice, and that when she'd pass riding or walking near to where I might be close enough for me to see her. So what I'm telling you is not truth that I know for myself, but—"

"Get on with it, Lizzie!"

"It was ma'am brought Lady Margaret here and insisted she stay. Lady Margaret's husband had been killed off in a war somewhere, and ma'am begged and begged her to come and live here. And . . ." —

Elizabeth's face had set. "How long was she here?"

"About two years, as I recall."

"Under what circumstances?"

Lizzie hesitated. "After a while, according to what was talked, I guess . . . like they got to be later . . . like . . ."

"Spare yourself and me, Lizzie! I never heard anybody try so hard to tell something by not telling it! I can guess what the circumstances were!"

"No one ever faulted his lordship about . . . her, Miss Stewart. It's God's own truth I'm saying! Nobody ever faulted him. Not the slightest bit, they didn't!"

"Very generous of them!"

"His lordship hadn't been living married—him and ma'am—since the time Master Colin came, was the talk, and so when—"

"I don't need to hear details!" The fact was that she couldn't bear to hear them. "I'm not interested in Lady Margaret!" Elizabeth suddenly went white. She took a step backward from Lizzie, as if backing off from the answer to the question she was about to ask. "These were Lady Margaret's rooms?" She thought she was going to choke.

"Yes, miss," Lizzie admitted reluctantly.

"Is that when the hidden stairway was built?" Elizabeth's voice had hard fury in it. "When she lived here? *Because* she lived here?"

"No, miss!" Lizzie said hastily. "No, Miss Stewart! The stairway was built when the manor house was built, the same as the stairs down the tower that go from his lordship's rooms to the ground. The manor house is hundreds of years old, you know, and they used to build in secret things like that. There are

stories that the Lord of Polreath who was living then
hid one of the Charleses here in the manor house and
saved him from capture and being killed when he was
in exile before he got to be king. And who's to know
but the stories might be true. His lordship's family
have always been strong Royalists . . . "

"Don't try to put me off with your fables! I'm not
interested in the political history of Polreath. That has
nothing to do with the fact that it was these rooms
that Lady Margaret lived in for two years with that
oh, so convenient stairway up to *his* rooms!"

"You're all upset about it, Miss Stewart, just like I
knew you would be."

Elizabeth took several agitated steps in one direction, and then several in another, holding her burning
face in her hands. "Go on about the headboard, Lizzie."

"Well, miss, Lady Margaret had a little dog that
she brought with her here. She always took it with her
when she traveled from her own house. She doted on
it. She kept it here in her rooms all the time. Her
ladyship is scared of dogs . . . something that happened
once years back when I was too little to know about
things going on here in the manor house, so I don't
know the full of it, nor any of it, but anyway it left
Lady Sarah scared of dogs, even little ones like Lady
Margaret's, and Lady Margaret knew it so that's why
she kept the little dog in here—so her ladyship—Lady
Sarah—wouldn't see it and have a fright . . . "

"Stop saying the same thing over a hundred times
and tell me what happened!"

" . . . One night Lady Sarah killed the little dog
with a knife. It was sleeping there on the bed where it
always slept—"

"One *night?*"

Lizzie hesitated. Then she tried to backtrack. "I'm not sure that I recall rightly that they said it was night. Now I think about it, it could have been morning they said."

"It was *night*, as you said the first time! While Lady Margaret was at the other end of that stairway!"

". . . Miss Stewart, it's finished now between his lordship and her. And what went on here was all long before he ever met you . . ."

"Don't take up for him!"

"You're faulting him when you shouldn't, miss."

"Don't cross me! Tell Thomas to take a message to the stables that I won't be riding!"

"Miss Stewart . . ."

"Do as I say!"

"You're not thinking of running, like you did the last time, are you, Miss Stewart? You'll only bring misery on yourself, and him. And all for something—"

"If I do run, I'll not take you with me to be plagued with your preachments!"

Lizzie burst into tears.

"What are you crying about?" Elizabeth screamed at her. "What have *you* got to be crying about! Go do what I told you to do!"

Lizzie brushed away her tears and went to find Thomas. When she came back Elizabeth was lying on her face on the bed, her shoulders convulsed with weeping. Lizzie went over to her. "Stop that crying now," she said. "You'll make your eyes all swollen and red." She massaged Elizabeth's shoulders gently, stopping now and then to pat her consolingly. "You'll soon be laughing about it all. You'll see."

"Stop pummeling me!" Elizabeth screamed at Lizzie. "Did you ever try to cry with somebody pounding you on the back?" she yelled.

* * *

Lord John rode with Colin, in order not to disappoint him. But they did not ride as long as usual, and he came immediately to Elizabeth's rooms when they returned from the ride. Elizabeth was sitting, stiff-backed, in her chair by the window.

"I thought I'd find you in bed, my sweet, or has your headache gone? I hope so. I'm glad if you're feeling—"

"Headache?" Elizabeth hadn't turned to look at him. Her face was as stiff as her back. She kept it turned from him and toward the window.

"Lizzie sent me a message that you had a headache."

"Ha!"

He came to stand in front of her. "What's the matter, Elizabeth? Why are you angry?"

"You thought I wouldn't find out, didn't you?"

"Find out what?"

"That these were *her* rooms! That for two years— two whole years—she—"

"That has nothing to do with you and me, Elizabeth!"

"It shows what small regard you have for me! that you would put me *here!* where she—"

"I put you here because I wanted you near me, and for no other reason!"

"And you put her here because you wanted—"

He cut her off again. "*I* didn't put her here. Try to show some sense, Elizabeth. Would you rather I had put you in rooms far separated from me? Would you like to move to other quarters? You have free choice of the house."

"You didn't offer me choice of the house before!"

"If you weren't so foolhardy in the things you do when you're in a fit of temper, I'd have to laugh, Elizabeth. Look, I'm sorry that you didn't learn from me that Margaret once had these rooms. I'm sorry that

I didn't think to mention it to you. To my mind, it wasn't important. I wasn't trying to hide anything from you."

"You don't have to explain yourself to me! I don't want explanations from you!"

"Then what is this quarrel about? I haven't seen Margaret since I saw her last in Brighton, and you know it. It's all over and done, and has been since then. I even put it in writing. I sent her a letter breaking off the friendship—"

"Ha! Friendship!"

"Why are you so stubborn, Elizabeth?" He grinned suddenly. "If I had been content to live a celibate life for the past nine years, I should think you would then have cause for worry," he said.

"How dare you say such a—a *bald* thing to me!"

"Because you push me to such limits with your unreasonableness. I have to dare."

He tried to take her in his arms, but she would not have it. She had shored up her anger with every mental image of Lady Margaret's life in those rooms—and in the ones above—that her versatile imagination could provide. Jealousy had never raged in her as it raged in her now. It had the upper hand of her completely.

"You kept everything in these rooms exactly the way they were when she was here! You couldn't bear to have a single thing changed! I can see you now, after she was gone—walking about these rooms and thinking about her, remembering her and missing her! Probably sleeping alone in the bed and wishing she were—"

"Stop this, Elizabeth!"

"Everything you see here reminds you of her! You kept everything as it was because you wanted to be reminded!"

"I could not have told you, if you had asked me, whether things were the same or not." He stood away from her and looked down at her. "I am not going to quarrel with you, Elizabeth. I will not let myself be drawn into a quarrel. I don't want to hear things said by you in anger, and I will not speak to you in anger."

"It's easy enough for you to take an above-it-all attitude! I haven't done anything to you!"

He continued to look down at her, but she would not meet his eyes. He sighed. "I'm not sure I can agree with that," he said. He sighed again. "I am going to leave you for a while," he said, "in hopes that when I come to you later you will be more calm."

When he came to her that night the door to the stairway was locked against him. He sent a note to her by Lizzie: *I must go to Plymouth tomorrow. Is this the way I am to leave you?* Elizabeth tore the note up and threw it in the fireplace. She told Lizzie to tell him that she had burned it without reading it. ❧

29

Elizabeth tossed and turned, unable to go to sleep. She twisted herself up in the covers and then threw them all off her and then snatched them over her again. Her mind was in a turmoil and her body in worse turmoil. She was not accustomed to sleeping by herself now, and her body was used to the relaxation of lovemaking, for she and Lord John never went to sleep without making love at least once. She ached with her need for him. She fell into a sleep of exhaustion near dawn, and when she awakened it was full daylight. She sat up in bed, staring frantically about her at the day that had come.

"Lizzie!" she called. "Lizzie!" Lizzie came running in from the dressing room. "What time is it, Lizzie?"

"The clock has just chimed eight, miss."

Elizabeth threw back the covers and scrambled out of the bed. "Get me dressed, Lizzie! Why did you let me sleep so late? Get me dressed!"

"He's gone, Miss Stewart," Lizzie said, as gently as she could.

"Oh, no! No, he can't have gone! He wouldn't have

left without seeing me! He wouldn't have left without saying good-bye to me!"

But she knew that he had. She sank back upon the bed. "Oh, Lizzie . . . What have I done?" She shivered as if taken by an ague. "What have I done?" she moaned. "What's the matter with me, Lizzie? What's wrong with me? How could I hurt him when I love him more than life? How could I turn him away when—"

"Because you do love him so, Miss Stewart. You're jealous of him in proportion. He'll be back, and he'll be over his hurt feelings by then. Try not to think about now. Think about when he'll be home again."

Elizabeth jumped up. "I'll go to Plymouth! I'll go to Plymouth after him!"

"He left orders special that you were not to come to Plymouth, Miss Stewart. Thomas told me that he gave strict orders to Oxford that you were not to be driven to Plymouth."

Elizabeth's hands went to her breast. She felt as if he had struck her a blow. "He doesn't want to see me. He doesn't want me near him."

"No, miss!" Lizzie said sharply. "Don't set yourself up for another one of your tantrums! He doesn't want you there because there's going to be rioting in the streets, and bloodshed likely. If you'd given him a chance to talk to you you'd know that he's gone there for the trial—"

"What trial?"

"They're trying six sailors and the mate from one of his merchant ships—*Sea Walk* I think's the name. The crew near mutinied. Did mutiny, I guess, but it was put down. They're trying six of the sailors and the mate."

A new fear came over Elizabeth, fear for Lord John's safety. "Why would that cause rioting?"

"Because, according to the man who came here to report of it to his lordship, the fault all lay with the captain, and he was deserving of worse than he got."

"What did they do to him?"

"They broke both his legs."

Elizabeth gasped.

"He'd flogged the cabin boy to death. With the cat-o'-nine-tails in his own hands, he flogged him to death!" Lizzie said vehemently. "Him a boy no older than Master Colin, or not by much if he was older! And all because he was hungry and had snitched for himself the crumbs of a biscuit that the captain had left on his plate!"

"Surely no one could be so heartless, Lizzie!"

"There's many could be, and many that are! How would you feel if it was Master Colin had been starved and beaten like that boy was?"

Elizabeth's stomach caved in at the thought of it. "Don't speak of that, Lizzie! Don't even speak of it!"

"I spoke of it so you'll know how the sailors feel, them was on the ship and knew the boy, and some of them heard it and saw it. Not only them from the *Sea Walk*, but from every ship in the harbor have banded together. They're ready to riot to see justice done. If a verdict is brought against the ones being tried—"

"But it won't be, Lizzie! His lordship would never allow it! He would never take the side of a man who has done what that captain has done!"

"*He* wouldn't, but the law might. There's no harder laws in England than them has to do with sailoring. One thing I have full confidence of—and Oxford and all of Polreath's people the same—if it comes to riot, his lordship will be the one leading the rioters!"

"Oh, my God, no! He might be hurt! He might be killed!"

"Would you want him to stand back, Miss Stewart?"

"Yes! I would! I want him safe!"

"He'll not stand back, but he'll be safe and return home safe. Oxford says there's not the man nor the mob in the kingdom can best his lordship."

"You've never seen a mob! I have! You've never been at the mercy of a mob! I have!"

"And so has Oxford, miss," Lizzie said quietly. "He came safe from it, and so did you—and so will his lordship."

"Oh, Lizzie, if I could be sure of that . . ."

"How could you not be sure of it? Could your confidence in his lordship be less than mine, or less than Oxford's, or less than anybody's in the world? It's you should have more confidence in him than any."

Elizabeth was weeping. "I want him safe home. Oh, dear God, let him come safe home. If anything should happen to him now . . . He left home thinking me angry with him, and hating him . . . Oh, dear God . . ." She rocked back and forth in her misery, her hands over her face. "I deserve what I'm feeling. I brought it on myself with my hatefulness. Yesterday I wanted to hurt him the worst way I could. He tried to make me be reasonable. I'd give my life to change things. I'd give my life if I could have back yesterday."

"That's a bargain he'd not make, nor let you make," Lizzie said. "I'm going to see to your tea and your bath now," she added briskly. "Master Colin sent word that there's something special in his plans for today for you and he'll be here early to fetch you. . . . Now, Miss Stewart, you'll not be wanting to upset Master Colin by letting him know you're in any way worried or out of sorts. If anything would be unpleasing to his lordship, that would. So brighten up your spirits now, and make yourself of a frame of mind that would please his lordship. You want to do for him all you can. So there! There's something you can do!"

"What kind of reasoning is that?" Elizabeth asked dully.

"It's a kind would please his lordship." Lizzie's voice was light, her own mercurial spirits noticeably brighter. "Do what I say, now. You've not time for sitting back and moping. Master Colin will be soon coming."

Colin did have something special in mind, something that meant a great deal to him. He'd gotten permission from his father to take Elizabeth to visit Jason. But he didn't tell Elizabeth. He had something to *show* her, he said, not tell her.

Daly had brought Colin from the gatehouse in the trap that he kept housed there along with the horse to pull it, and they rode back to the gatehouse in it. Elizabeth was beginning to have a suspicion of what the surprise was all about by the time they arrived there. When they alighted from the trap, Colin took her by the hand. "First I want you to see Guinevere," he said. "You've been here all this time and you haven't seen Guinevere yet!"

Colin led the way through the hall toward the back of the house. When they passed one door, he said, "That's their room—Daly and Mrs. Daly's."

"Their bedroom?"

"Yes. They call it the 'sun room' for a joke." He laughed, twinkling up at her. "Because it doesn't have any windows," he explained. He went on in a singsong voice, "On one side is the living room, and on one side is this hall we're in, and on one side is the storage room, and on one side is the enclosing wall," he sang. He lifted his hands and shrugged eloquently, his face an impish, smiling question mark. "So where could there be any windows?"

"It is a strange room to choose for a bedroom," Elizabeth said. "Where is yours?"

"Oh, mine's upstairs!"

"It looks from the outside as if there's room enough up there for the Dalys, too."

He didn't answer, but skipped to the back door and went springing out and down the steps of the porch and to a pen in one corner of the yard with a dog-house in the center of it.

"Guinevere! Hey, Guinevere! Where are you? Holed up again, are you?" He turned to Elizabeth who had come up beside him. "She's not like most dogs," he said. "She likes to be inside her house a lot of the time."

He said it as if it were the simplest and least meaningful sort of observation, but it gave Elizabeth a twinge. She had heard from Lord John about the other puppy.

"What does Daly have to say about that?" she asked.

"I haven't mentioned it to him."

"Hasn't he noticed?"

"No!" He spoke with emphasis. "I take care of Guinevere! It was promised me I would! But I have to tell Daly about her if she ever starts acting funny—you know, like the other one."

"I think perhaps you should tell him about her staying so much of the time in her house. Little puppies usually like to get out and run."

He twinkled up at her, his face impish again. "She's not a puppy anymore." He turned back and called out, "Guinevere! Come out and show how big you are! There she is! Come on, Guinevere! Come over here!" Guinevere came over and he petted her through the fence.

Elizabeth was amazed at the size of the animal.

"My goodness!" she said, "She's surely not a puppy. She must be full size."

"Almost, I guess."

The dog sniffed at Colin's hand and went back into her house.

"She doesn't take too much to strangers," Colin said.

"I'll have to see to not being such a stranger, I guess," Elizabeth said, "so she'll be friends with me."

"Don't be disappointed," Colin said, his little face serious. Then, as if making up to her for Guinevere's indifference to her, he said, "Anyway, I really brought you here to meet Jason!"

Elizabeth smiled down at him. "That's what I thought," she said.

He frowned at her, his black eyebrows and eyes accusing her. "You guessed my surprise!"

"I didn't really guess it. But I was hoping that was it."

"Oh! Well, all right then! If you were only hoping it!"

He took her hand and led the way and they went back inside and back along the hall. "I told him you were coming," Colin said, and started up the stairs.

When they reached the top of the stairs they were on a small landing about four feet square. There was a door facing them, and there was another door on the opposite wall in back of them. Apparently the wings on this floor were separated from each other.

Colin disentangled his hand from hers. Elizabeth hadn't realized that she had been clutching his. She had been remembering Lord John's face and voice when he had told her of how Jason had brought Colin to him.

"I'll tell him we're here," Colin said. He knocked on the door facing them and went inside, leaving the door open. Elizabeth could see part of the room. White curtains billowed outward from two open windows. There was a white wicker rocking chair facing toward the windows with a footstool of white wicker in front of it. On the wall to the right there was a heavy oak chest. There was a hand-hooked rug covering all of the floor that she could see.

Elizabeth heard Colin speaking in a low voice, but she heard no one answering him. Presently he came back to her. He took her hand and drew her inside and closed the door.

Elizabeth could scarcely credit her eyes. But they were not deceiving her. The room itself—the furnishings and hangings and other accessories—were exactly what one would expect to find in a pleasant bedroom in a pleasant and comfortable country house. It was the apparition in the bed that belied the reality of all around it. For could that be a living man lying there?

The wide-open staring eyes were gazing fixedly into her own. But they were the only part of the man that seemed alive and human.

It was not that the human form of the man was not discernible under the coverings protecting him. It was the very evidence of that form that was so distressing. It was skeletal. Of any robustness of form that might once have distinguished the man, there was no trace. There was no semblance of muscle, even wasted. There was the sharp outline of bone, from neck to stiffly jutting feet. The arms, lying outside the covers in the white sleeves of his nightdress, were extended straight along his sides. There might have been only gaunt and bleached bones inside the loose sleeves. The hands were exposed. They had been large hands. The skin that now wrinkled over the bones gave a graphic picture of the hands they had been. Working hands, rough with calluses and scars. The infinitely aged, infinitely wrinkled gaunt spidery fingers moved. Eliz-

abeth felt a start shoot through her. She stared in
fascination. Once the fingers started moving, they
didn't stop. They played a constant scrabble-scrabble.
Not as if the keyboard of a clavichord were positioned
under them, but as if they plucked the severed strings
of some broken lute. Plucked lightly and daintily. In
place, as one might run in place for exercise. For the
hands themselves never moved.

Colin tugged anxiously at Elizabeth's hand. "Aren't
you going to say hello to Jason?"

The face was a long one, on a long neck, the neck
enclosed in wasted lengthwise folds of skin. The bones
of the face thrust against the tightness of its covering
skin so strongly that one could be afraid that, even as
as he watched, the white-grayness of the sharp facial
bones would pierce the bloodless skin and so stand
exposed to the eye in unholy horror.

The hair was sparse, longish and wispy gray, and
that hair that there was, growing out of skin stretched
tightly over an elongated skull. The ears were overly
large for the head, though likely had not been before
the change that had taken place. The brow was prom-
inent. Had been before, and was the more so now.

"Leave her get her bearings, lad. She's not accustomed, as you be, to the sight o' me."

The mouth was a baleful covering over yellowed
teeth that showed like those of a skeleton when he
spoke. The lips were of the thinnest width, bluish in
hue, gray-blue in a gray face. The quality of the voice
was sonorous and full, belying the throat and the
mouth from which it came.

"It's doubting her own eyes, she be."

The large eyes were of the brightest blue. White-
blue fire blazing out of the cavernous face. The lids
were stretched tightly over the eyes so that little of
them was exposed to view. The sharp brightness of the

fire in them was in no way dimmed by the veiling lids.
The eyebrows were glowering, heavy and gray. They
were of a bushy thickness alien to the face otherwise
so wasted and deprived of any semblance of continuing vitality. Except for the fire of life in the eyes.

"It's not an apparition that you see, girl!"

There was nothing of the ascetic in the look of him,
but an aura of martyrdom was there. In the face and
in the voice, sharpened by sudden impatience.

"I'm sorry," Elizabeth whispered.

"There's no such thing as sorry, except if you be
speaking of your worth." He cackled. It was a ghastly
sound.

Colin laughed.

Elizabeth didn't.

"Jason's just making a joke," Colin said, trying to
prompt her to laugh. So she smiled for Colin's sake.

But the man had not been joking, at least not about
the reference to a person's worth. There had been an
underlying bitterness in his voice. He counted himself
of no worth.

"Colin tells me you've been to sea," Elizabeth said,
not knowing anything else to say to try to make conversation with the man, and not knowing how much
Colin knew of the story that Lord John had told her.

"Aye. I spent my life asea. When I had one."

"Jason was a sailor!" Obviously, Colin thought that
was a grand thing. "Weren't you, Jason?"

"Aye. That I was, lad."

"Next time he goes to sea, I'm going with him!"
Colin exclaimed. "I *am*, Jason!"

"I've told you, lad. I won't be goin' agin to sea."

"Yes, you will! You will! You'll get well, and when
you do—"

"I'll not live another sailin', lad."

"Don't *say* that, Jason!" Colin's voice cracked on a

sob. He ran to the bed and flung himself on the man, his arm across him, and his face pressed against the emaciated one.

"Is that what you've learned from what I've tried to teach you? Stop your crying, lad! You have to face up to things come to you! And all your crying won't stop them coming!"

"You're not going to die, Jason!"

"I told you, lad. I seen St. Elmo's fire. It come to me, a sure sign, and it beckoned. I want you ready for it, and not surprised by it, my going." The bright white eyes were staring at Elizabeth over Colin's head. "Take care of the lad when it happens," he said. "The way of my going won't be an easy one."

"I don't believe we can foresee things, Jason," Elizabeth said. "You had a dream, I expect."

"I'm charging you to take care of the lad!" Jason said, his voice sharp. "He holds you in trust and loving, so you owe it to him! You'll remember, when it happens, what I've charged you with!"

The unblinking eyes bore steadily into Elizabeth's. "The man as well," he said. "The lad's daddy. However a thing goes on the one, so it goes on the other. It's ever been so from the first. . . . Stand up, lad! You're next to smothering me! Wipe your face!"

Colin stood up and wiped his face. Then he sat down on the side of the bed and took Jason's hand.

Elizabeth went to stand by the window. What was the matter with Jason? Neither Lord John nor Colin had ever mentioned that he was a bedridden cripple. How had he come to be one? And how could he look so old? Ten years ago he had been a young and vigorous able-bodied seaman. Now he looked like an old, old man, ancient enough to be a hundred.

"I thought as you was goin' down to the cove today and bring me back the smell o' the sea," Jason said to

Colin. "What's gone with all your fine plans that you'd rather stay sittin' here sniveling?"

"I don't guess I want to go now."

"All your finaglin' o' your daddy, talkin' him into lettin' you show Miss Stewart the secret path, and you don't want to go now?"

"No."

"It was wastin' my time then, I was, figurin' out the times o' the tides for you." He raised his voice. "Are you hearin' what I'm saying to the lad, miss?"

"Yes, Jason." Elizabeth turned from the window. He was telling her to help him with Colin. "What secret path, Colin?" she asked. She made her voice animated. "A path that smugglers used to use? You have a smugglers' secret path right here at Polreath?"

Colin looked up at her. "I wonder if it could have been," he said. He became eager. "Was it, Jason? Do you think it might have been?"

"Might've. It's the only way in from the sea on this stretch o' coast."

"Maybe some of the smugglers who used Jamaica Inn for a hideout came ashore there!" Colin said. He had stood up, all excited. "What if they did? I'll bet they did! And pirates! Maybe that's how the path got to be there—pirates and smugglers made it so they could come ashore there!"

"Where is the path?" Elizabeth asked.

"It's just by Eagles' Aerie—that's just the kind of place where smugglers would want to come ashore! They might even have slept sometimes at Eagles' Aerie! Mightn't they, Jason?"

"Could be they might. Possible, anyway."

"I'll show you, Miss Stewart!" He couldn't wait to go now. He took Elizabeth's hand and pulled at her. "Come on!"

"Be remembering the times of the tides I told you,

lad. . . . And you, miss! You'll watch the lad careful, and you'll not be puttin' so much as a foot in the water, the neither of you. St. Elmo's fire that I seen come to me as warning as much as it come beckonin'."

30

"Look, Miss Stewart!" Colin was pointing excitedly. "There's a ship standing off the cove!"

Elizabeth had been paying so much attention to getting herself down the last few feet of the turnings of the path that she hadn't noticed anything but where she was putting her feet. When she was finally standing on the beach of the cove she looked toward where Colin was pointing.

"Why, so there is," she said, shading her eyes to see better, though the sun wasn't in them. "That's an ocean-going ship. Why do you suppose it's anchored there? Do they do that often?"

"I've never seen one off our cove before! It's a privateer! I'll bet it's a privateer!"

Elizabeth laughed. "And wouldn't you love it if it were! It must be one of your father's ships, come to Polreath on business of some kind."

"No, it isn't. It isn't flying my father's ensign. It isn't flying any ensign! It *is* a privateer! They fly whichever ensign suits their purposes. Jason's told me about that. They keep several aboard ready, so they can make you think they're friendly when they're getting ready to attack. If you're flying the British flag, they put up a British one—or French, or Spanish! They'll raise a British flag, I bet!"

There was activity on the deck of the ship. A small boat had been put over the gunwale and was being lowered. Elizabeth suddenly clutched Colin's shoulder. Her heart contracted with fright. A man she thought she recognized was standing by the railing of the ship. "Isn't that Mr. Hurford, Colin?"

"Hurford's on circuit of the mines with Mr. Calvin," Colin said, "and has been since the explosion at Wheal Craggen. It can't be Hurford!" It was obvious from his voice that he didn't want it to be Hurford, nor anyone he knew.

"I think we ought to go back up the path, Colin." Elizabeth didn't know why she was so frightened— perhaps it was because of the resemblance of the figure on the deck of the ship to Mr. Hurford. But Colin was right. It couldn't be Mr. Hurford. The long, thin, black-clad shape just resembled him. If she could get a close view, she'd probably laugh to see how little resemblance there really was.

All the same she didn't like their position—a strange ship in front of them, and walls of sheer rock on two sides and in back of them. "Let's go back up the path, Colin," she said, and took him by the hand to start back up. "We can watch from the top of the cliffs."

"The path's closed to you, you might say," a harsh voice in back of Elizabeth and Colin said.

The two wheeled around. A big burly man with a bushy black moustache and beard was standing a little above them on the last turn of the path. He wore a white shirt with a wide collar that was open at the neck. The sleeves of the shirt were full and the cuffs deep. He wore knee breeches of leather, and black stockings and buckled black shoes. On his head was a

black felt hat with a wide brim that was pinned up on
one side and trimmed with a long curving feather.

The man laughed. It was more a low growl deep in
his throat than it was a laugh.

Elizabeth clutched Colin tightly with both hands on
his shoulders. She looked back around toward the
ship. The small boat had covered half the distance between the ship and the cove.

"You look just like a pirate!" Colin said to the man.
His eyes were wide and blinking with his excitement.
"I've seen pictures of what pirates look like in my
books!"

"Shhh, Colin!" Elizabeth whispered. The man looked
like a caricature of a pirate to her, as if he'd put on
costume to play the part in a melodrama. Surely no
men went around in hats like that anymore.

"Did you come from the ship?" Colin asked. He was
trying to wriggle away from Elizabeth's hands.

"Else'n that or from the moon," the man said with a
sneer. His hands went to his hips with a swaggering
swing. Elizabeth's eyes riveted on his waist. A long-
bladed dagger was in a sheath that hung from his
wide leather belt and a pistol was tucked inside the
belt.

"What do you want? What are you doing here? Do
you realize you're on Polreath lands?" She was trying
to make her voice authoritative and commanding, but
she could barely speak. "What do you want?"

"You'll learn my business at my pleasure. I'll not be
telling it at yours," the man said. His eyes traveled the
length of Elizabeth as he spoke. They rose slowly back
up her body, an evil grin widening his mouth as they
did so. He opened his mouth and licked his bottom lip,
his eyes on her breasts. She shuddered. The way he
was looking at her and playing with his tongue on
his mouth told her plainer than any words could have

that in his mind his tongue and mouth were on her breasts. He continued to lick his tongue slowly back and forth across his bottom lip as his eyes moved up to Elizabeth's face. At her expression of shock and loathing, he laughed. It was the ugliest laugh Elizabeth had ever heard. Colin backed up close against her. His eyes on the man were no longer wide and excited and trustful. They were wary, the dark brows lowered.

The boat had come into the cove and two men had gotten out of it, leaving a third man in it. The two who had gotten out of the boat were wading toward the sandy beach where Elizabeth and Colin were. The three men who had come in the boat wore ragtag trousers and shirts of loose cut which left their limbs free for any movement. They were seasoned sailors.

"You'll be trespassing on Polreath lands the moment you set foot on shore!" Elizabeth shouted to the approaching men. Her warning did nothing to stop them. She felt Colin shiver and shrink closer to her. He was frightened now. Elizabeth turned again to the man behind them. "What do you want?" She tried to keep panic out of her voice because of Colin. "What do you want?" The man only laughed his ugly, jeering laugh. She swung her head back toward the silent men approaching from the shallow rippling waters of the cove. A boat that she had not seen put out from the ship was coming around the wall of rock to the right. It was from the ship because it was the same as the other. It must have been there all along but hidden beyond the wall, waiting until the other should come. The man on the path must have come ashore in it.

Elizabeth's heart was pounding from fear. Colin was clinging to her now, and whimpering. She held him as tightly as she could. She had no way to reassure him.

"I'll report you to the authorities!" Elizabeth

screamed. "Do you know what they will do to you?
You have no right to come ashore here! Your ship is
not disabled! I can see from here that it is not! You
have no right! . . ."

The man on the path stepped down suddenly to
the beach. He took hold of both of Elizabeth's arms
and pinioned them to her sides. Her arms were bent
at the elbows and she managed to keep her grip on
Colin. It was all she could do to keep from shrinking.
The man's hands felt as if they were breaking the
bones in her arms. The men from the boat were out
of the water and coming toward them across the narrow beach. They were silent, their faces set. Their
eyes were on Colin. Elizabeth gripped his shoulders as
hard as she could. She knew that she was hurting him
just as the man who held her was hurting her. Colin
was crying now, his body pressed with all his strength
against Elizabeth, his hands holding on to her skirt.
The two men were upon them.

"Let the boy go," the man who held Elizabeth said.

"No! No!" She tried to twist her arms from his grip
without letting go of Colin. Colin was crying in small
yelps, trying to back closer to her and away from the
men reaching toward him.

"Let the boy go!" the man barked. He jerked Elizabeth's arms backwards and up as if he would pull
her arms from their sockets. At the same time one of
the sailors grabbed her hands, one in each of his, in a
grip that felt as if it were crushing her fingers. Elizabeth screamed in pain. Between the two, the men
broke her hold on Colin. Colin tried to turn to face
her and fling his arms around her waist but one of the
sailors picked him up bodily and turned with him and
started back toward the water and the boat.

Colin was kicking and screaming. "Miss Stewart!

Miss Stewart!" he screamed. "Don't let them take me! Miss Stewart!" He was shrieking wildly between the words.

The sailor had let go of Elizabeth's hands and the man behind her had slid his hands to grip her wrists. She was struggling in his vicious grip. "Let him go! Make them let him go! Make them bring him back! Colin! Colin!" The man twisted both her wrists behind her back. She screamed in pain as much as in panic. "Colin! Colin!"

The man let go of her wrists and threw both his massive arms around her. He crushed his arms around her as if they were the coils of a python and crushed the breath from her lungs. As blackness overcame her, Colin's cries became fainter and fainter in her ears. "Miss Stewart! Don't let them take me! Miss Stewart!"

BOOK V

Kidnapping and Ravishment

31

Elizabeth could feel herself awakening with the coming of orgasm. She often was awakened so when Lord John was away and she dreamed of him. The dream was more real than most, and the feeling of orgasm stronger. She tried to keep from waking. She didn't want the dream to end. She felt him drive himself into her harder and faster. Her body convulsed when she felt the last powerful thrust and felt the hot wet juice of his body gush into her. She gave a strangled moan and strained her body upward as her orgasm culminated. She could feel the involuntary spasms of the muscles inside her on his organ as the nerves throughout her body relaxed. She drew a deep breath of contentment and made to stretch her arms and legs and to turn over on her side, to try to woo sleep back. . . . But she could not stretch nor turn.

She opened her eyes and was plunged into the pit of a nightmare for she thought that she was staring into the bearded face of a stranger. He pushed himself up from her and braced himself on his hands beside her head and looked down at her.

His mouth twitched in a sneering grimace. "Come

to herself in time for the fun, the high-and-mighty lady did," he sneered. "Not too much the lady to deny herself that!"

Elizabeth tried to turn her face from him, but his hands were flat on her loosened hair and she could not. She closed her eyes. It was a nightmare. It had to be!

"You should have been to yourself for the rest of it. You missed a lot, just coming to yourself for the finish." He laughed an ugly laugh. He got up from her body. Elizabeth opened her eyes, hoping against all hope that she would see the familiar ceiling and walls of her bedroom. But she saw the man slowly and casually put his limp organ back inside his pants and button the waistband. "The rest of the fun I had with you will come to you in your dreams," he said.

Elizabeth's mind had been too fogged for her to know where she was or who the man was. Suddenly everything came back to her and she tried to get to her feet. The man leaned down and pushed her to the ground. He jammed a wadded cloth against her mouth and nose. Fumes from the cloth smothered her and blackness overcame her again.

When she came to the next time, the man was gone. She was wrapped in the cloak that she had left in the large room at Eagles' Aerie when she and Colin had left there to go to the secret path. Lizzie was kneeling beside her. Elizabeth could see Daly standing at the edge of the cliff, a rigid figure staring out over the cove toward the sea. Oxford was standing a little distance away beside the straw cart. His head was bowed. His hands gripped the butt of his whip as if he strained to break it in two.

"You'll be all right, Miss Stewart," Lizzie was saying, "You'll be all right now. I'll not leave you for a minute. You've nothing to fear."

"Colinnnnnn!" The name was elongated scream that rose from Elizabeth when remembrance rushed back over her. She jerked and writhed herself from Lizzie's grasp and got to her feet and broke from Lizzie's grasping hands and ran toward the entrance to the path. Daly was there before her, in time to stop her headlong descent. She would have been killed if he hadn't been. He held her struggling form while Lizzie picked up the cloak that had fallen from her and brought it to wrap around her. Elizabeth stopped struggling with Daly. She bent over on herself, her arms against her stomach as if what she was feeling would otherwise tear her open. "No-o-o-o-o!" Her voice rose in wild wails piercing enough to reach the heavens. "No-o-o-o-o!" She raised her streaming, contorted face to the heavens. "No-o-o-o-o!" the wild wail rose again. She fell on her knees to the ground, too overcome with despair and grief to stand or even to cry his name.

The sky was a soft blue. Small white clouds, brightened by the sun, drifted between earth and heaven. The waters of the little cove were serene—and empty —as was the sea beyond them.

Lizzie wrapped the cloak more securely around Elizabeth and lifted her to her feet.

It was all too evident, the fun that the man had had with Elizabeth. When she was back in her bedroom with Lizzie—with Thomas standing outside the door in case more strength than Lizzie's might be needed— though her brain was dazed and numb, Elizabeth saw that her dress was ripped from neckline to waist and her chemise beneath it likewise ripped, and both ripped at the waist to the sides. Her skirts had not been torn and ripped but they were wrinkled and crushed and it was evident that they had been pulled up to her waist and wrinkled and crushed by the weight of the man's body falling with its pushing weight time after time upon her. Her breasts had darkening bruises all over them, and teeth marks. He had kneaded them and bitten them unmercifully. There were teeth marks on her throat and on her lower abdomen and on the insides of her thighs.

Lizzie's face was grim—and grew increasingly grim —as she bathed Elizabeth's bruised and scratched and bitten body. When she started to pat liniment into the breaks in her skin made by the man's biting teeth, she didn't warn Elizabeth. Elizabeth made no sound, not so much as a whimper. Lizzie had known that she was beyond any feeling. When she finished with the liniment, she dusted Elizabeth's body with a soft talcum. Then she dressed Elizabeth for traveling. Elizabeth lay, or sat, or stood—raised her arms, lifted a foot— did everything that Lizzie told her to do, as if she were an automaton. When she was dressed, Lizzie rapped on the door. "Go for Daly," she said to Thomas. Daly had been waiting at the top of the stairs in the great hall that led off the corridor from Elizabeth's rooms. He came to her dressing room and picked her up as if she were a child and took her down through the house and outside to the carriage. Luggage had already been stored in the racks.

Elizabeth sat upright, dry-eyed and unseeing, unspeaking, all the way to Plymouth. Daly sat watchful beside her, afraid that she might faint and topple from the seat. He held gripped in his fist an ornately carved gold ring that had been on Elizabeth's finger when they had found her. It was not Elizabeth's ring. It was the wedding ring with which Lord John had married the Indian princess.

Oxford was alone on the driver's seat. On a bed of

covers on the seat facing Elizabeth and Daly, lay Jason.

When they drove into Plymouth, the port city was quiet, but there were signs in the streets that it had not long been quiet. The mud and dirt of the main street were so trampled and disturbed that it was, in some places, impossible to tell where the street sides ended and the walks began. Broken wine bottles and flagons and other signs of drinking and debauchery littered the street and walks. Leavings of food and food wrappings were everywhere, and everywhere being set on by growling and snapping dogs, their rib structures showing under their mangy skin-coverings ample evidence of the reason for their growlings as they vied with each other for the meager scraps of food. Near the center of the town a makeshift gibbet had been erected. A corpse was still suspended from the crossbar. Drunken men were leaning against the uprights, or sprawled around them. Some macabre jokster had placed a visored cap on the back of the lolling head.

Those in the carriage were not much brought out of the misery in which they were sunk by the sight of the recent hanging.

"Be that law justice?" Oxford turned to ask Daly.

"No. Mob justice. But it was done with the law's eyes turned or there'd be others hanging beside him."

"It's the captain from the *Sea Walk* then?"

"Aye," Jason croaked, answering the question put to Daly. "Cork, by name."

"You knew him, Jason?"

"Sailed under him. If it's sympathy you're feeling, it's wasted. He's dancing now where he should've danced afore he ever set foot on a ship o' his command."

"If ye'd spoken that to his lordship—"

"He could bring a ship safe through any seas that Satan ever sent or will send," Jason said before Oxford could finish. "There was that about him, too."

If Elizabeth saw the gibbet and the body hanging from it, motionless except when one of the drunken men tugged it by the foot and set it swinging, she gave no sign that she did.

As they were passing the gibbet, Oxford had to pull up. His way was blocked by a wagon that came blind from a side street. It lumbered an ill-guided path over the ruts and rubble in the street, the reins in the hands of a gaunt black-clad woman. She was bent far forward in her efforts to guide the heavy mules in the traces, and her high black poke bonnet weaved back and forth with their plunges and halts. In the back of the wagon there was a long wooden box, a coffin. A boy sat on either side of it, hands braced on it to prevent its sliding about. Neither boy looked to be much into his teens.

"Him with tads of his own," Oxford muttered.

"Aye," Jason said, "and 'tweren't for them, she'd alone have to cut him down and box him, for there's not a man's finger will be lifted to help her."

"Poor woman. Poor woman," Oxford said and sent a ripple along his reins to set his horses forward again. &

32

"Be it I should make for dockside or for the Queen's Gate, Daly?" Oxford asked. A dread was in his voice, his own grief heavily back upon him and a mourning for the shock and sorrow they were bringing to his Lordship.

"For dockside!" Jason answered before Daly could. Whereas Oxford was sorrowful and grieving, Jason was agitated and impatient. "The *Sea Walk*'s refitted and ready, and captained a'ready, knowin' his lordship! We've no time for wastin'! Dockside!"

"Dockside, Oxford," Daly said. "It will be better if his lordship hears it in a place that's his own." His voice was heavier than Oxford's had been. To his own mind, next to Lord John, Colin was closer to him than to any. Jason would have argued the point.

Lord John wasn't aboard the *Sea Walk* when the little party boarded it. Jason was carried aboard, but Elizabeth walked. She walked with her face straight ahead of her, staring straight ahead of her. She might have been a condemned person, numbed by stupefying drugs, walking toward the execution block, from the look of her, but the fact was that she was simply doing what she was told to do and being guided to do.

" 'Tween decks!" Jason croaked. "We'll wait his comin' 'tween decks! He'll need his privacy, once come!"

And so Daly and Elizabeth and Jason waited in the low-ceilinged salon between decks while Oxford went to scout the town to find the Lord of Polreath.

Jason had been put to lie on one of the benches that lined the walls of the salon. Elizabeth sat on the bench at his feet. Daly stood at the table near the steps that came down to the salon from the upper deck. He had not moved since he had gone to stand there. Both of his hands were knotted into fists. One was on the table to his right, and the other, the one in which he held the ring, was stiffly down at his side. . . . Thus they were when the Lord of Polreath came down the steps, his feet appearing first and then his legs, then his hips and torso and neck . . . and then his face.

His face was as white as alabaster. His eyes were the color of ice. His limbs were so rigid from joint to joint that, except for propulsion outside himself, it seemed they would have been incapable of movement. His eyes were unfocused, staring into space as if he were a blind man. "I have it from Oxford," he said. "I forced him to tell me." His voice was hollow and was not recognizable as his own.

Elizabeth's eyes were on him, as were the eyes of the others. Her body made an involuntary movement toward him, and then halted in its movement, as if, in spite of her own numbed brain, she knew that she could not comfort him. It was from her that Colin had been taken. Even if that were not so—even if he were not beyond comfort—which he was—he would not want comfort at her hands.

Daly raised his left arm toward the Lord of Polreath.

He opened his hand. The ornately carved, heavy ring of gold lay upon his palm.

Lord John's face went whiter, if that was possible.

"There is no doubt then," he said. He took the ring from Daly and closed his own fist over it. "That was my first thought, and my worst fear," he said. "If it had been a kidnapping for ransom . . ."

Jason's head lifted and fell back and lifted again. His voice rasped. "The old rajah wanted his grandson back while he was still in his boyhood so he could be brought up as the prince he is!" His impatience was stronger in him than it had been. "He's got claim on him the same as you for his blood runs in him the same as yours! He's got a heritage for him equal yours for him. He's made his move. If you want that boy back, you'll make yours. Wallowin' in pity for yourself won't get him back!"

Both Daly and Elizabeth stared at Jason, aghast that he would dare to speak to the Lord of Polreath in such a manner. But it had its effect, for Lord John's eyes focused on Jason.

"Can this ship sail on the next tide?" Jason asked.

"It will," Lord John said. His voice showed some life now. It had been dull and dead before. "Is there any chance of overtaking them, Jason?"

"This is no attackin' ship! What guns she's got is little enough of defense for holdin' off attack. And if my suspicions is right, them that took Colin is sailing a fighting frigate. 'Sides that, it's too dangerous to try to take the boy on sea. You'd put him in jeopardy of his life. I say what we want to do is make all time we can and make port nigh on the time they do, so not to give them time to get him behind walls. The rajah'd not have thrown the ring in your face if he'd not been prepared with a surety against your comin'. The Red Fort's my guess. It'ud take an army to get him out of there. We've got to stop them clearing the port for inland!"

"What port would you say?"

"Surat! What other port would it be, man? Surat!"

An irrelevant thought came to Elizabeth. She remembered Colin's having said that he was going to sea with Jason the next time he went. If God were kind, Colin would sail back with Jason.

"Was the ship gunned, Elizabeth?" Lord John asked.

She didn't understand the question, and she hadn't been prepared to hear him speak to her. "What? . . ."

"You're the only one who saw the ship! Was it—"

Daly laid his hand on his arm. "Go gently with the lass, sir," he said, "She's been roughly used."

Lord John looked at Elizabeth as if really seeing her for the first time since he'd come aboard. "What do you mean, roughly used?" He started toward her. Elizabeth shrank from him and he wavered in his forward movement.

Jason halted him altogether. "This is not the time for commiserating on the ills of us here, nor the time for talk!" he said, "Gunned or not, we're going after her! There's things need doin'! You'll fly British colors, and that's all. Get every ensign of your own down and out of sight. Paint out the name and choose another. If we should come up on 'em, we don't want 'em guessin' who we are. Get topside, man! There's nothing here for you save talk!"

The name *Sea Walk* was painted out, and the name *Jason* painted on the ship. The name *Jason* for the ship was Oxford's idea. Oxford said that if the ship should pass close enough to the other on the sea, perhaps Colin might see it and see the name and guess that it was his father's ship, with Jason aboard, and that they were coming to take him from his captors and bring him home again.

Lord John stood beside Oxford, his arm across his shoulders in silent thanks and gratitude for the suggestion, and watched as the name was painted on. When it was done, he said, "That will remain her name for always."

"Ye can christen another *Sea Walk II*," Oxford said. "*Sea Walk*'s a fit name for a ship."

"The next ship of mine that's christened will be christened *Oxford*," Lord John said.

Tears came into the old man's eyes. "'Tis more honor than I ought be given," he said. "I never expected no such for meself."

"It's an honor I'm late in rendering you. This is not the first time—" He stopped, unable to finish. He pressed Oxford's shoulder. He was thinking of the time when Oxford had come to Wheal Maiden to call him home when Colin was lost on the cliffs, and of the time when Oxford had routed Hawkins from his bed and made him take up his gun and go with him to the manor house when the puppies had been brought there.

The *Jason* was larger than the average merchant ship, well over three hundred tons. There were two cabins in her wide, square stern, and two cabins on either side of the long salon between decks. She did not carry steerage passengers. All of the cabins had been booked for the passage to India. The bookings were all canceled and accommodations given in their stead on other Polreath ships. The furniture that had been put in the stern cabins by the people who had booked them was taken out and moved to the passengers' new accommodations. Furniture of Lord

John's selection was brought in for the emptied cabins. Two large double beds were brought aboard, one for each of the stern cabins; a wood-and-basketwork easy chair and a basketwork trunk for each. A high desk was put in one and a folding writing desk and folding chair in the other. A small sofa and a chest of drawers and china washbowls were placed in each, and gim-balled candlesticks. There were built-in stern lockers in the cabins under the long, steeply sloping stern windows. There were shelves along the bottoms of the windows on which the candlesticks were placed, and which could be used for books and telescopes and other objects wanted at hand. There were three win-dows in each of the stern cabins, each four panes in height and two panes in width. They would provide light and some degree of ventilation. The beams above them curved to the camber of the poopdeck, the under-side of which formed the ceiling of the cabins.

It wasn't necessary to bring aboard furniture for the cabins along the sides of the salon. They had built-in bunks with drawers for storage under them.

The luggage that had been brought from Polreath was brought aboard. Luggage for Elizabeth, Daly, and Jason had been packed and brought on Jason's orders.

Daly had been at work on his bailiff's records when Jason had sent for him.

"Things ain't right by the boy," Jason had said. "I sent him off to the cove when I never should've. I didn't take St. Elmo's warnin' strong as I should've. Be off with you to the cliffs and bring him back, for it's come to me he's in danger there."

Daly's face had gone stern and then white as he listened to Jason, for Jason never spoke to no purpose, and his words, whether prompted by superstition or

commonsense reasoning, had to be given full account.
Colin was as dear to Daly as a child could be that was
not his own. His daily life and safety were in his hands.
He was the son of the man whom Daly had been childhood servant and playmate to, and later valet to. He
had lived close by the side of the father of that son
throughout all the heartbreak and wildness of grief
that had almost wrenched his sanity from him when
he had lost the son's mother, and he had been with
him when Jason had brought the son to him. He had
seen him return to the strength of mind and will that
he had used to have, had seen purpose come back to
his life because of Colin. Lately, since he had brought
Miss Stewart to Polreath, the gaiety and zest for life
that had been his in his youth had been returning. . . .
If something happened now . . .

Daly's eyes were cold on Jason. "If a hair of the
boy's head is harmed, his lordship will have the whole
of yours for it! Why didn't you keep the boy safe with
you if you had feelings about him!"

"His lordship will need my head to think for him if
harm's come the boy, for he won't have his about him
at the first! Be off with you to the cliffs and fetch him
home!"

When Daly had returned with the grim news that
Colin had been taken from Polreath, he was in a state
of shock. Jason had no such reaction. Angry fire flashed
from his eyes. "He'll not be so easy took!" he flared out.
"Stow what'll be needed for you and myself! And
have done for the lass! Tell Oxford to harness up and
put his fastest teams to the coach. I'll see the road to
Plymouth before this hour's out. They'll not take him
to keep him! By God's stars, they won't! I didn't bring
him here and live crippled on this bed through these
years 'til now just to see him took!"

* * *

Lord John's luggage was brought from the Queen's Gate. Elizabeth's hatbox and other pieces were put in one of the stern cabins, and Lord John's luggage in the other. Jason's and Daly's were put in two of the narrow, windowless cabins on the sides of the salon. Luggage had not been brought for Oxford. He would be returning to Polreath.

Elizabeth had sat in silence at Jason's feet, watching all that was going on without seeming to comprehend the meaning of it. It wasn't until she became aware of activity on the upper deck, the running and scurrying about of sailors, who seemingly must crowd every inch of it and every foot upward of the spars, that she realized that she was about to undergo a sea voyage. She was afraid of the sea. She had made two sea voyages in her life. On one she had lost her mother and father, and on the other she had endured a storm at sea that had almost cost her her own life. Her fear of the sea was in her now, but it scarcely mattered to her. She wanted to know for herself that Lord John had Colin back safe with him, and then she didn't care what happened to her. He would never want her again, never love her again.

There were noises from the wharf and growing noise and movement on the ship. There was the creaking of wood and the whistling singing of lines and hawsers. There was the loud slapping crack of sail and the shuddering halt as the wind took them. There were calls and cries of sailors to dockhands. There was a sideways sluicing and then a forward running pull that could be felt along the length of the bottom of the ship. They were underway.

After some time Lord John and Daly came down between decks where Elizabeth and Jason were. Daly had not left Lord John's side since his Lordship had

come on board. When Lord John saw the disposition
of the luggage, he was not pleased. He silently began
to remove his luggage from the stern cabin where it
had been put. Daly hastened to help him. "Put it back
where it was!" Jason croaked. "A side cabin's fit for
me an' better than what I ever was used to! I'll get
plenty o' sight o' the sea. I don't intend spendin' me
days below here—it's topside I'll be riding! Put your
own things back where they was and where they ought
to be. I know you have in mind to put me there!"

"There likely will be weather this time of year. You
won't always be able to be on deck," Lord John said.

"That same weather that would put me belowdecks
is the same that would cause the deadlights to be put
in the windows, and that would be the worse for me,
to have windows on the sea blinded to me! Put your
own things back where they was and leave mine
where they be!"

In the end it had to be done. Jason would not give
in, and he was becoming feverish with his arguing.

33

"Do you feel strong enough to talk, Elizabeth?"
Lord John asked.

They were several days out to sea. This was the first
time that Lord John had made an approach to Elizabeth since he had moved toward her and she had
shrunk away from him on that awful afternoon when
they had had to tell him that Colin had been taken
by force from Polreath. He had rapped quietly on the
door of her cabin and had come in. Elizabeth was
sitting in the wood-and-basketwork easy chair, her
eyes on the windows, but not seeing the sea nor the
sky beyond them.

"Yes," she answered. Her voice was calm, but dull
and lifeless.

"I hope that I find you willing to talk to me." There
was great reserve in his voice and in his manner.

"Of course I am willing to talk to you."

"Jason tells me that there is nothing more that you
can tell me than what I have already learned, and that
you will not be able to be of help to us until we sight
a ship that you might be able to identify for us—but

I cannot be satisfied that there is nothing I can learn
from you until I have talked to you. . . . I hope you
understand and will bear with me."

"Of course I understand."

He stood with his back to her, staring out the
windows.

"You were the only one who saw the ship. Otherwise, I wouldn't trouble you."

"I know," she said. She knew that his need to learn
anything that he could that would help in his efforts
to get Colin back was all that had brought him to her.

"What colors were they flying?"

"They weren't flying colors."

"They must have been. Try to see the ship in your
mind, the way you saw it first. The flag probably
didn't register because it's such a normal thing to see
on a ship. Try to remember . . ."

"They weren't flying colors. Colin remarked on the
fact that they were not. That was what made him think
it was a privateer. He said Jason had told him that
they carry a number of different ensigns and put up
the one—"

"Colin noticed that there was no flag?"

"Yes."

"Then there wasn't," he said dully, finally. He believed it because it came from Colin, not because it
came from her, Elizabeth thought. He sighed heavily.
"I want to know what to look for, any identifying
things about the ship, if we should come up on it en
route, or if it should be in the harbor when we make
port. Would you recognize it if you saw it?"

"If the man is on it who was on it then—"

"The man . . . ?"

"There was a man at the rail who looked like Mr.
Hurford. I couldn't see his face from that far away,

but from his shape he looked like Mr. Hurford, and he was wearing the black clothes that Mr. Hurford wears. . . . But Colin said it wasn't . . ."

"No. It couldn't have been Hurford. But if you saw that man, you would recognize him as the one you saw on the ship?"

"I think so."

"That's at least something to go on." A little liveliness had come into his voice. "At least it's something. . . . Did you see any guns mounted on the ship?"

"I didn't notice any."

"Try again to see the ship in your mind. Gunports are something you would notice."

"I didn't notice any gunports." Elizabeth felt an overwhelming tiredness coming over her, the same kind that she had used to have when things were wrong between them, and that had so blessedly been absent from her these past months until the morning she had awakened to find that he had left for Plymouth without saying good-bye to her and thinking that she was still angry with him and hating him. It seemed to her now that that morning's awakening had signaled the end of her happiness and any hope for future happiness.

"Think, Elizabeth! Try to picture the ship!"

"I can see the railing and the man standing there. I can see them putting the boat over the side and lowering it. I can see the sailors in it rowing it across the water to the cove . . ." She didn't know how she could go on with the telling, how she could bear to live through it again by telling it. ". . . I can see the other boat coming from around the rocks to the right of us . . ."

"It's the ship itself I have to know about! The ship itself!"

She bowed her head and looked at her hands in her

lap. "I can't remember any more about the ship than I have already told you."

"Help me, Elizabeth! For God's sake!"

"I'm trying to. Don't you think I want to help you?" She couldn't speak above a whisper. "Do you think I wanted it to happen?"

"I can't hear what you say when you speak under your breath!" There was frustration in his voice, and anger with it.

She looked up, not meeting his eyes, but lifting her head. "I said I would help you if I could. Before I could get my bearings and could begin to realize what was happening, the man on the path behind us—"

"What man?"

Elizabeth felt the blood drain from her face. It felt as if it were draining from every vein in her body. She had thought that he had been told what had happened to her. She couldn't bear the feel of his eyes on her face. A terrible, unbearable guilt was on her as she remembered the convulsions of her own body under the onslaught of the man's body on hers. She bowed her head again. Even if her response had not been what it was, how could she ever face him again after he knew of the man's part? If there had been any hope that his feelings for her were still there and would come to the surface again after he had Colin safely back, all hope would be gone once he learned that her body had been defiled and forever tainted. . . . And he would have to learn it.

"What man, Elizabeth?"

". . . There was a man on the path. He wouldn't let us go back up the path. He . . ." She stopped.

"He what?"

"He held me while they took Colin . . ." She felt that she was choking on every word. "He squeezed the breath out of me . . ." She could hear Colin's cries

again, could hear his voice growing fainter as he
called to her.

"How many men were there?"

"Five altogether, but only three came ashore—the
one on the path and the two who got out of the boat
from the ship . . ."

"How were they dressed? Could you tell whose
countrymen they were?" Liveliness was in his voice
again, an eagerness, as if he saw in his questions a hope
of hearing something helpful. "Were they Indian?
Spanish? What language did they speak?"

"They weren't Indian. But other than that, I don't
know. They didn't speak. Except for the one on the
path. He spoke English—but with an accent . . . Spanish or French . . . I couldn't recognize it. It was very
slight, or might not have been one. He had an ugly,
guttural way of talking. He sounded—"

"Never mind that if you couldn't recognize an accent. I don't want guesses. They might be misleading.
Were they in uniform? Might they have been navy?"

"All of them wore a motley of sailors' garb, except
for the one on the path. He was dressed up like a
pirate—a buccaneer. Colin thought he was one . . ."

"Did he seem to be the leader?"

"I guess he was. The others seemed to be common
sailors. And it was obvious that they were under orders—from someone—him, I guess—to take Colin the
quickest way possible and get back to the ship with
him. They headed back to the ship and the man . . .
The man . . ."

She had been going to tell it all to him and get it
over with—tell him how she had been defiled and
forever tainted, and by herself as much as by the man,
for he would have to know sometime, and to put off
telling him would only prolong her agony.

But he cut her off, his mind taken over by his own thoughts.

"He hired a brigantine!" he said. "Spanish, probably!" He turned abruptly and strode to the door of the cabin. He seemed oblivious of even her presence. When he spoke, it was aloud to himself. "I must speak to Jason!"

He was out of the door and it had closed behind him while Elizabeth was still speaking, whatever she was saying now of no meaning or importance to him.

Elizabeth sat as if turned to stone where he had left her, struck the hardest blow that she had so far been struck by him. ⟡

34

"I tell you it's missing, Hurford!" Lady Sarah switched agitatedly back and forth, skirts swinging and eyes flashing. "It's missing!"

"You'll be overheard by Nonna, talking so loud," Hurford said. "Quiet yourself."

Mr. Hurford sat in a tall straight-backed chair, his long, thin legs crossed at the knees, his elbows on the wooden arms of the chair, his hands touching at the fingertips, forming a narrow triangle. He was seemingly unperturbed by the news. He and Lady Sarah were in her sitting room at her childhood home in Dunmavern in Scotland.

"Nonna is not about!" Lady Sarah snapped angrily.

Mr. Hurford leaned his head forward and rested his narrow chin on the points of his fingers, his eyes on Lady Sarah.

"Don't sit there and snicker at me! I tell you it's nowhere here!"

"Your voice, Sarah. Keep your voice down."

Lady Sarah slammed first one clenched palm into the flat of her other hand, and then that one into the first, and then clasped her hands together and wrung them. Her knuckles were white, her fingernails cutting into her own flesh. Hurford could see that he was going to have to bed her to calm her. One corner of his mouth drew up. It was not too unpleasant a prospect, bedding her. She was wild in bed, all over him, kissing and biting the length of his body. She was frenzied, taking the initiative as if she were the man, yelping like a dog and at him like a dog, as if she would devour him. She inflicted no small amount of pain. By the time she was ready for him to enter her, his body was patterned with fingernail slashes and teeth marks. The sheets were bloodied when he left them. He didn't always enter her. It wasn't necessary for either one of them. She came to climax almost immediately, once she was at him, and climaxed repeatedly during her maulings of him with her mouth and hands. If the progression of pain over his body was sharp enough and exquisite enough, he would ejaculate, and more than once. . . . He had been reluctant to enter into an affair with Lady Sarah—and had put off doing so in spite of her urgings—until frustration over his aborted dealings with Elizabeth Stewart had forced him to her bed. Had he known what waited for him in that bed, he would not have put it off so long.

He had tried to teach Sarah the use of the whip, but her interest in it was only half-hearted. She didn't get her pleasure from standing away and inflicting pain. She had to be at his body with her own. When their affair had first started, when she was still wooing him, she had let him use the whip on her, but now she wouldn't. It wasn't that she minded the pain. She didn't care how much pain he inflicted on her with his hands. She welcomed it. She wouldn't let him because her passions engulfed her like a floodtide. She went crazy with her greed. She had to grapple with him. The last time he had whipped her, she had come at him through the slashing swings of the leather thong of the whip. He had not been prepared for it and could not stop the wide, rushing, exhilarating sweep of his arm. He had struck her on the head with the leather-wrapped butt of the whip, knocking her to the floor, unconscious. He thought that he had killed her. He felt a sharper, sweeter ecstasy than he had ever felt and had ejaculated before the momentum of the whipping stroke of his arm could be halted and he could drop the whip and drop to his knees beside her to see whether she breathed or not.

After that, he had been afraid to use the whip. He would not have dared to use it even if she had begged him to. He knew that he would be driven to seek again the ecstasy that he had felt then. He sometimes lost all reason when the whip was brought up short in its vicious swing time after time by the soft quivering flesh of a cowering female form groveling at his feet. He might kill her. In the end, he knew he would, for he was jaded in his passions and it took more and more to satisfy him as time went on. He saved the whip for girls run away from the workhouse and other strays and vagrants and beggars who had no fathers or brothers to go in search of them once they were discovered missing. He'd left more than one bleeding all over her naked body and unconscious in the shadows of some rotting shed on some deserted farmstead or on the dark marsh grasses of some isolated bog. Whether they had still been breathing when he left them, he did not know. He hadn't needed to bother himself to find out. It was satisfaction enough that they seemed not to be. And once one had brought the supreme satisfaction to him, she was of no further use to him. He couldn't get it from her again.

Lady Sarah's voice brought Hurford out of his pleasant recollections. She stood before him, hands planted on her hips in the attitude of a belligerent, carping fishwife. Anger and threat were in equal portions in her voice.

"If it gets in the wrong hands, it will be more your loss than mine! You'll wind up with nothing!"

"Hardly, Lady Sarah. Whatever happens—in any event—I will wind up with half of what is yours."

"You'll be dead, and little good it will do you! You'll hang! Once your part in things is known, you'll hang!"

"And you. . . ?"

"I'm a Howard and the wife of the Lord of Polreath!" Her voice quavered as she said "wife," but it came out all the stronger to cover up the quaver. "No one would dare touch me!"

"Higher heads than yours have felt the block."

"These are not the days of the Henrys!"

Mr. Hurford leaned his head to his hands and bit at the tips of his fingers, showing his teeth as he did so and smiling slightly. His eyebrows raised in points as he surveyed the woman before him. He knew how to set her quivering with passion, inflamed and unmindful of anything except the cravings of her body. But it was not yet the time. He pushed himself up from the chair, to break the spell that he had begun to cast over her. He moved a few feet away from her and turned to look at her.

"What is in the letter that it is of such great matter to you?"

"You know what is in it!"

"I want to know in detail."

Her sharp eyes narrowed on him in suspicion. "Why do you ask to be told something that you know?"

"I told you. I want the details."

"What makes you pretend that there are details in the letter that you don't know?"

He shrugged and raised his hands, palms upward. "Perhaps there are none."

Her eyes slitted even narrower and accusation came into them. "You're trying to put me off!" she said, coming nearer to him and confronting him. "You have the letter!"

He made a deprecating gesture. He didn't answer the accusation.

She leaned toward him. "You have the letter!" she repeated, her voice an infuriated shriek.

Hurford pushed her aside with a backward brush of his arm and walked a few feet away from her. "Don't go off ranting half-cocked," he said. "How would I have come by it? You had it safely with you when you left London, did you not? You had it safely with you when you left Oban for Mull, did you not?"

She was sure that he had the letter. His complacency about it told her that he did.

"I had it safely with me when I left London, yes. I can't say the same for when I left Oban." She spaced her words deliberately. "The last time I saw the letter was when I was with you last, when you came to me at Lord Mowbray's at Mellonwood. I'm sure you will remember that you insisted that I should assure myself that it was safely where it should be in the leather sheath in my writing case. It *was* there. The leather sheath was in my writing case when I left Ogan, but *whether the letter was in it,* I do *not* know." Her eyes became like needles. "In fact, I think I *do* know," she said. "It was *not* there!"

He smiled at her. His smile was triumphant. "Evil match evil, evil catch evil," he said.

Sarah's breath hissed between her teeth. She was too furious with him to speak.

"I thought you were too clever for that, my dear Sarah," Hurford said. "In truth, you must take yourself in hand and learn to be as clever as I had thought you. You would have given me your soul's last secret that night, if I had demanded it. What if there should happen in your path another man who can serve your body as well as I? You would do the same for him."

"How dare you!"

His mouth became hard. "If my neck is ever put in a noose," he said, "it will not be by reason of betrayal by a woman whose pantings after lust blind her to everything except satisfying that lust."

"How *dare* you!" She struck out at him, but he caught her wrist before the blow landed.

"I took the letter that night," he said, "while you lay swooning on the bed still in your raptures! Any other man could have done the same!" His voice was facetious at first and then sneering and contemptuous. His thin lips curled and his cold eyes bored into hers. "Do you think I'm such a fool that I don't know that?" His fingers tightened on her wrist like iron claws ready to snap the narrow bones of it.

She cringed before him, passion beginning to rise in her. "There would be no other man," she whimpered.

"I have no guarantee of that! Or, that is to say, I had none. Now I have!"

"There could never be anyone else!" She reached her free hand toward him and tried to move her body close to his, but he held her away. "Don't torture me," she begged, her voice still a whimper. "Be good to me. Don't torture me."

"Control your lust and keep your reason about you!" he sneered. "We have matters to discuss.'

She continued to whimper wordlessly. His grip tightened savagely on her wrist. The pain drove her to her knees. My God! Hurford realized he had brought on the very thing he had wanted to prevent. She was going into a frenzy of lust. He threw her backward away from him as she made a grab for his knees. She fell on her back, and he felt a danger from himself, for his own lust rose at the sight of her helpless on her back at his feet.

"Stand up! Get up!" He was beating back the drivings of his own body as he tried to beat back the drivings of hers. "Control yourself! Control yourself or I will leave you alone with your insatiable cravings!"

"No! No! Don't go!" Sarah rolled over and pushed herself up on her hands and knees. It was all Hurford could do to control himself when he saw her on her hands and knees. He itched for the feel of the whip in his hand. He could feel, almost as if it were happening, the snapping of the whip against the buttocks reared before him, could see the skirts that covered it slashed to ribbons and the blood rising in the welts and cuts in the white flesh. He had to tear his eyes from the sight and turn his back to her until she was on her feet again.

"Don't go!" she repeated. She was breathing hard, but making every effort that she could to bring herself under control. She knew that he had not made an idle threat. He would leave. But if she did what he demanded that she do—if she kept herself in hand for now, until they had discussed whatever it was that he wanted to talk about—then . . . She slowed her breathing and showed every evidence of composure. She moved to her writing desk and picked up her fan that was lying on it. She fluttered it casually back and forth at her throat as she walked to the window. "Would you care for tea? Or a sherry, perhaps?" she asked.

She gazed out upon the scene before her, the wide, flat lawn stretching to the still water of the loch. It was near noon, but it seemed more like the first hour

of dawn that awakens daylight. The skies were gray.
The day was gray. The air was dank and chill. There
was a stillness over everything—the grass, the leaves
and limbs of the bushes, the gaunt bareness of the
limbs and trunks of the trees, the hard pungent green
of the firs. The water of the loch was as flat as a mirror and glimmered through the gray and mist of the
day as if backed and silvered like the glass of a mirror. She heard Hurford stir behind her, heard him
move to resume his seat in the chair. She knew that he
did not want refreshment. She did not expect an answer to her question. She had asked it only to give
him proof that she had her senses about her, that her
reasoning was clear and that she was ready for conversation.

"What is your latest news from Polreath, Lady
Sarah?"

"The same as that I sent you in my message—that
he has her there with him and has had since he sent
me here to Dunmavern and took her back with him
there."

"I have later news."

She turned to face him. What was it she had heard
in his voice? Urgency? Gloating? "What later news?"

A sardonic smile thinned Hurford's mouth. "The
light of his life has been kidnapped from him."

"Kidnapped? By whom? Who knows that she—"

"Not *she!* Colin!"

Sarah's hand flew to her throat. "Oh, my God! He'll
think I did it! He'll kill me!"

"He doesn't think you did it—or had it done. The
boy's grandfather, the maharajah, had him taken from
Polreath. He left token that it was his doing—the wedding ring from his daughter's finger that your *loving
spouse*"—he sneered the words—"had placed there."

Sarah sagged against the frame of the window in

relief. "Thank God there's proof it wasn't my doing," she said.

"Don't feel so confident that you're out of it. You may be in it the worse!"

Sarah paled. "What do you mean?"

"He's on his way after him! To India!"

Sarah's pallow deepened. "He swore he would never return." She felt strangled. "He has always sworn that he would never return to India."

"I'm sure that he meant the vow when he made it. But nothing could keep him out of India, and Colin there. He's gone to fetch him back and you can be sure that he'll turn heaven and hell to get him."

"But if that's all it is—if it's only Colin—if that's all his mind is on, then what is the concern there? Why . . ."

"*She* is with him!"

Sarah clutched the frame of the window behind her. "Are you sure? Maybe your information is wrong. Maybe—"

"My information is not wrong. She is with him."

"Even so. She came here from Calcutta. His lordship was stationed in Bombay and Delhi. The whole country of India lies between." She was trying desperately to find relief from the fright that had come upon her.

"His lordship put me hard to task once about her origins," Hurford said. "He was determined then to find out who she is. It's likely that he still is. I've never known him to put a determination aside, even if he's years in the carrying out of it. Where better to look for information on her origins than in India?"

"But they're dead! The Reverend and Mrs. Stewart are dead!"

"What, my dear Sarah, if the return to the scenes of her childhood awakens her memory?"

"She won't be going to Calcutta! The brat wouldn't be taken there, he'd be taken to Baglidore. That's to the west, according to information that I have from you yourself."

"All very true, but the Marathas are not famous for staying within their own borders. The Rajah Sirijavi could be anywhere, although I will grant that it is not likely that he is as far east as Calcutta."

"I think you are needlessly trying to upset me."

"I'm simply pointing out to you your position."

"*And* yours!"

"Not necessarily. I have alternatives."

"Indeed? And they are . . . ?"

"In due time, Lady Sarah. In due time."

She tossed her head. "If you think to frighten me and threaten me, you are mistaken to think you can. As I said before, the Reverend and Mrs. Stewart are dead, and they—"

He interrupted coldly. "The solicitor who handled the transfer of funds for Miss Stewart's keep in England is not dead. And he has known through all the years how the conduct of her affairs was proceeding. Until Miss Stewart graduated from the school, he had a report yearly from his partner in London who met the ship in Plymouth and took Miss Stewart in hand when she arrived there. There are three people who know for certain fact that she was put on the boat in Calcutta and that she arrived safely here and was safely lodged at Miss Holybrook's school."

"Three. . . ?"

"The London solicitor's wife met the ship with him when Miss Stewart arrived in Plymouth." His tone became sarcastic. "To lend a woman's mothering touch, I would assume."

"But they don't know but what the Stewarts were her parents! They don't know—"

Hurford slid an envelope from the pocket of his coat. It was old and yellowed and spongy from much handling. Lady Sarah recognized it before she saw it fully. It was a letter that she had received from a Reverend Stewart, probably on the same day that Elizabeth Stewart had been enrolled in Miss Holy-brook's School for Young Ladies. The letter had trav-eled to England on the same ship on which Elizabeth Stewart had traveled to England.

"The information in this letter, Lady Sarah, is not the sort that is of such small importance that it does not require to be put in duplicate. We should never have stopped in our efforts to find out where that du-plicate was—in whose hands—and get it into our own . . ."

He stopped. There was no good in recriminations. He had had the issue out with Sarah many times be-fore, cautioning her that just such a day as the one now upon them might come to be. Reminding her of that fact would not solve the problem nor in any way ease his anxieties. He drew the letter from the enve-lope. He unfolded it and read, beginning his reading at a point halfway through the second page, " 'I would have sent this plea to Lord Moulton himself, if I could have done so in conscience. But I swore on my oath to the child's mother that I would not make known to him the whereabouts of the child. What her reasons were for keeping the child from her rightful father, I do not know, for she would not tell me. She came to me as a man of God, in repentance and confession, but for her sins only and not to lay before me any sins against her. Perhaps you know the reason for the quarrel between Lady Moulton and her husband. If you do, I will leave it to your judgment as to whether to intercede with him on behalf of his daughter. The child is undeserving of having her rightful heritage taken from her. She is, and ever has been, and will be until she comes to the age of reason, free of any guilt and should not be penalized for the sins of others.' "

As he read, Lady Sarah sank farther and farther within the recess of the window. None of the words that he read were new words to her, but the dread that they brought came ever anew to her each time that she was reminded of them.

Hurford's voice was relentless. "This letter states without equivocation that Elizabeth Stewart is, in fact and in truth, Rosamond Howard, the legitimate daughter of Lord Moulton, and as much a rightful heiress of Clarwicke as you, my dear." He stood up. He folded the letter and put it back in its envelope and returned the envelope to his pocket. "Do you think that there is not a copy of it somewhere?"

Sarah tried to find strength in the argument that she had always put forth. "The Reverend Stewart was a minister, as he says in the letter—a man of God. He was not a businessman. It would not have occurred to him that a copy need be made. And the letter was written in confidence to me. There is no duplicate!"

A sardonic, triumphant, complacent look came over Hurford's face. "I hope that what you say is true. I hope that I worry myself needlessly, and that you are right and I am wrong. I will concede, as I have before, that there is reason and logic in your contention. . . . In that case, my dear Sarah, I have sole possession of proof of the truth. So, my dear Sarah, whether you inherit from the Earl of Clarwicke depends upon my whim."

Lady Sarah's lip curled in scorn. "It depends upon your greed, Hurford! And since it does, the inheritance is vouchsafed to me! You will never reap a farthing of it except through me!" She snorted in derision. "You will not divert it from me!"

"Lord Moulton has mourned his daughter since the day she was taken from him. You are as well aware of that as I. More so. You know from your intimacy with him how often her name is upon his lips. You know of the good he squanders on orphans in hopes that the good will be returned in measure to his Rosamond. You know better than I can tell you what it would mean to Lord Moulton to have his daughter returned safe to him. . . . What, my dear Sarah . . ." A slow, confident smile thinned his lips. There was a threat in it. ". . . I told you that I had alternatives. . . . What, my dear Sarah, do you think his daughter's safe return to him would be worth to Lord Moulton—in far-things. . . . ?" He repeated the word she had used sarcastically.

"You wouldn't! You wouldn't dare! I would expose you for fortune seeker you are—for the would-be murderer you are! I would expose your part in his lord-ship's accident at the mine. I would expose your part in the ambush by the tinners! I would expose every-thing! Everything, I tell you!"

Hurford shrugged nonchalantly. He was not touched by her threats. His manner became brisk. "As a busi-nessman I prefer the arrangement that I have with you. Of course, it lacks the humanitarianism that my going to Lord Moulton would show, but then it has other compensations . . . for both of us . . . Does it not, Lady Polreath?"

Sarah felt her loins tighten hotly and a trembling start in them and spread throughout her. She stood up from the windowsill that she had been leaning into.

"Not so eager!" Hurford barked. "We have not reached terms!"

"What do you mean? What terms?"

"It doesn't seem to have come to your recognition, my dear Sarah, that you no longer hold the ante."

"What are you talking about?"

"I'm talking about this. I can take my chances that there is no copy of this letter—" he tapped his pocket "—and that Elizabeth Stewart's memory will remain blank as to her origins. In the case of those two eventualities, I will share your inheritance *in equal parts* with you when it comes to you. . . . Or, without taking any chances, I can go to Lord Moulton with this letter and reap a handsome reward for the doing. If I decide to hazard my chances, I will require further recompense."

"More than half? You must be mad!"

"Merely a good businessman. I know the worth of what I hold in bargain."

"What more are you asking?"

"I haven't decided yet. It may be the Polreath lands that will strike my fancy . . . Or the mines, perhaps . . . Or both. I've not thought much as regards the fleet. But perhaps . . ."

"The Polreath inheritance will not come to me!"

He lifted his eyebrows. "To whom then, pray, if there is no *Master Colin* to inherit?"

Sarah turned from him. She didn't want him to read anything in her face that might give her away.

"The Lord of Polreath has no other possible heirs," Hurford said. "His son . . . and his wife . . . And if there is no son . . ."

"There is very much a son! And very fate seems to stand on his right hand in protection! All of my attempts to get rid of him have failed!"

"So far your attempts have been inept and amateurish. And that business on the boat with Miss Stewart showed even less finesse!"

"If you had not already failed in attempts of your own, I would not have had to make one!"

There was a pause, and then Hurford said, "We are

speaking of things a little off the point. Both Master
Colin and Miss Stewart will be taken care of. When
they have been taken care of, the Polreath holdings
will be as clear in title to you as those of Clarwicke—
on my sufferance, of course."

Sarah kept her face turned from him. A secret triumph of her own had come over it. He would not miss
it if he should catch a glimpse of her expression.

"Well, Lady Sarah? Do you accept my terms?"

"I haven't heard your terms."

"My terms are the right of choice of what I would
have of the Polreath inheritance."

Sarah smiled, keeping her face rigidly turned from
him. She made her voice sound grudging. "You leave
me no choice," she said. "I have to accept your terms
whether I would or not."

"Now that we understand each other," Hurford
said, "we will put business aside. I feel a need of relaxation." He came up behind her and took her waist
in his hands and crushed it between them and then
took handfuls of flesh in a vicious grip, his fingernails
like knives through the layers of her clothing, his hands
twisting as if he would tear the flesh from her.

Before she would let herself give in to him, Sarah
said, "The Polreath inheritance will be long leaving
the hands of its present lord. You may not live . . ."

His hands released her waist and moved to the front
of her body and took hold of her breasts, cruelly
clenching and tightening upon them, finger and thumb
pinching the nipples while she gasped and writhed and
sagged in pain against him.

"Mining is a dangerous business," Hurford said. He
held the writhing woman upright against him, his
hands gripping ever tighter on the softness of her
breasts, his fingers and thumbs on her nipples pinching
and twisting. Her moans were mingled with keening,

low-voiced screams. "Is it not, Lady Sarah?" He flung
her to the floor away from him. He watched her turn
to him, her face avid and working, her eyes gleaming
with lust and craving. He stood where he was while
she crawled to him. He felt in himself a hotter lust
than she had caused in him since the last time with
the whip. When she grabbed his knees and started
crawling up his body to bring herself to her feet
against him, he reached down and jerked her up by
the arms. The marks from the grip of his fingers would
be visible on her arms for days. He turned her and
pushed her before him toward the bedroom. She would
get worse from him now than he had ever gotten from
her! If it gave her more the pleasure, then that was into the bargain. Whatever her pleasure, it would be in
small measure compared to that he intended to take!

35

Mr. Hurford and Lady Sarah were alone at breakfast. Lady Sarah had dismissed the butler and the footmen after they had been served.

"What do you think we should do, Hurford? We have made no plans."

"If fortune smiles on us . . ." He broke off and laughed. The sound was more bark than laugh. ". . . If *fortune* smiles on us, we won't have to do anything. A squall will take the three of them as they sail happily homeward."

"Your attitude little suits you!"

"Levity does not become me?"

"This is not the time for it!"

". . . Or you prefer another attitude from my part?"

"I have never known you to be so vile!"

He laughed the short bark again. He was well pleased and well content this morning. His body was still sated with the pleasures of the long night before. For the first time he had driven Lady Sarah to beg for mercy, to beg for rest instead of for more. But he had given her no rest, not the long night through. That she had been able to stand on her feet that morning was a miracle. A woman of lesser strength would have had to keep to her bed for a fortnight. And even she showed exhaustion in the lines of her face and the drooping of her body. Yes, he had mastered her. Too bad, in a way. He would never be able to wrest from her body more pleasure than he had wrested from it the night before. The danger was that he now might tire of her . . . Well, if he did, he would put her off when he could and take her when he had to. It was all a matter of business. He would protect his investment to whatever degree he must.

"Please speak seriously with me, Hurford. You don't realize how hard it is for me, far away from things, being here in Scotland and not learning of things until well after the event. I pass my days not knowing what is going on with you wherever you are, not knowing what is going on at Polreath . . ."

"Nothing prevents your returning to Polreath. Lord Moulton has been gone from there since a month after you left for London."

"I am prevented. He prevents me. In the press of other things, I forgot to tell you that my uncle has been here to talk with me about the girls. He is well enough satisfied for me to to have them with me as long as I am home here. If I bring them back to Cornwall, he wants them with him at Baloorin."

"Then you must remain here if you want to keep them with you. I agree with you on that. In fact, I insist upon it. Either keep them with you here, or give them over to Baloorin upon your return to Cornwall."

"I will not give up the girls!"

"There's no need to become heated. You have no argument from me on the point. What I am saying is that it would not be wise to go contrariwise to Lord Moulton's wishes regarding the girls."

"I could take his dictates concerning them more

easily if he had any claim to them. But he has *none!*
None whatever!"

"He is godfather to them."

"He has no blood claim to them!"

Hurford was thoughtful for a moment. "There might
be a way there that has never occurred to me. There is
no way, is there, that the inheritance could bypass
you and go to the girls?"

"No! They are not Howards! I call them my nieces,
but they are first cousin to me. They are the children
of my mother's sister."

Hurford's face cleared of the worried look that had
come over it. "Why has it suited you, up to now, to be
dark about the connection?"

"I have not been dark about it. It hasn't come up for
mention before now."

"You have been dark about it, and I will tell you
why. If it were known that Lord Moulton's concern
for the girls was toward two who are not blood-related,
support would be lent to the contention that some hold
that you are one of the 'mad Howards.'"

Lady Sarah's face whitened and the lines in it deepened. She did not become angry as he had expected
that she might. She simply looked more tired and exhausted.

"I am not mad," she said.

"Whether you are or not is of little matter to me.
What matters to me is that we have the truth clear
between us." His eyes grew cold, all levity gone from
them. "I have to know what I am dealing with, and the
whole of what I am dealing with! What other secrets
have you?"

Lady Sarah's lips trembled when she tried to speak.
She felt that he could see into her mind, and would
know the lie for the lie it was when she uttered it.
"None," she said.

She waited for him to throw the lie back at her, but he did not. He seemed to accept it—at least, for then.

"Keep in mind for now and for the future, that I will deal with you only if there is full and open truth between us," he said.

"I have no reason to keep anything from you."

"See that none arises!"

Lady Sarah sighed. She lifted her cup of tea, but before she touched it to her lips, she returned it to the saucer. The effects of the tortures of the night before and her present mental stress were causing a weariness almost to paralysis to come over her mind and body.

"You spoke earlier of making plans," Hurford said. "We have no need to hurry ourselves to do it. We have time to relax and think and let things come to us. His lordship and the others will be long coming back to England. We've no need to rush to put together ill-advised schemes. That has been our failing up to now —the reason for our several failures." He took pity on her to the extent that it was in him to take pity on anyone. "Consider that you have been given respite, Lady Sarah. They will be months away."

"I wish they would never come back," she said. "That was what I thought we might do something about. That would solve everything."

"Yes. As I said before myself, it would. But we cannot bring that about. It would take the intervention of providence. . . . Or did you have in mind that I trail them to India? If anything so preposterous *has* been in your head, then I must agree with those who think that indeed you are mad. India is not a lawless jungle. Murder is no more easily accomplished there than in England, and no less harshly dealt with. If such idiocy—"

Anger flooded Lady Sarah and gave her strength. She rose from her chair. "Watch your tongue! Have a care for the words you use in my presence. I'll not listen to talk of murder! I'll not listen to talk of idiocy! Have a mind whom you address! You are a common man in my husband's employ, and nothing more than that! I have suffered you to speak to me as an equal, and you have repaid the condescension on my part by overstepping the bounds. In future, you will keep to your place!"

Hurford had not risen to his feet when she arose, and he did not rise now. He rested against the back of his chair and watched her silently while she railed out her tirade against him. When she had finished, he said, "Sit down, Lady Sarah."

"I will sit when it pleases me to do so, and not on your order! How dare you sit in my presence!"

His eyes remained on her. He relaxed farther into his chair. "Sit down, Lady Sarah."

She snapped her face away from him and walked on rapid, agitated feet to the broad windows.

"It is long past the day when you could take on and put off the attitude of the lady-born with me, Lady Sarah," Hurford said. "When I've the time for it, I rather enjoy your airs and condenscensions, but I've no time this morning. I want a full day's journey behind me before nightfall tonight."

Lady Sarah swung around. "You're not leaving today!"

"I am."

"You promised me! You said you would keep with me for a fortnight!"

"That was before I came here and before I had completed my business there. My plans have changed."

"But why! What have I done?"

He let out an exasperated breath. "You're beginning to bore me with your vagaries of mind. Sit down, or else I will leave without further word with you!"

Lady Sarah returned to her chair and sat down. Her eyes were hurt and accusing. "What harm would it do you to stay for a while with me?" she asked. "How much time have I asked of you in all the time I've been here? . . . I have no one else . . . I'm lonely. No one else knows me as you do. You're the only one in the world that I can speak to freely. You—"

"Spare me your whinings, Sarah. I cannot idle here for two weeks with you. There are things important to us both that need doing. I go directly from here to Plymouth. The lugger *Spindrift* sails in eight days' time. She can overtake the *Sea Walk*, winds favoring, I'm told. We need an eye on—"

"His lordship sailed on the *Sea Walk?* But that's a merchant tub!"

"That may be, but that's what he sailed on. There's no ship safer. Perhaps his lordship was more concerned with getting there safely than with the time spent in doing it. What good would he have been to Colin shipwrecked in some gale? . . . Incidentally, the *Sea Walk* sailed as the *Jason*. Touching, don't you think? Also incidentally, I failed to mention, I believe, that Jason is aboard."

"Then they will be successful," Lady Sarah said in a flat, dull voice.

"Don't be stupid. If anything, Jason will only hinder them in their movements. A crippled man to cart about . . ."

"They will be successful."

"If you want to entertain your superstitions to do with Jason, do so, but don't take up my time with them. . . . As I started to say, we need an eye on their doings, insofar as we can keep one on them. I have hired a man—a sailor who has lost his papers and can't get berth on any ship in any port in Britain. He's a man of some years who knows the ports of India and has some knowledge of the inland parts of the country. He has spent time on a brigantine. He is well qualified for what we need him for. He is sailing on the *Spindrift*. I want to have another talk with him before the ship sails. . . . I thought that news might comfort you."

"I would feel more comforted if I thought his qualifications included more than acting the spy."

"Perhaps they do, Lady Sarah. Comfort yourself with thinking that perhaps they do."

"But you said before that it's no different in India than it is in—"

"I was speaking of yourself and me, Lady Sarah— yourself and me, not the good man Luke Balsam."

Sarah's face brightened, and a crafty, appreciative light came into her eyes.

"I thought that news would please you," Hurford said. "And I have yet a further stroke for you. Years back Balsam sailed with Jason. Knows him well, and better than he would like to. Jason testified against him, played no small part in his losing his papers and losing all chance of ever having them restored. I'm sure that I need not add that Balsam holds no love for Jason." &

36

When Elizabeth had sailed from India to England when she was a child, she had not even been aware that there was such comfort to be had on a sailing ship as that in which she traveled now. Then, she had been one of the mass of humanity—men, women and children—crowded together in the narrow space of the intermediate cargo deck. Her living—and sleeping— quarters had been a rough box berth nailed together from softwood. It was a piece of temporary construction, as were all the others. There were tiers of three crowded on the walls on each side of the cargo deck. The aisle between was so narrow that two could not walk along it side by side. The berths were not any wider than a healthy man's body, and a man of even medium height could not sit upright in one but must sit bending over while he dressed or undressed—and the extent of that was to take off or put on his shoes and outer coat or mantle. The headroom of each berth was less than two feet.

There was no furniture. The life that was lived in the cargo deck was lived in the berths—the children played at their games in them, the women mended or strained their eyes in the dim light at petit point, the men talked and argued and drank what spirits they had brought with them or could come by. What space there was along the aisle was taken up with the traveling chests and barrels and boxes of the passengers. There was no room to store them under the bunks for the bottom ones were built flush to the floor. The passengers drove pegs into the walls and into the uprights of the berths and everything imaginable hung from the pegs and from the bulkheads—garments and hats and baskets and bundles. Cooking utensils and tea-making equipment sat about on the boxes and barrels. She remembered the smell of the cramped space as vividly as she remembered any of the rest of it—the smell of human bodies that hadn't been washed since the journey had begun, the smell of cooking food that was being cooked in air still cloyed with the smell of foods previously cooked, the smell of chamber pots that were not emptied until full to the lids and were never washed, the smell of vomit that could not be scrubbed from the spongy, always damp wood of the floor.

She remembered her aloneness in all that crowded humanity. There had been others traveling on the ship who were not a part of it. On the few times when she was allowed on the upper deck she would see them taking the air at the railing or walking about in the little space that there was for walking. They had accommodations somewhere else on the ship but she didn't know where nor what they were like, but she knew that they must be better than those she was acquainted with. It was obvious from the look of them.

She remembered four people who were not cargo-deck passengers. There had been a man and his wife. They always looked freshly bathed and dressed, and satisfied and smiling as if they had just come from a well-laden dining table. Elizabeth imagined that the way they were traveling was the way she had traveled when she had been a passenger on board ship with her mother and father. She liked to imagine her mother and father looking as light-hearted and happy and smiling as the man and his wife looked to her—and from the stories she had been told, that was how they had looked and been.

Besides the man and his wife there had been a man —two men, but only one had made an impression on her. When she would see him he would be standing at the rail, gazing in the direction from which they had come, morose and silent, or he would be striding the deck, wrapped in a long black cape with high upright collar that shadowed his face, a black-brimmed hat pulled low over his brow, and always, standing stiffly at the rail or striding the deck, morose and silent. The other man was always close beside him or following close behind. Even so, the tall, angry man—as she thought of him—in spite of the man always with him, seemed to her as turned within himself and as lonely as she was. He had been on the upper deck when a storm had hit suddenly and without warning. It had come first from the sea itself and then the wind and rain had come. A wave had washed the deck and, except for the quickness of the man in reaching her, it would have taken her back to sea with it. After that, when she was on the upper deck he would always appear. He wouldn't speak to her, but he would keep a watchful eye on her until she was safely down from the deck.

He hadn't been about when the ship had landed at Plymouth. She had looked for him. She had felt more familiar with him than she had with any of the people with whom she had lived in the cargo deck. She had wanted to see his familiar figure, simply because it was familiar, and the place where she had come was strange and alien. She also had wanted to see what his face looked like, for she had never really seen it. His cloak and hat had shielded it from view—what view there was, for the entire passage had been made in dull and stormy weather. Fog and mist had obscured everything. She remembered him as a dark and shadowy form of a man whose black cloak billowed about him in the storm-driven winds.

While she was standing with her traveling trunk beside her, looking around for him, a man and woman had come aboard the ship asking for her. They had been appalled to learn the conditions of her travel. The captain of the ship had been apologetic. The space had been preempted, he explained, on very short notice, by the owner. A berth in the cargo deck was all that he could secure for the child. He would have left her to be assigned cabin space on a vessel sailing at a later date, but he had understood that the overriding consideration had been that she sail immediately. She had suffered no neglect, he assured them. The steward had attended her every need. The man who had come for Elizabeth had demanded immediate return of funds—the difference between the amount that had been paid for cabin passage for her and the amount chargeable for berth passage in the cargo deck. The captain, grudgingly, and with marked ill humor, had made refund.

"I am not unaware of the methods by which ship's captains are wont to fill their purses!" Elizabeth heard the man who had come for her say as the lady who had come with him led her down the gangplank. "This incident will be reported to the owner of your vessel!"

"I will remind you, squire," the captain returned,

"that it was the owner himself who preempted her space."

That voyage stayed ever-present on Elizabeth's mind as she traveled now in the comfort of her cabin, sitting most always in the easy chair with the tall, sloping windows before her giving her long and slanting views of the sky and the bright white clouds, the sea, and the playing spray. She had been miserable and alone on that voyage. She had thought then that she would never be more miserable nor more alone. But she was. She was more miserable and more alone in her present comfort than she had ever been in her life.

Elizabeth spent almost all of the time alone in her cabin. The steward brought her fresh water every morning and brought her tea and her meals on a tray. For the first week she had been too ill and weak and sore in her body to be up from her bed or from her chair. Finally the soreness had left her body, but her spirit stayed as bruised and damaged as it had been. There was nothing that she could do to restore it, and nothing that *he* would do.

During the first several days after he had come the first time, Lord John came to her cabin often to question her, to ask new questions, and to ask again questions that he had already asked her, as if hoping that her memory might dredge up something that had not come to her before. Each time he came, she had to endure the knowledge that she was failing him. He came to her for help, and there was no help that she could give him. His visits became more painful to her than his absence. She became convinced that he did not believe her, that he thought she was keeping something back from him. She even began to wonder if he thought that she had been one of the conspirators who

had taken Coliin from him. Finally, during one of his
visits, her nerves had splintered under his relentless
questioning and she had screamed at him, "Why do
you come to me to badger me with questions when
you don't believe the answers I give you!"

"I should think you would understand why I come,
Elizabeth," he had said quietly, and had left her. He
had not come back.

After Lord John stopped coming to her cabin Daly
came twice daily to inquire if there were anything
she needed or wanted. There was never anything she
wanted. He would stand about for a bit as if reluctant
to leave without doing something for her.

She never saw Jason though sometimes, above all
the noises of the ship, she would hear the croak of his
voice. Usually that would be when they were later
about taking him to the upper deck than he wanted
them to be. He had had a bed rigged up for himself in
a boat carried outward on the starboard quarter and,
so far, the weather had been fine and he had spent all
of the daylight hours there. His head was elevated and
he could see out to the horizon over the foaming V of
spray that the heavy bow of the ship plowed through
the water.

One morning Jason had himself brought to her cabin
when he was being taken to the upper deck.

"You'll come topside," he said.

"No, Jason."

"You'll come smell the salt air and get some health
and strength back in you. You're making yourself a
hindrance on us, and we've no need o' that. Stir yourself!"

Elizabeth had followed the sailor taking Jason to
the improvised bed in the little boat topside. She
stayed there by him most of that day, and most of
every day after it, leaving him only to go down to the

salon at mealtimes to eat, or try to, with Captain Colfax and Lord John and Daly. The first day, when she
had gone down on Jason's orders, a place had been
set for her and her presence accepted as if there was
nothing unusual about it. Lord John and Captain Colfax talked about the progress the ship was making that
day and the progress they could expect to make the
next. Otherwise there was little or no conversation.
Captain Colfax was a very polite and friendly man,
but not jovial nor outgoing, a little too naturally stern
to relax easily.

Lord John was polite to Elizabeth, even solicitous of
her, but he was withdrawn from her. The meals were
a torture for her. Her days with Jason were also a torture for her, for Lord John often came to him. He
seemed to draw his only hope and comfort from him.

Each long day dragged out in the endless sameness
as the day before it. The weather held fine. Elizabeth
began to feel that rough seas would be a blessing.
Anything to ease the slow dragging through of day
after endless day.

Lord John's body was becoming thinner and more
taut of muscle with each day that passed. His eyes
were becoming more deeply sunken in his head and
more haunted in their expression.

Elizabeth slept badly, and she sensed that he was
not sleeping at all. Sometimes in the brief lulls of quiet
in the night she thought she could hear him pacing
back and forth across the space at the foot of the windows of his cabin, staring out at the empty moonlight
and the silent stars.

Daly stayed close by Lord John. It was seldom that
he was out of his sight. One night, when Lord John
went into Jason's cabin to spend an hour or so alone
with him, as he did every night, Daly did not sit reading at the table as he usually did until he had said

good night to his lordship and seen him into his cabin.
He knocked on Elizabeth's door and asked to speak
to her.

"Of course, Daly."

He came inside and closed the door. He had made
up his mind to speak, and he was not hesitant. "I don't
know what's gone bad between you and his lordship,"
he said, "I begin to see that it's more than just the
boy, and had already happened before what happened
to the boy. Whatever it is, is it something so much
that you can't put it behind you? Must you hold hard
feelings against him? You see how it is with him."

"I don't have hard feelings against him, Daly."

"Have you such a wealth of pride then that you can't
go to him and make things right between yourself
and him?"

"No . . . It isn't pride . . ."

"What, then?"

"He would turn me away if I went to him."

"Was it him turning you away that was the start of
whatever went wrong between you?"

"No . . ." she whispered, remembering the stupid
quarrel, the hot rage and jealousy that had blinded
her to all reason. It had all been on her part and
not his.

"Then it must have been you turned him away." He
looked at her. "So it's your place to go to him," he said.

". . . He doesn't want . . . I'm afraid . . ."

"I've lived with his lordship man and boy, Miss
Stewart, all my life and his. I know him as no other
knows him. The heart and will's gone out of him, now
when he needs it most. He's not acting like the man
he is. You could quarrel with him at your pleasure, if
such be your pleasure, and with no thought nor word
from me about it, if things were otherwise all right

with him. But they aren't." He looked at her steadily.
"Will you go to him?"

Elizabeth's heart was beating in ragged jerks. She
had wanted a thousand times to go to him, but she
had been held back by fear of being rejected by him.

"Daly . . ."

Daly drew himself a little away, as if his own pride
had been offended. "Is it such a sacrifice that I ask,
Miss Stewart?"

"No! No, it isn't that!"

"Would it be in contrariness to your feelings towards
him?"

"No! Oh, no!"

"Then I beg you. I beg you for his sake. Will
you go?"

Elizabeth clasped her hands tightly to try to stop
their trembling. ". . . Yes," she whispered. "I will go
to him."

Daly's relief relaxed his strained face. His voice was
kindly when he spoke next. "You've no cause to be
agitated in yourself," he said, "You'll find it's truth I've
spoken." He turned to go.

Before Daly closed the door behind him, Elizabeth
said, "Thank you, Daly."

"I should have made bold to speak to you sooner,"
Daly said, "I see that now. For the sake of both of
you."

Elizabeth knocked lightly on the door of Lord
John's cabin. She opened the door and entered before
he could answer. She was afraid a coldness or impatience might be in his voice, and if there was it
would shatter the wavering strength of will that she
had been able to summon.

He was standing before the windows, but he had

turned his head toward the door at the sound of the knock. When he saw Elizabeth, he turned fully. He did not move toward her.

Elizabeth closed the door and stood just inside it, as he had stood at the closed door of her room at the Caledonian in Oban. Their eyes met and locked, as they had then. Elizabeth said what she had planned to say, scarcely aware that she was saying it. "I don't have anything new to tell you. I haven't been able to remember anything more." The words were static and uninflected as if uttered by an automaton. She had decided that she should tell him that immediately so that he wouldn't have his hopes raised on seeing her and then be disappointed.

He nodded slightly, his eyes, looking even more sunken than they were because of the dark circles around them, never leaving hers. Their eyes remained locked. Neither spoke.

Elizabeth's eyes were as sunken and as haunted as his. And there was fear in hers. The fear of being rejected by him. She made a small gesture with one hand. She couldn't speak.

The same fear that was in her eyes came into his. He was afraid to speak. But he was stronger than she.

"Have you forgiven me, Elizabeth?"

With a cry she ran to him. He opened his arms to her and enclosed her within them.

"Forgiven *you*. . . ?" She sobbed uncontrollably. "Forgiven you when you have done nothing. . . !" Convulsive sobs wracked her body. "How can you ever forgive *me*?"

He held her gently and soothed her with his hands, caressing her hair, her back.

"I thought that it was over between us," he said. "I thought that I had lost you. It seemed to me that if I had, then I had forever lost Colin."

Elizabeth raised her face to his and pressed her cheek against his. The hot tears on his face mingled with her own.

"Don't cry," she whispered. "Oh, my love!" She wiped the tears from his cheeks with one hand. He caught it in his and crushed it against his mouth. His head was bowed over hers and tears continued to flow from his eyes. She felt the tremors of his crying in the length of his body against hers and in his shoulders. "Oh, my love!" she whispered. "My love!" She was not crying now. All thoughts of herself and her own misery were gone from her. Her only wish was to comfort him. "We'll find Colin! We'll bring him home to Polreath! Try to think about that, my love. Don't think of now. Think of how it will be when we find him and have him safe with us again." With a stab, she remembered when Lizzie had said something much the same to her, and remembered why she had said it. "I'm sorry for the jealousy I showed. I'm sorry for what it made me do. I'll make up for it a thousand times! I swear I will! I'd had too much happiness, and it had spoiled me! I'll never do that again—I swear I never will!"

He drew a deep, shuddering breath. His body was still now, the crying over. "My life is bound up in you and Colin, Elizabeth. My will to live and my wish to live are bound up in you and Colin."

He held her closer, straining her to him. They were silent for a moment. Then Elizabeth said, "Colin knows that you will come for him. However long it takes us to find him, he will be waiting for that day. He knows that you are coming. Wherever he is and wherever they take him, he knows that you will come for him. He has told me of times when he has been in danger and some miracle of God has brought you to him, and just in time. He has every faith that it will always be so. He has said as much to me."

"I trust and pray that that is true. I cannot bear to think that he—"

"Don't speak of his doubting that you will come for him. Don't even say it." She touched his face tenderly. "His one great trust in life is you."

He held her hand against his face with his own. "You are balm to me, Elizabeth, my resurrection. You are my life given back to me." He looked into her eyes while he spoke and then pressed her close to him. "Jason has been telling me to bide—and wait—but I felt that he didn't know you as I do, and I was afraid."

"Jason is the wisest of all of us."

"Sometimes I think that he is. I thank God for Jason. Every day of my life I thank God for him. I owe him a debt such as I will never owe another. I owe him for my son. If not for Jason, my son would have been alive in this world for these ten years past, half the world away from me, and I would not have known of his existence."

"Do you know what Jason said when he learned that the rajah had stolen Colin? Daly repeated it to me. Jason said to Daly that he hadn't lived all these years through the struggle that living has been for him just to see Colin taken from you. It was Jason who planned everything—the coming to Plymouth—everything. Poor Daly was stupefied with shock and grief. He hardly had his senses about him. But Jason . . ." She had felt his body begin to lose some of it rigidness as she talked, and so she continued to talk, trying to ease him further. ". . . Jason's head, if anything, was clearer than usual, and it is always clear. Every move we made, from the time they found me . . ."

Suddenly Lord John's hands gripped her shoulders and he held her away from him. All of the pallor that had been in his face was back. His eyes were as deeply sunken in his head as they had been. They were staring piercingly at her, but they seemed to be seeing past her, staring into some bottomless pit of dread and horror. There was something of desperation in them. "If they had taken you too, Elizabeth . . ." He swayed on his feet, clutching her still, causing her to sway also. ". . . If they had taken you too . . ."

He crushed her to him, his arms straining her to him as if he would force her body inside his own.

"I could not have borne it," he said. "I could not have borne the double loss!"

He was kissing her—her eyes, her mouth, her throat. Passion overcame him. He picked her up and carried her the few steps to the wide double bed. He laid her upon the bed and leaned over it and began to work with the fastening of her clothes, his fingers clumsy in their haste. The buttons and hooks and ribbons that would not give instantly were broken from their holding threads. Her dress and petticoats and chemise and her stockings and shoes were as much ripped from her as removed from her. He ridded himself of his own clothes in the same frantic way. And then he was with her on the bed. He was on top of her, not beside her. He smothered the length of her body with the length of his. His arms were around her again as if again he sought to force her body into his own. His mouth was on hers as if with his mouth he would take her into him. He was inside her as soon as he was on her.

He took her with a force that he had never taken her with before. Every hurt, every fear, every grief that he had bottled up inside him during the last several weeks, he poured out from him by the means of her body. He seemed oblivious of her as anything other than a vessel for his need. He gave her no chance to respond. He gave her no room to move beneath him. She felt the hot force of his ejaculation within her and felt the weight of his body come down on hers. She realized then that he had been hurting her. Even after he was still, her loins and the soft woman parts of her body ached dully as if from the effects of a beating.

He had never taken her so brutally before. He was always vigorous with his thrustings and overstrong for her, but, except for the first time that he had taken her, he had always restrained himself enough to keep from hurting her. And, always, except for that first time and this one, he had caressed her and kissed her and tantalized her until she was as eager for him as he was for her. This time there had been no foreplay, no lovemaking—only the coming into her, the forceful pouring of himself into her.

His head was on the bed beside hers. He turned his face to her. "I swore to myself that first time," he said, "that I would never have to ask you again to forgive me, for I swore then that I would never again give myself cause. But I have. . . . Forgive me, Elizabeth."

"Make love to me," Elizabeth said softly, "as you did after that first time . . ."

He raised himself to lean above her and look down at her. His eyes were as soft as she had ever seen them. His voice was as tender as she had ever heard it. "Elizabeth," he said, as he had said it that first time. "My Elizabeth . . ."

He kissed her eyes with soft kisses, to close them. "My sweet Elizabeth," he whispered. "The love for me that I see in your eyes sometimes is more than I can bear. . . . If I ever had to be without you, my Elizabeth . . ."

His hands moved softly over her body. His mouth moved softly over her face and throat. He was arousing in her and in himself the tenderness of desire and not the raging fires of passion that usually overcame them both when they made love.

He came into her with gentlest love and took her with gentlest movements of love. The orgasm that he brought her to was the sweetest, the most long-drawn-out quivering thrill of ecstasy that she had ever experienced. It was a lovetide that he planted at the core of her and slowly and sweetly caused to spread throughout her. It brought her fulfillment beyond any that he had ever brought her and left a beatitude upon her. She was more his than she had ever been.

Afterward, he held her softly close. "The way that you show your love for me humbles me, Elizabeth," he said. "I have been blessed. My world will come right with you beside me. You were meant to be beside me and a part of me. Else God would not have given me the depth of love I feel for you, nor given me the love you have for me."   ℰ

37

Lord John was a different man after his reconciliation with Elizabeth. There was purpose in his steps and a briskness in his voice. His eyes were sharp and clear, a brilliant translucent gray, the black streaks in them more defined than Elizabeth had ever seen them. His shoulders had never been bowed, but they seemed more squared and straighter now. The pallor left his face, and it began to take on color from the sun and wind. Confidence was in his every move and gesture. There was no gaiety about him. A smile was never seen to light his eyes, and laughter was never heard from him. But there was assurance in him where there had been desperation, and there was strength and determination where there had been debilitation brought on by overwhelming loss and sorrow. His former arrogance wasn't back, but it was just beneath the surface.

The attitude of everyone on the ship changed because of the change in Lord John. A pall seemed to have been lifted from the very ship itself. Spirits were lifted and hopeful instead of downcast and fearful. Jason's querulous croaks and impatient demands ceased. He was outgoing toward the sailors and, when they were free from duties, one or two were almost always to be seen standing at the rail beside the small boat where he spent his days, listening to his tales of his seafaring days and telling him tales in return. Daly relaxed his watchfulness over Lord John. The strain of it had shown on him, but most of the traces of the strain disappeared. He still kept his eye on him, but it was care and loving concern that were in them now and not anxiety and despair.

The weather continued good. The ship—being the flat-bottomed, massively hulled, full-bowed merchant ship that she was—rode the waters like a cork. She was a good ship and a safe ship, as ships of her kind were, if they were kept in good condition and manned by a skilled crew and a knowledgeable captain—and the *Jason* was. Even in heavy seas she could drift for days slant bowed on to the wind and stay righted. . . . She had her drawbacks. She shipped little water but still required continuous pumping. Her speed was not great; it was slowed up by the huge bow wave that she plowed before her. And there was no such thing as shipshaping the complicated standing rigging that supported her three masts, each composed of three parts joined with long overlaps, and leaving the rigging to stay so, for it would not. It required the constant attention of the crew. Constant vigil must be kept and precautions taken that a fire not catch. She would not easily be rescued from fire, and was susceptible to it.

The *Jason* was loved by her crew. The sailors went about their care of her with willing, skillful hands and strongly muscled legs. She was new to one or two of the crew, but she was home to others. All of them who swarmed so strong-limbed and so nimble-fingered about her now had been among those who had strung

her former captain to the gibbet under the scowling
gray skies in the drizzling rain on the street in the
town of Plymouth. But that deed was behind them,
and there was no cabin boy on the *Jason* to remind
them of the cabin boy who had died under the merci-
less hands of Captain Cork of the *Sea Walk*. The new
captain commanding, Captain Colfax, was not a hero
to his crew. He'd had no challenge yet by which to
prove himself to them, but he was known by reputation
to be a fair and just man if a shade overrigid in his
standards. He wasn't one to mingle, even with his
mates. All the signs boded well for the success of his
command.

The *Jason* carried ballast. She would bring no return
in sovereigns for this passage. Her intended cargo had
not been laded when the decision had been made to
put out to sea two days before the scheduled time of
sailing. Lord John had ordered that her hold be filled
with sand and gravel, as it would cut the lading time
by more than half. She sailed without paying passengers and without paying cargo—but she would bring
Colin home.

The *Jason* didn't have to bypass her straight route
by the thousand and more miles sometimes required
in seeking out the most favorable winds. She made the
port city of Surat in just over two months.

Elizabeth and Lord John stood together at the railing of the ship from the moment of first landfall. Even
if Colin had been in no way involved, this arrival in
India would have been a tense and unnerving and
apprehensive experience for both of them. Each was
returning to a place of unhappy memory and loss. They
saw first the peaks and crags of the surrounding mountains and then the mists at the middle heights that
obscured their view. Then the deep semicircle of the

city came into sight, its business buildings and offices
and warehouses and factories crowding down to the
waterfront.

"My happy memories of India, as you know, Elizabeth," Lord John said, "are overshadowed by sad
ones. I would never have returned here, given choice,
but when I set foot on land, I will be on the same
continent where Colin is, and that makes it all well
worth . . ."

He paused. Elizabeth thought that he would continue, but he did not. It came to her for the first time
that the man beside her, who was so much a part of
her and of her life, didn't know what feelings her
memories of India brought to her. They had never
talked about her early life. Her happy memories of
India were also overshadowed by sad ones. But she
made no mention of that to him. Someday she would
talk to him and tell him the little about herself that
she remembered. Some of the loneliness and the feeling
of not having roots in family and of not belonging
would leave her once the knowledge was shared with
him.

"You see the mountains there, Elizabeth? That's the
beginning of Maratha country. Colin could be anywhere up there." He put his arm around her waist, as
if for support. "He could be watching us come into
port. You can see the harbor and the ships from many
points up there."

"You don't seem to think there's any chance that
Colin might still be in Surat," Elizabeth said.

"I've never thought that we would catch up with
him here. Even Jason admits that the chances are slim
enough to be almost nonexistent. My guess is that they
took him ashore by small boat somewhere up the coast
before they came into the harbor. Still, Surat has to be
our starting point because we have no other."

* * *

From a distance it seemed to Elizabeth that there
would not be room in the harbor to take them. Ships
and vessels of every kind crowded every inch of the
surface of the water, and masts of every height closely
stippled the air above. As they came nearer, she could
make out dhows and galleons and junks, barks and
frigates and luggers and sampans. There must be trad-
ing ships in the hundreds in the harbor. The whole of
the scene before her was astir with the bustle of the
busy port. Figures of men and boys bent to their work
were running about on the lading wharfs and on the
long piers, and on the decks of the anchored and
berthed and beached vessels. They swarmed over
water and land alike. Owners and brokers and traders
in tophats and skirted coats stood head to head, deep
in talk of their business. Vessels were being laded and
unladed. Masts were being stripped of their canvas
and unsectioned. There was a ringing of iron on iron
and steel on steel that carried all the way across the
distance to her ears. A smell of rotted wood and freshly
cut timber came to her, a smell of kerosene and oil
and bilge water, of acrid sacking fiber and greased
hemp, a smell of fish and of chicken coops and rusty
wire, and a smell of cooking food that floated on the
small dark gray columns of smoke that rose in awkward gyrations from the sampans and dissipated into
the clearer air about them. Where were the smells of
tangy spices, of teakwood and balsam, and the sweet
scents of flowering plants and trees that were so much
a part of the India that she had known?

The *Jason* stood at anchor some distance out from
shore. The longboat was lowered and Captain Colfax,
with his oilskin of ship's papers, and Lord John and
Daly and several chosen sailors were rowed ashore.

Elizabeth stood beside Jason's little boat and

watched the longboat as it was propelled neatly across the water. She was very depressed and bitterly disappointed in herself. They had scanned every seagoing vessel in the harbor with glasses and telescopes, a dozen times each, looking for something recognizable to her. They had played the glasses over every figure of a man, stout or lean, who was dressed in gentleman's garb, black or not, in search of the figure of the man she had seen at the railing of the ship off the cove. There had been nothing. Nothing. Nothing recognizable on any ship and nothing recognizable about any man.

"Did you think they was going to hang out signs for you to read?" Jason asked gruffly.

"He thought I would see something!" Tears stung Elizabeth's eyes. "He thought I would be able to point out the ship to him! I wasn't any help at all!"

"You're no help to me now, splittin' my eardrums with your screechin'."

"I might as well have not come if I'm not going to be any help to him!" Elizabeth didn't try to hold back her tears. "I'll just be in his way, somebody he has to worry about taking care of!"

"According to your thinking, I reckon that makes two of us."

"Oh, Jason, I'm sorry!" Elizabeth apologized, aghast at how unthinking she could be. She reached to take his hand in hers and leaned over and laid her cheek against his. "I didn't mean that! I'm sorry!" When Elizabeth had seen Colin lean his cheek against Jason's the first time, it had shocked her. Now she was doing it and didn't even realize that she was.

"First thing I ever heard you say was you was sorry. Get your face off me if it's got to be wet!"

Elizabeth stood up and wiped Jason's cheek dry with one hand. With the other she kept holding his.

She wiped her own face. Jason said, "I know you was disappointed," and that almost set her off to crying again.

"Do you think he'll be able to find out anything in town?" she asked.

"Not him. But the boys might."

The "boys" were the sailors who had been chosen from among the crew to make themselves at home and friendly at every grog shop and tavern and pub and waterfront dive, and every brothel and opium parlor, and every other sailors' gathering place in the town to gather any information that might be helpful. They ranged in age from early twenties to late forties. They were hardly boys.

"He won't come to any harm, will he? You don't think anybody will recognize him and—"

He interrupted her. "Hand me the glasses! Quick!"

Elizabeth quickly picked up the spyglasses that were lying beside him and helped him hold them to his eyes. Jason had some use of his hands, but not enough strength in his arms to hold the glasses up to his eyes for any length of time. She held them and he focused them on what he wanted to see.

"What do you see, Jason? What are you looking at?"

He didn't answer. He was too intent on trying to see clearly. Elizabeth could see easily enough for herself what he was looking at. One of the ships that had been close in was pulling back, apparently giving up its dock space and coming back to anchor. There wasn't anything familiar about the ship to her.

"You see that lugger comin' out?" Jason said finally.

"Lugger. . . ?"

"That one comin' up on our quarter!" Jason said impatiently.

"Yes. Yes, I see it."

"She was in the harbor at Plymouth. We left her sittin' there."

"That ship looks like it's been here for a while, Jason. It's been refitted already. It's got new paint and canvas."

"That's the *Spindrift*, and we left her sittin' in Plymouth harbor!"

"How could she get here before we did?"

"She's faster than we are by a wide margin! That's how!"

Elizabeth couldn't understand why Jason should be so interested in the lugger. It wasn't anything like the ship that had been off the cove at Polreath. She had already pointed out the ones in the harbor that were similar to it.

"That ship's not anything like—" Elizabeth stopped, her breath choked in her throat. She whirled around so that her back was to the approaching ship and clutched Jason's arm. "That's the man! That's the man who was on the path! That's the man, Jason!" She started to run, to hide herself, but Jason's clawlike fingers closed over her wrist. "Keep still!" he said. "Don't draw him to notice you! Keep still!"

It was all Elizabeth could do to stand there quietly, but she did.

"Move yourself enough in front of me to keep them from seein' me," Jason said. He pulled her by the wrist to where he wanted her to stand.

"The one just come on deck?" he asked.

"Yes."

Jason squinted into the glasses. Even with the glasses, seeing any distance was difficult for him. ". . . Black beard? . . . Silk collar and tailcoat?"

"He wasn't dressed like that then." Elizabeth was shaking all over. "He was dressed like a pirate. But that's the—"

"Be still! Be quiet!"

The ship had come to a stop, and the anchor was being run out. Then the ship was still in the water and Jason had the glasses in good focus and could see.

". . . Luke Balsam . . ." he said.

"Who?"

"Somebody I thought would end his days in chains . . . or had."

"Who is he, Jason?"

"He's somebody would hire out for just what he done. Sold his soul once and was ready enough to do it agin for the one that got him out of his chains. Stands to pick up a fat purse for himself for doing it. Dressed the fine squire. Next thing, he'll be pinchin' snuff."

". . . Jason . . ."

"He's the one we want. Knew when I seen the *Spindrift* she was carrying prize."

". . . Jason . . ."

"They ought to'uv hung him like I voted hanging. Was dealing in humans then, and still doin' it."

". . . I don't think I can stand here any longer, Jason."

"Don't faint on me, girl!" Jason's mind came back from wherever it had been. "Stay put on your feet where you are!"

Elizabeth tried to put down the light-headedness that threatened her. She tried to lock her knees in standing position so they wouldn't give way under her. ". . . What is he doing? Is he looking over here? Do you think he saw me?"

"He's lightin' himself a rich-man's smoke and takin' his enjoyment of the evenin' breeze like the fine gentleman he's pretending to be. He's not thinking on us and won't start 'less you give him cause. Just stand there quiet. Dark's comin' down. Comes down in a hurry here."

Almost with his saying it darkness fell over the harbor. Through the darkness, the light of lamps and candles that had been lit in anticipation of its coming shone in dottings about the harbor, some shining from the ships and other vessels in the water and some from the windows and porches of the buildings on land.

"Matey!" Jason called.

The sailor who usually attended Jason was there suddenly enough to have materialized from the darkness. "I've been close by," he said. "I seen who you was watching."

"Take me below afore they start that harbor light turnin'. I don't think he'd know me—way I am—but it all fits too close not to mean somethin'. You walk behind, Miss Stewart, and keep between me and him."

When they were below in Jason's cabin, Elizabeth asked again who the man was.

"In a minute. In a minute," Jason said to her. Then to the sailor, "You know that man, matey?"

"I wouldn't claim knowin' 'im," the sailor answered. He wasn't being disrespectful toward Jason, but scornful toward the man.

"What do you know about him? Any of his doins you know, I want to hear them."

"He was scullin' 'round Plymouth all the while we were put in there, keeping himself out of sight mostly. I don't know what he was up to, but whatever it was, it wasn't to no good."

"He wasn't in Plymouth all the time," Elizabeth said, trying to keep her voice even. "He was at Polreath. He was . . ."

The sailor looked at her. "You're right, miss," he said. "Come to think on it, he was nowhere abouts the day of the hangin'."

"Go topside, matey," Jason said, "and keep your

eye peeled on him. Tell Mr. Forster I said send a boat
in to shore to find his lordship and get him back on
the double quick. The boats'll come back separate and
easylike, like there's no rushin' about it. You get me?"

"Aye, sir."

"Off with you then!"

"Who *is* he, Jason?" Elizabeth asked as soon as the
sailor—Tobey was his name—was gone.

"He's Luke Balsam. He was all right a man once,
'til greed got the best of him. I knew him years back,
sailed with him on the *Mary Kelso*. He got somebody
with a pocketful of money—stole likely—to back him
buying the *Mary Kelso* off the old lord—this one's
daddy—when he was ready to junk her for salvage.
Talked me into leavin' Polreath's lines where I'd been
in ships's service from the first I sailed. The captain
of his hire took me on at premium—I was greedy myself. But I didn't know what he was up to. Got up-
river off the coast of Africa and I found out. He turned
the *Mary Kelso* into a slaver, and after the good ship
she'd been all her life before . . ." He referred to the
ship as if she had been a living person. "It took me
making two runs with her before I had something
on Balsam could get his neck broke for him. . . . I don't
hold with slaving."

"But—"

"I didn't get him on slaving. He killed the captain.
Maybe he did and maybe he didn't. He claimed he
didn't. Claimed his death was accidental. Fell through
the open scuttle, he claimed, and broke his neck. Could
be. I didn't see it. The captain wasn't known to be
sober much of the time. But the way I told it when he
come up for trial was how he'd bragged more than
once about how he was going to kill the captain and
walk away from it like he'd done no more than snap
a flint in two. Maybe he did it and maybe he didn't.

But there weren't no maybe about him runnin' slaves, and dirtyin' my hands with doin' it, and that's what I wanted him hung for. Should've been hung. . . . But some of his slavin' money changed hands, and he got off with a sentence—life sentence it was, so money's changed hands on his behalf agin, or he wouldn't be out and free."

"Do you think he's after you, Jason?"

"He'd like to get his own back out of my hide. But that would be gravy for him. What he's here for is gold, the same thing he turned slaver for. Either to get paid his own self, or to be delivered the gold to take back to whoever hired him on the other side and get his split from him."

"How do you know that, Jason?"

"Don't take a brain to figger it. Was he already paid in full, he wouldn't be here."

"Maybe whoever hired him sent him after us to try to keep us from getting to Colin! They may attack us, Jason!" She clutched Jason's arm, fear coming over her. She and Jason were on the ship with less than half its full complement of crew. "Do you think they will? Do you think they'd dare to, right here in the harbor?"

"Might . . ." Jason muttered, as if to himself, not seeming himself alarmed, nor even taking notice of her alarm. "Might . . ." He was scowling, thinking. "Something don't figure. . . . Why'd he not come on the same ship brought Colin? . . . Why'd he hang back and not come 'til we'd already put out to sea? . . . Unless 'twas they were waitin' to see if his lordship was for sure comin'. . . . But they *knew* he'd come! They'd baited him to come!"

"Who's 'they'? Are you talking about the rajah?"

"I'm talkin' about him and about whoever it is on the other side who's in cahoots with him. . . . You were

quick to recognize Balsam, and from some distance—
and you say you thought you saw Mr. Hurford on the
ship off from the cove. . . . It's more than once I've
suspicioned Mr. Hurford, one thing or another."

"But his lordship said Mr. Hurford—" She broke off,
listening. "The boats are already back!" she cried, relief flooding through her. "His lordship is back!" She
stood up. "Thank God!" She turned and opened the
door to run to the upper deck. "How did they get back
so soon? The boat you sent must have met him on the
way coming back!"

"Hold on!" Jason's harsh croak stopped her. "Close
that door and lock it! Brace it with something! Pull
one of the drawers out from under the bunk and brace
the door with it! That's not but one boat boarding us,
and it's not ours!"

Elizabeth was huddled, too panic-stricken to take a
deep breath, on the edge of Jason's bunk, holding one
of his hands tightly in both of hers. A drawer was
braced under the handle of the door, and her feet were
pushing against the drawer. A furious, harsh scuffling
and shouting had erupted on the upper deck and had
lasted for some time. The worst of the noise had died
down now, but there were still the sounds of heavy
feet moving about and of heavy weights being dragged
across the deck.

"Can't the people on the other boats see the fighting, Jason? Why doesn't somebody come to help us?
Why . . ."

"It's dark out, for one thing, and what's a little
tussle the light might pick up in its sweeps? Com-
monest sight on a waterfront is a brawl."

"It's not just a brawl going on up there!"

"Only thing we couldn't've done was send up a flare,

and I guess they got to all of ours 'fore they had a chance."

"I'm scared, Jason!"

"Keep a hold on yorself! He'll come!"

"It's just you and me, Jason! They must have killed all the others!"

"They wouldn't be that much fools. Tied 'em up is all they've done."

"What do they *want*?"

"That's somethin' I can't figure. 'Pears to me like they're givin' away their hand. Could be Balsam recognized me for who I am. He'll come after me any first chance he gets. An' if they've been watchin' us, this is as good a one as he'll likely get and he knows it. We're not likely to have to be sittin' like a duck, shorthanded again fer his convenience."

They could hear coarse laughter now and the sound of rough voices of men talking among themselves. . . . And then there was the sound of boots thumping sharply almost overhead. Someone was coming down the hatch!

Elizabeth's throat was so dry that she couldn't swallow. She clutched Jason's hand as tightly as she could.

Only one person had come down to the between decks. It was the man, Luke Balsam. They both knew it as well as if they had seen him. Was he after Jason, or was he after Elizabeth? It wouldn't matter. Once he found them—the two of them—they'd both be at his mercy. They could hear him opening first the door of one stern cabin and then the door of the other. He opened the doors of the two cabins opposite them, and then he was walking toward their door. He tried the door. They could see the handle of the locked door turning slightly until it hit the bar of the lock. It was jiggled several times. "Open up!" a harsh, ugly voice ordered.

"That's him!" Elizabeth whispered. "That's his voice!" Her eyes were staring at the handle of the lock as if it were a cobra.

The door was kicked a hard, vicious blow that rattled it in its frame.

"Open up or I'll break it down!"

It was all Elizabeth could do to keep from shrieking. She bit her bottom lip until she could taste blood. The man heaved the full force of his body against the door once, and then a second time. They could hear his angry, muttered curses.

Elizabeth was backed as far back against Jason as she could back herself and still push against the drawer braced against the door with her feet. She heard herself whimpering with each breath she drew, but the whimpering was more of her breathing than her breathing itself. She couldn't stop the sounds of it from coming from her.

They heard running feet on the deck above their heads. "Come on! Come, man, or we're leaving you!" a voice called down the open hatch. "There's boats headin' this way! Come now or we're goin' without you!"

Luke Balsam heaved himself against the door again, ignoring the man calling to him. He picked up something heavy and slammed it against the door. It must have been a heavy metal locker that was kept in the salon—everything else heavy was secured. The man cursed aloud and kicked the door as hard as he could. He must have hit it in its most vulnerable spot because the door buckled a little, but by some miracle the lock held.

"Come, man! For the last time, come!"

There was a full second of silence. They could hear Luke Balsam's heavy breathing on the other side of the door. "I know it's you in there, Jason Niles," he said, between breaths. "I stepped too fast this time, but I won't the next! Fourteen years out of my life I owe you for! I've waited that long, planning every day of it how I'd pay you back when I got free! I can wait . . ."

"I ain't stayin' longer!" the man at the hatch yelled, and they heard his running feet.

"I'm coming!" Luke Balsam bawled after him. "I ain't done with you, Jason Niles!" he snarled through the door. Then they heard his booted feet going at a fast clip up the ladder and across the deck. They strained to hear or feel them going over the side and down and to hear the splashing of the oars as the boat pushed away but they could not.

Their ship seemed wrapped up in an awful shroud of silence in spite of its creakings and gurglings and sighings as it swayed on its anchor in the shallow sloughs of the water. It might have been a derelict except for the two in the barricaded cabin, for there was no sound anywhere on the ship of any other human being. It seemed an eternity to Elizabeth before their own boats reached the ship and she heard Lord John and the others come aboard. ☙

BOOK VI

Pursuit to India

&

38

None of those who had returned to the *Jason* had come back empty-handed of information. It almost seemed that they could have stayed on the decks of their ship and learned what they wanted to know. It was no secret that the Maharajah of Baglidore had sent to England and rescued his grandson. The Rajah Sirivaji had held a durbar on the day he had been returned to him for the purpose of presenting his grandson to his court. There had been a procession in the streets of his capital city of Amphat so that his people could see his grandson—his heir and successor —in the flesh.

Whether the half-caste was really to be his heir and succeed him to the throne was readily accepted as fact by some and angrily denied by others. The old rajah was using the half-caste as a ploy, his opponents said, to throw a scare into his son Shallabhugi, who was out of favor at the moment—and periodically was out of favor—because of his profligacy and his abandoned and debauched way of life. But whatever the reason behind it, the rajah had his half-English grandson with him. There wasn't any doubt of that.

The question was—where?

In celebration of his greatness and in the renewed
conceit of his belief in his invincibility, the rajah had
moved out by night from his stronghold in the mountains and, with his guerrillas spread out and moving
invisibly across hills and plains, had advanced upon
Delhi and, due to the surprise of his attack, had taken
the city and secured it to himself and had moved on to
take Agra, the most precious jewel in the crown of
the once-mighty Moguls—all of this done while he
was assumed by his enemies to be resting from the
rigors of his days of jubilee.

Some said that the rajah was now fortified against
attack in the Red Fort in Delhi, some said that he
had taken possession of the palace across the Jumma
and was in residence there, and others said that he
had taken up residence in the Taj Mahal in Agra.
Wherever he was, his grandson was with him.

There were disconcerting rumors that he was holed
up in his palace at Amphat and had never left it.
That rumor was disconcerting to Lord John because
Amphat was far removed from the other three places
where the rajah was rumored to be. The other three
were in manageable proximity, Agra being only some
hundred miles or so to the south and east of Delhi,
while the fort was in Delhi and the palace was just
across the river. The party of rescuers was not large
enough to split up and set out in two directions.

Lord John hoped that the Rajah Sirivaji had Colin
in Delhi or in Agra because Amphat—while it was
between Surat and Delhi, and thus Agra, to the west
of the route to the two northern cities—was situated
in the rugged mountains and enclosed and protected
by the surrounding crags and peaks. Approach would
be difficult and extremely dangerous if not downright

impossible, for the rajah's capital was strongly guarded
by his highly skilled and much-experienced guerrillas
who knew every stone and leaf of wildlife and foot-
hold and chasm of the treacherous heights they
guarded as well as they knew their own mothers' faces.

The difficulties of effecting Colin's rescue made it
seem impossible. There was no remotest hope of ne-
gotiating for his release, and Lord John had not the
strength of men and arms to take him by force. It was
going to have to be done by intrigue. He was going to
have to kidnap him. He was going to have to get him
back by the same methods by which he had lost him.
In order to do that he had to have information from a
knowledgeable source—from someone who had exact
information as to the rajah's whereabouts and who had
access to him. He was galled by his seeming helplessness, but in no way to be thwarted from his purpose
by it. He could have walked into any court in England and made claim to his son, and his son would
have been taken by legal means and according to
writ of law from those who held him and handed over
to his rightful father. But his claims of fatherhood
meant nothing here in the face of the rajah's claims of
right to have his succession assured by the bodily
presence with him of the blood prince of the realm that
he had chosen to succeed him. And he had demon-
strated that he would hold him by force of arms if
need be.

When Lord John had returned to the *Jason* from
his trip ashore into the city of Surat and had heard
from Jason and Elizabeth about Luke Balsam, he had
known for a surety that that was his man, his avenue
to the rajah. In spite of Elizabeth's protests, and
against the advice of Jason, he had had himself rowed

in the longboat to within hailing distance of the
Spindrift, had hailed the ship and asked permission to
come aboard. Permission had been denied.

Lord John had wanted to make a deal with Luke
Balsam, and that was what he still wanted. He and
his party, bolstered by a number of cutthroats and
mercenaries he had hired in Surat, and hampered by
the presence of the crippled Jason and the female
Elizabeth, had tracked Luke Balsam's movements.
When he left his ship, they left theirs. When he left
the confines of the city, they left. When Balsam and his
cohorts made camp, they made camp. When Balsam
struck camp and moved on, they followed. It was not a
matter of tracking him as much as it was a matter of
dogging his footsteps. Balsam knew their every move
as well as they knew his. He was laughing at them.
Lord John knew that he was, and knew that he thought
he was leading them into a trap. But Luke Balsam was
leading them to the rajah and Colin, and Lord John
didn't care how much Balsam laughed.

It was evident from the first that the rajah was not
in his capital city Amphat in Baglidore, for the direction they followed was always northward. And it continued directly northward, after a slight veering to the
east, when, if the destination had been Agra, a direct
turning eastward would have been made. The rajah
had Colin in Delhi, either within the walls of the Red
Fort or in the palace across the Jumma.

Lord John remembered that Jason had mentioned
the Red Fort early on. He had dismissed it out of mind,
thinking that Jason had little knowledge of the
Maratha states and their locations and didn't realize
that Delhi was far removed from Baglidore and that,
further, Baglidore was bordered on the north by
Kalphum whose rajah, Singal Jan, while himself a
prince of the Marathas, was deadly foe to Sirivaji.

Singal Jan coveted Delhi and Agra and always had. He'd won and lost them more than once.

"How happened you to mention the Red Fort, Jason?" Lord John asked him. Jason's former mention of the Red Fort was no longer an observation to be taken lightly.

"Way she talked . . . the boy's mother," Jason said. "There was three things her daddy, the rajah, wanted before he died. He wanted to make as big a name for himself as the man he claimed he was descended from —Shivaji was his name. He wanted to be the greatest of the Maratha princes of his time, like Shivaji was. Second he wanted to leave enough male descendants that there wouldn't be any chance his line would die out. And he wanted to take Delhi and Agra and hold them, to settle some kind of old score had been hanging 'round since the time of the Moguls. . . . He never has made himself as big a name as he wanted. That's number one he wanted and hasn't got yet—or maybe he thinks he has. He never had but one son—got hisself gelded in a too-close fight afore he could spawn more. That's number two he wanted and hasn't got yet and never will. That Shalla-however-his-name-goes ought to 'uv been dead of high livin' back that ten years ago, and must be close on to bein' dead from it while you and me's talkin'. Number three I reckon he's got—leastways for long enough to warm up the throne seat with his backside. He won't have it no longer'n that 'cause the East India Company ain't about to sit back long for his playactin'. They'll rile up old Singal Jan and sent him after him to rout him out from Dehli, and then they'll tell old Jan that's part payment on what he's back due on. That's the way they been doin' things for two hundred years. . . . But right now the old rajah thinks he's ridin' high. He's hoodwinked a British lord, and to him that's the same as the whole of the kingdom. He's got fresh blood for his succession. He's sittin' where he wanted to sit in Delhi—and that's in the palace in the Red Fort. It's safer there than in the palace across the river. Besides, some Hindus is superstitious about the Red Fort. That's where he is, and feeling well pleased with himself. He's got a last insult to himself to square though, and that's the one you dealt him. He's got hisself all set up to square it—or thinks he has. You're not mistaken about what he got you over here for, are you?"

"That's beside the point."

"It's a point got always to be kept in mind. He don't plan for you to leave here walkin'."

"He took what was mine once, Jason. I don't intend for it to happen again."

"I don't expect you to let it happen again. I'm just remindin' you about bein' careful is all."

Lord John was glad that Elizabeth was not present for the conversation. Otherwise he would not have felt free to say what he said next. "You seem to know a great deal about the rajah, Jason."

"For two months, your lordship—the last part of while I was sick, and especially after she got sick herself, Miss Santha talked about yourself and the baby and her daddy, and mostly about her daddy—like she was trying to find out some reason strong enough for him to have done what he did to you and her . . . like . . ."

Lord John stood up and touched Jason's shoulder. He didn't want to hear more.

Now that Lord John knew for certain that their destination was Delhi, it was time for him to have a talk with Luke Balsam—by force, if necessary. He walked into Luke Balsam's dark tent that night and shook him roughly awake. "I've come to talk business,"

he said. When Balsam started to make outcry, to call
his men, Lord John said, "My men have yours in
hand."

"You lie!"

"I am here in your tent, am I not?"

"My guard is asleep at his post again! Damn
scourge! You, Rufus!" he yelled. "Rufus!"

There was no answer.

"It's just the two of us," Lord John said. "No one
is coming in here on my behalf, and no one *can*
come on yours. We can talk, and come to terms
through talk, or—"

Balsam was off his cot and on his feet and slugging.
"You're off your turf, man! You may give the orders
at Polreath, but you ain't at Polreath!"

The two men fought in the near-dark, blows sometimes making contact and sometimes whizzing sharply
through empty air. Lord John kept himself always between his opponent and the exit from the tent. The
fight ended in a wrestling match, two bodies grap-
pling. In the end, it was Lord John who got to his feet,
his breath coming heavily, Balsam unconscious on the
ground. "Grober!" Lord John called. "Nate Grober!" A
gross, hulking man came into the tent, first having lit a
torch that he had held in readiness. He handed the
Lord of Polreath a length of rope also brought in
readiness, in the event Balsam would not be willing to
talk. Balsam's hands were bound behind him. He was
brought back to consciousness and made to walk to the
camp five hundred yards distant from his own. He was
bound to a chair and left there until the morning.

Now it was morning, and Lord John stood facing
Balsam. Lord John had not come out of the fight
unmarked. There was a livid and darkening bruise
that started at the point of his left cheekbone and extended to his temple, and there was a cut on the left

side of his lower lip that extended below his lip and
that would leave a scar he would wear the rest of his
life.

"I want my son," he said to Balsam. "You can help
me or you can further hinder me. If you will help me,
I'll forget your part in his kidnapping. I'll not prosecute
you nor in any way endanger you. I know you had
part—"

"You know nothing!" Balsam spit out. One of his
eyes was badly swollen from a blow received in the
fight. There was a large swelling below his left ear
that looked like a misplaced, monstrous goiter, and
there was a cut across his broad nose that could not
stay closed because of the way he continually wrinkled
and then stretched the skin of his nose. Every time he
stretched it, the cut gleamed wetly with fresh blood.
"You talk about part! Part in what?"

Lord John continued as if Balsam had not interrupted. "I can give you more in money and in sub-
stance than the rajah can, and I will. I came here to
get my son back and I'm going to get him back, but
I don't want any danger to him in the getting. That's
why I'm willing to make an agreement with you, and
that's the only reason. My one concern is for his safety.
. . . Will you talk?"

Balsam let out an ugly, belittling laugh. "You think
because you've got me tied on this chair"—he jerked
his body about on the camp chair—"that you've got
me done for?" He snorted. "First place, you got the
wrong man! What you're talking about I didn't have
a hand in. Kidnapping. . . . ? Kidnapping ain't my
business!"

"I haven't got you here to waste time listening to
your denials."

With that, Lord John turned and went to the opening of the tent. "Would you come in, Elizabeth,

please," he said. He turned back to Luke Balsam. "I
have someone who can identify you and prove your
part in the business," he said. He turned back to take
Elizabeth's arm as she entered the tent and to bring
her to stand beside him in front of Luke Balsam.

Balsam's eyes flared at the sight of Elizabeth and
then narrowed. A leering, knowing, ugly smile spread
his mouth in a grimace. He snorted. "Yeah, she could
identify me," he said. "Sure could." He drew the two
words out in a lewd, suggestive drawl when he said
them. "Not much about me she couldn't identify." His
eyes raked Elizabeth up and down. "Nor *nothing* about
her I couldn't." His eyes slid over her body and up to
her face. "That's right, ain't it, girlie?"

Elizabeth stood petrified, turned to stone. Lord John,
who had been standing beside her, moved in front of
her, between her and the leering man in the chair.

"You're not so valuable to me that I won't kill you
where you sit," he said in a deadly voice. "More dis-
respect to her and I will! . . . Is this the man, Elizabeth?"

". . . Yes," Elizabeth said. She had to try several
times before she could get the one whispered word out.

"If you've got to open your mouth and spill something, girlie, spill the truth!" Luke Balsam sneered.
"Don't try to put my tail in a crack just 'cause you've
got yours in one! He caught you out, didn't he? You
funned yourself once too often!"

Lord John's body had become as rigid as stone.
"What is he talking about, Elizabeth?" His voice was
deadly quiet. He didn't look at her. His eyes stayed on
Luke Balsam. When Elizabeth didn't answer, he repeated the question. "What is he talking about, Elizabeth?"

". . . He . . . He . . . After they took Colin, he—"

"*After!*" Luke Balsam snorted again. "After! Oh, no!

You're not going to keep on getting away with your lies! Tell him the truth of it! *While*, not after! It was while you were funning yourself with me that the boy was taken!" He leaned his head as far to one side as he could and looked at Elizabeth, who was still to the rear of Lord John and partially hidden from Balsam's view. "Come out from behind him and face me. Then repeat the lie you told him if you can! Come on out! Show yourself up for the wanton you are!"

". . . I haven't told him anything. . . . He doesn't know . . ."

"You told him something, girlie! You told him something makes him think I'm connected up with old Sirivaji getting hold of his kid! I didn't have nothing to do with it, and you know it better'n anybody!"

"You know the rajah's name," Lord John said. "And you're on your way to him."

"So what? This ain't the first time I've been on my way to see him. I been doin' business with him two years now. If you'd asked around about that in Surat while you were asking around about everything else, you could've found it out quick enough. I ain't got nothing to hide."

"What kind of business do you have with him?" Lord John's voice was cold and removed. His face was as rigid as his body.

"The kind that's his and mine! That's what kind!"

"Two years you say you've been doing business with him? You haven't been out of chains two years."

"Is that a fact? Show me raw chain marks on me!" He thrust out a leg. "Show me a raw chain mark on that ankle!"

Lord John ignored the outthrust leg. He had gotten the impression from what Jason had said that the man was only recently out of prison—but Jason had not

said that. "What were you doing on Polreath lands?"
he asked.

"What was I doin'?" Luke Balsam peered around at
Elizabeth again. "Ask her."

"I asked you."

Luke Balsam looked up at the Lord of Polreath. His
eyes narrowed. "I was *on Polreath lands . . .*" he
mimicked, "visiting a lady who was expecting me,
with her skirts already up ready for me to get under
them. Why do you think she told you the lie she did?
Did you think she was going to tell you that?"

Lord John's body jerked more stiffly upright than it
had been.

"She's a piece of tail I'd go out of my way to
Polreath lands for," Balsam leered. "Ain't many likes
it much as she does. Get her going and she'll outrun
you. Ain't a hotter hole nowheres that I've come across.
That hole of hers grabs onto you, you know you been
grabbed. She like to tore my knob off." He looked the
man in front of him up and down. "Reckon you hadn't
been takin' good enough care of her wants," he said.

Lord John did not answer. Elizabeth was too stunned
by what the man had been saying to have her senses
about her. She had come out from behind Lord John
and was staring at the man in the chair. What he had
said was so beyond reason that she couldn't believe he
had said it.

"Leave us, Elizabeth," Lord John said.

"No! No, I won't leave!" Lord John's cold voice
speaking to her had brought her to herself. "He's
lying! Everything he's said is a lie!"

"It's a lie that you and me was up on top of the
cliffs and the kid was down below, and that's where
they took him from?" Luke Balsam laughed, low and
ugly in his throat.

"I was with him! I was with him when they took him! You know that I was! It was you who—"

"You was up on the top of the cliffs, girlie, flat on your back, and me on top of you. If it hadn't been for the way you were screaming and moaning and carrying on and forcing me on long after any normal woman would have had more than she could stand, I might've took some notice of what was happening to the kid."

"That's a lie!" Elizabeth screamed. "That's a lie!"

"Is that a fact?" Luke Balsam's eyes went down to Lord John's crotch. "He knows it's not a lie. He knows what I'm talking about. He's had some of it for himself. Just hearing it talked sets him off." Lord John's penis was not concealed by the tight cut of his pants. It was in erection. Luke Balsam looked at the long, full bulge of it and then looked up at Lord John. "She's not ruined you yet," he said, "I can see you're still full equipped and itching right now for her to make your equipment tingle." His heavy lips curled and his nostrils widened. "Toss you for who gets in her first," he said.

"Leave us, Elizabeth!" Lord John's words were a harsh, cold order.

"No! I will *not* leave! He's lying, and I will not leave to have you listen to more of his lies! He—"

Balsam's ugly voice cut her off. "You wasn't on the top of the cliffs with me?"

"Not then! Not when you said I was! Not when they took Colin!"

"Then you're sayin' that after they took him you come up to the top of the cliffs to party yourself with me?"

"No, I'm not saying that!" Oh, God, why hadn't she told Lord John what had happened? Why . . .

"Are you sayin' you wasn't on the top of the cliffs with me?"

"No! You know I can't say that! But I wasn't there with you because I—"

"Are you sayin' I don't know your titties are the same on both sides and not lop-weighted like some? Are you sayin' I don't know the color of your woman-hair is the same almost as your hair on your head? Are you sayin' I don't have scars down my back now from fingernail cuts you put there?"

"I didn't put cuts on you! If I did, I—"

"The longer you keep from admitting to him what you was doin' with me topside them cliffs, the more I'm going to prove to him that you was doin' it! I know some more of your secrets that he thought 'til now he was the only one knew them!"

"Leave us, Elizabeth," Lord John said. She had heard his voice cold before, but she had never heard the coldness that she heard in it now.

"It wasn't the way he said it was," Elizabeth said, her voice small and hopeless. She didn't expect him to believe her. How could he?

"Leave us." ❧

39

When Elizabeth walked, vacant-eyed and numb, out of the tent, Daly came to her side. He took her arm. She tried to shake his holding hand away.

"Stay with him, Daly," she said.

"I'll come back to him after I take you to Jason," Daly said, "Jason's been asking to see you."

"Go back to him now," Elizabeth said.

Daly kept his grasp of her arm and didn't answer.

"The greatest kindness you could do me would be to leave me to do as I will," Elizabeth said.

"The greatest disservice I could do to you and to him, and to Master Colin, would be to let you do yourself harm. You'll come and stay with Jason. He will tell you the same as I'm telling you—that things will come right."

"Things will never be right again, Daly."

"They will. Once he's done with him in there, he'll be himself again. Standing outside the tent and listening, I blamed myself that his lordship was hearing something he ought to have heard as soon as he heard about Master Colin—but it seemed to me then that it would be asking the man to stand too much—to tell

him his son had been taken and then tell him what
had been done to you. I figured let him handle the
one and then would be time enough to tell him the
other."

"It wouldn't have made any difference if he had
learned about it then instead of now. It wouldn't have
changed things."

"Balsam would have been dead the first minute his
lordship laid eyes on him, and would have been no
good to us. The truth not coming out 'til it did he was
left alive long enough to bring us to where Master
Colin is."

"The truth? Do you believe what he said, too, Daly?"

"I'm not talking about what he claims is truth. I
wouldn't believe his lies even if I didn't know the
truth for myself—which truth I do know. Wasn't I one
of the ones who found you? His lordship doesn't believe his lies either. That's not what's put him out of
himself. It's knowing somebody touched a finger to
you. Once he's taken care of the one did it, he'll come
back to being himself."

"He despises me. You heard the way he spoke to
me."

"What he *said* was to you, not the way he said it.
Miss Stewart, if somebody took Master Colin's hand
and gripped a knife in his hand and stabbed somebody
dead with the knife, his hand holding the knife in
Master Colin's hand, would his lordship despise Colin?
He can no more despise you than he could Colin. It
would be despising his own heart."

"Things will never be the same again. He'll never
feel about me again the way he did."

"Things will never be the same for he'll have even
more of anxiety about your safekeeping than he's had
up to now. He'll ever have in his mind how close a
call he had. Balsam could easy enough have thrown

you off the cliffs. I've wondered at it myself that he left you alive to tell the tale. As for his lordship's feelings, they don't lie so shallow in him that they could be uprooted by something of your own doing, and surely nothing of Balsam's doing can uproot them."

"It's over. Everything is over between us. I know that it is," Elizabeth said. She didn't say it hoping for Daly's denial of it nor asking for further reassurances and comfort. Nothing he had already said had reassured nor comforted her. She believed it, and so she said it.

"We're here at Jason's," Daly said. "Don't talk such foolishness to him. Foolishness is what it is and he'll round on you proper if he hears one word of it. You stay here and keep company with him. I'll be back here directly, and his lordship with me."

Lord John turned his back on Luke Balsam and strode out of the tent. He came back with a long-bladed knife and slashed through the ropes that bound Balsam's hands and then through those that bound him to the chair.

Balsam watched Lord John's grim, set face. When he was free he stood up and stretched himself and switched his shoulders and hips back and forth to get the kinks out of his muscles. He kept his eyes on the man with him and on the knife in his hand.

"I knowed you'd come round to being reasonable," Balsam said, feeling his way. He didn't know what was behind the white mask of the man's face, but he knew that he wasn't being set free to go his way. "No reasonable man'd let a chit of a girl—"

"Do you want to fight with weapons? If you do, what is your choice?"

"Wha-at. . . ? What kind of talk is that? You can't duel with me. You can't challenge me. I know the rules on that. You can't challenge somebody ain't a peer like yourself."

"I'm not challenging you. I'm going to kill you. I'm giving you your choice of weapons for defending yourself."

"Aw, come on! Come on now! Defending myself? I've lived my whole life defending myself. You don't want to take me on. Look! What's a woman? What's one woman? It's not like she was your wife and married to you. You take some tasties on the side, she takes some tasties on the side. What's the difference?"

Lord John backhanded Balsam with his left hand with a blow to the side of his head that staggered him. Before he could fall, Lord John grabbed his shirt front. His eyes blazed. "One more filthy insinuation about her and I'll slit your throat! Take back your lies about her!"

Balsam's eyes were on the knife. "All right! All right! I got overexcited tussling with her! She got me heated up fighting me! I'm a natural man! I—"

Lord John threw him down. Luke Balsam crouched, taking stock of the man confronting him. He wasn't afraid of a fight, but he was accustomed to fighting on his own terms. He was used to having the advantage— the advantage of a sneak attack. He wasn't going to let himself be set up for maybe getting more of what he'd got the night before. The man in front of him could handle himself in a fight. And there wasn't any doubt that he was looking to kill. One of them would be dead before it was over. He'd be smart like he'd always been, Luke Balsam decided. He'd back down now and take his advantage later.

"Look! Now lookee here . . . You wanted to talk deal, you said. Now you're a reasonable man . . ."

Lord John threw the knife through the open flap of the tent to the ground outside. He advanced on Balsam.

"Wait now! Wait a minute! You want your boy, I'll help you get him!"

"You've led me to him. Now that I know where he is, I'll find others to spy for me. Using you would have made it easier, but I don't want your services!"

"Might be others can help you with getting your boy, but ain't no others can help you on the business I got in India to do with her."

The man before him stopped short. Balsam pressed his advantage. What would it matter if he opened up to Polreath? He wasn't leaving India alive.

"If she means all that much to you as she seems to," he said, "you'll want to know about my business to do with her."

"You have none! You're lying in your teeth to save your skin!"

"Give yourself some chance to listen and I'll tell you enough about her to prove I'm not lying. I can tell you that she took ship at Calcutta some ten years or more back on a merchantman that put in at Surat before starting the long haul. She was orphaned and being sent back home to England . . ."

Balsam saw the man take a short step backward, saw him shake his head and rub his hand across his eyes as if to clear his mind and his sight of something or to bring it more clearly to him. He thought he had him. A crafty, satisfied look came over his face. "Don't what I've told you prove I ain't lyin'?"

Lord John's eyes cleared. His confusion had been momentary. "You haven't told me anything," he said. "What you've told me is common knowledge."

"I reckon you think it's common knowledge nobody knows who she is and can't nobody find out." He eyed Lord John a long minute. "What if I told you there's them *do* know who she is?"

Lord John returned Balsam's stare, his eyes cold.

"There's no bargain can be had with me on the matter of Miss Stewart's origins," he said. "It is no longer a matter of any importance to me."

"You'd change your mind about that if you knew what else I could tell you."

"I've had enough of your stalling and enough of your lies!" Lord John strode to the front of the tent and dropped the flap. He turned. "You're warned to defend yourself!"

Balsam backed away. "Hold on! I've got proof!" He jerked out from under his shirt front a small object suspended from a thin leather thong around his neck. It was a gold locket. He held it toward Lord John and sprung the catch that opened it. "There! There's proof!"

Inside the locket was a gold disc. The coat of arms of the House of Clarwicke was engraved on the disc.

"Where did you get that?"

Balsam took his time answering, savoring his triumph. His voice was smug when he spoke. "From the one that hired me," he said.

The sight of the disc threw a cold fear into Lord John, fear for Elizabeth's safety. He didn't recognize the locket, but the disc was Sarah's. For a black moment, panic surged up in him. He felt a tidal wave of evil swelling up from Scotland and heaving across the seas to India, rushing even then to wash over and engulf Elizabeth.

"Grober!" he called out, throwing open the tent flap. "Nate Grober! Bring two men with you and guard this man!" He headed for the center of the compound on the run, calling to Daly as he ran.

"Here, your lordship! Coming!" Daly answered, running to meet him.

"Where is Miss Stewart?"

"With Jason, sir," Daly answered, turning to stride

hurriedly beside his lordship, who headed for Jason's
tent. "I took her to stay with him. I didn't think she
ought to be by herself."

Jason was alone in his tent. He was in such a state
of anger that a red light flashed from his eyes. The
tightly stretched skin of his forehead quivered. "Time
somebody answered me!" he rasped out. "I want a
horn given me I can blow, make somebody hear
me! . . ."

"I thought Miss Stewart was with you!" Lord John
interrupted. "Where is she?"

"That's what I was trying to get somebody in here
to find out! Where is she?"

Lord John looked wildly around the tent as if he
would see Elizabeth if he looked hard enough.

"How long has she been gone from here?" Daly
asked Jason.

"Long enough for you to quit your gawking 'round
in here and start looking for her! Don't waste your time
lookin' in the camp—you won't find her in it!"

But Lord John ran first to Elizabeth's tent, hoping
against hope that he would find her there.

"Where did she say she was going, Jason?" Daly
asked.

"To fetch the tea," Jason said. All of his impatience
and anger had left him, and all of his energy as well.
He lay in his cot bed looking even more shrunken
than he usually looked. He cast his eyes around dully
at empty space.

Daly asked a question that he dreaded to hear the
answer to. "Do you think she ran?"

"I wish I did," Jason said. "She'd be easy enough to
track down and find. She didn't run. She wouldn't've
brought more trouble on him. She's got iron where
most have guts. She'd have stuck it out 'til he got
Colin back."

"Do you think the rajah . . ."

"I'm hoping that, and you'd better. If it wasn't him, it was marauders or guerrillas."

Lord John did not find Elizabeth in her tent. The camp was searched and all the surrounding area. She was nowhere and there was no sign of where she had been. There was no trace of how she had left—or been taken from—the campsite, and there was no trace to indicate the direction in which she had disappeared.

40

The man's short breaths in Elizabeth's ear were maddening to her. His arms around her, holding her on the saddle before him, were a physical torture to her. They were not tight, but she was the more physically uncomfortable than she would have been if they had been tight. She had just enough slack that if she kept her spine absolutely straight, she could keep her breasts from touching his arms and could keep the upper part of her back from touching his chest. If she leaned forward, she would lean into his arms; if she relaxed backward, she would be resting against his chest. It was all she could do to keep from slumping forward or sagging back; they had been riding the better part of the day.

The sun was going down now almost directly to the rear of them. Elizabeth could see their shadow and the shadows of the growth around them stretching ever longer before them.

They had ridden through arid plains covered with coarse grass and prickly bushes, and through tangled forests of tamarisk. Sometimes the dusty plains had extended beyond view and sometimes to the right and

left hills of bald red rock could be seen. The heat had
been smothering. Her skin felt as if it had been pulled
to the limit of its elasticity on her face and hands. Her
eyes ached from the steady relentless pressure of the
heat against them. The ground over which they rode,
even in the near distance, was a shimmering mirage
varying in color from black to brown and from red to
yellow. Now and then hot winds would rise from the
earth and carry the earth's colors with it to howl and
hiss around them and envelop them and cut off the
light from the sun—but not the heat of it—wrapping
them in a smothering swirl of dun-colored dust that
coated bodies and face and left its grit in nostrils and
mouths and eyes.

As the sun went down behind them, they entered a
different landscape. They rode through shadowed
meadows and over grassy hillocks and wove their way
through thickly wooded copses, through orange groves
and pomegranate groves.

Elizabeth was amazed at the endurance of the man,
and at her own. They had stopped only once. The
man had pushed her into a narrow space that cut into
a solid rock and had placed his horse to stand before
it, cutting off her exit. The man then disappeared
around the rock. The horse would not move from
where it had been stationed. When she tried to push
it away, it pawed the earth and tossed its head, whinnying and snorting loudly. She could hear the man
behind the rock laughing. His needs taken care of he
returned. He pantomimed a lifting of skirts and a
squatting position to indicate to Elizabeth that she was
to take advantage of the stop. Elizabeth's insides felt
as dry and tight as her skin. She glared angrily at the
man and ignored his grins and pantomimes. He
shrugged and led her to a small running stream, pulling the guardian horse along behind her. He knelt and

washed his face and hands and pointed to her and to the water, inviting her to do the same. She stood stiffly on the low bank that was almost level with the water of the stream and ignored him again. From a silk scarf tied to the back of the saddle, he took two oranges and handed her one. She could not resist the orange. She had never been so thirsty. The juice of it was sweet and seemed cool, though it was not. When she finished the orange, her fingers were sticky with oil from the skin of it and from some of the juice which, in her haste to peel and eat it, she had wasted. Also the small measure of relief from thirst that the sweet, thick juice of the orange had given her had weakened her will to resist the water. She knelt down and dipped her hands into the stream. She cupped them and brought up water to drink, but he slapped at her hands so that she lost the water. He shook his head and made motions that she was to use the water only to cool and wash her face and hands.

The horse was fed—two hard black spice balls. The base might have been made from peas, Elizabeth couldn't tell from the look of them, but she could smell the garlic and pepper that they were spiced with. The horse was allowed to drink, but sparingly.

That stop had been made about halfway through their ride. There had not been one since. The man and the horse—it was a light pony—apparently were accustomed to such extended rides.

It was when the short-lasting gloom of twilight was beginning to dissipate the heat somewhat that the pony began to lift his head every few paces and sniff the air. His step became a prance at times. He was giving evidence that his stall and feedbag were near and that he was impatient for them. The man chuckled and let him have his head.

Soon, in the distance, Elizabeth could see a mulberry

grove. She could see the peaks of tents rising above
the tops of the trees and could see movement. There
seemed to be a large encampment there and it was
obviously their destination. The pony snorted and
broke from a walking trot into a fast trot. Elizabeth
expected him to lengthen and run for home, but he
did not. He continued his elegant trot as if he were
on show, smartly crossing the open ground closing the
hundred or so yards to the edge of the grove. They
passed several sentries at their posts and entered the
grove and traversed half the length of a wide path
that seemed to separate it neatly into halves and came
to a stop at some command from the man that Elizabeth was not aware of in front of a tent in the center
of the path. For grandeur, it was like no tent that
Elizabeth had ever seen.

A heavy figure of a man came out of the tent and
stood under the canopy that extended six feet beyond
the main body of it. The canopy was of scarlet velvet.
It was supported by angled gilded poles and festooned
with gold fringe and golden tassels. A carpet of shades
of scarlet, red, and purple covered the ground under it.

Except for gleaming patent leather boots, the man
was dressed in scarlet and gold. His wrapped turban
was of scarlet satin. It was heavily rounded on one
side and covered his head to below the ear. On the
other side it was flatter and did not cover the whole
of the ear. In every fold and twist of it there were
ropes of gold and pearls. Black ringlets showed from
under the turban on the flatter side. His legs were
encased in wrappings of scarlet silk, and his calf-length
tunic was of the same fabric. The hems of the sleeves
and of the skirt for a width of five inches were banded
in gold inset with precious stones—emeralds, rubies,
and pearls. He wore a gold breastplate of fleurs-de-lis.
(He wasn't as unfriendly as some to the hated French,

Elizabeth thought, or else the breastplate had been stolen. Such a breastplate was a traditional present from the French. She did not think it had been stolen. She was in the presence of royalty. Her heart squeezed tight within her. If this was the Maharajah Sirivaji, Colin must be near!)

The man had the fairer skin of the Marathas, but his face was heavy and florid, as his body was loosely heavy under his clothes. His nose was small and thin and deeply hooked. A short beard covered his chin and extended in a thin line that outlined his jowls to just below his ears. He had a heavy, neatly combed and oiled moustache that extended to thick points well beyond his mouth. His eyes were black and narrow. They stared without blinking and without a hint of expression. There might have been lust behind them, or there might have been indifference.

The man behind Elizabeth on the horse half-pushed and half-threw her from her position in front of him. She fell on her hands and knees before the man in scarlet and gold. When she looked up at him, he had not changed expression. He spoke to a man standing a reverential distance behind him. The man signaled with the slightest gesture of his hand, and the man on the horse was suddenly surrounded by a dozen or more soldiers. The soldiers were unlike as to face and physique, for there were Europeans among the Indians. But they were dressed identically in scarlet coats with white crossbelts, white trousers and black boots, and wore tall shakos on their heads. They were members of the royal guard, all spit and polish, looking ready for parade.

The man on the horse was speaking rapidly and agitatedly in a language that Elizabeth did not understand. It was not the language of the Indians of Calcutta that her ear had become attuned to in her child-

hood and that she had some understanding of. It must
be the Maratha Hind.

The royal presence ignored the incoherent bab-
blings of the man on the horse and ignored what was
being done to him as he was pulled roughly from his
horse and kicked and shoved, screaming now and holding back, along the path away from the tent. His pony
followed at the heels of the soldiers surrounding him.
His cries could be heard even after he had disappeared
from sight.

"Get up," the man in scarlet said to Elizabeth in
English. Before she could get to her feet he had turned
from her and returned inside the tent.

"His Royal Highness, the prince, would speak with
you," the man who had been standing behind him said.
He had learned his English at Oxford. It was clipped
and very little accented. He waited for Elizabeth to
follow the prince inside the tent and then came inside
himself.

The prince was seated cross-legged on a gold chair
which was on a gold brocade carpet of ceremony.

"You come from the white man's camp, the one who
follows the renegade?" he asked.

Elizabeth nodded numbly.

"He stole you?" He gestured with his head in the
direction in which the unfortunate horseman had been
taken.

Elizabeth nodded again.

The prince conferred with the other man—who was
not the menial that Elizabeth had thought him—for
some time. Elizabeth knew that they were discussing
her abduction, but could guess very little of the par-
ticulars of what they were saying. At first the prince's
face remained as unreadable and inscrutable as it had
been from the moment she'd seen him, and then it
became animated by an unconcealed cunning and

craftiness. From the treatment of the man who had
brought her there, and from the prince's questions to
her, it was easy enough for Elizabeth to know that he
had not had any part in her abduction and had been
displeased by it to the extreme of summarily ordering
the death of her abductor. It would seem now, however, that there were aspects of it that were not
entirely displeasing to him. The skin on her body
prickled. Her hands grew cold and her breath shortened as fear grew in her. Had he decided to take advantage of the plaything thrown his way? True, he
had scarcely glanced at her, but that was no reassurance.

As the two men talked on Elizabeth's weariness of
body began to make itself felt again, and more
strongly than at any time during the ride. She felt
herself sinking to her knees and could do nothing to
stop herself. She fell prone on the carpet before the
prince. He took no notice. She lay in a strange sort of
semiconsciousness. She was not in a faint. Blackness
had not overcome her. Her limbs simply couldn't support her weight any longer. She had a certain amount
of awareness and she tried to keep her mind riveted
to the talk between the men but remembrance of the
scene that morning between herself and Lord John
and Luke Balsam crowded out everything else.

A thousand pictures of what must have happened
when she was discovered missing crowded through
her mind. Not once did she think that the truth of why
she was gone from the campsite would occur to Lord
John. She was sure that his only thought would be
that she had run away. She could only see him as
angrier than ever and hating and despising her more
than ever for visiting more trouble on him. She could
see him flicking her from his life as he might flick away
a pesky gnat and ordering that her tent and all of her

belongings be burned and the remains removed from
his sight. He would certainly not detour from his purpose to try to find her—nor would she wish him to.

After what seemed hours to Elizabeth, during which
time she could not summon enough strength to her
bones and muscles nor salvage enough pride from her
wounded spirit to give herself the will to make
her raise herself from her abject position at the feet of
the prince, the prince snapped his fingers. Immediately
a woman appeared from the recesses behind the
screening silken hangings to the rear of the gold brocade of the carpet. He spoke to her and she disappeared, returning immediately with a goblet fashioned of beaten gold and encrusted with jewels. She
came to Elizabeth and knelt beside her and lifted her
head and held the goblet to her lips. The fiery liquid
gagged Elizabeth. She tried to push the goblet from
her mouth, but the woman was stronger than she was.
The woman held the goblet slanted against her lips,
and Elizabeth had to swallow or choke. The woman
did not stop forcing her until she had drained all of
the liquid from the goblet. A light-headedness came
over her. Her physical self seemed to detach itself and
float away from the shell of her body. Her mind was
outside both, only her spirit remaining with her. It
was a frightening sensation. She felt herself divided—
body from mind, spirit from physical self, and mind
from spirit. The sensation was gone of a sudden, and
she had strength of body and clarity of mind. She got
to her feet. The woman brought two deep pillows and
placed them, one on top of the other, in front of the
prince, leaving a space of six feet between the chair
of gold and the pillows, and indicated that Elizabeth
should sit upon them. Then she disappeared again behind the silken hangings.

After Elizabeth had seated herself somewhat clumsily upon the pillows—her legs and feet tucked under her for otherwise her knees would have been on a level with her nose—the prince turned his attention to her.

"You are the wife of the Englishman?" he asked.

"No."

The prince and the other man exchanged significant glances. The man inclined his head to one side and scratched beneath his ear. He smiled. "All the better," he said in English.

The prince's eyes narrowed. "It would not be like an Englishman to hamper himself with a woman's presence as a necessary for his gratification," he said. "The English, as we know, are a cold race."

"Well reasoned, Revered One. She has a value to him that exceeds that of woman."

The prince's eyes had not left Elizabeth. "Why has he brought you with him?" The question was blunt, as if he expected a blunt and ready answer.

Elizabeth had determined not to answer any questions that could in any way do harm to Lord John. She was sorry she had answered any, and especially the last. She sat mute.

"You will answer me!"

"I will tell you nothing."

The prince's eyes narrowed in quick anger. He was not accustomed to being crossed. Elizabeth thought that he would issue a clipped order that would bring a dozen of his soldiers to pounce upon her and drag her off as they had dragged the horseman. But the prince threw back his head and laughed. The laugh was short and without mirth, but when his head came down and his eyes returned to hers, the anger was gone from them. "You think I want the Englishman's hide? You mistake me! He is my unwitting ally!"

Elizabeth did not let the expression on her face

change. She was not going to be taken in by any lies
nor blandishments from him, not let him think that
she was.

The prince's face became hard. "I am Shallabhugi,
Prince of Baglidore," he said. "I am heir to the throne
of Baglidore. Do you think that I will let the throne be
usurped from me by one whose Maratha blood is polluted by the blood of the English? He is not Maratha,
nor yet Indian! I am Indian, and a thousand times Indian, for I am Maratha! The upstart is less than
pariah! He is the lowest of the low and the dregs of
the earth! His blood is polluted by the blood of the
race of monkeys! He is the leavings of the carrion crow
and the excrement of the lice that infest the pigeons!
He—"

Elizabeth almost came up from the pillows in defense of Colin. "The blood that flows in him is none
of his own doing!" she lashed out. "It may be mixed,
but it is purer than yours because it is not corrupted
by greed! His worth as an Indian and as a Maratha is
a thousand times your worth!" She looked straight at
the prince. "The rajah, your father, obviously thinks
the same!"

The prince came out of his chair and stood over her.
His eyes were murderous. But again, before he caused
harm to be done to her, he threw back his head and
laughed.

"My father, the rajah, has lost the use of his faculties
in his old age," he said. "He thinks to turn the people
of Baglidore against me and to put in my place on
the throne a red-faced English! But it will not be so!
Half my people are with me already!" He swung an
arm to indicate the other man. "Molkar was his
peshwa! Do you understand what that means that he
stands here beside me? It means that the strongest
man in all Baglidore sides with me! In my personal

guard alone I have two thousand of the finest soldiers of Baglidore! My guerrillas blanket the land from here to Delhi and from Delhi all the way to the mountains and Baglidore!"

"Tut," the other man kept repeating all the while the Prince was making his declarations. "Tut."

"I will not be silenced!" the prince exclaimed in anger when the sound finally came to his ears.

"I would remind you that His Majesty has thirty thousand of the finest soldiers of Baglidore in his personal guard," the Peshwa Molkar said softly. His attitude was that of a schoolmaster whose knowledge was as the contents of a vast caldron and the knowledge of the pupil he addressed only a drop from the caldron. "And we are far from Baglidore and from the people of Baglidore. Our way must be paved with guile. It cannot be forced by strength of numbers."

"As you say. As you say," the prince answered. He subsided and returned to the gold chair and resumed his seat cross-legged upon it.

The Peshwa stood between him and Elizabeth. In appearance, he had the look of the menial that Elizabeth had thought he was. He wore the coarse garb of a beggar monk—a loose garment of coarsely woven wool that hung from his neck in long, loose sleeves to his wrists and in long, loose folds to his ankles. It was caught in low on the hips with a rope of hemp. He wore crude goatskin sandals on his feet and an over-large skullcap of the same skin on his head. His hair under it was gray and hung to his shoulders. He was clean-shaven. He was of medium height and medium build. His complexion was a shade darker than that of the prince. None of his features stood out. He was totally nondescript. If Elizabeth had had to turn her back to him and describe him, she would have had difficulty trying to bring a mental picture of him to her mind. But there was no doubting his power and his authority when he spoke.

He stood between the prince and Elizabeth and addressed Elizabeth. "This Englishman—this Lord of Polreath—is giving every appearance of being a very stupid man," he said. "Once he found out that it was known and far broadcast that His Majesty had his son, he began to flaunt his own presence. He made a loud noise of the business of setting himself up to travel in caravan and made an unseemly display of letting it be known that he followed the brigand and why he followed him. I am informed that representatives of His Majesty the King of England have called upon him to try to dissuade him from approaching His Majesty the Maharajah. He has ignored their warning. He has ignored the warnings of a deputation from the East India Company. He cannot be unaware that the maharajah wants him to make an attempt upon his person. He cannot be unaware that such an attempt will mean his certain death.

"I am puzzled. I cannot fathom the meaning in his method. If he thinks to kidnap his son, as he was kidnapped from him, he will not find it possible to do. He is as well guarded as His Majesty himself. If the Lord of Polreath should, somehow, in spite of all odds and all precautions, succeed in obtaining his son, there is no way possible that he could get safely away with him. He travels in a party of two able-bodied men—himself and his man called Daly—one cripple and one woman—two who can only hamper him. He will have another hindrance in the person of his son, once obtained. He is protected by no more than a score of hired mercenaries." He spread his hands. "It seems a fool's way. It seems so much a fool's way that I cannot think it is."

"He is not a fool," Elizabeth said.

"It little matters, fool or not fool," the prince said. "He is here. He is in good time. He can be of use to us. . . . If he refuses, we have the means to change his mind." He looked at Elizabeth. "And I will not hesitate to avail myself of the means." There was no mistaking that Elizabeth was the means and that her life was held in forfeit.

41

"Our thinking has been all wrong, Jason! We're the fools and idiots that we've been playing at!"

Lord John had not reacted to Elizabeth's being taken as he had reacted to Colin's. Once he had had to accept that she truly was gone, a hard, cold anger had come over him.

"If you think you're a fool, maybe you'll play the part better," Jason said.

"We're close enough to have been approached by somebody! Even the old woman could have come this far!"

"The old amah may be dead."

"All the disaffected Baglidori aren't dead!"

"Your best bet is still Shallabhugi."

"In the end, yes! But I need fresh information, and from the source. And I need it now!"

"You better see if you can't get a holt on your patience. You've come along just right and easy, so far, like you said you was comin'. You don't want to jump the gun now and ruin any chance you had."

"If Shallabhugi is as far gone in wine and opium as you claim he must be by now . . ."

"If he is, he's all the more desperate, and will take more desperate steps. I'm having to repeat your own arguments back to you."

"I can't sit here and wait, Jason!"

"What's in your mind then? To call in the redcoats? They'll help to find Miss Stewart. An Englishwoman taken, they'll turn every rock in India to get her back. But a rajah's rightful grandson . . ." He didn't finish the sentence.

Lord John had worn a groove in the dirt floor with his pacing. "If I could be sure that he's the one who has her, then I could bear the waiting. I could feel some assurance that harm would not be done her. I'd know she was only being held hostage. . . . He *must* have her! He's trying to force my hand!"

"You're acting like you're ready to let him." Jason changed the subject. "We been travelin' in the sight and sound o' Balsam all this time now. What's his reason, do you think, for not makin' a try at gettin' to me?"

"The man's an innate coward. He was waiting until I'd be gone from camp and some of the men with me."

"He'd likely be gone the same time."

"All of his men wouldn't."

"He'll not leave it to his men to do. He wants the enjoyment of doin' it himself."

"Then he was waiting until he knew me dead. He expects me dead. He told me things he wouldn't have if he didn't."

"What are you going to do with him? Keep on keeping him prisoner and harness yourself with him too?"

"I'm not finished with him. There's more he knows that I want to know. I have no choice but to keep him prisoner until the other business is taken care of."

"Are you sure all chance is gone of using him for spy?"

"No sum of gold that I could offer him would bring him back out of Delhi once he had the rajah's protection. His sorry life is at stake and he knows it."

"If we made a mistake it was countin' on him as the only one could get inside the rajah's court."

"No Baglidori could get anywhere near the rajah's court—none that we could hire who was stranger to the court. The rajah is more leery of his own people than he is of the worst of his enemies."

"That ain't what you told Balsam. You said you told him you'd hire others."

Lord John paced and didn't answer Jason. He knew that Jason was purposely trying to keep his mind distracted from what was of foremost importance to him. "Sirivaji must have Shallabhugi under guard at the palace—or imprisoned somewhere. That's the only thing that would explain his not having gotten to me himself or gotten word to me."

"I'd think there'd have been noise abroad about it if the old man had done anything out of the usual to him. Hasn't tried to hide any other of his doings."

"There hasn't been anything said of Shallabhugi and his whereabouts. That's peculiar in itself."

"Wouldn't seem to me to mean nothin' more than that things was going along with him same as they usually do—on the outside, anyway. Closer he keeps his doins to himself, better it reads for us, seems to me."

"For how long? I can't keep sending Lagrosse to every corner of India looking for him!"

"When Lagrosse gets back from Amphat—if he comes back saying he's not there—then you said yourself the only other place he might be is Agra. That's saying a course that he's not in Delhi. If he's not in one of those three, he's holed up in the mountains. I'm not a land man, but I know enough to know there won't be any getting to him if he's in the mountains."

"Agra is less than a day's ride—"

"Don't start thinkin' of riding yourself to Agra.
You're readier every minute passes to let the old rajah
call the turn. Lagrosse can't be much longer gettin'
back from Amphat. He's the one to send, and you
know it. What good could you do yourself except lay
yourself open to getting yourself killed? Lagrosse has
been in this country nigh on twenty years. He knows
his way around the Indians. He speaks the Maratha
lingo. And there ain't none can beat a Frenchy for lyin'
and devious ways. You ain't worth as much to yourself
in that respect as he is."

Lord John walked outside and looked up at the wide
spread of the dark heavens. There were few stars. The
sky was unusually dark. Elizabeth had been missing
since morning. He had done nothing. Nothing but tear
around the camp like a madman, throwing things aside
and asunder looking for her. Nothing but race the
wind out of his horse riding for hours in widening
circles around the campsite looking for any sign of
the way she might have been taken. His helplessness in
the face of the black empty distances around him was
driving him crazy. He knew he had to get hold of
himself. He knew he had to be calm and clear-headed.
He knew that the only sure way to get Colin back—
and now Elizabeth—was the way he had planned all
along . . . if he could be sure that it was the rajah who
had her. . . Why hadn't he kept her guarded? Why
hadn't he guarded her as carefully as he had guarded
Jason? But there hadn't been any reason to. She hadn't
had an ever-present enemy who had sworn to kill her.
Was she terrified, wherever she was . . . terrified and
helpless and hoping with every breath that she drew
that he would come with her next breath? . . . She must
know that he would turn heaven and hell to find her.

. . . She might be in Delhi by now, with Colin. He prayed God that she was with Colin in Delhi. It was the only thought that comforted him.

The camp was quiet. The camp across the way was deserted. The four who had been with Balsam had taken everything of value and fled the place the moment they'd been freed the night before when they found out that Balsam was being held prisoner. They would spent the rest of their lives hiding from him and in fear for their lives. He'd sworn to kill every one of them. They hadn't heard him, but they knew the man.

Hoofbeats sounded on the quiet night. They were coming from the west, not from the side of the deserted camp. Lagrosse!

"Lagrosse is back," Jason called out to Lord John.

"Halt! Stop where you are!" the posted guard yelled to the approaching horseman. "Stop and state your bus—"

"Get out of my way before I ride you down, you bloomin' ape! It's me! Lagrosse!"

Lagrosse talked between gulps of food and swallows of gin that Lord John had had brought into Jason's tent. Daly was also present.

Prince Shallabhugi was not in Amphat. The people in the capital and all over the state were taking sides, some with the old rajah and some with the prince. Lagrosse couldn't find out which way the weight was swinging, feelings hadn't stabilized in the people themselves and strength could go either way. But the feelings were strong and tempers short. There was fighting in the streets among factions. From the way it looked to him, the one that showed his face there first was the one they would swing to. Still you never could guess ahead on an Indian's mind, nor expect him to hold to it once he ever made it up.

"I'd stake my eyes Shallabhugi ain't prisoned," La-grosse said. "The old one never has yet locked him up. He's soft on him and ever has been. That's why he's been let to go as wild as he has."

"Did you get any lead on his whereabouts at all?" Lord John was growing impatient with the man. He was making all too much of his moment of importance and giving expression to his opinions when all Lord John wanted was facts.

"If the old one's done what he usually does when he goes on one of his raids, he's give him a soft sop guarding some outpost with ten times more soldiers than he needs to guard it. Not but one outlying place he's holding this time, and that's Agra."

"You think he's in Agra then?"

"That's my guess."

"How large an army would you say he has with him?"

An evil grin came over Lagrosse's face. His lips smiled but his eyes showed malice. "Altogether?"

"Certainly altogether!"

"Well . . . the reason I asked that . . ." The grin widened. "Shallabhugi's got himself two armies now. He's got the one give him by the old one . . . and he's got his own. Leastways he's got a good beginning on his own."

"You seem to take pleasure from the fact."

"I'll take more when the old one's army comes over to Shallabhugi. Had a good berth in that army once myself 'til the old one give me walkin' papers."

"Do you have any basis for thinking the rajah's army might go over to Prince Shallabhugi? I don't want to hear anything that there's no basis for thinking. All I want to hear is fact."

"It's a fact makes me think it." The malice in his eyes deepened as he looked straight at Lord John. "I

wish it was the old raj I was tellin' it to 'stead of you,"
he said. "I'd like to be the one he hears it from. I
found out a little something would rock him right off
his jewels on his trone." He paused for emphasis. Then:
"Molkar ain't in Amphat. Three guesses where he is."

"Who is this Molkar you speak of?" The question
was brusque, no attempt being made to conceal the
impatience Lord John felt. "I've no time for games!"

"Molkar was Sirivaji's peshwa! That's who Molkar
was! He was to him what the prime minister of England is to your king, except a peshwa, if he's smart as
Molkar, has got more power than a prime minister
'cause there ain't no parliament to gainsay him. Molkar run Sirivaji's government while Sirivaji scuttled
around making dirty war like the mountain rat he
claims his bloodline come from. Word ain't out on it,
but Molkar's gone over to Shallabhugi. When the rajah
brought the half-breed . . ." he caught himself. " 'Scuse
me. I'm saying it like Molkar sees it. . . . That's when
he decided to go over to Shallabhugi. He's like a lot
that's half-breeds themselves—his blood ain't all
Maratha—he's stronger for the blood than the bloods."

"Are you saying that Prince Shallabhugi and this
Molkar are plotting to overthrow Sirivaji?"

"That's about the size of it. You're close to finding
yourself in the middle of an insurrection."

"That puts me ahead," the Lord of Polreath said, "if
I find myself in the middle of it. I came here to start it."

Lagrosse stared at him, then shrugged. "English is
English," he said.

"I can guess what you mean by that, but I have no
care for your good opinion."

"Split 'em up, set 'em against each other, and get 'em
fighting. After it's over, step in and take the spoils."

"I came here to get what is mine. The spoils can fall
as they will." &

42

Elizabeth was taken by the woman to a room in the tent behind the silken tapestries. The earthen floor of it was overlaid with thick carpets to a depth of six inches. In it there was a bed of pillows the size of mattresses. They were upholstered in scarlet silk embroidered in floral designs of every hue. A canopy of scarlet velvet with gold fringe and golden tassels, the same as the canopy at the entrance of the tent, upheld by gilded poles, sheltered the bed. Curtains of sheer muslin were caught to the poles with rings of pure gold. There was a small low table of carved teak beside the bed on which there was a hookah. There were a number of large standing mirrors with frames of gold picked out with diamonds and shells. The only other furnishings were large pillows of velvet and silk and brocade stacked in twos, some in front of the mirrors and some along the walls.

A low table was brought in and placed in one corner. All the things necessary for bodily comfort and cleanliness were brought in and placed on and about the table by Indian boys clad in white wrapped trou-

sers which extended from waist to mid-calf, and white
turbans. The rest of their bodies were bare. Their eyes
did not lift from the things they carried before them.
Not one of them looked at Elizabeth. The woman
brought in bowls of attar and flagons of scented oil.
She brought in a bodice of cloth of gold and a long
skirt of multicolored silk. Elizabeth was sure that it
was straight from the harem, and wondered if he carried his harem around with him. From the stories she
had heard of him, he probably did. That, or he kept
a wardrobe in readiness, as Madame Labouille kept
one in readiness in her establishment in the Haymarket
in London.

Elizabeth bathed herself and used the chamber pot
of beaten gold, but she refused the attars and oils and
the change of clothing. The woman received her re-
fusal in silence and did not insist.

The things for the toilette were removed, and a tray
of food and wine was brought. The wine was sweet
and cooling, but, as hungry as she was, Elizabeth
could hardly eat the food. There were meatballs so
heavily spiked with pepper that she thought she could
feel the heat of it on her fingers. There was a quail,
oozing fat, stuffed with spices. And there was a platter
of greasy sweetmeats and a bowl of pears. No implements were brought her. After she had eaten what she
could of the meal, the woman brought a bowl of
warm lemon-scented water to wash the grease from
her hands and mouth. The wine and pears were left,
and the rest of the platters of food removed. Elizabeth
was left alone. She walked about the room unable to
sit and unable to lie down. She could hear the voices
of the two men murmuring beyond the hanging tapestries and silks. They were speaking in their native
tongue. She could not make out a word of what they

were saying. Molkar was doing most of the talking, his voice a steady murmur, never raised in anger nor heightened by excitement.

Outside the tent there was great activity. There was a continuous moving about and the sound of shouted orders. From the sounds there was no doubt that they were breaking camp.

"English! Here! Come here!"

Elizabeth was startled to hear herself being called. She had been expecting every minute that the prince would come to where she was, expecting to find her dressed in the outfit that had been brought her and oiled and scented and waiting for his pleasure. She had determined that he would kill her before she would submit to him. She pushed aside the tapestry and walked into the main chamber of the tent. If the prince noticed that she was not apparelled for his pleasure, he gave no sign of it. In fact, it was not he who addressed her.

"I am informed," Molkar said, "that the Englishman has brought with him gold in a sum that would ransom a king or procure for himself the services of an army. Which did he intend it for?"

"If he had such a sum with him, he would have been set on by your ruffians, and the gold taken," Elizabeth said. Her tone was as full of contempt as she could make it.

The peshwa was not disturbed. "It is in the vault in the bank in Surat, of course. The one who receives it must see the man safely back to Surat or he cannot come by it."

"I know nothing of gold that he has brought."

"Are you informed as to his plans?"

"No! And if I were, I would tell you nothing!"

Again the peshwa was not disturbed, neither by her tone of voice nor by what she said. She was a woman, after all. It was not surprising to him that the man had not revealed his mind to her. He hadn't asked the questions expecting information. He was gauging the character of the female he was dealing with.

"The Revered One and I have decided to help the Englishman," Molkar said. "He will help us. We will help him. Our aims, in the end, are the same."

"If you think to use me to make him help you you're wasting your time. He has no more use for me. He has tired of me."

"You speak a truth from the heart, and yet the words you speak are false to the truth," the peshwa said. "But that is something that I cannot convince you of and that you will learn for yourself. As I said, we can be of mutual aid. We have decided to return you to him as pledge of good faith and proof that we will deal with him on equal terms and not from point of advantage."

Elizabeth's heart skipped. "When? Now?" The words spilled involuntarily from her, but something in her shrank back. Apprehension filled her. What would be his reaction when he saw her returned to him? What would she see in his face? What would be the sound of his voice when he spoke to her?

"In time. When the time is right. We must be in touch with him first."

Elizabeth's mind pictured the bedchamber of the tent. There was the rest of the night to be gotten through, and the bedchamber was obviously that of the prince.

"Why can't I go now? Why do you have to be in touch with him first? Where's the good faith you were talking about?" Her mind was still on the bedchamber. "Why was I brought here?"

"The first two questions I will answer by saying for reasons of my own. The third I will not deign to answer. As for the last . . .". The peshwa shrugged. "The servant thought to please his master."

"And was killed for it? That was his reward for trying to please his master?"

"He was punished, and deservedly punished, for actions exceeding his master's orders. If a servant fails to carry out the fullness of his orders, he disobeys. If his actions exceed the fullness of his orders, he disobeys."

"But he wasn't even given a chance to defend himself! What if I had asked him to bring me here?"

"It is not you who commands him."

Elizabeth had been prepared to stand there until the morning came asking questions, but the quiet finality of the words stopped her.

The peshwa indicated a writing desk and chair that had been brought in and placed on one side of the carpet. The desk and chair were of ebony inlaid with mother-of-pearl that gleamed in many-colored softness in the wavering light of the candles of the tall candelabra that stood near.

"You will write the Englishman that you are well and are being treated well. You will say that you long to return to him—"

"No! I will not!"

"You wish to return to him. Why do you wish not to write to him?"

"I do not wish to return to him!"

"You were eager when told—"

"I was eager to get away from *him!*" She flung a gesture toward the prince.

Molkar smiled. "You have nothing to fear from the Revered One." The smile left his face. "Write!"

It would do Elizabeth little good to try to refuse, and she knew it. She sat down at the desk with a heavy sigh. "I will say that I am well and being treated well. I will not say more!"

Molkar regarded her for a long minute. "Your pride being such as it is, I would prefer that you do not. Your pride has been stirred against him and I'm sure he must be aware that it has. If you write what he will know you would not have written if not forced, he will know that it was forced, and he will think the other also forced. Write only of your well-being."

Elizabeth scratched out the few words that she was willing to say, just as he had said them to her. She threw the quill pen aside and thrust the sheet of paper toward the peshwa. He glanced at it. "Your signature, please," he said.

Elizabeth didn't want to write her name. She had started to write it before, but the sound of the gentle voice that she loved saying softly ". . . My Elizabeth . . ." had come to her and tears had come into her eyes and her hand had started to shake. "I don't need to sign it," she said. She couldn't keep her lips from trembling. "He will know it's from me."

"Can you manage the initial?"

Elizabeth knew that the man guessed what she was feeling. Why was everything she ever felt as readable as the open pages of a book to some people? She scrawled an "E" angrily and stood up to hand the sheet of paper back to the peshwa. She had more command of herself when standing.

"Go now and rest," the peshwa said. "The ride back will likely be soon, and it will be long, as you know."

Lagrosse slept for a few hours and set out before dawn for Agra. He arrived back at the campsite about the time he would have been coming up on the camp outside Agra if he had continued on his way. With him was the emissary of Prince Shallabhugi. They had met at midpoint.

Lord John broke the seal of the official-looking docu-

ment first and started reading it. Part way through the
reading, he thrust it into Daly's hands and tore open
the envelope of embossed white vellum that had also
been handed him and took out the single sheet of
paper.

Daly hastily and worriedly scanned the lines of the
paper that he held until he came to those that had
stopped Lord John. The worried look left his face. He
laid his hand on Jason's shoulder. "She's safe," he said.
"She's well and safe and coming back."

Lord John stood staring at the scant one and one-
half lines of Elizabeth's writing and at the scrawled,
angry-looking "E." The sheet of paper was like a slap
in the face. There was no message there from Elizabeth to him. There were a few cold words that stated
a cold impersonal fact.

"Give orders to strike camp and to pack to move out,
Daly!" Lord John's voice was clipped. "See that all
haste is made!"

Daly looked up at Lord John, frankly puzzled, both
by his attitude and by the order. He had expected his
lordship to be elated at the news, vastly relieved. But
an impatient black scowl was on his face, and anxiety
and hurt were in his eyes.

"But, your lordship, Miss Stewart is being returned.
A message sent from you to Prince Shallabhugi by his
messenger here will bring her—"

"I send no message! I go myself! Follow as soon as
you can!" He was striding out and calling for his
horse to be saddled, Daly following. "Keep Balsam
well bound and well guarded. Keep three men guarding him and tie his horse to one of theirs. I want him
alive when he gets there. Keep him at the front of the
caravan and Jason well away from him. Take no
chances!"

Lord John went to the tent where Luke Balsam was

being held and took him from the locket with the disc inside. It had come to him several times since he had known that Balsam had it that he must take it from him, but something had always come up to intervene, and he had failed to do it. He didn't know why he remembered about it now, but he was glad that he had. He wanted it in his hands. He went to his own tent and took an extra supply of bullets for the pistol he wore in his belt and took up his rifle to have strapped to his saddle. Then he went to have a last word with Jason before leaving.

"It's right you go," Jason said. "It's wasting time, messages sent back and forth, back and forth. It was to him we been headin' from the first, ain't it?" He peered up at Lord John. "Miss Stewart ain't one to beg," he said. "That don't mean she don't want what she won't beg for."

"I would not expect, nor want—"

"You wanted more than you got in that letter she wrote. I'm just warnin' you not to at first expect any more from her than you got from it. She ain't had time yet to come round to thinking better of herself. She's got to do that afore she can start believing you never thought the worse of her."

Lord John and Lagrosse and the prince's emissary rode off as dark was settling over the campsite. They would have no sleep that night, nor would anyone in the camp. Tent canvas was already collapsing into center poles and sagging against side poles as the mercenaries and Indian boys who had been hired as servants scurried around breaking camp. It would take the caravan all night and all the following day to reach Agra. Lord John had every intention of being there himself well before sunup. &

BOOK VII

Final Reckoning at the Taj Mahal

త

43

The sounds of activity that Elizabeth had heard had been what she thought they were. When she was awakened just before dawn, the campground was empty of every tent except the one in which she had slept. When she was brought outside by the woman, the prince and his peshwa were mounted, and a saddled horse was waiting for her. From the sea of men around the three horses, it was her impression that all two thousand of the prince's personal guard were in attendance on their safety.

The sun had not risen and did not rise until they had reached the outlying grounds and gardens of what, to Elizabeth, was the most beautiful sight she had ever seen or ever would see. From a distance, shrouded in the morning mists, she could see a dome with a slender minaret on each side at some remove from it. It did not occur to her that it was the Taj Mahal until two more slender minarets showed at some distance to the rear and two smaller domes appeared on either side of the large one.

As they rode up and the main body of the building came into view, the sun came up. Elizabeth reined her

horse in and sat staring in awe at the sight before her.
It seemed meant for the eyes of gods and not for the
eyes of mortals. There was an ethereal quality in the
delicate beauty of the great tomb. A million iridescent
delicate colors danced and sparkled from countless
facets in the carvings on the marble walls and arches.
She hardly noticed when her horse was nudged on.
She was still well within view of the building and still
lost in admiration of the beauty of it.

They did not approach the building from the front
but rode around it—Elizabeth thought that they were
passing it—and approached it from the rear. She was
surprised to see that it was situated high on the bank
of the river—the Jumna, she knew the river to be. The
great tomb reflected in the water of the river and
seemed on first sight to rise from the water and to
float suspended between earth and heaven. The ethereal quality of its beauty was even stronger here than
it had been from the front.

But what were they doing here? They hadn't
brought her here because they wished to impress her
with the great masterpiece.

They were stopping. The soldiers of the guard were
already dismounting. Beyond, Elizabeth could see bul-
lock-drawn carts and pack animals. More came up as
she watched. From one of the carts the mirrors and
the pillows, the bed canopy and the poles, the mattress pillows and the teakwood table were unloaded
and carried into the Taj Mahal. The gold chair and the
ceremonial rug were carried in. Household furnishings
that she hadn't seen before were unloaded and carried
in. She couldn't believe what she was seeing. The
activity that she watched was that of a dwelling being
taken possession of by its new owner and furnished
with his belongings! Surely even the son of a maha-

rajah would not commit such a sacrilege on the Taj
Mahal! But that was what was happening.

The woman came to her horse with two running
servant boys who clasped each other's wrists to make
a support to give her a foot down. She dismounted and
was led up to the Taj. It was as beautiful on close inspection as it had been from a distance. It was on a
raised marble platform which extended beyond the
octagon of the building. The slender, delicate minarets
that she had seen from the distance rose from the four
corners of the platform. She couldn't see the large
dome nor the smaller domes from where she was now.
There were arches in each of the walls which were
patterned similarly, but there was not a monotonous
sameness about them.. The spandrels of the arches
were inlaid with precious or semiprecious stones de-
signed to represent bouquets and wreaths and plant
designs. Everywhere she looked it seemed there were
designs in colored gems, exquisite tracery, scrolls and
frets in relief. Nothing that she had ever heard or read
of the Taj Mahal had given her to realize the true
beauty of it. No painting could ever capture it, no
matter the genius of the artist, for a great part of its
glory was the delicate and constant changings of its
colorings. With the clear bright rising sun of morning
sparkling on the clinging dew and the pure white
marble and on the facets of the gems and the delicate
planes of the traceries, it was enough to take her
breath away.

Elizabeth was led around to the front of the building. She saw the famous reflecting pool then, but a
a haze came between earth and the sun, and there was
no reflection. It could have been that there would not
have been one in any case because of the time of day
and the low height of the sun—she didn't know—
but still it seemed to her an ill omen, for when she

was inside, the sun came out again. The bright light of it shone through the marble screens.

She followed the woman past the cenotaphs of Mumtaz Mahal, the wife for whom the Taj Mahal had been built, and of Shah Jehan, the grieving husband who had caused it to be built. The cenotaph of Mumtaz Mahal was in the center of the great room and that of Shah Jehan, the last of the great Moguls, to one side of it, throwing off the symmetry but somehow not disturbing the balance. The mausoleum of contrasting black marble that he had planned to build for himself across the river had not been built in his lifetime, and his son Aurangzeb, who had wrested control from his three brothers and had ruled after Shah Jehan, had not seen fit to honor his father after his death by having the mausoleum built for him. Perhaps it was more fitting that the shah lay beside the wife he had loved so much.

There were four chambers inside the Taj. Elizabeth was led to one of them. The furnishings from the bed-chamber in the tent had already been placed inside it. The beauty of the room was no less than that of the outside of the building. The walls were inlaid with six-foot-high marble plates on which were designs of flowers executed in gems. There were elaborate traceries and patterned designs on the floor and on the ceiling. Trelliswork in marble broke up the extent of the room.

Elizabeth felt that she was treading—trespassing—on sacred and hallowed ground and wondered at the supreme arrogance and self-pride of the prince. And then she remembered that the great Jehan had been Moslem. The prince was Hindu. This was no shrine to him. It was a building of sufficient beauty—lacking as it might be in accommodation—to serve as residence for a Prince of the Blood Royal. She couldn't help but think, though, that it fed his arrogance and self-pride to take possession of and make himself at home in and master of the greatest masterpiece of art produced by the Moslems in all their history.

With every moment that passed, Elizabeth wondered whether the messenger from the prince had reached Lord John's campsite. In answer to her question that morning at the beginning of their ride to the Taj Mahal, Molkar had said that he had just dispatched the document from himself and her letter by emissary of the prince and that the time he would arrive would depend on how straight a way he took—meaning, she was sure, that it would depend on whether he had to make detours in order to keep clear of any guerrillas loyal to the maharajah. He couldn't be there yet. If he took the straight route, he probably wouldn't arrive there before middle or late afternoon.

Elizabeth regretted with everything in her the curt note that she had written to Lord John. She berated herself a thousand times for the formal, standoffish "E" with which she had signed it. She had had a chance to say something to him and she had said nothing. At least she could have said that she had not come where she was of her own accord. Molkar's message to him regarding her was only that they were returning her safely to where she had come from. There was nothing in it to indicate how she had gotten where she was. For all Lord John knew, she might have bribed the horseman to bring her there. Her feelings were no longer at war inside her. She no longer had any pride where Lord John was concerned. She wanted to be with him. On any terms. Even if he loathed her and thought her the defiled and tainted thing that she thought herself to be, still she wanted to be near him. She ached for the sight of him and the feel of him.

There was only emptiness inside her. She had no being when she was without him.

The day passed in waiting for Elizabeth, and most
of the night passed in waiting. She was awake and
still dressed when two soldiers came to her chamber at
some time in the night.

"You come," one of the soldiers said. "We go."

Elizabeth's heart leapt within her. She was going
back! She went eagerly with the soldiers. She gave no
thought to it and attached no importance to it when
they cautioned her to be quiet. She crept as silently
as they from her chamber and past the two cenotaphs
and through one of the long wings that stretched away
from the Taj Mahal. She allowed it when they
wrapped a long length of wool about her, arranging
the folds so that her head and body and all of her face
except her eyes were covered and her eyes shadowed
by a drooping hood of the fabric. She stood impatiently by while they exchanged a few whispered
words with the sentries that they passed. She walked
with them in the dark through the trees and shrubs.
She didn't notice that they kept themselves and her
always hidden in the shadows even though the night
was dark. There were few stars. They came at last to a
close clump of trees well beyond the gardens and the
grounds of the Taj Mahal. Three horses were tethered
there. They mounted and were off. Elizabeth wondered at the pace they kept. They had started out at
full gallop and they continued at full gallop. They had
a day's ride before them. They couldn't run the horses
all the way. When they finally slowed down it was to
stop and change mounts. A little cluster of soldiers was
waiting with three fresh horses in the shadows of a
wooded knoll. There was little talk, only a few short
words exchanged while the change of mounts was be-

ing made. Elizabeth was offered wine from a goatskin. It smelled acrid and raw. She refused it. The two
soldiers who were escorting her took long drinks of
it after they were mounted. And then they were off
again, and again at full gallop. Elizabeth began to
sense that something was wrong, and when the sun
came up she knew that there was. They were not
headed west toward the campsite. They were headed
north toward Delhi.

By the time Lord John arrived in Agra, Elizabeth's
absence had been discovered and the reason for it
determined. Prince Shallabhugi had moved out of the
Taj Mahal and he, Molkar, his retinue of servants and
attendants and amusers, his personal guard of two
thousand soldiers and the greater part of the ten
thousand soldiers who had been detailed to the holding—and defense if need be—of Agra by the maharajah were barricaded within the walls of Agra's own
Red Fort. Battle had not been joined, but the Maharajah Sirivaji and his son Prince Shallabhugi were at
war.

Prince Shallabhugi sat at one end of the carpet of
ceremony, cross-legged on the carpet, not in his chair
of gold. Lord John sat in like manner at the other end
of the carpet. They were conferring as equals, in the
manner of princes. Molkar stood, sometimes near the
one, sometimes near the other. He was no longer
dressed as he had been when Elizabeth had seen him,
for he was no longer in disguise. On his hairless head
he wore a black brushed felt hat with a shallow crown
and a wide flat three-cornered brim. He wore a robe
of cloth of gold heavily embroidered with filament of
gold and patterned over its entirety with pearls and
diamonds. On his upper right arm he wore a band of

gold from which was suspended an emerald the size
of a baby's clenched fist. At his waist was a curved
Genoa blade eighteen inches from hilt to tip. The hilt
was of gold, striated for grip. It was sheathed in a
scabbard of gold encrusted and inset with rubies,
emeralds, topazes, amethysts, aquamarines, cat's-eyes,
sapphires, garnets, and pearls. On his feet were boots
fashioned from unborn kid. The splendor of his garb
shaded that of the prince, and his complexion was
lighter than that of the Prince.

With his own skin color, there was nothing nondescript about his face. His eyebrows were not heavy
but were very black. There were few eyelashes on his
eyelids but there were dark, almost black half-moons
under his eyes. His cheekbones were high and flat,
and there were deep hollows under them. His nose was
long and thin and black at the nostrils. His lips were
thin and red almost to purple. Elizabeth would not
have recognized him.

A sorry remnant of a man was on his knees in the
center of the carpet. His head was bowed down almost
to the level of the carpet. His uniform, or what was
left of it, was in strips and was blood-caked. There
were swollen bruises and gashes on his head and face.
His right hand had been severed at the wrist in such
a way that a flap of skin had been left appended which
had been folded over the stump and bound with a
leather thong to hold in the bleeding.

Lagrosse stood beside the mutilated soldier. Lord
John had wanted his translation of what the soldier
said.

"Are you satisfied, my lord of England," Prince
Shallabhugi asked, "that this sinful dog and scourge
of the earth conspired against me, he and the two who
took Miss Stewart and the fourteen others that he
named?"

"Yes, I am satisfied of that," Lord John said. His face was strained, but he showed no tiredness of body or will.

"The fourteen others have received the same deserved reward as he. Would it please you to see that they have?"

"No."

"They will be hung on posts and their traitor's hearts cut out and hung beside them in full sight of their once-brethren as a signal example to them. Would it please you to watch that done?"

"No."

"When I have the two in hand who took Miss Stewart to the maharajah my father, they will die deaths of less grace and swiftness. Does my assurance of that satisfy you?"

"I would like now to move on to other matters."

"As you say." The prince lifted his hand and a group of soldiers came into the room. They pulled the condemned soldier to his feet. He couldn't walk, nor even keep to his feet. They dragged him from the room.

Lagrosse started to follow after the soldiers, thinking that no more was required of him. "Stay, Lagrosse," Lord John said.

"Yes, do stay," the prince said, "in the event my peshwa and I forget ourselves and neglect to speak the English. I want no misunderstandings nor suspicions between my lord of England, my peshwa and myself."

Lagrosse came back inside the room and stood behind Lord John.

"Miss Stewart was with my son when my son was taken," Lord John said. "The maharajah did not take her then. Why has he taken her now?"

"When my father took your son, I had not the support to wage successful war against him. I had not the soldiers, and, most important, I had not Molkar. Also, I had no pressing need to rise against him. The throne was not in peril. My father had no need then of—what would you say in English—leverage."

"He mistakes me if he thinks to bargain the one for the other."

"You had two. Now you have none. One is times into infinitude more than none."

"There will be no bargain."

Molkar made a slight movement and the eyes of both seated men turned to him. "Have you someone you can send to the maharajah, my lord?"

"For what purpose?"

Molkar smiled. "To open negotiations on this bargain that you will not make."

"I see no reason to waste time with diversionary tactics."

The smile left Molkar's face. "The ploy has a twofold value. It will divert some part of the maharajah's concentration from his preparations for defense, and it will ensure Miss Stewart's value to him." He paused. "If he cannot use her for bargain, she is of no value to him. It grieves me to speak thus bluntly, but I know the rajah's mind, and I know his reactions when angered by frustration. If you refuse at the outset to treat with him . . ." He shrugged and spread his hands.

"Miss Stewart is a British subject," Lord John said. "Does that guarantee her nothing?"

"There are always many unaccountable accidents in time of war, my lord. There is always a slaughter of a certain number of innocents. Is it not so?"

Lord John stood up. With some difficulty, the prince got to his feet. Two servants ran in to help him, but he was already up and brushed them impatiently aside.

"How soon can you be ready to attack?" Lord John asked.

"When I receive word that Delhi is equidistant between where we are here in Agra and the regiments
from Baglidore and the forces of guerrillas from the
mountains, we march. My armies move as one man
and with the speed of one. We will be outside Delhi
in two days' time."

"I have a man that I can send, but I don't want him
to get there in time to complete his business with the
maharajah and leave before the fort is besieged. I
don't want him to get free to go his way. I have un-
finished business with him."

"The one you hold prisoner?"

"Yes."

"Why have you confidence that he will go to the
maharajah? Why would he not make his escape immediately you free him?"

"He was in on the plot to kidnap my son. He was
on his way to the maharajah for the gold promised.
Greed will guarantee that he goes to him."

"Would not greed bring him back to you?"

"No."

"He seems to me a poor choice, and dangerous. He
could as easily tell His Highness that you refuse to
bargain as tell him that you wish to bargain."

"He will tell the maharajah what he knows he wants
to hear. He has no thought except for gain. I have it
from him that the maharajah wants me to forswear
my son so that my son will feel abandoned by me and
will turn against me and feel no loyalty toward me,
his father, nor toward England, his country. The man
will lead the rajah to believe that through his per-
suasiveness such terms can be had. His greed will convince him that he is bringing about such terms. He
had demented visions of himself possessed of a wealth
to equal all the diamond mines of India."

"You intend, then, to stay here to receive the pro-

posals when they come? I had thought to send word
that you wished to meet in person with the maharajah
—with a representative of your country's government,
of course, for guarantee that no attempt on your life
would be made."

"I go to Delhi. I have someone who will stay here
to carry on negotiations as if he were I."

"The man Daly?"

"Jason."

Molkar shook his head. He walked about shaking it.
"I will never understand you English," he said. "No, I
will never understand you. The man is crippled and
old and querulous, and given to impatience and rash
temper. He is a man of no education, a common sailor
by background—and you would trust him to nego-
tiate for the lives of those you hold most dear . . ."

"I would if it were necessary, but in this case he will
be acting merely to stall."

"That is true, but if he is not adept, the maharajah
will quickly recognize the stall for what it is. Do not
mistake His Majesty. He is not an undiscerning man.
Baglidore has not retained its supremacy among the
Maratha states and all the other states of India by my
wits alone."

"Jason has, more than once, proved himself possessed of more common sense than I and wiser than I."

"I think I begin to see. You hold in you the superstitious worship of the old and enfeebled."

"I hold no such superstitious awe of him. If I did,
it would be misplaced. Jason is not an old man. His
crippled state and the illnesses he has endured make
him seem so. He is a man of only some forty years . . ."

Molkar stopped and stood still before Lord John.
"Is it so as you say? I do not like the sound of it. No,
I do not like the sound of it. A man not aged, and paid

the veneration of the aged. No, I do not like it. It bodes ill."

"Jason has never brought me else than good."

The prince had been standing aside switching his hands back and forth and plucking at the skirt of his tunic. He had lost interest in joining in the talk, and in the talk itself. He had followed it, not listening to it but waiting for it to be finished, looking from one to the other of the two men, impatience and eagerness mixed in his face. He seemed to feel that he could interrupt at this point.

"I have been thinking and thinking, my lord of England," he said, "on the pleasures of my court and wondering what most would please you as entertainment. Business, business. It cannot always be business Come! Let us retire to the salon! You see, I remember my days in your England. To the *salon* then!" He clapped his hands sharply and a dozen servants appeared, bowing with heads almost at right angles to their feet while they waited to hear his orders. "Supper! We will sup now. Bring wine and prepare the hookahs. The performing monkeys I'll want first and then the dervishes. Tell the nautch girls they must dance tonight as they have never danced! Tonight they dance for a lord of England! Come, my Lord of England! Let me entertain you! Come!"

The semicircle of bowed white turbans popped up, and the servants ran in every direction at once to carry out their master's bidding. They laughed as they ran in appreciation of the pleasure they were about to bring him.

If Baglidore retained its supremacy among the Maratha states and all the states of India after the prince was on the throne, Lord John thought, it would retain it through the wits of the Peshwa Molkar, without any aid from the wits of the prince. ᴇᴏ

44

The Maharajah Sirivaji was nothing like his son Prince Shallabhugi and looked of an age to be his brother instead of his father. The maharajah was short and slight of build. He seemed to be strung together of wires inside his skin. His skin was as fair as Shallabhugi's, but there all physical resemblance ended. His face and hands were fine-boned. His nose was more deeply hooked and longer than Shallabhugi's. His face was smooth and clean-shaven, except for a heavy, drooping moustache which covered his lips. His dark eyes were hooded and opaque and had about them a look of melancholy. He was dressed all in white— this in imitation of Shivaji, the noted ancestor that he claimed. His turban was of white silk that had the sheen of satin. His floor-length robe was of the same material. His turban was jeweled and plumed, but the glossy material of his robe was not ornamented with embroideries and jewels. He wore the ropes of large pearls that marked him as the personage he was —the reigning prince of a major Maratha state. He wore a jeweled dagger at his waist but no sword—this also in imitation of his illustrious ancestor. He shared one peculiarity of dress with his son. Ringlets of black hair fell from one side of his turban.

Elizabeth's mind had been too occupied with other things, and her body had been too exhausted from the grueling ride—which had lasted two days and part of two nights—she had slept when sleep had overcome her in the saddle—for her to be able to take in the massive size and seemingly impregnable strength of the red sandstone walls of the Red Fort or to realize, once inside them, that they enclosed a small city. She had wanted to memorize every wall and every corner and every passage of the place where they would take her—which she had assumed would be the maharajah's palace. She wanted to be able to make her way around in it if she ever got the chance—to find Colin, who was surely there—and to be able to retrace the way she had come, to get them both out.

It was stupid to think that she would ever be able to do either, and she knew it, but that was what she had wanted to set her mind to. She couldn't. Her mind was all confusion. Once inside the massive walls they had ridden through many streets, past palaces and gardens and military barracks, even a mosque. It would have been difficult for her to form a picture of the place if she had had her clearest wits about her, for soldiers swarmed everywhere. The majority of the soldiers wore dun-colored jackets and dun-colored trousers tucked into mid-calf boots and black berets, and looked more French than Indian, at least in dress. They wore crisscrossed ammunition belts and carried heavy-duty rifles. They were not wandering aimlessly around. Some were standing guard, some were walking sentry, some were at drill. Cannon were being limbered, ammunition stacked, and horses shod and caparisoned.

As Elizabeth and her escorts neared the opposite

wall from the one where they had entered the fort, the balance switched and the majority of the soldiers were members of the maharajah's personal guard. They were not uniformed in imitation of the British red-coats, as were Prince Shallabhugi's personal guard. They wore tunics of yellow satin with narrow collars of precious stones. The trousers that bloused over their shiny black knee-high boots were of white patterned in purple. They wore small black visored caps strapped under their chins. They wore swords and carried long rifles ready bayoneted. The eyes of all of them were alert and darting, their bodies were tensed and poised to strike. The very air was crisp with their readiness. The Peshwa Molkar had said that there were ten thousand of them, and Elizabeth had no cause to doubt him.

The Maharajah Sirivaji did not speak English, or, if he did, he did not choose to avail himself of use of the language to speak directly to Elizabeth. The extended questioning that she had to undergo was extended further because everything said had to pass through the rajah's translator. There was very little that Elizabeth could tell the maharajah, and he was not satisfied with the little that he was hearing. He was more concerned with Lord John and his plans than he was with Prince Shallabhugi and what he was up to, and, strangely enough, Elizabeth knew, or could guess, more of the prince's plans than she knew or could guess of Lord John's. She realized early in the questioning that the rajah felt that he had little to fear from his son. If he expected attack—and from the atmosphere around him, it would seem that he did—he expected it from a different quarter. He brought up the state of Kalphum and the Maharajah Singal Jan more than once, and was impatient and unbelieving when Elizabeth showed an honest ignorance of anything to do with the state and its ruler.

Elizabeth was not allowed to speak except to answer the questions put to her. When she tried, the translator simply turned from her and acted as if she weren't speaking. She lost her temper and started to move toward the maharajah to scream her anger at him. Two rifles were crossed in front of her before she had put down the first foot she had lifted. She leaned forward over the ugly sharp blades of the bayonets and shouted, "Colin! I want to see Colin! Do you understand me? Colin!!"

A hand was clapped over her mouth. The maharajah made a slight shake of his head and the hand was removed.

"The name is unknown to me," Maharajah Sirivaji said.

"Whatever name you call him by, I want to see him!"

The maharajah lifted one crooked finger and Elizabeth was hustled from the audience room. She was taken down a long corridor and through several large chambers and along another corridor and thrust through a door. The door was closed behind her and she found herself alone in a courtyard. The buildings that enclosed the courtyard rose two stories above it. There was a balcony on the second floor that extended all the way around the four walls. It was colonnaded to the roof above it and to the ground below, which was tiled from wall to colonnade and was a promenade to be used in inclement weather. The slender columns of the colonnade were looped with flowering vines. The pattern of the tiles was a delicate floral. Traceried marble screens hid the windows and the doors of all the rooms on all four sides of the second floor. She was in the courtyard of the harem.

After Elizabeth finally calmed herself, she examined

the place where she was. There was only one door on
the ground floor—the one that led back into the palace
—and it was locked. There was a marble stairway that
led to the balcony. There was a heavily carved teakwood door at the top of it, and she did not have to try
it to know that it was locked. She became aware of—
or sensed—movement behind the marble screens on
the balcony. She stayed very still and listened. She
could hear the swish of beaded skirts and the soft
jingle of metal on metal as braceleted arms were
lifted. She heard the muted tinkle of bells when braceleted ankles moved. She heard lilting voices and flut-
ing, quickly quieted laughter. She was being watched.

After a long time, the ground floor door was opened
and an elderly woman came into the courtyard. She
wore a black long-sleeved and high-necked under-
bodice and a black sari. A black shawl was over her
shoulders and a long black veil—it might have been
part of the sari—over her head, but her face was not
covered. Her face was brown and heavily lined. Her
skin was like crepe. She was very small, though not
bent with age. She came only to Elizabeth's shoulder.

The old woman took Elizabeth by the arm and led
her to a marble bench beneath the balcony. She
jabbered away in whatever language she spoke with
a few words of English here and there. After they were
seated she turned to Elizabeth. Her face was very intent, very concentrated. Her eyes were on Elizabeth's
mouth as if she could better understand what Elizabeth said if she saw it said rather than heard it.

"The boy," she said, "He like . . . ?" She made
motions of feeding herself with her fingers and chew-
ing.

"Colin. . . ?" Elizabeth grabbed the woman's arm.
"Are you talking about Colin? Where is he? Take me
to him!"

"He like. . . ?" She made the motions again. She disengaged her arm from Elizabeth's hands and took a rolled parchment and a slender length of charcoal from under her shawl and put them into Elizabeth's hands. She made the motions of writing. "He like. . . ?"

"He's sick!" Elizabeth said. "He's not eating!" She tried to hand the parchment and the charcoal to the woman but the woman pushed them back toward her. Elizabeth threw them on the ground beyond the tiles and stood up. "You'd better take me to him!" She pulled the woman to her feet. "I know how to take care of him! You'd better take me to him!"

The woman pulled away from Elizabeth, shaking her head at her outburst or else in understanding of what she meant.

"Do you want him to die?" Elizabeth was screaming. "Is that what you want? How long has it been since he's eaten? How long has he been sick?" She stretched out her arm and pointed toward the door and the direction of the audience room. "You go tell that maharajah that if he doesn't let me see Colin, he'll die! Die! He's homesick and heartbroken! How does he expect him to eat! You go tell him—"

There was a commotion outside the door. Feet were shuffling aside, and sharp footsteps were coming down the corridor. The door opened and the translator stood in the opening.

"His Majesty has asked me to say, Miss Stewart, that if you will control yourself, and keep yourself under control, you may wait upon His Royal Highness the prince."

Elizabeth turned on him. "I don't want—" she yelled and then stopped. She realized that he was speaking of Colin. She took a deep breath and got control of herself. "I would certainly not act in any way in front of him that would upset him," she said. "My concern for his welfare is as great as the maharajah's."

"His Royal Highness the prince understands that his only relation now is his grandfather the maharajah, and that his duty is to him and to the throne that he will inherit. You will say nothing to him that would be in contradiction to that."

Elizabeth stared at the man. "The maharajah is not his only relation," she said. "He is not his nearest relation. Colin's father—"

"His Royal Highness the prince has no father. His father has relinquished claim to him."

"That's not true." Elizabeth shook her head. "That's not true."

"It seems that we cannot understand each other, Miss Stewart," the translator said. He bowed and withdrew from the doorway.

"Wait!" Elizabeth ran to the door. "Wait! I'll do whatever you say!"

The man stopped. "I will be present," he said.

Elizabeth nodded. She wasn't surprised that there would be a watchdog over them, and it would necessarily be one who spoke English.

The translator—who must be more than just that, must be high in the maharajah's councils and privy to him—swept his arm to one side indicating that she could come out. The soldiers of the guard moved aside to make a path for her through them. She walked along the corridor beside the translator. "He is His Royal Highness the Prince Paniphi," the man said. "You will address him 'Your Royal Highness.'"

Elizabeth nodded again, as if in agreement. She told herself that she wouldn't call him anything out loud and would whisper his own name to him.

*   *   *

Elizabeth had expected to find Colin ill in bed, but he was standing by a tall window looking down on the courtyard below him where there was a cavalry drill in progress. He was dressed in a long white robe, tight-sleeved and narrow-skirted and of a thick satin-sheened silk, a miniature of the one the rajah wore. The tip of a small jeweled scabbard showed at his hip. He was not wearing a turban, but his hair had been oiled and dressed in ringlets. The oil made it look black instead of the dark brown that it was. But there was no mistaking that it was Colin, even got up as he was and seeing him from the back. He looked small and forlorn, the room so huge around him, the window so tall above him. He had not been told that she was coming. He didn't turn when the door was opened, and she and the translator entered the room.

The translator bowed as low as if he had been bowing to the maharajah. "With Your Royal Highness's permission," he said, "Miss Stewart seeks audience."

Colin turned around as if he had been spun by a bullet. "Miss Stewart!" he cried. "Miss Stewart!" He ran across the room to her, arms wide. Elizabeth dropped to her knees and caught him to her. Tears were running down Elizabeth's cheeks. She expected Colin to burst into wild crying. But he didn't cry. His arms were tight enough around her neck at first to choke her, but almost immediately he took his arms from around her and stepped back from her embrace. "I'm pleased you've come, Miss Stewart," he said, and then, as if he addressed a stranger. "What has brought you to India?"

". . . Why, I—I came for a visit. I—My first years were spent in India. I came back for a visit."

Colin was looking beyond her toward the door, now closed. "I thought my—" He caught himself. The word

father was denied him. "I thought someone might be
with you," he said. "But I am not expecting him. He
is not coming." His little face was pinched and miserable. He held it straight before him and lifted, trying
to look regal and proud and disdainful of feelings, as
they had taught him he should look, trying to hide
his misery. Elizabeth reached toward him to take him
in her arms again, but the translator took her by the
elbow. "If you would rise, please, Miss Stewart," he
said. He bowed low again before Colin, still holding
Elizabeth's arm. "If that is His Royal Highness's pleasure," he addressed Colin.

"Yes," Colin said. "Do rise, Miss Stewart."

Elizabeth and Colin sat before the window, a table
between them. A silver tea service was on the table, a
plate of sweet cakes, a bowl of dates, and a platter of
fruits. Elizabeth drank tea and forced herself to swallow cakes and fruit and dates, trying to tempt Colin
to do the same. He sipped some of the tea and broke
open a pomegranate, but he only picked it apart and
didn't eat any of it. They were having a hard time
finding things to say. The only person they wanted to
talk about could not be mentioned. And even if he
could, Elizabeth felt that Colin's pride would not let
him mention him again. What on earth could they have
said to him to convince him? He believed himself
abandoned by his father.

Elizabeth was sick with disappointment in herself
that she couldn't think of some way of getting a message across to Colin in words that would be meaning-
less to the translator. There must be a million things
that she could say that only she and Colin would
understand. Finally she hit on what should have been
the most obvious thing.

"I had an interesting sailing," she said. Colin only

looked at her. They had already gone through the usual questions and answers and remarks about a voyager's journey, Colin polite and formal, sounding as if he were ninety years old. "I don't believe I mentioned the name of the ship. It was the *Jason*."

Colin's brow puckered. "I don't remember that any—"

Elizabeth spoke up hurriedly, interrupting Colin before he could say more. "It's newly christened," she said. Colin had assumed that it was a Polreath ship that she had sailed on. He naturally would. She didn't want the translator to guess that they were talking about one of his father's ships. "An honored friend of the owner was making the voyage," she went on quickly. "It was the first time he had been to sea in a long time, and as a gesture of"—she slowed down so that Colin would be sure to hear every word—"well, I suppose because he was glad to have his company, and his advice on a matter that was bringing him to India, he renamed the ship and named it for him." She added, trying to make what she had just said seem only of casual and impersonal interest to her. "I've never had a ship named after me. I don't suppose I ever will."

Colin had turned his head to the window, away from the man across the room. His chin quivered and he kept swallowing. Elizabeth didn't know whether he had understood what she was trying to tell him, or whether the thought of Jason was making him want to cry. She wanted to say more, but she didn't know how far she could go because she didn't know how much the translator knew. The Peshwa Molkar had seemed to know as much about things as she did.

Colin leaned toward the window and looked down into the courtyard as if something happening there had drawn his attention. "The owner came on the ship?" he asked. There was a catch in his voice, but he spoke in a low, almost lost little voice, and the translator might have missed the catch.

Elizabeth could have shouted for joy. Colin had understood. She had a hard time keeping her face from showing the relief and gladness that she felt. And she had a hard time keeping her voice casual and uninvolved. "Yes," she said. "He had business here, I believe—or no, I believe it was a personal matter, something to do with someone in his family who was going to go back to England with him. But I'm good at mixing things up. I may have it all wrong." She laughed lightly.

"Maybe that person in his family doesn't like it here and wants to go home," Colin said.

A lump rose in Elizabeth's throat. It was a moment before she could speak. "Perhaps," she said. "Whatever the problem, he and his friend Jason are going to set it all to rights." ૭

45

Elizabeth had hoped that she would be allowed to spend most of every day with Colin. He was pale and thin, and she had hoped that she would be allowed to take him out into the sunshine to get some color in his face and to bring back some robustness to his body. She wanted to do with him the things they had used to do at home—picnic and take long walks and go for rides that would last the morning. He needed fresh air and open spaces. He was accustomed to an outdoor life. But she was allowed to go to his rooms each day for afternoon tea, and that was all.

Colin spent most of every day at the side of the maharajah. He was being given an intensive education in court protocol and the duties, prerogatives, privileges, and obligations of a reigning monarch. He was being indoctrinated in the Hindu religion, and was being taught to speak and read and write Maratha Hind. He was learning to defend himself as well as to attack with the dagger, the curved blade, and sword—on foot and from the saddle. He was learning to load and cock and shoot pistol, rifle, and long bore, although how he could manage the latter two unless they were scaled to size Elizabeth could not imagine.

Elizabeth was quartered in the harem and spent most of her time there, where she had to endure the malevolent glances and pointing fingers and snickering remarks of the women of the harem. She couldn't understand the words, but there was no doubt of the meaning behind them. Even after days had passed and she was not taken into the room set aside for the purpose and given instructions on how to comport herself in a maharajah's bed, was not taught the delicate and different ways of tempting and teasing and titillating and rousing a man who had already countless times been tempted and teased and titillated and roused— and sated with sex to exhaustion—the attitude of the women did not change. They thought that she was being treated differently because she was different. There were Moslem women as well as Hindu in the harem—they could be differentiated because the Moslems wore blouses and trousers and the Hindus wore bodices and long skirts—and other Asiatics, but there were no Europeans or English.

The ladies of the harem had nothing but leisure. They strolled in the courtyard or in the enclosed gardens and terraces adjoining the harem on the outer side of the building where they were housed. They reclined on pillows and chaises in the columned rooms and on the screened and fretted verandah and dreamed and languished in studied poses on the balustrades of the balconies. They played chess and parcheesi and flew pigeons and kites. They smoked the hookah. Hours were spent soaking in marble baths in warm scented water and dressing and undressing in lavishly decorated many-hued silks and muslins and cloths of gold.

They adorned themselves with dangling earrings in the shape of flowers and birds, the crescent moon and stars. They wore multiple bracelets of gold and silver on upper arms and wrists and belted their costumes with loops of tinkling bells. They wore belled bracelets on their ankles and hollow circlets of jingling beads. Some had pearls on their foreheads and sprinkled or coiled in ropes in their hair. The Moslems stained their fingers and toes with henna. The Hindus stained the parting of their hair with vermilion. Some of the women glued on artificial eyebrows and some blackened their teeth with a powder prepared for the purpose. Most used kohl to line their eyes—and used it for a contraceptive when needed.

The heavily perfumed air of the harem rooms was cloying to Elizabeth—it was not at all the same, but it reminded her of the perfumed air in Lady Margaret's house in London. The air in Lady Margaret's house had been heavy with the scent of an overabundance of fresh and hothouse flowers. The air in the harem was perfumed with scented candles, incense, shavings of sandalwood that had been set to smoke, the oils that the women rubbed into themselves, and the salves of musk with which they coated themselves. Rosewater was sprinkled over pillows, upholsteries, drapes and hangings, and on the garments of the women. There was also the scent of the betel nut. Some of the women were addicted to it and some used it only for the sweet scent and to redden their lips.

The women of the harem dined on the full range of foods that India and her neighbors and the incoming ships to her harbors could provide, from the daintiest of delicately sugared violet petals to the most succulent of fowls and meat, including whole roast wild boar. They dined on Chinese porcelain with plate of solid gold and drank from golden goblets. They were surrounded with every ease and lavished with every

luxury, and they were petulant and jealous and scheming amid all their ease and luxury, divided into cliques
and couples pitted against each other—but they were
united against Elizabeth.

Nothing could be seen from the harem or from its
courtyard or gardens or terraces of what was going
on outside those confines, but every change in the air
and atmosphere outside was felt in the harem. On one
day Elizabeth noticed that the women were quieter
than usual and more watchful and alert, most closely
drawn together in their groups and pairs. As each day
passed the atmosphere became more tense. She learned
what was going on from Colin.

When she was taken to Colin's rooms for tea, the
translator was not present. It was the first time that he
had not been. Colin was withdrawn and aloof. He
would not permit Elizabeth's kiss. He did not invite
her to sit for tea.

"What they told me would happen has happened,"
he said.

Elizabeth was taken aback by his attitude. He
wanted no part of her. He was cold and arrogant.
He resembled Lord John at that moment more than
he ever had.

"What, that they told you would happen?"

"He has abandoned me, the same as he abandoned
my mother."

"He did not abandon your mother, and he has not
abandoned you. They lied to you!"

"He has sent a man here to arrange for you to be
sent back to him. You are to go and I am to stay. That
is his choice."

"He would not make that choice! Don't you see
what they're trying to do? They're trying to turn you

against him. They've told you all manner of lies, and they'll keep on telling you lies—"

"It is not a lie that the man is here. I have seen him and I have heard him talk. He is the same man who was there when His Majesty the maharajah my grandfather sent for me."

Elizabeth felt fear prickle at her. "Luke Balsam?"

"The names of men like that one are not told to me. He is not worthy of name, nor to be called 'man.' All I know of him is that *he* sent him here to trade me for you."

"Your father would never do that!"

"I heard him speak. I saw the envelope with my . . . with his handwriting on it. I saw the letter that said the man was empowered to represent him to His Majesty the maharajah."

"Colin, you've known your father all your life. You know the kind of man he is. You know his loyalty to those he loves. However things may look now or seem to be—"

"I have no father. I have not had since the day he abandoned my mother. He despised her, and left her to be despised. He—"

"That is not true! I will not listen to you say such things about your father! He loved your mother as few women are ever loved! He loves you more than any father ever loved a son!"

"He used me for his amusement the same as he used her. He tired of her. Englishmen always tire of their Indian women. Now he is tired of me. Englishmen never keep the sons of their Indian women once they start to become of age. That is why my grandfather sent for me when he did, because I was starting to become of age."

"If that is true why do you think your father is here? Why do you think he came to India? Colin—"

"My name is Paniphi."

"Your name is *Colin!* Your own mother gave you the name! Do you think she would have given you an English name if—"

The door to the room was flung open and the translator burst into the room. "Who brought you here when I could not be present?" His eyes on Elizabeth flashed with deadly anger. Elizabeth knew that he had heard at least the last part of what she had been saying.

"Why, the same—"

A volley of rifle shots exploded on the air. The force of the repercussion seemed to shake the foundations of the building. Elizabeth and Colin ran to the window. The translator ran after them and pulled Colin away from it. "Get down!" he shouted to Elizabeth. "Stay away from the window!"

Elizabeth couldn't move. She stared in fascination and horror at the scene in the courtyard. Dead and wounded lay under the feet of soldiers struggling hand-to-hand. Blood was everywhere—in pools and streams on the flagstones and on the earth and trampled grass of the gardens, on the dead and wounded, and on some of the men on their feet and fighting. The soldiers of the maharajah's personal guard were fighting each other. Soldiers in the dun-colored uniforms of the regular army were crowding into the courtyard, pouring over the walls and streaming through the gates and arches.

The translator grabbed Elizabeth's arm and pulled her from the window.

The sounds of gunshots and of running feet and shouted orders and the neighing and snorting of horses came from every corner of the fort. The booming of cannon sounded through the other noises.

"What's happening?" Colin was shouting to be heard above the noise. "What's happening?"

"The fort has been besieged for three days," the translator said. "They are attacking."

"There's fighting inside the fort!" Elizabeth said. "The soldiers of the maharajah's guard—"

"The attackers are not inside yet. His Majesty's forces have been infiltrated. Some of his own have been persuaded to turn traitor. They are being put down. The fighting inside the fort is only a skirmish."

A loud, rising yell rose from the opposite wall of the fort and rode the billows of noise inside the fort to reach and fill every space of air and every ear. It sounded as if it must be coming from a horde numbering into millions.

"They're breaching the wall!" Elizabeth exclaimed.

"The walls cannot be breached! They've forced the gate—or the traitors have opened it to them!"

A name was called from the door—apparently the translator's—in clipped, military tones. The three in the room turned. A captain of the maharajah's personal guard was standing in the door. All the space behind him was filled with soldiers in the yellow satin and white and purple of the guard. The captain of the guard spoke to the translator. Elizabeth understood nothing of what he said, but she heard the name of the maharajah—Sirivaji.

"You will go with him," the translator said to Elizabeth. "You will be taken to a place of safety."

"What about . . . His Royal Highness?" Elizabeth forced herself to use the title.

"His place is beside His Majesty."

"To be killed if he is killed?"

"You know nothing of war! All the same . . ." He spoke to the captain of the guard. They conferred briefly and then the translator bowed low before Colin. "With Your Royal Highness's permission, please accompany the captain."

Colin drew himself up straight, his hand on the hilt of the dagger at his waist. "Where will His Majesty my grandfather be?"

"At the front of battle, Your Royal Highness."

"I will be with him."

"Colin, no!" Elizabeth cried out.

Colin ignored her. "Take me to His Majesty my grandfather," he said to the translator.

Elizabeth rushed to him and took his shoulders and turned him to face her. All had suddenly come clearly to her—Lord John's secret plans. "Don't you know who's out there? Your father! He's come to take you back! He's joined forces with—"

A blow to the side of Elizabeth's head knocked her to the floor. "No! Don't do that!" she heard Colin scream, and then blackness descended on her.

When Elizabeth came to, she was lying on a long low couch of pillows in a large room lit by candles in sconces on the walls. She looked around herself, dazed. She couldn't make things come back to her. She thought that she was awakening from a bad dream— a nightmare—and that soon she would be fully awake and things would right themselves. Soon she would hear Lizzie's voice and see her familiar things about her. What she could see of the room must be part of her dream, for there were no windows on the walls— nor doors. She closed her eyes and mentally willed herself to awaken and opened her eyes again.

All was still the same. She turned her head and looked about her. She saw the indolent form of a man lounging against the wall opposite where she was. He was smiling a lewd, lip-licking smile that she had seen before, feasting his eyes on her face and body. It was Luke Balsam!

Elizabeth sat up. She started to get to her feet, but everything around her swam in dizzying circles. She sank back on the couch, her head in her hands. She felt the bruise where she had been struck. She remembered Colin and lifted her swimming head to look around for him. He was not in the room, but two soldiers of the guard stood at the entrance. Relief flooded her. Relief that she was not alone with Luke Balsam. Fear for Colin crowded out the momentary relief. But almost immediately she heard him. He was speaking in a high, piping treble full of wrath and fury that had been his voice of anger at Polreath. It was the first time she had heard him sound like himself. He was using single words and memorized phrases parroted phonetically, and repeating them several times, as one will when trying to make himself understood in a language that he has little familiarity with. The words were strange, but the voice was Colin's. His anger got the better of him, and he reverted to English. "She's dead! That's why you won't let me see her! You're afraid to! Get away from the door! Let me out of here!"

Elizabeth wanted to call to Colin, but she couldn't break through the nausea and dizziness that gripped her. She could hear scuffling as Colin was being held from running from where he was. Luke Balsam chuckled.

"My father will kill you!" Colin screamed. "He'll find me, and he'll find her, too! You can't hide us where he can't find us!"

Elizabeth struggled to her feet, to go to the entrance and call to Colin, but the dizziness over came her and darkness enveloped her. She sank to the floor beside the couch. &

46

Elizabeth awakened feeling that she was choking. A gag was in her mouth, held there by a cloth tightly bound across her face and tied in back of her head. The first thing that she saw when she opened her eyes was a blood-swollen, heavily corded penis jutting from a mass of black pubic hair. She heard a man's coarse laughter and saw the organ strained forward with the force of the laughter. She heard soft, high-pitched, womanish giggles coming from in back of her beyond the head of the couch. The sounds in the dead quiet told her something that she hadn't noticed when she had returned to consciousness before, and that was that no sounds of what was going on outside in the fort could be heard. Where she and Colin were being held was underground, and, apparently, the underground rooms were soundproof. She was cut off from any help from outside—and it was Luke Balsam who was standing, naked, beside the couch. It was the two guards at the entrance to the room who were giggling.

Elizabeth jerked herself upright on the couch and backed as far away from Balsam as she could. She tried to scramble to the foot of the couch to get off it and run, but he caught her. He laughed at her desperate efforts to free herself. His laugh was heavy now, lewd cackles between harsh, fast-coming breaths.

"Come to yourself this time for all the fun, did you?" he grunted out between breaths as he pulled her to him. He held her with her back against him with one arm pinioning both of hers to her sides. He turned himself and her to face the guards. "Told you she was a spitfire, didn't I?" The guards couldn't understand what he was saying, but they giggled in anticipation of the show that was coming. "Wait'll you see her when I get her going. Ain't many takes to it like her." He leaned his head down to Elizabeth's ear. "Ain't that right, cock-lover?" He stuck his thick wet tongue in Elizabeth's ear, bending his head with hers when she cringed, trying to pull away from his sickening, hateful mouth. He explored every curve of her ear with his tongue before he pulled his mouth away. "If I have to knock you out to get you going, I will. Don't think I won't," he said. "We're going to give them two a show like they ain't never seen."

He pulled her straight back up against him and held her so that the front of her body was toward the guards and her back against him. He ran his free hand over her body. He cupped each breast with his palm and played with it, making smacking sounds with his lips and grunting. He rubbed his hand in circles over her abdomen and up and down her thighs, pushing the folds of her skirts, and his hand, deeper between her legs with each upward and downward stroke. Elizabeth writhed and struggled, kicking backward with her feet, but her heels when they struck Luke Balsam's shins and ankles did nothing more than make him laugh. Her shoes had been taken off. She hadn't realized it until she had started trying to hit the tender places on his shins with her heels. She knew that if she hadn't awakened when she did, she would have been as naked now as Luke Balsam was himself.

Luke Balsam leaned himself and Elizabeth forward and reached to the bottom of her skirts and lifted them, slowly, making a long-drawn-out, lascivious thing of it to give a higher pitch to the soldiers' enjoyment. The eyes of both were bulging, following Luke Balsam's hand. Their expressions had become avid and feverish. Their eyes glinted. Their breaths were short, hissed between saliva-slick parted lips. Balsam raised Elizabeth's skirts slowly to one knee, his hand beneath her skirts. He picked her leg up at the ankle, forcing her to bend it backward at the knee. He pulled down her stocking and pulled it from her foot and threw it toward the soldiers with a low, sly laugh. He put his hand on Elizabeth's other ankle and went through the same slow process.

Elizabeth got her foot free and stamped as hard as she could on his hand. He jerked his hand from under her foot and ran it up to her bare thigh and gripped the flesh of her thigh in a vicious grip. "You're going to get everything you ask for!" he snarled in her ear. "You better keep remembering that!" He released his grip on her flesh and stroked his hand up and down on her bare thighs, caressing one and then the other. He tantalized the soldiers, keeping his arm well bent up under Elizabeth's skirts, not letting them see her legs, not letting them know exactly what he was doing nor how high up her legs he was reaching. The soldiers each had caught a stocking. In their excitement they had balled them up in their hands and were kneading them, making motions the while for Balsam to raise Elizabeth's skirts and let them see him play with her. "Not so fast, my mateys," Balsam said, "Not so fast. Don't do to hurry this little game." He took his hands from under Elizabeth's skirts and stood the two of them straight. He made thrusting motions against her back with his pelvis, his swollen organ jabbing into the small of her back against her clothes. He put his free hand back on her breasts. He played with each nipple until he made it hard, laughing lewdly and thrusting all the while.

Elizabeth's throat was raw with her attempts to scream. Only a faint thin sound would come from her throat, and it tore at the soft flesh of it. Her arms and back and waist felt as if the skin had been abraded from them by the fabric of her clothes in her frantic twisting and turning, trying to free herself. Luke Balsam started to unbutton the throat-high buttons of the bodice of her dress, and she struggled harder. He was so involved with his pleasure in what he was doing that he didn't notice that his arm holding her arms pinioned to her sides had slid above her elbows. She ducked her head and threw her hands up before he was aware of what she was doing, and jerked the binding cloth and the gag from her mouth and screamed one scream after the other before he could clap a hand over her mouth. "Bitch!" he hissed between clenched teeth. He jerked her hard enough to snap her backbone. "Bitch!"

Answering screams came from the room adjoining. "Miss Stewart!" Colin screamed. "Miss Stewart!" The scuffling sounds that Elizabeth had heard before from where Colin was started again. The sounds were drowned out by a thundering of feet coming down a stair and turning into the corridor that led to the underground rooms.

The soldiers at the entrance threw the balled stockings from them and stood at stiff attention. The approaching noise became the sound of many individual footsteps, some striding sharply, some scraping as if being dragged. Balsam clutched Elizabeth more tightly against him, trying to cover his nakedness with her body. The door of the room was pushed forcibly inward, knocking aside the soldiers.

Lord John stood in the doorway. He was hatless and was bleeding from a wound in the head. There were bayonet slashes in the hunting jacket that he wore. He was breathing hard, and the sweat on his face mingled with the blood from his temple that ran down his cheek. He held a bloodied sword in his hand: Soldiers in red jackets with crossbelts crowded the space behind him. Two of the soldiers held between them the drooping form of the translator.

Lord John's face turned white and contorted with anger at the sight before him. His eyes narrowed with the white fire of hate. He said no word. He strode the space between them in two strides and tore Elizabeth from Luke Balsam's grasp and pushed her behind him with a backward motion of his arm. His sword arm flashed upward and down again. Luke Balsam swirled away, cringing and bent almost double. The blade of Lord John's sword landed on the back of Balsam's shoulder cutting through flesh and sinew and muscle to the bone. The point of contact had been the curve of the shoulder, on the joint, and the blow had landed with such force that the arm was almost severed at the shoulder. It dangled, held to Balsam's body only by skin and muscle. Balsam howled, grabbing at the useless arm and holding it against his side. Blubbering, yowling, animal cries went up from him.

Hysterical cries came from the adjoining room to mingle with Balsam's. "Miss Stewart!" Colin screamed. "Miss Stewart . . . !"

Lord John turned his back on Balsam. "Tie him up!" he ordered. He ran toward the sound of Colin's screams. "Watch her! Take care of her!" he ordered

the redcoats who had made a protective circle about
Elizabeth.

There was a sudden quiet overall. And then:
"Sir . . ." Elizabeth heard. It was almost like a question.
And then high and joyous. "Sir!"

"My son!" Elizabeth heard, clearly said. And then
muffled, "My son!" She knew that Lord John had knelt
to open his arms to Colin and was holding him close
against himself with his face pressed against him, as
she had done when she had first seen Colin. She heard
the wild, heartbroken but rejoicing crying burst from
Colin now that she had expected to hear when she
had gone to him.

Presently Lord John came from the room carrying
Colin, who was sobbing quietly now, in his arms.
Lord John smiled at Elizabeth, tears streaming down
his face. She ran to him from the circle of soldiers.
Lord John released one arm from Colin and encircled
her with it, holding her close against him. The soldiers made a way for them and they walked through
the long corridor and up a long flight of stairs and
out into the sunshine.

The fighting was over. The forces of Prince Shallabhugi and the Peshwa Molkar had defeated the forces
who had remained loyal to the maharajah. It had been
done quickly. The Maharajah Sirivaji had lost heart
when he had witnessed his son the prince, his peshwa,
and more than half his army arrayed against him. He
was a prisoner in the fort that he had so recently and
so pridefully gained possession of. The translator was
sent to join him there. Lord John had no more use for
him. Luke Balsam was taken in hand by Lord John's
own mercenaries. ☙

47

Elizabeth was overcome by the sight before her. Colin—himself again now that he had his father in his sight and sound and touch—was chattering a mile a minute, running back and forth to point out things, explaining everything to Elizabeth. Lord John stood beside Elizabeth, smiling, amused at Elizabeth's trepidation and at Colin's pleasure in being the one who was an old hand at what was happening, the one who would explain and direct.

A royal procession was about to begin, and the three would be participants. Colin's departure from Baglidore was being attended by a fanfare to equal that with which his arrival had been attended. Lord John had refused the fortune in precious stones and works of art and native crafts that Prince Shallabhugi had wanted to present to Colin, and to himself and Elizabeth, but he had agreed to the procession. He had allowed Colin one present: a miniature of his mother in a frame of gold picked out with pearls and emeralds. It was the only likeness that the prince had of his sister. Lord John had offered to have it copied and to send the copy to the prince. He had been shaken by the dealings to do with the miniature. It was the first time he had seen it. But he had wanted Colin to have it, and to have the original, for that was the one his mother had posed for and it seemed to him that something of Santha herself was captured in it.

"Everything is just about ready," Colin said.

Twenty-two elephants were in the wide square. Twenty were arranged in a semicircle and two were at midpoint of the semicircle and in front of the others.

"Those two in the front," Colin said. "You can see they're the biggest and the oldest. They're the royal elephants. They carry royalty. They say that one on the far side is over eighty years old. He looks like he is, doesn't he?"

The backs and flanks of the two lead elephants were covered with scarlet silk trimmed with gold fringe and hung with golden tassels. Their legs were caked with gold paint. Wide scarlet circles had been painted around their eyes. Their tusks had been plugged with gold and bands of gold bound the pairs of tusks at intervals from root to tip. Their mammoth foreheads were covered with fresh gold dust, and a design of it continued halfway along their trunks. The back of their ears also were coated with gold dust. Atop their backs were howdahs of gold—which looked to Elizabeth to be the size of small gazebos and had somewhat the appearance of gazebos. They had peaked roofs of carved and gilded spokes overlaid with canopies of scarlet silk, tasseled and fringed in gold. Inside the gilded railings on the sides were seats upholstered in gold brocade. A carpet of scarlet and gold overlaid the floor.

"The other elephants carry the noblemen of the nawab's court," Colin said. "And visiting noblemen, if there are any."

Ten of the twenty minor beasts were crusted with

silver paint. Their silken coverings were of silver cloth,
as were their trimmings of fringe and tassels. The
howdahs on their backs were silver and canopied with
silver. If the sun had been glaring, few eyes could
have stayed long on the sight of them. The other ten
were crusted with the same silver paint and bore silver
howdahs. Their cloth coverings and the canopies of
their howdahs were scarlet silk tasseled and fringed
with silver.

"They will be made to kneel when it's time for us to
get up in the howdahs," Colin said, "and ladders put
up. Don't worry. The ladders will hold you. They
don't look like it, but they will."

As if that had been their command, the two lead
elephants were prodded by their attendants into kneeling position, their forelegs outstretched and their hind
legs folded under them. The howdahs still looked
awfully high to Elizabeth, and insecurely perched on
their backs for they had swayed sideways and to back
and front with the movements of the elephants. She
clutched Lord John's arm. He placed his hand reas-
suringly over hers and pressed it. He didn't speak for
Prince Shallabhugi—now Maharajah of Baglidore—
and the Peshwa Molkar were approaching them from
across the square, the noblemen of the court in twos
to the rear of them.

The maharajah stopped before his guests. Elizabeth
gave him the low curtsy which she had learned that
day at tea in Lady Margaret's salon was due majesty.
Lord John and Colin bowed. The maharajah bowed in
turn. It was not a low bow but it was lower than protocol demanded and showed that he wished to express
extraordinary grace.

"Will you change your mind, Master Colin, and ride
with me?" the maharajah asked.

Colin's dark brows lowered. His face clouded over.

"I will ride with my father," he said. "We will ride together. We three."

The maharajah laid his hand on Colin's shoulder. "As you say," he said. "When I have sons, I could only wish . . ." His face was thoughtful and a little wistful. He broke off what he was saying, and his thoughts, and smiled broadly. "If you will mount, then." He turned and with his peshwa beside him and his noblemen falling in line behind him went to the elephant on the far side and climbed the ladder that had been placed against the elephant's massive ribs and settled himself in the howdah. His Peshwa Molkar climbed up to join him.

Lord John climbed first into the howdah on the other elephant and assisted Elizabeth to climb up. Colin climbed up after her. He was bright-eyed and eager, delighted with everything again.

A blast from a hundred clarion trumpets sounded on the air and the great forelegs of the elephants bumbled into ponderous movement. Elizabeth clutched the railing of the howdah as the great beast beneath her heaved upwards, rocking up on his forelegs, and rose. The howdah rocked and swayed with the elephant's every move. Colin laughed when she squinched her eyes tightly closed. When she opened them, she was even higher off the ground than she had imagined she would be. A man could have stood on the shoulders of the keeper below, and his head would not have been on a level with hers.

The two royal elephants moved out, and the others followed in twos behind them. The trumpets continued their clarion call. The members of the royal guard marched in columns of two along the sides of the elephants and in rows of twenty to the rear of the elephants. A phalanx of the guard had materialized seemingly from nowhere and was marching ahead.

The crowds that had stood silently massed on the outer perimeters of the huge square and along the street burst into wild cheering. The skirling of bagpipes— one of the few foreign musical instruments that produced a sound in kinship with the musical sounds familiar to Indian ears, and thus a favorite—was heard coming from all directions, the shrill piercing tones pleasing the maharajah for he smiled and nodded in the direction of the piper when he picked one out in the crowd.

Crimson bougainvillaea was spread like a carpet along the royal way. Blossoms of every kind were strewn in the path as the royal elephants approached, tossed over the heads of the marching guard. The air was sweet with the scent of flowers. No dust rose from under the petals, for the way of the approach was wetted down by hundreds of scurrying boys with goatskin bags of water. As each emptied his goatskin bag he ran to one of the roadside troughs, placed there for the purpose, and refilled the bag and ran to do his share of wetting down the dust ahead.

Colin reached out and caught an errantly tossed frangipani blossom and waved it at the crowd, laughing and holding out his arms in invitation for more. Blossoms of every hue and scent were tossed at him by the delighted crowd. Most fell short, but enough reached the howdah to cover the laps of the riders and the floor beneath their feet.

"Do you think you will miss all of this, Colin?" Elizabeth asked. It had occurred to her more than once that the little taste he had had of being treated as royalty might have a stronger and more lasting effect on Colin than Lord John might wish.

Colin playfully fluttered the frangipani under her nose. "Do you think you will?" he teased, his eyes sparkling at her.

"I don't suppose I shall miss it, but I will surely think about it," Elizabeth said. He had missed her point. She didn't know whether that was good or bad. "It's not something one would likely forget," she said.

Colin looked around him at the crowd and at the maharajah on the elephant lumbering along beside theirs. The sparkle left his eyes. He dropped the flower and moved across in front of Elizabeth to stand between his father's knees. Lord John pulled him up to sit on his lap. Elizabeth looked around at Lord John. He smiled at her. He had understood what she had been asking Colin. And he had Colin's answer.

After a while of silence Colin said, looking at the maharajah who was smiling and nodding at the crowd, "He looks lonesome. He doesn't have anybody, like we have."

Lord John looked at the maharajah, wondering at Colin's astuteness that he could see beyond the outer facade. "Do you realize, Colin," he asked, "that he is your uncle?"

Colin sat up, his eyes wide with surprise and questioning. "Like Oxford is Thomas's uncle?"

"Yes."

Colin looked back and forth between the maharajah and his father. "He is?"

"He is your mother's brother."

"I didn't ever put it together like that, to make him come out to be my uncle. I didn't think I had any."

Nothing more was said for a while. Then Colin said, "If I ride back with him, will you stay close beside?"

"Of course."

". . . I guess I ought to . . ."

"He would be very pleased. It would be the nicest parting gesture you could make to him."

Colin sat quietly on his father's lap for a moment, and then a mischievous twinkle came into his eyes.

He stood up and and leaned over the railing. "Hey, uncle!" he yelled.

Prince Shallabhugi looked around in surprise. Then a wide grin came over his broad face. "Yes, nephew?"

"May I ride back with you?" ॐ

48

All was in readiness for the trip down the mountain from Amphat. Colin was already in the saddle and every moment becoming more impatient to be gone. He couldn't wait to see Jason and Daly who had gone directly from Agra back to Surat and were waiting for them there. He couldn't wait to board ship and sail from India. He sat on the sure-footed mountain pony prancing under him, watching his father and Elizabeth through the open doors of the verandah, trying to hurry them by showing them how ready he was to go.

They were going to sail home on the *Jason*. Lord John had spoken of taking a faster ship, one of his Indiamen, but Colin wanted to sail on the *Jason*. Lord John had given in to his wishes in spite of his own reasons for wanting to reach England as soon as possible.

Lord John had learned much from Luke Balsam. The swaggering braggart—his strong right arm amputated and a fever on him—had shown himself to be the craven coward that he innately was. He had babbled everything he knew in the hope of saving what

miserable life was left to him. He was being returned
to England, but not aboard the *Jason*. He was a
prisoner on board a ship of the line of His Majesty's
Navy. There was a doctor on board the frigate who
would do what he could to keep him alive and return
him to some degree of health. Lord John fully intended
to see him dead, but not yet.

Lord John knew now that Balsam had indeed had
dealings with the old maharajah for the two years
past. Hurford had paid for his release from his prison
chains (the jailer would be called to account for that)
with money supplied by Sarah (where else would he
have gotten such an amount?) and, between Hurford
and the maharajah, with Balsam acting as contact,
Colin's kidnapping had been plotted and carried out.
Hurford had made the original approach and had offered his services to the maharajah, for a fee.

The timing of the approach could not have been
more propitious—for the success of Hurford's scheme.
Prince Shallabhugi had just refused to enter into the
royal marriage that his father had arranged for him.
Facing him with a bona fide alternate heir to the
throne would show him the extent of the old maharajah's displeasure with him. By tradition, the reigning monarch could appoint the successor of his choice,
even adopting as a son someone outside the family if
need be. It suited Sirivaji far better to propose as heir
someone of his own blood—Colin.

Lord John didn't know how deeply Sarah was involved in the plot to kidnap Colin. He doubted that
she was at all involved. That wasn't her way of
handling things. She wasn't clever enough to scheme
and plot. Or she wasn't patient enough. Her homicidal
mania took over. She rushed into foolhardy attempts
of her own to try to get rid of someone she thought

was in her way. He'd had enough experience of that to know it.

Lord John saw many things now that he considered himself a blind fool for not having seen before. He could lay the failing to nothing but his excess of sentiment. He loved too deeply when he loved. He couldn't see the dangers—see the realness of them and accept the truth of them—to those he loved because he was too involved with his feelings for them. First there had been Santha, and then Colin, and now Colin and Elizabeth. Was he called upon to love less? He didn't know. At any rate, he could not. But he could stop being a blind fool and open his eyes.

He could see now a pattern of intrigue between Hurford and Lady Sarah going back to the time when Sarah had first become patroness of Miss Holybrook's School for Young Ladies—and that had been when Elizabeth had come there. It was Elizabeth's presence in the school that had drawn Lady Sarah's interest, and not any feeling of commitment on her part to the school. He had no doubt that Lady Sarah's interest in Elizabeth had to do with Elizabeth's origins. He suspected that they connected with Sarah, and, if his suspicions were founded in fact, he knew what the connection was. And he knew why Sarah had tried to get rid of Elizabeth.

Lord John could see Hurford's hand and Sarah's hand in his accident in the mine, in the ambush by the tinners, and in the explosion at Wheal Craggen. Why Sarah would want to bring about his own early death and lay her position open to exposure he could not imagine. Perhaps Hurford had persuaded her that she would be safe from exposure.

Every word that Elizabeth had said to him about Hurford's treatment of her had been true. Now that he knew Hurford to be evil in one respect he could see him as evil in all respects. Hurford had much to answer for. He would rot in chains. Death was too good for him.

As for Sarah . . . He was of two minds about Sarah. He felt a certain responsibility for her condition, but he no longer felt obligated to her. He had obligations to others—to Colin and to Elizabeth—that far outweighed any obligations he might once have had to Sarah. His course of action where she was concerned would come clear to him when he faced her with the proof of her scheming. He had that proof in his pocket —the disc with the coat of arms of the House of Clarwicke. Elizabeth had no need for the Clarwicke fortune, for all that was his and Colin's would be equally hers; but she had the right to her true name and family heritage, and Lord Moulton had the right to his daughter.

Lord John had told Elizabeth nothing of what he knew or suspected. He was not going to hand her speculations and suspicions. He wanted the certainty of it—solid proof—to give her. It would be his wedding present to her.

Lord John stood waiting while Elizabeth pulled on her riding gloves and adjusted her hat and veil. He could see Colin through the open door of the verandah impatiently beckoning to him to hurry. He smiled at Elizabeth's reflection in the mirror. "I have the feeling I have a lot of this ahead of me," he said.

"What? Waiting for me and being hurried by Colin?"

"That and everything else that a man goes through when he's pulled between two he wants to please. I hope I will have found an easy way by the time I'm old so I can enjoy my tottering years in peace."

Elizabeth had been looking at him in the mirror.

Now she turned to him. "Will we still be together when we are old? You are braver than I am, that you can think about our future. I'm afraid to think beyond the day."

"The time will come when you won't have to be afraid. And soon. We are going to marry, my Elizabeth."

Elizabeth took a step backward from him. A stricken look came over her face, and she clutched her hands to her heart. He had never seen her so deeply vulnerable to hurt. "Don't say it if it isn't true," she whispered. "I could not bear to expect it and then not—"

"Sarah no longer has the right of claim to me nor to my protection. She has forfeited all right. I have proof."

"You would go through—" She could not bring herself to say "the scandal of divorce."

"I will marry you. Whatever it takes to bring that about, I will go through. I will marry you."

Tears gathered in Elizabeth's eyes and spilled down her cheeks. She had to remove her veil to wipe them away.

Colin's patience ran out and he jumped off his pony and came running inside. "Come on!" he said, "Everyone else is ready to go and waiting on you!" He saw Elizabeth's tears. "What are you crying about?" he asked in amazement. "We're going home! That's not something to cry about!"

MARA

Kathleen Morris

Mara McQuaid is a blackhaired Irish beauty caught up in the raging fever of a passion that will not die. This book has all the blazing romantic action of LOVE'S TENDER FURY and SAVAGE SURRENDER.

This virginal child-woman, ravished on her eighteenth birthday by her rakehell cousin, leaves her native land to travel to the American frontier in search of her long-lost father. She becomes first the unwilling "bride" of a powerful Cheyenne chief, then the captive of a brutish mountain man, later a Faro dealer and courtesan in San Francisco and finally, Queen of Circle City—the wicked "Paris of the Klondike".

Through all of Mara's adventures runs the whitehot bond of passion for the man named Desmond, a bond as immortal as love itself.